MYTHOMANIA

W H ROSE

MYTHOMANIA

Copyright © 2020 by W. H. Rose

First paperback edition January 2020

Cover Design and Interior Book Design by: Kristina Hack of Temys Designs

www.whysteriarose.com
Paperback ISBN: 978-1-7342739-2-2
Ebook ISBN: 978-1-7342739-0-8

For Lauren

wisteria
rose 🌸

Terms

Bias: Your favorite member of a K-pop group.

Fan Meeting/Fanmeet: An event where fans get to meet their idols and get albums signed by them.

Hyung: An honorific suffix used from a younger male to an older male. It literally means older brother, but is used when referring to friends or acquaintances as well.

Jagi/Jagiya: A Korean endearment used by couples.

Lightstick: A flashlight type device used by fans at a concert to show their support and interact with the concert's lightshow. Each group has a unique design.

LiVe: A fictional streaming platform that allows fans to connect with their idols by watching them livestream or airing prerecorded episodes of shows the idols and/or their company has created.

Maknae: The youngest member in a group.

Nim: An honorific used when referring to someone who has superiority or is otherwise at a higher level than you in a business or organizational setting. A newly debuted idol group will refer to another idol group which has been in the business for longer using this honorific, for example.

OT_: A phrase used to refer to the entirety of a K-pop group.

The number of members in the group goes in the blank. It's most commonly used when the group does something as a whole, like taking photos.

Ssi: An honorific suffix. Loosely translates to Mr. or Ms., but is not necessarily that formal.

Sasaeng: A 'fan' who crosses boundaries with idols. They frequently stalk, harass, and make idols uncomfortable and/or scared by doing extreme things to get their attention, like breaking into their homes or stealing their personal belongings.

Things to know

In Korea, people are referred to by their family name first, then their given name. EX: Matoi Jaemin. 'Jaemin' is the given name while 'Matoi' is the last or family name. First names are only used when people are really close, or the same age.

People bow to others when being polite, usually when meeting or leaving each other, but people also bow in other occasions, like accidentally inconveniencing their peers.

As a general disclaimer, I have taken a few liberties when writing this book to achieve certain plot points. This is a work of fiction and thus is not 100% factual when referring to the idol industry or Korean culture. Regardless, I hope you enjoy the story.

It's Saturday morning at eleven AM when Isla Montgomery finally rolls out of bed and shoves her cold feet into a pair of pink fluffy house shoes she bought from Goodwill. Yawning and rubbing the sleep out of her eyes, the nineteen-year-old girl lumbers across the crooked floors and into the shoddy kitchen, filling her dented kettle and waiting sleepily for the water to boil. She quickly grows impatient, grabbing an apple from the counter and rinsing it off, slicing the fruit into small chunks and rummaging through her disorganized pantry to find some peanut butter.

Isla settles onto the flat, floral couch in her tiny living room with her breakfast and a warm blanket thrown across her legs. She reclines and grabs her phone, smiling at the adorable photo of Jaemin she has as her lock screen before punching in her passcode and checking her notifications. With a small frown, Isla realizes that she slept through a LiVe. She clicks the link anyway, only to be told that the livestream is currently being re-uploaded. She shrugs, deciding to simply watch it later.

Isla has been a fan of OT2B for four years, ever since the K-pop band was first formed. It consists of five members - three singers - Kim Seojoon, Park Woojin, and Matoi Jaemin and two rappers - Han Leo and Bae Daehyun. She remembers those early days vividly, smiling to herself as she recalls the bizarre hairstyles and questionable outfit choices the boys donned. Their music was always phenomenal, even if it wasn't popular, their lyrics filled with meaning and their melodies memorable. Their lyrics always seemed to resonate with her, encouraging her to do her best and uplifting her spirits whenever she felt down. The band has become such a large part of her life that Isla doesn't know who she would be without them and without their work.

Beyond their musical prowess, the band members themselves bring light into Isla's life. Their energetic and bubbly personalities always make her laugh and smile, seeming to connect with them on a personal level. Through the years, they've become friends for Isla, people she reaches for, even if that just means watching videos or liking tweets.

But in the last year or so, the foreign band has become increasingly popular abroad, their lovingly named fans - the Starlights - popping up everywhere. On one hand, Isla couldn't be prouder of them. The band's successes feel like her own, their triumph making her heart race with pride. But on the other hand, Isla feels a bit apprehensive, sitting through forced and awkward interviews as everyone tries to get their hands on the group, using their name for views and clicks.

She sighs, clicking off the LiVe app and looking at her phone, noticing the lack of notifications. It's another one of those weekends where the young lady has no plans, no friends to hang out with, and no errands to run. Isla could stop by and visit her family, but it would be a waste of time to visit people who don't care about her. Since graduating high school a year ago and forgoing the traditional college route, Isla has desperately been searching for her life's purpose, for what makes her tick. But she's been entirely unsuccessful, stuck working a waitressing job to afford her tiny, run-down apartment only an hour's drive away from the hometown she hates. OT2B is the perfect distraction from reality.

The girl is completely free of commitments, whether she wants to be or not. With nothing better to do, Isla decides to spend her time binge-watching the new kdrama she's heard so much about - something involving a chaebol falling in love with a waitress. She makes it half an hour through the first episode before a Twitter notification interrupts the funny scene the main character experiences.

It's a message. That's quite odd as Isla's Twitter is purely for her to be able to keep up with the OT2B boys and to host her LiVe account. She only has six followers and has never spoken to any of them or anyone else for that matter. Curious, she clicks the notification, tsking in annoyance when it takes too long to load. When it finally does, she finds herself wishing she'd just continued with her show.

'A whore like you doesn't deserve Jaemin. I hope you choke on your own spit.'

Isla just stares at the message, not sure what to do. It doesn't make any sense at all. She doesn't deserve Jaemin? What do they mean?

After another moment of deliberation, she decides to ignore it, blocking the hateful person and continuing with her show. The message couldn't have been meant for her, and if it was, it must have been a troll who sent it, just choosing a random account to try and start shit with.

But she doesn't get another five seconds in before her phone seems to spazz out, a million notifications coming at once. Thousands of messages all pop up and her follower count skyrockets from six to sixty thousand.

She shakes her phone, thinking it's glitching out. When the notifications keep flooding in, Isla goes to her Twitter, finding among all the new followers, comments, and DMs, a post notification from OT2B's official account.

She nearly drops her phone when the tweet loads, her fingers shaking badly as she stares at the photo that was tweeted out.

It's a photo of her, one her outgoing coworker took two weeks ago when the two of them spent a Saturday afternoon shopping at the strip mall near her home. She'd dressed up that day and had felt pretty, smiling widely towards the camera and situated beside one of the trees growing inside of the building.

The caption has her feeling sick to her stomach.

'This is her, my beautiful girlfriend. Thank you @islaliving for always being there and supporting me. I love you! #Jaeminie'

They must have been hacked, right? There's no way this is happening, there's been some terrible mistake. Convinced that she's dreaming, Isla downs the last of her coffee in one gulp, turns off her TV and heads back to bed. When she wakes up, it'll all be over, or so she believes.

But, it's not a dream. The messages keep coming, her phone keeps ringing until she wants to chuck the metal through the window. She doesn't dare to even open her Twitter, fearful of more unsolicited hate comments. She goes so far as to disable her notifications. None of her other social media accounts are any better, her photo is posted everywhere on every account. Hell, even Billboard has an article up: 'Idol Matoi Jaemin of OT2B announces his relationship with foreign girlfriend, Isla Montgomery, this morning on LiVe'.

Seeing the title, Isla immediately opens up the app, sighing in relief when the livestream has been re-uploaded. Her breaths are short as the video loads.

When it finally flickers on, Isla is blessed with the sight of a very happy looking Matoi Jaemin, the man grinning at the camera with his face cradled in his hands. He looks casual, dressed in a simple white t-shirt, face bare and hair messy. His dark locks fall right above his eyes, so the idol tilts his head to the side to get them out of his way. His nose is adorable, rounded and delicate, almost as cute as the twin dimples that imprint his cheeks when he smiles. It's obvious why he's a fan favorite. Jaemin is everything a girl could dream of: filthy rich, super talented, sickly sweet, and unbelievably sexy when he wants to be. He's in direct contrast to Isla's meeker, shyer personality. She wishes she could have some of the charisma he possesses.

Jaemin leans closer to the camera, giving the viewers a closer look at his neck and collarbones as he adjusts the lamp behind his phone, necklaces brushing together. As always, he waits a few minutes for the livestream to get more viewers, humming some tune she recognizes as one of her favorite songs.

An uncomfortable chill runs down her spine and she burrows deeper under the covers, subconsciously attempting to hide from it.

Another minute passes before he begins, sitting up straight and flashing an even wider smile. He looks absolutely ecstatic.

"Hello, everyone," he begins, Isla being more thankful for subtitles than she ever has been in her entire life, "It's late, isn't it? Ah, I hope I didn't wake any of you. Usually, I'd be getting ready to go to bed too, but I had a thought I just had to share with my Starlights."

He pauses as if pondering his next words.

"I," he bites his full, pink lips, rubbing his hands together, "I have an announcement."

The comments must have surged because he laughs, scrolling on the screen.

"No, don't worry! I'm not leaving OT2B, no way. And I'm okay, better than okay. It's something good, I promise."

Isla feels herself growing irritated. Usually, she'd love to see him ramble, but now is not the time. She can't scroll forward either, as she could miss something important.

"Yes, it's something very good indeed. Starlights have been there to support me these last years and I couldn't have been more thankful. I wouldn't have been here without you. For whatever reason, whatever time, each one of you found One Thousand Times Bright. It was fate for us to be together, for us to spend our youth together, to give and take love to and from each other. . ." He trails off, doll-like eyes looking dazed.

"And now, now I ask you to support me in my next endeavor. There's this special path I hope each of you can walk down one day. I've stumbled across it, accidentally. I never meant for it to happen, but I'm so glad it did."

He takes another breath, heat rising to his cheeks in the form of a beautiful blush as thoughts race through his head, loud, all shouting the same thing.

Isla is startled when the next words out of his mouth are in English, spoken clear as water.

"I'm in love."

Isla pauses the video, overcome with some sort of emotion. She doesn't know how to react. She stands up from her bed and leaves her phone frozen on Jaemin's glowing face, her hands shaking as she paces across her bedroom floor.

"This is okay. This is fine. There's some sort of misunderstanding. Maybe he's going to say he's in love with a new hobby, career or something. Maybe he's fallen for Woojin. Yes, it's something like that, isn't it? I'll go over there and press play and he'll say he's dating Woojinnie. Anyone but me. Maybe it's another idol? Or a childhood friend? He probably just used my Twitter handle by accident. It must have been close to someone else's. Yeah, that's it," she convinces herself.

Clutching her fists together, she retrieves her phone, resuming the video.

"Her name is—"

Isla flings her phone across the room, wiping at her face.

"You know, I think I need to have a social media break today. That sounds great. I'll read that new book I ordered, yeah. I'll do that."

She grabs the book and walks back into the living room, nearly tripping. Isla flops down onto the recliner and opens up the first page.

Fifteen minutes in, it's clear that this isn't working at all. She's reread the first line at least a hundred times.

"Fuck it!"

Isla storms back upstairs and grabs her phone, sitting on her hands to prevent herself from tossing it again.

"—Isla," Jaemin plays with his fingers, looking bashful, "She's the most wonderful person I've ever met. I couldn't keep it inside of me anymore. I want to show her off to the world, hold her hand confidently, let everyone know that she's my baby."

He's grinning so widely now, it looks like his cheeks might burst.

"I love her so much, I want to be with her forever . . . and I really hope my Starlights can grow to love her as much as I do. Please continue to send your love and support . . . I'm sorry if this seems selfish, but I can't help feeling the way I do. I can't help falling in love with her," he licks his lips.

Isla feels herself grow warm, some indescribable electricity running through her veins. She lifts a hand to her mouth, feeling embarrassed that someone could say those things about anyone, especially her, even if it is a lie.

"Isla," he says, and it feels like he's looking right through her and into some part of her she didn't know she had, "I hope I did okay. English is really hard," he laughs, "but you know I'll do anything for you. I've been studying like crazy, so I hope I don't sound too weird! I love you so much. See you soon."

He grins again and blows a kiss to the screen, hiding his face in his shirt as he turns the screen off.

For a moment, Isla just sits where she is, mind blown. She replays the video once, then again, and once more. A part of her refuses to believe that it's her he's talking about, but there's no way he could mean anyone else. He used her name, her photograph, her username. Maybe one of these could be a mistake, but surely not all of them.

She's stumped. How is one supposed to react when your idol who you've never met, never spoken to, suddenly outs the nonexistent relationship between the two of you?

She can't exactly deny it, can she? It'll make her look like she broke his heart, wouldn't it? No one will believe that it's not real if Jaemin says it is.

Why would he do this anyway? It makes no sense! Why jeopardize his career like that, especially for a relationship that isn't even real?

And why her, of all people? He could have chosen a million other people to have this fake relationship with. She wasn't even informed about it. Surely, to have a plot like this, the other person has to be in on it.

Maybe she should just delete her Twitter, lay low for a while. She should be safe, right?

But how did he get that photo anyway? The only people who follow her on Instagram are people she knows, just a few acquaintances.

It hits her like a bolt of lightning.

Her coworker.

Hurriedly, she pulls up her account, and lo and behold, her coworker (who doesn't believe in putting anything on private) has that photo posted. And worse, she's been tagged. Just as she realizes this, follower requests flood in like a hurricane.

Isla feels sick to her stomach.

As if to make things worse, a text message comes in. A text from her crush who she had finally went on a date with only yesterday.

'Didn't know you were the cheating type. Don't talk to me again'

She wants to scream. None of this makes sense in the slightest. How would someone like her ever be able to date an idol? Especially if that idol is Matoi Jaemin, beloved by millions. They're on two entirely different wavelengths, living in separate worlds. How can anyone take his announcement seriously? How had Isla's boring Saturday turned into the worst day of her life? How, how, how?

But a disaster cake isn't done without the icing on top.

She receives an email from Smash Entertainment, OT2B's company.

"Fuck."

2

She tried her hardest to ignore the situation, ignore everything and pretend that nothing was out of the ordinary.

Her little bubble of denial was soon ruptured when the media began hounding her, sitting in front of her apartment with their cameras and following her when she went to work. The owner of the diner didn't seem to mind much as business boomed.

And even worse, the emails from Smash Entertainment kept coming, before they turned into phone calls. She could no longer ignore the matter once the priority letters showed up at her house. It made the impossible situation real and caused chill-bumps to race up and down her skin. Isla grew paranoid, the fear that someone would knock on her door and rough her up caused her to finally reply to Smash.

Even when the line of communication was forced open just a week after the LiVe, Isla tried to explain that everything was a mistake, tried to get them to understand the confusion over the phone.

The company wasn't having it. Smash Entertainment demanded she fly to Korea to sort everything out in person, and with no other real option, frightened that someone would show up at her apartment and drag her out, she relented. The arrangements were made for her to fly out the coming weekend.

And now she's here, standing in a busy airport in South Korea, ignoring the shouting the Starlights direct at her as she shuffles between large bodyguards, the camera flashes giving her a headache.

Isla had hoped her impromptu arrival would be kept a secret, that everything would be done off the books without anyone knowing. But lately, nothing has been going to plan.

So really, she shouldn't be all that surprised by the obscenities being yelled at her, should she? The hateful signs, with blown-up photos of her face defamed with streaks of violent red paint. The tears, both angry and sad, all running down swollen pink cheeks. None of this should be a surprise, none of this should affect her. Isla told herself that she'd stay strong on the exhausting plane ride over, that none of it matters and everything will be explained and eventually return back to normal.

And yet it feels like she's been thrown in front of some blinded jury, accusations being screamed at her, a life sentence she doesn't deserve for a crime she didn't commit. It's scary. So scary that her hands shake and her breaths are uneven under the stuffy cloth mask they made her wear. Black dots fill her eyes as they speed through the airport, the girl jumping into their black van and ripping off her mask, struggling to calm herself down. She can't pass out, not here, not in front of these people. Not in a foreign country, squished between two strange and muscled men. She pulls out the water she'd stashed in her bag, spilling a bit of it on her legs as it sloshes about. She downs the whole thing without breaking for air and places a cool hand on her forehead then each of her cheeks, attempting to fully chill out.

Isla is not sure how long the drive takes, her fractured state of mind blurring and pausing time as it sees fit. They arrive eventually though - thankfully before she pukes on one of the poor bodyguards - and rush through some sort of secret entrance.

She's not even given any time to get her bearings before being more or less shoved into a massive boardroom. Several impressive looking men and women in harsh suits all stare at her, unamused.

Isla tries to straighten up her lousy attire, a band t-shirt wrinkled from the long journey and some plain bottoms, curly hair in all sorts of ebony disarray. No doubt the locks have worked their way into painful knots she'll have to grit her teeth and detangle later and her toffee-colored skin is oily. She's a far cry from impressive, unintentionally presenting herself more like a homebody and less like the dazzling temptress they'd all expected her to be. After all, Isla Montgomery must have been astounding for Matoi Jaemin to break the number one rule of idoldom - no relationships.

Someone gestures to an empty chair and she takes it, plopping down, drained of energy. It's clear that these company heads already have a clear impression of her and it's unlikely that sitting down properly would change that in the slightest.

"Let's just get down to business, shall we? Now that everyone has arrived," says a blonde man, relatively young and with a haughty accent, possibly an Aussie.

Isla feels immense relief at his words. If 'everyone' is here already, then OT2B won't be showing up - Jaemin won't be showing up.

She never thought she'd be so relieved to miss out on meeting her bias, the man she'd daydreamed about dating since she was fifteen years old.

"You need to break up with Matoi Jaemin," the blonde man says, disdain coating every syllable.

"That's the thing though, we were never together in the first place. That's what I've been trying to tell you guys. I don't know what went through your idol's head, but we are not dating. We're not even friends! I don't know Jaemin personally. All I know of him is what any other Starlight does," Isla says, hoping that they'll hear her out now that they're face to face.

"Playing innocent won't help you."

"I AM INNOCENT!" Isla can't help but shout, "I don't know him! I don't know him at all! We've never spoken, he's never gotten in contact with me, none of them have! Until this week, I didn't know he even knew who I was!"

A quiet murmur rises above the room as her words get translated, executives trying to make sense of the situation.

"So, you're saying that our idol made all of this up and put the careers of himself and his members in jeopardy for some elaborate prank?"

Isla nods frantically.

"I swear it."

"That doesn't make any sense. If you expect us to believe that, you're quite frankly out of your mind."

"What do I have to gain from calling him a liar? What do I have to gain from any of this? Do you know how much hate I've received? How afraid I've been that some psychopathic fan would break into my house and murder me in my sleep?"

The room falls silent.

"I will say this for the last time. I do not know Matoi Jaemin. I am not his—"

The door to the boardroom swings open, hitting the wall with a bang. A very flustered looking guard chases weakly after the idol in question, Matoi Jaemin stepping into the room. Isla is immediately bombarded, Jaemin bounding towards her with a relieved and excited smile, immediately gathering her in his arms. "Baby!" he exclaims, squeezing her tightly, "I've missed you so much!" "Jaemin," Isla begins, attempting to untangle herself from his vice and wrap her head around what's going on, "I don't know you."

He just smiles at her, eyes darting over every single inch of her face.

"It's okay, Isla, we can stop pretending now. That's why I went on LiVe to tell everyone about us."

Everything is a blur. Matoi Jaemin is holding her.

Matoi Jaemin is holding her.

Matoi

Jaemin

Is

Holding

Her.

Rapid and angry-sounding Korean flies over her head, Jaemin arguing with the man Isla recognizes as Hwang Hyungmin. His beautiful face twists into an expression so livid, fear licks Isla's belly, her instincts screaming that she's in danger. She tries to pull away from him but the idol's grip on her only tightens until it's nearly painful.

"Let's go, Isla. You're not signing that fucking paper. She's not signing it, do you understand me?!" He yells in clipped Korean-accented English.

Matoi Jaemin entangles his fingers with Isla's, hauling the two off somewhere. Isla digs her heels into the floor, but the combination of the slippery tile and Jaemin's fierce grip prevents her from doing anything.

"Matoi Jaemin!" Isla shouts, finally ripping her hand away from his warm, soft one.

The man turns around, meeting her eyes.

"I'm sorry about them, angel. I'm sorry they were pressuring you to leave me. But that'll never happen, I know. I'm not mad at you at all,"

She eyes him, looking him up and down, feeling sick to her stomach.

"What is wrong with you? Why are you doing this?"

Jaemin tilts his head, the soft look she adores falling onto his features. Up close, Jaemin is even more beautiful than she thought he'd be, all soft and pretty, reminding her of a fairytale princess more than a prince.

"What do you mean?"

His words are accented, though significantly less than what she had expected considering she hadn't known he could speak English at all.

Isla takes a step back from the man, the uneasy feeling taking over her.

"Why do all of this? Why make a fake relationship and tell everyone about it? You put yourself on the line, put your members on the line, jeopardized my relationship . . . why? You don't know me. I don't know you. Why do all of this?"

"Isla . . . of course I know you. I know everything about you. You're my girlfriend," he says sweetly, confusion in his words.

The girl just stares at him, realizing with a sudden, terrifying epiphany that Matoi Jaemin is completely out of his mind. His eyes, his posture, hell, even the smile on his face. He genuinely believes that she's his girlfriend. Truly.

Pity wells up inside of her, a sick feeling in her stomach.

"Jaemin."

"Yes, angel?"

"We should break up. I think it'll be best for both of us," she says, words tumbling out of her mouth before she can think them through.

There's silence for a moment, then seven more, as Jaemin just stares at her, attempting to understand what she said.

"You want . . . to leave me?"

His words are quiet, hushed under the fluorescent lighting.

This is a pinnacle moment, Isla's sure.

"Yes . . ."

Too bad she made the wrong choice.

The tears are instantaneous, Jaemin seeming to collapse onto himself, nearly falling to the ground.

Isla rushes to help him, only to meet his tear-filled gaze, his dark eyes seeming so utterly broken.

"What's wrong with me? Why don't you love me anymore, Isla? You said you'd always be with me, even when no one else was. You said it! You said it!"

His grip on her wrists is strangling despite the shakiness of his fingers.

"I what? Jaemin, don't cry, please don't cry!"

He continues to sob loudly, people from the boardroom exiting and seeing the two in such a state, Jaemin defeated on the floor and sobbing while a panicked Isla tries in vain to comfort him.

"What's wrong with him? Jaemin? Jaemin, are you okay?"

He ignores his superiors, clinging onto Isla like a lifeline.

There's more yelling, Jaemin's voice wavering in and out as he crushes Isla to his chest, the girl feeling claustrophobic.

"Look what you did!" He gasps out, barely able to take a breath, "Look what you monsters caused! She's going to leave me! Leave because you won't accept that I'm in love with her!"

Isla tries to pull away from the hysterical man with no success, despite his deep trembling.

"If you won't let us be together, I'll leave OT2B," he says, fingers pressing too hard into her hips.

A strangled gasp leaves Isla as Jaemin says the words every Starlight fears hearing.

"Jaemin, don't!" She says, managing to wiggle free enough to cradle his face in her hands.

His cheeks are flushed, and red hot, salty tears slip down and leave streaks. Isla brushes them away frantically, trying to get him to calm down.

"Don't go saying stuff like that, okay? We can still be friends, alright?" Isla scrambles, disregarding that they were never friends in the first place, "So, don't go saying that! Leaving OT2B?! What about the boys?"

The idol shakes his head violently, still crying. He grasps her hands in his, pulling them away from his face.

"No. No. The boys understand. They know how much I love you. More than anything, more than anyone. I won't let that be tampered with, no matter what."

Isla shoots a terrified look at the horde of suits still gawking, praying they'd save the day. But alas, they do nothing.

"Jaeminie, darling."

His face brightens a bit at her softening tone.

"I can't be the cause of all of your dreams, all of everyone's dreams, to go down the drain. It hurts right now, but I promise you'll feel better in no time. It'll hurt for me too, but we'll heal. Trust me."

Never in her life did she think she'd dump Matoi Jaemin, the man she's admired for so long, the one she thinks about every day, the one who can make her smile like no one else. She's not lying. It hurts. It really hurts her soul to see him so wrecked. If Isla didn't know he was sick, that he needed help, she could never have had the courage.

He's crushed. Jaemin's precious face crumples and he collapses onto the floor, undoubtedly bruising his flawless skin. He doesn't speak for a moment and it seems that everyone holds their breath, hoping that her words finally got through to him.

"If you leave me," he says, voice so quiet she can barely hear it, looking up at her with eyes too strong, too invasive, "I'll jump."

His eyes pan to the window beside her, the glass displaying a large balcony at the side of the building.

Ice runs through her veins and she shrieks, launching herself at him and holding on like her life depends on it (maybe it does) and squeezing, the emotional rollercoaster she's experiencing causing tears of her own to fall down her cheeks.

The man below her looks at her tears like they're a marvel, some strange, incomprehensible item.

"Why are you crying? Didn't you want me to leave?" He asks, genuine confusion in his tone.

He hates seeing Isla cry, it hurts him more than anything.

"No. No, no, no, no, no. You can't do that, Jaemin. Never, never think about that. You - you have to live, okay? You have to."

"What for?" He asks, thumb gliding across her wrist.

He's too calm for a person who'd just threatened suicide.

Her brain is fried.

"For me!" She pleads, unaware of the gravity of her words, "Live for me until you can live for yourself, okay? Please?"

He seems to contemplate her words.

"So . . . you're not going to leave me?"

Isla shakes her head.

"I'll stay."

Her hands are shaking but she doesn't notice, looking at his face intensely, searching for confirmation.

"You'll still be my girlfriend?"

"Yes. Yes, I'll be your girlfriend,"

He grins then, that familiar smile she has saved a thousand times on her phone.

"I love you so much, Isla," he replies, finally returning her vice grip of a hug, "So, so much."

Isla doesn't resist when he kisses her, slowly for a moment before pulling away, only to dive back in, the couple making out on the floor. She doesn't know if she enjoys it or hates it, zoning out so completely that she can't even feel him against her skin.

She's painfully aware that she just made everything worse, that she's sucked herself into a pit without an end in sight and no one to help her.

But what could she do? What else could she do but tell him everything he wanted to hear when he dangled his very life in front of her eyes?

When they finally break apart, Isla's lips are sore and bruised and a dead feeling lurks in her stomach.

"I love you too, Jaemin,"

Needless to say, she never signs those papers, not daring to look at the shell-shocked execs.

"Where are we going, Jaemin?" Isla asks, squeezing his hands tightly, afraid he'll snatch it away and do something awful.

"Home, baby. The boys are so excited to finally meet you."

3

The company van is silent except for the happy humming of Jaemin, the man's fingers entangled with Isla's. His hand is warm and pink, but Isla isn't sure how much longer it'll stay that way. One wrong step and all the warmth from his body could disappear.

Isla swallows, squeezing Jaemin's hand tightly and not letting go. She's sure her grip is hurting him, but Jaemin just smiles at her and doesn't complain, his happy tune soon returning.

While Jaemin is off in lalaland, thinking whatever, Isla's thoughts swarm with questions and concerns.

How much do the rest of OT2B know about her? Surely, they're aware he's sick, right? What if they're not? Could she convince them? Maybe if she speaks with Leo, the only other member in the group who is fluent in English, she can explain what has really happened.

There's a slim chance that it'll change anything, but it's all Isla has at the moment, all she has to cling onto in order to keep herself sane.

"We're here, Isla, darling!" Jaemin suddenly announces, startling her.

"What? Oh, right," Isla stammers, freeing her head of thoughts.

Jaemin can't get suspicious.

"The boys are so excited! Everyone's actually at home for once. Everyone goes their separate ways a lot, ya know?" Even though he's still smiling, Isla notices something sad in his gaze.

She wets her lips.

"Do they–" she begins, not sure how to put her words, "Not spend a lot of time together? With you?"

"Mm," Jaemin says, "Everyone needs alone time. We're always together. We can't help but get sick of each other from time to time."

"Oh, yeah," Isla agrees, "My friends like having breaks too. Keeps it fresh."

Her words are a lie, a hollow attempt at relating to him. Isla doesn't have any true friends, only acquaintances, so she isn't sure if long stretches of time apart is what usually happens in a functional relationship.

Jaemin's hand tightens now, Isla's bones pushed closer together than what's natural. It's not enough to cause any real pain, but it certainly causes Isla to wince.

"Good thing we won't need any breaks, though, right, Isla? I love you too much to ever get tired of being around you," his words are light, no hint of something under them.

"M-me too, Minie," Isla replies, trying to prevent herself from ripping her hand out of his grasp.

She tosses in the nickname randomly after coming up with it on the spot. Couples have pet names for each other, don't they?

He hums again, blushing at the new name he's been given and releases her hand, bringing it up to his lips and kissing her knuckles.

"Let's not keep them waiting."

In all honesty, Isla is less terrified of meeting OT2B than she would have been a month ago. Back then, when she still retained her sense of anonymity, Isla always daydreamed about meeting her idols, always feared saying something inappropriate or accidentally tripping over her feet. But now they're a welcome presence as Jaemin's focus is shifted off of her for the first time since they've met.

She almost sags from relief but holds firm, not wanting the boys to get alarmed, at least not until she knows how mindful they are of the situation. For all she knows, the rest of OT2B could have easily been the one to push Jaemin in this direction.

"Jaeminie! We were getting worried! What took you so long?" Seojoon asks in rapid Korean, not giving Isla the chance to even pretend to understand.

Kim Seojoon, age twenty - six, is rather tall and broad, shoulders giving him a more traditionally masculine shape than the other members. His legs are long and hugged beautifully by a pair of ripped skinny jeans, a giant bright yellow knit sweater making him appear sweeter than he usually is on stage. His hair is buzzed in the back, a mop of curly midnight blue locks plopped on the crown of his head. It stops right below his dark eyebrows, not quite brushing his downturned eyes, a feature that always makes him look sad even if he's grinning one of his infamous smiles.

"Nothing much. Just the execs being assholes. But don't fret, they couldn't do anything about us. Isla wouldn't sign those papers, would you, baby?" Jaemin asks, the latter half of his statement in English.

She just shakes her head, suddenly shy over having all five pairs of eyes on her frame. Isla doesn't really know what to say, not having had any time to prepare for this abrupt meeting.

"Don't be so stressed, Isla, lighten up," Leo says jokingly, extending his hand.

Despite being the only one in the band with a white parent, Han Leo has beautifully melanated skin, the color of a beach washed in sunshine. He's dressed simply in a white shirt with a Versace jacket hanging loosely around his shoulders, jeans and a pair of Chucks rounding it out. His hair is golden yellow and cut bluntly across his forehead, giving him the stereotypical Asian bowl cut.

She takes his hand and squeezes once, shaking it.

"Sorry, just . . . a lot has changed lately. The meeting was kind of rough."

She's getting better at lying. Shocker what fear can do.

"Sorry 'bout it. Dating an idol is always rough. Seems it was exceptionally difficult this time," Leo says, a bit of pity in his words.

Isla's silly hope flares. Maybe Leo does know something's off.

"But it's worth it! Getting to tell the whole world she's mine is worth the hardship," Jaemin says, wrapping his arms around her waist protectively - possessively - and placing a kiss on her cheek.

She blushes furiously, the PDA embarrassing her.

"I hate that it dragged you guys into it, though. I wish it wasn't so messy."

Leo opens his mouth to say something but Jaemin's phone rings, interrupting him. Jaemin apologizes, stepping into another room to answer it, agitation clear on his features.

Isla jumps at her chance.

"Leo," she says, quieter than before in an attempt to prevent Jaemin from overhearing, "You've got to help me."

The urgency in her tone has the leader frowning, unsettled by her sudden change in attitude. Even the other boys pick up on it, eyeing each other.

"What?" Leo asks, confused.

"I don't know any of this. The things he's told you about me aren't true."

She opens her mouth to continue but Jaemin steps back into the room, hands empty of a phone.

"She's right, you know," He says, once again trapping her in his grasp, "She's taller than I told you she'd be."

He hangs his head as if ashamed.

"I just didn't want to admit how short I am, ugh. But it's okay. Everything else I told you guys about her is true. Her favorite food, favorite color, the posters of us she has on her wall . . ."

Pure terror strikes her, Isla frozen in place.

A sudden alarm rings through the air and Isla jumps up, startled. Seojoon mutters something and rises to his feet, exiting the room.

"Food's done! I know you've got to be starving after such a long flight," Jaemin remarks, leading her gently to the table.

Everything's been set. Forks and spoons sit next to glittering silver plates, not a chopstick in sight. Small dishes are already on the table, but Seojoon brings in a large dish, revealing her favorite pasta. Now that she thinks about it, all of the foods are on her top ten list.

She's going to puke.

"Let's get to know you more, Isla," Leo says once everyone's settled in and eating.

"Like what?" she asks, not really looking at him.

She hasn't looked at any of them, any of the dazzling men she's longed to be near for years.

"Are you excited to be moving to Korea?" Daehyun asks, looking proud of himself.

The Starlight in her is proud too. His pronunciation is really good.

Bae Daehyun, aged twenty - six, is the shortest member of OT2B, but it never seemed to bother him. At times, he was rather proud of his smaller figure as it automatically made him look less gangly and awkward than the others when dancing. His hair has been dyed cotton candy pink and looks just as soft and airy, little more than a floofy poof on his head. His smile is sweet as sugar in bright contrast to the rather deep baritone in his voice and his role as the main rapper in the group.

"Oh, I'm not moving here. Just here to visit for a bit," she says, popping a forkful of food in her mouth to hide the anxiety the man's words cause.

She wants out of Korea as soon as possible, the mere thought of her staying makes her want to spit out the bite she'd just forced herself to take.

"But didn't you rent that apartment upstairs with Jaemin?" Leo asks in confusion, munching away in a fashion that would be unappealing if it were done by anyone else.

"Ah," she squeaks out, looking at the man next to her as he chews happily, soft eyes daring her to elaborate.

Happy, happy, happy. She never thought she'd hope for Matoi Jaemin to be anything but happy.

"Yeah, but that's just for visiting. So we can have some us time while I'm here," she explains, pulling something out of thin air.

Jaemin stops chewing.

"I thought you were moving here? That's what you told me, jagi."

The Korean endearment sounds heavenly coming out of his mouth but Isla does anything but swoon. Pure panic surges through her system. No way in hell she's staying here.

"Yeah, but then I told you something came up and I couldn't," she scrambles, fighting to keep her voice from rising.

Jaemin frowns, Leo looks uncomfortable, and Isla's stomach sinks to her feet.

He's in so deep.

"I don't remember that."

"I told you. We were on the phone for almost an hour," Isla says, hoping that's not too outrageous; she has no idea how long she and Jaemin supposedly talk for or if they talk at all.

"Oh, yeah," Jaemin says after a moment, tilting his head, "That thing with your job, right? How could I forget?"

How could he indeed.

But Jaemin brightens just as quickly.

"And then you had to go before I could tell you I talked with one of my managers. He said you could get an internship working under him. It's unpaid, of course, but don't worry, I'll support you."

Isla feels like a caged animal, desperately searching for an escape.

"Let's . . . talk it over after dinner, okay? I don't want Seojoon's delicious food to get cold," Isla says, purposefully speaking the elder's name louder than necessary and catching his attention.

"You like?" Seojoon asks eagerly.

Isla nods and takes another bite. It's the first time she's told the truth all evening.

"Yes, it's very good. Thank you for cooking it."

Seojoon's chest seems to swell with pride and he grins. Isla is momentarily taken aback. There's always this untouchable aura surrounding them when they're all dolled up with staff members swarming them constantly. But here, in their home, they seem real.

And so Isla allows herself to relax if for no other reason than to keep herself from passing out right in her food, finally falling naturally into a half-understood conversation with everyone (after all, Jaemin won't try anything in front of them . . . right?). Jaemin beams as his members and the love of his life converse, making each other laugh and smile. It's just like he knew it'd be.

Isla really is perfect.

After everyone is stuffed and the table's cleaned, Isla stands up and stretches, gathering her few essentials.

"Where are you going, baby?" Jaemin asks, coming to stand by her.

"Oh, ah, just to my hotel. I can catch a taxi no problem," she says, hoping Jaemin won't make a fuss of it and she can leave once and for all.

In all honesty, she has no idea how to do that at all. Isla just plans on walking back to her company-provided hotel. She knows it can't be too far from here.

"Nonsense, Isla," Leo says, "You're our guest."

"Yeah, baby, just stay here for the night," Jaemin says, cradling her hand gently.

He really is obsessed with it.

"Oh no, I don't want to be a bother," Isla stammers, trying to step back.

"It's no bother at all, Jaemin says, "And besides, I want to take you to our apartment. You haven't seen it in person yet."

Isla blinks, rapidly fishing for an excuse.

"I don't have any of my things," she says, smiling sheepishly.

"You can just borrow mine," he offers simply.

Isla can't think of another thing to say, so she gives in, seeing no real other choice.

"Okay."

She'll just have to sneak out while he's sleeping. Her flight home is in the morning after all.

4

Isla thought she could do it. She really did. She thought she'd be able to stand a few more hours in Jaemin's stifling presence, smile pretty and laugh like nothing's wrong.

But as soon as she sees "their" new apartment, her heart drops into her stomach and dread fills her to the brim.

Jaemin's hand is hot on the small of her back.

"Do you like it?" he whispers, mouth against her ear in a smile, always a smile.

She's paralyzed. The apartment is huge and modern with high ceilings and lots of windows. The walls are decorated with paintings and photographs - paintings she's made and sold throughout the years for extra cash, photos Jaemin has photoshopped himself into.

Her mouth is dry and she feels like she's about to pass out.

"Our bedroom's over this way," Jaemin says, guiding her throughout the giant space and either being oblivious to or completely ignoring her paralyzed state.

The bedroom is even worse. Her exact lamp sits mirrored on both of the nightstands, glowing softly like someone turned it on in preparation. The bed is huge and unmade on one side, the side she always sleeps on left pristine and untouched.

Waiting for her.

She's afraid to open any of the dresser drawers, already knowing what she'll find. But Jaemin gently pulls her to what must be the closet.

"I bought you something," he says excitedly, grinning to himself, "As a celebration."

His words are background noise. Isla's full attention is on the half of the closet that must be her half - every piece of clothing she's ever wanted, every bag, every pair of shoes, every fucking piece of jewelry is there.

A loud buzzing noise arises in her ears and she zones out, unable to cope with the madness surrounding her.

It's the shock of cold metal against her skin that brings her back to the present moment, Jaemin securing a necklace around her nape. All the hair on her arms rises as he places a gentle kiss on her temple, looking into the mirror Isla hadn't even noticed they were standing in front of.

"Welcome home, angel."

She has to get out of here.

Now.

Isla puts all of her energy into restraining herself from shaking.

"It's beautiful," she says, finally looking at the simple chain with a small "J" pendant resting in the dip of her cleavage.

It really is. It's the most expensive, most exquisite collar she's ever seen.

"You like it?"

She nods, licking her lips. Jaemin's too close for her to make a run for it. Her eyes settle on the smiling man and she feels a sharp wave of hatred wash over her.

Why'd it have to be her? What's she ever done to deserve this nightmare?

"Why don't I run us a bath? You must be exhausted from such a long day," Jaemin purrs, fingers falling away from her collarbone.

She jumps at the chance.

"Yes, that would be lovely. I'll explore a bit more while you get it set up, yeah?" she says, internally praying he complies.

Jaemin pouts, the same puppy expression that would have melted her heart a month ago.

"Why not do it together? It's been so long since the last time."

Even though his words are cutesy, Isla detects the hidden meaning and nearly gags.

"Last time?"

"A bath is a perfect way to set the mood," he says, voice suddenly lower, a bit of his Busan accent coming out, "Then we can break this new bed in, hm?"

She'd fantasized about this a million times. Who hasn't dreamt about sleeping with their bias? With Jaemin? But now? Now she'd rather fling herself off the nearest bridge than let him touch her. The kisses were already too much.

"I-I'm kinda tired, Minie. I really just want to go to bed. We have plenty of time to break whatever in, alright?" Isla prays that Jaemin doesn't hear the shake in her words.

Jaemin pauses and looks her all over, analyzing her. Isla comes to the sudden and awful realization that they're completely alone - that he may not listen to her words and try and force it.

He wouldn't, would he? Jaemin's not that guy.

But he's not the type of guy to stalk a random fan and fake being in a long-term relationship either.

Her anxiety shoots through the roof.

"Okay," he says, smiling softly, "Rest is important. Health always comes first."

She could fall out from relief.

"But we'll make sure to leave no piece of furniture untouched once you're adjusted,"

Isla's half a second from saying fuck it and running for her life, but Jaemin's blocking her way.

So the girl stands fearfully in the bathroom as her 'boyfriend' runs them a bath in the huge bathtub. He pours sweet-smelling stuff into the water and tosses in rose petals as he talks excitedly about the new comeback he and the other boys are working on.

"And the choreo for the title track is amazing, Isla, you're going to love it," he says, turning off the tap and facing her.

"Water's ready," he says, but she doesn't plan on moving.

"Um . . . aren't you going to leave?" she asks softly, toying with the hem of her shirt.

He giggles cutely, a lighthearted sound, one much too happy for the current situation.

"Why would I? Come here, baby."

Isla hesitates but moves to obey his actions, a sudden flash of Jaemin committing suicide via bathtub (even if it was only for a role he'd played in a drama) causing her to panic slightly.

Jaemin wraps his arms around her waist from his position perched on the bathtub, head laying against her breast gently. He hums a bit, leaning in to hear the somewhat steady pounding of her heart.

He pulls away and looks up at her.

His eyes are so pretty, dark, inky, and endless.

"You don't have to be afraid, baby, it's okay. You're absolutely perfect just the way you are," he says, standing.

Her heart lurches.

She's never been naked in front of a guy and never in her wildest dreams did she think Jaemin would be the first one to see her in her most vulnerable state, especially not under these circumstances.

She says nothing as his warm fingers slide under the material of her shirt and glide it above her head. She holds her breath as the button to her pants pops open, the sound of the zipper seeming painfully loud. The jeans slide down her legs and hit the ground with a dull thump as her heart starts beating erratically. He looks at her face as his hand reaches around to undo the clasp of her bra. He kisses her cheek as his ringed fingers slide down her sides and hook onto the elastic waistband of her underwear, dragging them just far down enough to fall off on their own.

He's still gazing at her face as he helps her step into the warm water, Isla's quivering form sinking under the suds.

He hadn't looked. He saw no more than what everyone else did every time she went to the beach. And yet she feels as if she's just had the most intrusive experience ever.

Isla can't help but look at him, though. She can't stop her eyes from following the way he effortlessly discards every piece of clothing, maintaining his modesty.

God, his thighs.

Her gaze snaps up to catch his own when the last piece of clothing comes off. She's absolutely certain that if she had continued looking, she'd end up in that new bed and not the airplane out of here.

Insane or not, Matoi Jaemin is a tempting man.

The first few moments of the bath are quiet and tranquil, Jaemin relaxing into the water and letting all the stress from today go. Isla sits as far away as possible, pulling her knees up and tucking them under her chin, watching his every move.

Jaemin's eyes are closed. She could make a run for it now, couldn't she? But there's no way she could put anything on to leave before he caught her, and running through the streets of Seoul naked is not an option.

A moment later, Jaemin opens his eyes again with a pleased sigh. "This is nice, isn't it, angel?"

"Mm," she replies, gripping her knees tighter.

"It's been so long since I've had a bath. Usually, all I can take is a five-minute shower before I have to get going."

"Mm," she repeats, unsure of what else to say.

"You're really tired, huh?"

"Yeah. It was a long flight."

"Why don't I spoil my princess then, hm? Let me take care of you tonight."

And then he's scooting closer in the tub, a rag with coconut-smelling body wash in his hand.

"I can do—"

"Nonsense," Jaemin cuts her off, grabbing one arm and beginning to bathe her.

Isla freezes. This can't be real.

But it is. It's so real. Jaemin's fantasies and dreams are finally coming true. He's wanted to spoil Isla even before he fell in love with her and now he finally can. He's careful to avoid wetting her curly hair, knowing that it's not wash day for her yet. He ignores the noises of protest she emits when he grabs her ankle to wash her legs, laughing at the cute blush that spreads across her cheeks.

"You're so cute, Isla," he says, pulling her into a hug she tries to wiggle out of.

Instead, he just pulls her closer until their chests are smashed together and she's sitting on his lap and straddling something that makes her eyes pop open in alarm.

Isla is stiff as a board as Jaemin kisses her neck softly before placing another kiss on her forehead.

All of this would be incredibly romantic and sexy if not for the fact that he's tripping monkey balls.

"Let's go to bed, Minie," Isla suggests, trying desperately hard to apply as little pressure against his lap and separate their chests.

Is this really happening? This can't be happening! No way is she really sitting on his penis with her boobs smashed against his very toned chest. No way in hell!

Right?

Wrong!

Jaemin hums -

What's with all the humming?

- and nods, releasing his grip on Isla and letting her float to the other side of the tub once more.

He rubs himself down with the rag quickly before standing and stepping out, barely giving Isla enough time to avert her eyes. He snags a towel from the rack hung on the wall, drying off swiftly before tying the plush fabric around his hips, the very tops of his v line still visible.

Isla wraps her own towel around herself as she stands up, resulting in the ends of it being soaked, and toddles after Jaemin, mentally scheduling a therapy session for as soon as she steps foot back home.

Unsurprisingly, Isla is able to find copies of her favorite pajamas in their closet, but she decides to wear something completely different, not wanting to give Jaemin the satisfaction.

The sheets are pulled back when she exits and Jaemin is propped up in bed wearing some reading glasses and reading a book in Korean she's (thankfully) never heard of.

The lamplight casts a pleasant glow across his features and Isla's breath catches in her throat, stunned by how gorgeous and normal he looks. She could almost believe he was her boyfriend come to visit, not the mentally ill Matoi Jaemin of OT2B.

He looks up and pats the space on the mattress gently, smiling at her.

If only this were normal. If only.

She takes the spot and slides under the sinfully soft sheets, staring at the ceiling as Jaemin continues to read.

"Jaemin?" she asks him, gaze never leaving the smooth plaster, momentarily comparing it to her cracked one at home.

"Hm?"

"Why do you love me?"

She's been wondering why it was her of all people that Jaemin decided to "fall in love" with. Maybe there's some sort of reason, some explanation that will help her figure out how to escape.

He pauses in his actions and turns his head to look at her.

"What a silly question."

She doesn't say anything.

"It's because you were there for me when no one else was. You stuck around even when I turned my back on myself. It's because you're a beautiful human being with a beautiful soul and every day I wake up and remember you exist and everything stops hurting. How lucky am I to be alive at the same time as you? And there are a million other reasons to go with it and I find more every day."

Oh how she wishes this were real.

"You should get some rest, Minie," she says, blinking away the burn in her eyes and resisting the frog in her throat.

She turns off her lamp and he does as well, removing his glasses and pulling her tight against him.

"I love you."

He falls asleep near-instantly and she sobs quietly, trying desperately not to wake him.

She cries for him. She cries for the beautiful broken boy clinging onto her. She cries for her love for him. She cries for his pain and she cries for herself.

But mostly, she cries because she's going to leave and that's going to break both of them - shatter whatever delusion Jaemin has and haunt her for the rest of her life.

It's easier to slip out of his grasp than she had expected. It's loose, being in his arms is comfortable.

He trusts her, she realizes.

The tears threaten to leave again.

She quickly scribbles out a half-assed excuse and leaves it on her pillow, citing a family emergency as her reason for leaving him in the middle of the night.

Isla looks back at the peaceful Jaemin once more before exiting the bedroom with her old clothes, leaving her pajamas in a crumpled pile on the floor in her haste.

She checks her purse and thankfully everything is still inside. No taxis are running at this time of night (or day, rather, as it's just past one a.m.), so Isla makes a quick return to her hotel, promptly checking out and catching the subway to the airport.

Inside of the empty car, she gnaws her lip, guilt eating away at her. She knows she's doing the right thing but it still feels wrong.

She sends a quick email to Smash Entertainment explaining her actions and begging them to give the boys a break and get Jaemin the professional help he needs. She also warns them of his suicide threats, fearful he may really toss himself off of a building due to her departure.

And with that, she's done. Isla makes up her mind that this will be the last time she has anything to do with OT2B, anything to do with Jaemin, no matter how much the band's existence has comforted her when nothing else could.

She prays for everything to work out okay as Seoul disappears under the clouds.

5

Jaemin adjusts himself in bed, subconsciously rolling over a bit to snuggle into Isla's warmth. But no matter how far he seems to roll, he doesn't feel anything but the cold sheets. It startles him awake, and he rubs his bleary eyes as he tries in vain to see in the darkness. He runs his hand to his left, pressing firmly into the bed.

"Isla?" he calls out once it's evident that she's no longer in bed. There's no response.

"Isla?" he calls again, this time louder.

The only thing that greets him is silence. Panic starts to bubble up inside of him as he rolls back over to his side of the bed, tugging the string of his lamp and flooding the room with light. It's empty, just as he feared.

Frantically trying to prevent himself from having an anxiety attack, the idol slips out of bed and opens their bathroom door, switching the light on. Empty.

"Isla?! Baby, where are you?!" he shouts, abandoning all of his attempts to stay calm.

Jaemin runs through the apartment, throwing open every door and flicking every switch, but every time it's the same thing - empty, empty, empty.

"This can't be happening. This can't be happening," he mutters, hands stuck in his hair as he tries to keep a hold of his sanity.

Jaemin shakes his head harshly, trying to drown out the sudden static in his ears.

"She's here. She's here," he chants, spinning around in a circle in the living room and trying to locate her on the walls.

"Come out! Baby, come out! This isn't funny."

Silence.

He explodes.

"THIS ISN'T FUCKING FUNNY! COME OUT RIGHT NOW!"

Nothing.

Jaemin starts to shake, holding himself tightly.

"No. No. She promised. She promised, she did!" he assures himself, dragging his feet back to their bedroom, "Someone must have taken her. She must have been taken. Someone took her," he concludes, throat dry.

The room is closing in quickly. Jaemin trips over his own feet and crashes into the wall, landing harshly on a pile of clothes he hadn't noticed before. They're hers. Jaemin lifts the fabric in front of his face, brown eyes blown out. It's what she had been sleeping in.

"Oh God," he says, tears springing into his eyes and breath leaving him, "Oh, God!"

Someone had really taken her. They had robbed Jaemin blind in his sleep.

He struggles to his feet and stumbles over to their bed in an attempt to retrieve his phone and call the authorities. Before he can dial the number, he notices a slip of paper crumpled in the destroyed comforter. A ransom note, perhaps?

Jaemin snatches the note and spreads it out on the bedside table using the lamplight to reveal the words.

It's a note from her. Jaemin could practically cry in relief, but he has to read it first. When he's done, he sinks onto the floor, taking the piece of paper with him.

"Family emergency?" he asks himself in confusion.

Jaemin grabs his phone and unlocks it, scrolling rapidly on the screen. Just as it was yesterday, none of Isla's family are hurt or in some sort of predicament. He sees no new notices from any of their social media, nothing from any of their text messages he's had rerouted to his phone. Everyone is perfectly fine. He's glad for it - he wouldn't want any of her family to be hurt - but what can this mean?

"Did she *lie* to me?" he asks himself quietly, "No way. She wouldn't do that."

But what other explanation could there be? Now that he's calmed down a bit, he checks and notices that the front door has no sign of forced entry. No one has been inside of their home and the note is definitely written by her hand - he's seen her writing enough to know for sure.

Jaemin dials her number but is told that her phone is out of service. She's already on the plane. He sits in silence as the moments pass, mind completely empty. After a million moments, a chuckle begins deep in his chest before spiraling into intense laughter, Jaemin folded in half as loud, insane laughter tumbles out of his mouth. He laughs until tears pour down his face, until he can no longer breathe.

"No. Not my baby, no. Not my Isla. She loves me. She loves me. She said so. She promised," he rises to his feet suddenly and latches onto the nearest thing to him - a large, ornate vase, "SHE PROMISED!" he screams, tossing the vase so hard into the wall across from him that it shatters into a million pieces of ceramic on the floor.

He doesn't notice, walking barefoot through the wreckage to grab another item - a decorative plate he'd hung so lovingly on the wall only weeks before - and smashes it onto the ground, hunting through the apartment for more things to destroy.

He screams as he smashes all the glasses in the cupboards, cries as he rips her clothes from their hangers, laughs as he drags thick butcher knives through their photos on the wall. He slashes his own face out of them, stabbing the sharp end into the canvas again and again until he's a tattered, ruined mess. Jaemin can't help but think it looks better that way.

The cuts on his legs and feet sting but he revels in the feeling, brandishing the knife recklessly through the air before lodging it into a wall all the way to the handle.

"It's not enough. It's not enough! The clothes aren't enough. The house isn't enough, you're not enough. You!" Jaemin accuses, looking at the cracked mirror in their bathroom.

"It's your fault," he says, jabbing a finger into the glass, "Yours. You fucked it up like you always do. You always fuck everything up! You useless, despicable bastard!"

His reflection only smirks at him, wide and happy.

"Stop it. STOP IT!" Jaemin shouts, beating his fists against the countertop and stomping his sliced feet against the cold ground, "STOP SMILING! STOP FUCKING SMILING! STOP IT!"

The reflection doesn't pay Jaemin's tantrum any mind, joyous smile still in place, taunting it.

"I'm not the problem, Jaemin," it says in that sing-song voice it has, "You are. You're the issue. You're the reason she left. One look at your pathetic self and she bolted - the girl who said she'd love you always and forever. You drove even her away, Jaemin. You did, you did."

"No!" Jaemin exclaims, backing away from the mirror in fear and falling to the ground, "No!"

"Yes," the reflection hisses, pressing a hand against the glass before pushing through it, its body melting through the mirror and onto the counter.

"NO! Stay away! Stay away!" Jaemin sobs, pushing himself along the bloodied floor.

"I can't stay away, Jaemin. I can't. I'm part of you. I am you, Jaemin. I'm the real you."

"No!" Jaemin cries, shoulders shaking tremendously, "No!"

"Stop denying it. It's futile. You can't block me out anymore. You can't drown me out," the reflection says, happy smile on his face as his hand snaps tight around Jaemin's ankle.

"I can. I can get rid of you. I can!" Jaemin insists, shaking his leg as hard as he can, wincing at the pain the reflection's sudden claws cause him.

"It's you and me, baby. I'm all you have left."

"No!" Jaemin screams, managing to shake it off long enough to stumble into the bathtub, "I can kill you. I can!"

"Oh?" the reflection asks, propping itself up on the side of the tub he'd been in only hours before.

It's obvious he doesn't believe Jaemin.

Jaemin grasps onto the handle of the faucet, turning the cold water on full blast.

"I can. I can. I can kill you. I can do it," Jaemin repeats, keeping his eyes on the reflection as the tub steadily fills with water.

Jaemin doesn't feel it. He doesn't feel anything.

"You won't do it. You don't have the courage," the reflection states as unbothered as ever.

"I will!"

"You won't. You haven't even said goodbye yet," the reflection says, nodding his head to Jaemin's cracked and abandoned cellphone on the edge of the tub.

Jaemin doesn't know when it got there.

"You...you're right. I have to say goodbye. I have to say goodbye."

With wet fingers, Jaemin once more grabs his phone, pulling up Isla's contact. He stares at the screen for a moment, looking at her smiling face.

"I can't do it. I can't do it," he chokes out, guilt coursing through his veins, "She asked me to live for her. I can't. I can't kill you."

The reflection's face smiles so hard, his cheeks crack.

"I know," he says, "I know. Get out of the tub, Jaemin. Get out. Clean this mess up. Aren't you ashamed of yourself? You can't do anything. You can't even kill yourself. How pathetic," the reflection says, placing a hand on Jaemin's cheek gently, "Like a kicked puppy, still keeping your promises after she broke hers. How pathetic."

Jaemin sniffles. His head hurts.

"I know. I know."

The reflection stands up.

"Clean this shit up, Jaemin. Clean it up. Stop being such a damn nuisance," he says, making his way back over to the mirror, "Do better."

Hours later, as Jaemin is finishing straightening up their bedroom to the best of his ability, feeling completely numb, he receives a call from CEO Hwang.

"Hello?" Jaemin asks, his voice small and weak compared to the strength he had only yesterday.

Had it been only yesterday?

"Jaemin," CEO Hwang says, sounding relieved, "Where are you?"

"I'm at home."

"Good, good. I was worried. I want you to come on in today. I think I need to talk to you."

Stop being such a damn nuisance.

"Why? Is something wrong?" Jaemin asks.

"I sent Leo to come get you," he says, leaving the idol's question unanswered.

"Okay," Jaemin says, "Okay."

Moments later, the doorbell rings and Jaemin opens the door to see a concerned-looking Leo standing on his doorstep.

"Hey, Jae," Leo says, eyes searching his face.

"Hi, Leo. I guess CEO Hwang sent you to babysit me," Jaemin jokes, smiling so widely at his friend that his cheeks hurt.

Leo is silent. After a moment, he opens his mouth.

"Let's go."

When the duo arrives at the entertainment company, Jaemin is sent up to the boss' office. Inside, a strange woman stands wordlessly beside the uncomfortable looking CEO.

"Hello, Jaemin. This is Doctor Moon," he introduces, gesturing to the lady.

She steps forward.

"Hello, Jaemin. I have a few questions for you. Why don't you take a seat?"

6

Fear constantly haunts her. After she got off the plane three weeks ago, paranoia has rested on Isla's shoulders constantly. She deleted all of her social media and even changed her phone number and email address. She also refused to go back to her crappy apartment in favor of hiding out at her aunt's house under the guise of making a visit. Isla even went so far as to quit her waitressing job altogether, internally blaming her coworker for everything that had happened to her.

Her aunt is single and childless, preferring the company of horrid historical romances and foreign teas. She doesn't spend much time arms, not questioning why Isla showed up out of the blue. Through teatimes and meaningless discussions on B roll romcoms, thoughts of the future torment her.

What now? What does she do? Meeting Jaemin and becoming his 'girlfriend' has thoroughly wrecked her shoddily put together life. She can't even go outside for fear of being recognized and mauled for stealing some fanatic's oppa.

Out of morbid curiosity and complete and utter boredom, Isla hops on her aunt's ancient computer, waiting for what seems like hours for it to boot up and load. She doesn't touch any of her normal accounts, instead logging into an account she created like eight years ago. Quickly, so she doesn't talk herself out of it, she searches OT2B's account and clicks on it, scrolling to see what the members have posted in the time she's been gone. It would be a lot easier and not take so damn long if she'd used her phone, but she stays away from it as much as possible, even with the new number.

There are quite a lot of posts, even more than their usual amount. She'd expected a handful of things, but there are dozens of updates. There's a short video of Seojoon dancing to some unnamed song (maybe the one Jaemin was telling her about), some photos of Seojoon and his dog, Woojin messing around with Daehyun when the rapper's asleep and Daehyun's playfully angry replies. Leo has posted some deep thoughts that Starlights are convinced are hints for the comeback and Seojoon posted an update about his new favorite restaurant. There's only one post from Jaemin. The video is kind of grainy due to the darkness of it, but Isla can make out

Jaemin's form. A closer look reveals that he's sitting on the railing of 'their' apartment, swinging his legs without a care. Due to the angle and the poor quality of the shot, no one else would really be able to tell he's not sitting on a bench.

Panic shoots through her and she yelps, lurching forward like she can save him through the screen.

But he doesn't fall. His butt stays planted firmly on the railing, legs swinging gently. After she's calmed down and her heart no longer feels like it's going to dive after him, Isla notices the audio on the clip. She turns up the old computer's speakers as much as she can, faintly hearing Jaemin begin to sing.

"Just let me love you~" he croons, head tilted up and staring at the moon, "Let me hold you the way I need to~"

The comments are filled with cute messages and proclamations of love and adoration, but the message is clear. Isla notices the slight warble in his voice, the way his legs begin to swing slightly out of sync, and the way his shoulders are sloped slightly.

He's crying.

Pain shoots through Isla as she grips her shirt, balling the fabric up in her fist. It hurts, it hurts her. He's broken, she knows that. Something deep in Matoi Jaemin is broken and she prays that someone will be able to help him fix himself.

She moves the mouse to exit the video but can't quite bring herself to, watching the crappy video loop over and over and hearing the hurt in his voice more each time it replays. Even though she knows she did the right thing, guilt rises in her like a violent flame, licking every inch of her until she has been entirely consumed. Her full lips tremble and green eyes begin to burn, a sure-fire sign that she's only moments away from bursting into tears. Just as the first drop spills down her face, a voice comes from behind her, thoroughly startling her.

Isla jumps, turning around quickly to see her aunt holding her phone.

"Your phone's been ringing nonstop for the past ten minutes," she says, the device in her hand, "It must be pretty important."

"Oh, right, thank you," Isla says, standing up and taking her phone.

"Hey, you okay? Your eyes are kinda red," her aunt asks, sounding concerned.

"Yeah, I'm okay. I just saw something sad online," Isla explains, offering a somewhat weak smile.

"Alright then. Try watching something happier. Those cat videos always cheer me up."

"I'll try that, yeah, thank you," Isla says, smiling one more time just as her phone rings loudly.

Her aunt leaves the room and Isla stares at her phone screen for a moment, debating what to do. She doesn't recognize the number at all, but she has just changed phones and doesn't have anybody's number saved.

Then again, she hasn't given it out to anyone either. The ring cuts off and her screen darkens only for it to light up again seconds later, the same number calling once more.

Based on the thirteen missed calls from this number, Isla can tell that this person isn't giving up anytime soon, so she answers.

"Don't hang up."

As soon as the voice registers in her head, she does exactly as she was told not to, hanging up on the person as quickly as possible. Her heart is back to beating rapidly, shock coursing through her.

"No, no, no, no, no," she chants to herself, willing her phone not to ring again.

If she was thinking properly, she would have blocked the number and taken the battery out of her phone, but her mind's a tangled mess, sirens wailing in her brain.

The phone rings again and in her shaky attempt to dismiss it, Isla once more answers the phone.

"Something'swrongwithJaemin," Leo rushes up in an attempt to get her to stay on the line.

Isla pauses.

"What?"

Leo takes a deep breath, thankful that she hasn't dropped his call yet.

"Smash Ent got your email. He's been getting help. There's a famous psychologist working with him."

"Good," Isla says, relieved.

She'd been so worried he'd do something dumb before someone could stop him.

"That's good," she says, pressing her free hand to her face in an effort to cool down her skin some, "But why are you calling me? You've got to know that everything he said was fake, right? How'd you even get my number? I changed it," Isla asks.

"It's not so good, Isla," Joon says, ignoring her questions, "It's not. He has–"

The word Leo utters has static loud in Isla's ears.

"What?!" Isla practically shouts, Jaemin's diagnosis startling her.

"Yes," Leo says, sounding very worn out, "And it's only getting worse. Apparently, he's had it for years now. Years. It's only progressed so slowly because he's been projecting onto you. It's been keeping the voices in his head quieter than they would have been."

A bad feeling starts in Isla's stomach.

"But since you've left, he's deteriorating at an alarming rate, Isla. He's barely himself. It's scary. It's so scary to see him like this, Isla."

"Isn't there anything the doctor can do? Some sort of medication?" Isla asks, trying in vain to fight what she knows is coming.

"He is on medication and he's abusing it. When I found out . . . he got this big-eyed look on his face and burst into tears, crying over some guy and blaming him about everything that's happened. When I asked who the guy was, he . . . he pointed at the mirror. He was a shaking, blubbering mess. It was like someone else entirely was living in Jaemin's body. I never want to see that again, I never want him to do that again," Leo says firmly, fear present in his tone, "When I told the doctor, she suggested to all of us that having you around could help. Having you around might keep him stable."

"He doesn't know me, Leo, he doesn't know me! I don't know him, Leo. I can't go back there, I can't. I get that you're worried for him but he terrifies me. I've never been so afraid as I was being near him."

"You do know him, Isla. You do. That person you've seen through videos is real. He's in there, Isla, Jaemin is still in there."

There's a pause. Isla feels overwhelmed.

"I know this is scary. It's utterly terrifying, and under normal circumstances, I wouldn't even dream of asking someone to do something like this but he's like my brother, Isla. Jaemin's my family and I love him. I need him to be okay."

Another pause.

"Please, search within yourself somewhere and find the love for him I know you have. I've seen all your old posts, I know you've been supporting us for a long time and I ask you to still support us through this," Leo pleads.

"What if . . . what if he hurts me?" Isla asks, afraid that one of Jaemin's mood swings could end up having her battered and bruised on the ground.

"Jaemin only hurts himself," Leo says quietly, "Only himself."

Isla is silent once more. In the hours she'd been with him, she could see the vulnerability he had, the way he clung to her and looked to her for validation.

Could she really turn away from him? Could she really abandon him after he's given her all his trust, even if she never wanted it? Would she be able to live with herself if something happened to him and she stayed away? The rational part of her knows that this isn't her fight, that she ought to just chuck her phone across the room and change her name and pretend that nothing ever happened. But the image of Jaemin sprawled out, completely lifeless and broken against the hard ground prevents her from being rational.

Because as afraid of him as she is, Isla can't help but be more afraid for him if for no reason other than the way he made her feel when her father's drunken screaming was too loud to drown out.

"Okay," she whispers into the phone, "Okay. But we're doing this on my terms."

It's only two days later that Isla once again stands in Seoul, only this time, she's here to stay. She didn't bring anything more than her purse, Leo having informed her that Jaemin still had a whole wardrobe and other necessities set up for her even though she hasn't seen him in nearly a month. It creeps her out, but she figured Jaemin would be less emotional if she relented on that much.

Besides, all the clothes are brand-new, never worn by anyone. All she has to do is forget who bought them.

Her rules for coming back were very clear:

She'd play Jaemin's fake girlfriend but she's not crossing any lines with him. No way in hell.

She has to be able to maintain her independence. No having someone hovering over her 24/7 or having a tracker on her phone.

She has to receive a salary. A very, very generous salary to put up with all of this and to make sure she can afford to move back home and set herself up better than she ever thought she would be able to.

If things go south and she has to get physical in order to protect herself, she can without fear of any sort of punishment.

She can bail at any time.

Five basic rules and a bunch of little details and paperwork and she's here, nervously awaiting being picked up. No one outside the company knows she's supposed to be coming but she still was picked up on a private jet and sent to wait in a private room.

Her phone dings to let her know someone's outside waiting for her, so Isla shuffles out of the airport as quickly as she can without drawing attention to herself.

Inside the very normal looking but heavily tinted car, Isla is greeted by a smartly dressed man who is busy typing away on his tablet, speaking rapid Korean into his phone that he has wedged between his ear and right shoulder. It makes her feel very awkward as if she'd interrupted him.

Isla clasps her hands together and places them on her lap, fidgeting.

In an effort to be taken more seriously by the executives at Smash Entertainment now that she'll be here for an unknown amount of time, she'd traded in her Goodwill outfit from before and used some of her advance allowance to buy herself something a little nicer - a pretty yellow sundress that compliments her skin tone and a pair of brown strappy sandals. She's fussed with her hair as well, piling the dark curls up on top of her head like the Pinterest girls do and adding some white and yellow daisy clips. Even her nails were painted a matching shade.

The nineteen year old's mind briefly drifts to the last time she put any real effort into her attire, feeling bitter when she realized it was the date she'd gone on.

To think that she'd gone from having one date in her entire life to 'dating' an international superstar.

The man beside her finishes up his phone conversation, pocketing the device and placing his tablet aside.

"I apologize," he says, momentarily surprising Isla.

She hadn't expected him to be able to speak English.

"Ah, it's alright," she says, feeling awkward.

"I'm OT2B's international manager. You can call me Calm."

"Calm?" Isla asks.

For a moment, the man smiles briefly.

"It's a nickname the boys gave me and it stuck. Everyone just calls me Manager Calm now."

"Okay, Manager Calm," Isla says, smiling slightly.

"I've been tasked to brief you - explain some company rules and such that weren't in the contract."

Isla's heart drops and that must have shown on her face because Calm quickly reassures her.

"It's nothing big. Just a few rules to make sure both Jaemin and your privacy is maintained."

"Okay. Let's hear it then."

"You are not to interact with any of the other idols in the company beyond what is required for general politeness."

"That won't be too hard," Isla says, feeling grumpy, "I couldn't even speak to them if I wanted to."

Honestly, the language barrier is Isla's biggest fear, right after Jaemin going hysterical and leaping head-first off a balcony. It doesn't sit right with her that she'll only be able to talk to a handful of people.

"You must act the part of Jaemin's girlfriend whenever you're in public, even if you think no one is around. There cannot be any rumors about the stability of your relationship."

Isla nods, biting her lip, hoping she won't regret this any more than she already is.

"And, of course, you must follow all the rules all other employees do. That means no social media unless it's been approved, no wandering about without proper guards, no communicating the details of your relationship or any company activities to anyone, not even your friends or family."

A part of her wants to tell Calm that he doesn't have to worry about that last part since there's only one person in her entire family she can stand and she has absolutely zero friends, but she holds her tongue.

"I can do that."

"And this should go without saying, but you absolutely cannot tell Jaemin about your contract or the fact that your entire relationship is only a figment of his imagination. There's a very good chance such information could push him off the deep end if he finds out before he's ready."

"Are we going to see them now?" Isla asks, suddenly unsure if she can face him.

"Yes. We're headed to the company. We would stop by the apartment to give you a chance to freshen up and maybe grab a bite to eat, but it's probably best if you see the boys right away. They're currently at practice."

"Right," Isla says, mentally preparing herself to see Jaemin again.

"It's not his fault," she thinks, *"It's not his fault. He's the victim, he's the victim."*

Much too quickly for comfort, the huge car arrives at Smash Entertainment and Isla and Calm exit, Isla swallowing in an attempt to clear the desert in her throat.

"Ready?" Calm asks, searching her expression.

"As ever."

Isla hears him before she sees him. Music seeps through the door of the practice room and drifts down the hallway, an unknown song floating through the air.

Jaemin's singing in the audio, voice lower than usual and more sensual, easily fitting the vibe of the song.

The hallway seems to stretch on forever and take no time at all, Isla's hand coming in contact with the doorknob in what feels like an immeasurable amount of time.

She looks back to see Calm waving at her in encouragement on the other side of the hall, far away from her.

Shaking slightly, she swings the door open.

The music's volume amplifies as the door opens, the new song blaring at a level that must be too loud for the human ear.

The boys inside don't seem to mind it. All five of them are present but they aren't together. Seojoon and Leo stand talking with two people unfamiliar to her (most likely choreographers of some sort), while Daehyun is practicing some moves in formation. Woojin is guzzling water from a large bottle, hair stuck to his forehead with sweat.

And Jaemin . . . Jaemin stands in front of the large wall to wall mirror, face pressed against the glass. He's singing something so softly his words are completely inaudible, hardly vocalized at all. His breath fogging up the mirror right in front of him, hair is on the messier side, but it's obvious it started off well-groomed and lost its shape due to what must be hours of practicing.

The moment is surreal. Isla's heart races just being within a hundred feet of him, hands subconsciously reaching up to grip her dress tightly. She'd imagined how this reunion would go down a million times on the long flight to Korea, but standing behind him washes all of her plans and all of her words away.

Her eyes dart across his form, noticing the way he's a bit skinnier than usual, the way his naturally lightly tanned skin has faded and become dull. Even his shoulders droop, exhaustion evident in the way he leans most of his weight on the glass. He's deteriorating, rotting from the inside out.

She takes a deep breath and calms her nerves to the best of her abilities and speaks.

"Jaemin."

The man's eyes open instantly, brown irises connecting with hers through the mirror's reflection.

"Isla," he breathes out in near disbelief.

In a moment, he's turned around and launched himself at the girl at full speed, thin arms wrapping around her frame and squeezing like a vice. He's speaking so rapidly, she can't keep up, can't even tell if he's speaking English or Korean. Isla returns his hug, squeezing him just as tightly, pretending that she can't feel his bones under her fingertips.

"Hi, Minie," she says, rubbing circles on his back, warmth sinking into his cold body.

"You came back. You came back!" he says, pulling back only enough to look at her face before placing his head back in the crook of her neck.

There's not a stitch of space between them, Jaemin nearly suffocating her. By now, the couple has attracted the interest of everyone else, all the other members looking at the scene with emotions Isla doesn't want to think about. She shuts her eyes.

"Of course I did," she swallows, "I promised."

"And you're never going to break any promises again," he states, tone leaving no room for debate.

"Right," she says, "No more lying."

And then he's kissing her, fingers digging into her cheeks too hard, lips bruising hers, noses knocking together. There's nothing sweet about it, nothing romantic, no butterflies in her stomach. Disgust wells up inside her and Isla fights against the urge to shove him off, the urge to gag as his tongue snakes into her mouth forcibly despite her trying to keep it out. This is not a kiss that should be done in public and the fact that she knows people are watching makes heat rise in her face, Jaemin mistaking her embarrassment for arousal. He moans, low and quiet enough for only her to be able to hear, but that's the last straw. She pulls away and looks to her left, away from everyone else.

"I'm sorry," she says, wishing she could wipe her mouth without hurting his feelings, "I'm sorry, Jaemin."

He shakes his head.

"I'm the one who should be sorry. I know I don't deserve you. I know you left because I wasn't enough. But you came back! You came back, so you must love me too! I'll earn it, I swear. I'll make sure you never want anyone else," he reassures her, tone bright despite the words he's just spoken.

Isla looks at him in alarm, hand going up to his face and feeling how thin his cheeks have become.

"That's not why I left, Minie. Didn't you get my note? And you're perfect just the way you are, Jaemin. You shouldn't change anything."

He grins at her.

"I'll be whatever you want me to be," he says, completely dismissing her words, "And you just said you weren't going to lie to me anymore, Isla."

Her throat feels dry, the girl watching in unease as the happiness in his eyes shifts to something darker, something nearly cruel. Her internal panicking must be pretty evident because Leo speaks up from across the large room.

"Hey, Isla! You must be pretty tired from the flight, huh? Why don't you go downstairs to the cafeteria and get a refresher?" he asks, the slight off-tone in his voice making it clear what a 'refresher' really is.

"Oh, yeah," Isla says, brightening up and looking back to Jaemin, "I'll just go get something to eat then head back home, eh? You guys continue practice," she turns to face everyone else finally, still refusing to make eye contact, "Sorry for interrupting, everyone!"

Isla bows respectfully and moves to make a quick getaway but Jaemin doesn't let her go, fingers wrapped around her wrist.

"I'll come with you," he says.

"No, Jaemin, you're in the middle of work. I shouldn't have even come here in the first place, but I thought it'd be a good surprise. I'll see you in just a bit, okay? I promise."

Jaemin holds on even tighter.

"No. You just got here. You can't leave again this quickly," he says, attempting to sound calm but the shakiness in his tone still evident.

Isla's been back together with Jaemin for less than ten minutes and she's already ready to pack her bags and hop on a plane again.

"Well, how about I go and get something to eat and wait for you to be done with practice? We can go home together?" she suggests, still trying to find a way to get out of his sight.

"No. I want to come with you," Jaemin insists, unwilling to compromise.

She's only just returned, only just stepped into his embrace again but already he feels calmer and happier than he's been in a month, the constant cloud fogging up his mind parting just from her being near. Jaemin can't let her leave, not when he's only just gotten her back.

Isla looks to Leo for support, only to be jerked back to facing Jaemin, the grip he has on her becoming more and more painful. She looks towards the boys one more time and locks eyes with Woojin, who has a perplexed look on his face. She knows that expression. He's thinking about something, running it over in his head. Woojin has always been the most perceptive of the members.

"Why are you looking at them?" he asks, suspicion rising up in him, "Aren't you happy to see me? Didn't you miss me? I missed you every damn day, even moment. All I thought about was you and you don't even want to spend time with me?"

"No," she says, feeling small, "I just don't want you to get in trouble," she says, chewing on her lip.

If this keeps going on, it'll only be a moment before she starts crying and everything goes to hell.

"If Woojin can be an hour late to practice because he was fucking some stylist, I can certainly miss the last half hour of it," his voice is cheery but there's a clear edge to his words.

The Jaemin she knew would never have spoken so brashly, especially not about his beloved Woojin, but this isn't the Jaemin she knows.

"I - okay. Let's go then," Isla relents, not wanting this to go on for even a second more.

Jaemin smiles brightly and lets go of her wrist in favor of tangling his fingers with hers, leaving the practice room without so much as even looking at anyone else. The walk to the cafeteria seems to be taking forever, stark silence and the tightness of his grip being the only things Isla can focus on. She has no idea where he's taking her, half certain Jaemin will end up dragging her off to some abandoned storage closet to either murder her or rip off every piece of clothing she's wearing.

Both possibilities are horrifying and she feels herself begin to sweat, feet dragging against the floor in an attempt to slow down Jaemin's determined stride.

Despite the idol not being particularly tall, his stride rivals that of someone over six foot, managing to cover an incredible distance in a short time. He doesn't look at her, eyes boring straight ahead even though she's sure he can navigate this whole building with his eyes closed and his hands tied behind his back.

But thankfully, the couple arrives at a cafeteria, the space empty of everyone, even staff. Jaemin gently guides Isla to a table close to the food line, pulling out a chair for her and helping her sit down.

"What would you like? We mostly have sandwiches and there might be something else hidden in the back somewhere," Jaemin says, sounding completely normal.

He's sat her down in a position where he can still see her even as he rummages through the food selection.

"Whatever's fine," she says, not feeling hungry at all.

Jaemin hums, choosing a plastic-wrapped sandwich and snatching a can of Coke before sitting across from her.

"I'll make something better for dinner. I've been practicing more recipes and I think I've gotten quite a few of them down packed," Jaemin says as Isla unwraps the food, taking a mouse-sized nibble.

As she pops the tab on the can, Jaemin rests his elbows on the white table, head resting on his tangled hands. His sneaker-clad foot sneaking towards hers and trapping one of her ankles. He smiles sweetly but somewhat vacantly at her, sending chills through her entire body.

"You're not eating?" Isla asks.

"I'm on a diet."

"What if we shared?" Isla suggests, "My stomach feels a little uneasy from the flight."

Not quite an entire lie.

Jaemin lights up.

"Okay. Half a sandwich won't make much of a difference, will it?" he says, already taking it out of her hands.

"No, it won't. Besides, why are you even on a diet, Jaemin? You already look too thin," Isla points out, concerned.

He shrugs and takes a large bite from the side she's already bitten off of.

"Needed to lose weight."

"No, you didn't," Isla says, watching him scarf down most of the sandwich.

"May I?" he asks, gesturing towards her soda.

"I can get you a full one," Isla offers.

"I just want a sip."

"Well … okay, I guess," Isla says, watching him practically snatch the drink and down at least half of it, lips pressed against the metal instead of waterfalling it.

He slides both items back over to Isla, picking up her hand and rubbing it with his thumb.

"You know," he says, speaking quietly despite the two of them being the only people in a thousand-foot radius, "I almost drowned."

Isla freezes up instantly, eyes blown wide.

"What?!"

"I haven't told anyone but you. But I almost . . . it hurt. I felt abandoned, completely tossed aside and trodden on."

"Jaemin–"

"But I didn't. I didn't because all I could do was think about you, think about how sad you'd be if I broke my promise. So, I didn't."

"Jaemin–"

"I don't think I can do that again," he says, tone flat and lifeless, "I don't think I'm strong enough to keep that promise again," he says.

The threat is clear.

"We'll go through it together," Isla says, not sure what else she can say, "You're not alone, Jaemin."

"Okay," he says, back to smiling.

He takes her other hand as well, cradling it.

"Okay. I trust you," he says, so much innocence riding on those four words.

Isla smiles back, lips trembling slightly.

"Isla?"

"Hm?"

"I love you. More than anyone, more than anything. I will never stop loving you. Every breath you make, every step you take, I'll be right beside you. I'm never leaving you," he says, the poetic words making her sick to her stomach.

"I love you too, Jaemin," she says, squeezing his hands to hide the way hers shake.

"More than anyone?"

She nods.

"Say it," he demands.

"More than anyone."

"More than anything?" he asks.

"More than anything."

"And?"

"And I'll never stop loving you," she says, licking her suddenly parched lips.

Jaemin stands slightly and leans over the clean surface of the table. He moves his hands to cup her chin. His eyes flutter closed and Isla's widen, staring at his forehead as he connects his plump lips with hers softly, sweetly.

"Never."

7

Isla takes as much time as she can to finish the small amount of food Jaemin left her, chewing so slowly her mouth only moves every couple of seconds. She's stalling going back to 'their' apartment, dreading seeing the photos of the two of them hung up on the wall, displaying now deep in Jaemin really is.

But as much as she doesn't want to go there, sitting here in this empty cafeteria with Jaemin watching her so intently that he's counting each time her chest moves to take a breath isn't much better. It's only been minutes but she already feels suffocated by his presence.

She smiles at him hesitantly and places the empty can down, cringing at the loud sound it makes against the table.

Jaemin doesn't react to the noise at all, still staring at her.

"Would . . . do you want to get out of here?"

Jaemin raises a single eyebrow, a slow, lazy smile on his face.

"I-no, I meant did you want to leave this place and go somewhere else? I–" Isla panics, heat rushing to her face.

The last thing she needs is to have another bathtub incident.

"Relax, baby, I know what you meant," he laughs, standing up and reaching out to her, "Let's head back, yeah? It hasn't been home without you there."

Isla takes a breath before standing up and taking his hand, attempting to keep the grip as loose as possible but it's futile. Jaemin clutches her hand so tightly, it turns white.

"I can call the van and it'll be here in about five minutes," Jaemin suggests, swinging their hands back and forth like a small child would do.

"Can we just walk instead? The weather is really nice today," Isla asks, not wanting to endure another stifling car ride.

"Anything you want, angel. Our bodyguards will have to follow behind though, just to be sure."

"Our bodyguards? Is that really necessary?" Isla asks, feeling uncomfortable at the thought of being followed by large men in uniform, especially with the way Jaemin acts.

"Of course," he says, holding the door open for the two of them, "Some people are just crazy, you know? I don't want to take any chances of you getting hurt," Jaemin says with genuine concern in his tone.

"Of course," Isla mutters, "We wouldn't want any crazy people around."

Jaemin smiles as he backs out of Smash Ent, sunlight streaming beautifully across his soft features as the sound of birdsong floats through the air.

"There's so much that I want to tell you, so much I want to show you," he says, "but I still can't believe that you're here. While you were gone, I came up with so much stuff we can do."

Jaemin leans against the side of the building still holding onto her, the two of them apparently waiting for their bodyguards out in the open.

"Since you never got to go anywhere while you were here last time, I thought of a million places I want to bring you – oh, and you haven't met my parents yet, my mother already loves you so much and–"

Thankfully, two tall and bulky-looking men exit the building, each wearing not so discreet black shirts and tight pants, looking like they're straight out of a *Men in Black* movie or something. Jaemin doesn't even acknowledge their presence, just pushing off the wall gently and guiding them all down the sidewalk, still talking, talking, talking.

Isla nods occasionally and adds in a few hums of agreement every time he pauses in his speech. She knows she should be listening as he'll probably ask her about it later, but all she can do is focus on keeping her breathing even and putting one foot in front of the other so she doesn't pass out.

"–okay?" Jaemin asks, coming to a stop under the shade of a large tree, their two companions silently standing a few feet back.

"Huh?" Isla asks, looking away from the concrete she hadn't realized she was focusing on so intently and into Jaemin's eyes.

"Are you okay? You're zoning out and you look a little ill."

"I-I'm just tired, I guess. It was a really long flight," she says, both paranoid and slightly touched that he noticed she isn't feeling well.

Jaemin frowns.

"I'm sorry. I got ahead of myself. Of course you're not feeling so great, this is only the second time you've taken such a long trip. Even I get worn out from cross global fights and I've done them like a hundred times. Forget anything I just said, okay? Let's not worry about doing anything today."

He wanted to do stuff today?!

Isla wants to beat herself over the head with a book.

"We can just relax at home. You can take a bath and just go straight to sleep, alright?" he asks, rubbing her cheek gently.

"Are you sure? It's not even late in the afternoon yet," Isla asks.

It's not as if she's trying to talk herself out of resting in favor of playing pretend happy girlfriend, but she's hesitant, not wanting him to change his mind suddenly. And the thought of the bathtub brings back traumatic memories.

"Of course! It'll probably be a few days until you're properly adjusted. I don't want you to end up getting sick. We have all the time in the world to do things together," he says, reassuring her.

All the time in the world.

Isla nods, feeling even sicker than before.

"Yes, we do. All the time," she says.

Not too much later, they arrive at the apartment complex and go through the usual security, the guard keeping himself expressionless but nonetheless giving Isla a creeped out feel. She can feel the uncomfortable tingle of being watched, but when she turns her head, the man is facing forward and not looking her way at all.

Paranoia.

Not a single thing is different in the apartment. Not one. Every picture is in the exact same place. The exact same roses sit on the coffee table, wilted and dead and the same dishes are placed on the same spots on the counter.

It's inhumanly the same as before. It almost looks like nothing has even been touched since she ran out.

"Why don't you go get reacquainted with our room? I'll run you some bath water," Jaemin suggests sweetly.

"Actually," Isla begins, "I think that it'll be better if we have separate bedrooms."

Jaemin's face falls, features pulling downwards.

"Why?" he asks, voice small.

"I think we're moving a bit too fast," she says, stumbling to come up with a valid sounding reason.

"What do you mean? How can we not share a bedroom in our own apartment?"

"It's just ... I think it's a good idea to have our own space, ya know?"

Jaemin shakes his head.

"No, I don't know. Our own space? Why? This apartment is our own space. Just me and you. Why would you want your own bedroom?"

"Well, I—"

"Is it me? Do I snore too loudly? Do I talk in my sleep? I could have sworn I stopped doing that years ago. I can call my doctor and see if—"

"You know what, never mind," Isla says, seeing that she's just making things worse, "I'm just tired. I don't know what I'm saying," Isla yields.

It's clear that her words either aren't getting through or he's blatantly misunderstanding. Either way, he's won this round.

All the apprehension melts away from the idol and he giggles adorably, gently booping her on her nose.

"That's jet lag for you," he says, dismissing the situation, "Now, let's get that bath going, shall we?"

Jaemin insists that Isla keeps the bathroom door wide open while she bathes. When she questions him, he explains that he doesn't want her to pass out from the steam.

It's a valid reason on paper, but Isla notices how he tenses slightly, the way his words are ever so slightly strained.

And now she's here, nose deep in the familiar bathtub, listening to Jaemin whistling happily in the bedroom as he flips through the hangers in the closet. Isla's relieved that he hadn't asked to join her again, stating that he's going to be taking care of her instead.

"Here's something for you to put on, angel," Jaemin announces, walking into the room with full arms and placing a neatly folded stack of clothes on the vanity.

Isla watches him silently from the water, eyes tracking every move he makes. Even though Leo and Jaemin's psychologist was resolute in him not being dangerous, Isla can't help but feel uneasy being around him, especially in such a vulnerable state.

"Take your time," he says, exiting just as quickly as he came.

No lingering, no wandering gaze, no suggestive remarks. Nothing.

Isla sits in the water until it turns cold and her toes turn into raisins, reluctantly exiting while watching the door like a hawk for an unwelcome visitor. Jaemin doesn't pop in while she's stark naked (thank God). Isla doesn't see him until she exits the bathroom, the idol fussing with the covers on the bed.

"Jaemin?" she asks, hugging herself tightly.

"Hey, baby! Do you feel better? Does your head hurt? I have some ibuprofen in the medicine cabinet if it does," he asks, wandering over to her and pulling her into his arms.

"Yes, I feel better, thank you, Minie. No, my head's okay," she says, allowing herself to melt into his arms and comfort as genuinely as she can, proud of herself for not trembling.

For a moment, only briefly, Isla wonders what it would be like for this to be real. To be held so lovingly by someone who truly cared for her, to experience that type of intimacy.

"Alright. You should take a nap, okay? Sleep as long as you'd like, Isla," he says, kissing her head and gesturing to the pull backed covers on her side of the bed.

"Okay."

"I love you," he says, backing away and closing the door softly.

"If only," she whispers to herself, climbing into bed and

immediately falling asleep, exhausted.

8

Jaemin took the next week off and didn't leave Isla's side for seven days straight. At first, Isla had been terrified to have him so near her for so long but she quickly realized he was more or less harmless as long as she did what he asked of her - letting him cuddle her while they watched her favorite movies on the expensive couch. He makes her dry his hair when he leaves the shower and insists on redoing her nail polish every afternoon, being sure to blow on the wet lacquer every time. They sip tea together at lunchtime and she listens to him recounting various tales she would have killed to hear months ago. He cooks three times a day and never asks her to assist him, even though she does anyway, if only to feel less like a doll and more like a human.

But, apparently, Smash Entertainment's leniency has been stretched to the max because, after days of radio silence, Isla finally receives a text from Leo. She's careful to check it while Jaemin is whistling happily as he stirs lunch on the stove, hips swaying slightly to his own music.

Is everything okay? Jaemin hasn't been answering his phone.

Isla glances up slightly to see that Jaemin is still preoccupied with cooking.

Okay as it can be, ig. He's mostly just been really clingy.

The rapper's reply is instantaneous.

Do you think you could convince him to come to practice? It's pretty clear that he doesn't feel like talking to any of us.

Jaemin being at dance practice would be a much-deserved break for Isla. Even if her 'boyfriend' forces her to sit and watch the whole thing, he'll be more than two feet away from her.

I can try

Isla waits until after lunch, the couple cleaning up the kitchen together.

"Hey, Minie," Isla begins, rubbing a sponge across a dinner plate, "Why don't you go to practice today, huh? It's been a while since you've gone," she suggests lightly, already tensing up in case this goes south.

"Practice?" he questions, looking at her with those eyes, "But why? I'm having such an amazing time with you, baby."

"It's just . . . well, don't you miss the others? I know they miss you," she says, looking away from him.

"No," he says, tone flat and without room for argument.

Isla is slightly startled, not expecting the hostility.

"I . . . you've been talking about the new comeback dance a lot. I'd like to see you guys do it," she says, nervously pulling on one of her curls.

If she's learned anything about Jaemin in the last week, it's that he responds best to flattery.

Jaemin brightens instantly.

"Really?"

"Of course," Isla says, still mindlessly returning to scrubbing the same plate.

"Let's go then!" He exclaims energetically, tossing the dish towel aside and grabbing her hand.

He immediately starts to pull her out of the apartment, barely giving her enough time to shove her shoes on, let alone grab her purse or phone from where she left it on the table. He talks the whole way out of the complex, continuing to yap her ear off in the company van as well. Isla, now well-adjusted to this, just nods and smiles occasionally, pretending to pay attention even though all she wants to do is yell at him to shut up.

After what seems like an eternity, they arrive at Smash Entertainment, passing several staff members who look at the couple strangely, some even whispering silently. One woman, a short thing with too pale lips and too straight hair, not so quietly whispers something to her coworker that causes Jaemin's smile to drop instantly. He stops walking abruptly, which causes Isla to run straight into his back. Any joy from Jaemin's eyes has been replaced with pure emptiness as he glares at the lady with such ferocity that she's taken aback, unintentionally stepping backwards.

His tone is clipped and simmering as he speaks to her. Isla doesn't understand a word but she understands the way the woman's already pale face turns ghostly white and she bows excessively, the rest of the room deadly silent as tears start to gather in her eyes.

"Jaemin," she whispers, pulling his sleeve slightly.

She doesn't like the way everyone refuses to look at them now, faces glancing at the floor.

"Jaemin," she tries again, the idol still speaking to the woman who looks like she'd give anything to be anywhere else right now.

Still no reaction.

Isla swallows, mentally cringing for what she's about to do. She wraps her arms around his small waist, leaning forward to place a kiss on his neck, feeling his heartbeat spike under her lips.

"Let's go, Jaeminie. I really want to see you dance," she whispers so only he can hear, wishing she could join the pale lady in a hole somewhere underground.

Any harshness flees as he giggles, quickly turning around to hug her tightly.

"Okay, let's go, baby," he says, refusing to let her go as he waddles backward.

By the time they get to the practice room, Isla's face is so red that it burns, the girl wishing she had a paper bag to stick her head in and disappear.

Apparently, everyone is surprised to see Jaemin as they all stop their movements, Seojoon ending up awkwardly with one leg half in the air.

"Isla wanted to see the dance!" he says, smiling widely and finally letting her go but still holding her hand.

Everyone pretends like everything is okay, Leo sending her a thankful smile as Isla nods, taking her spot as far as she thinks Jaemin will let her go. The practice goes by in a flash, everyone working hard. Jaemin is putting his all into every choreo, going all out. He's gonna wear himself out and Isla is thankful. Hopefully, he'll pass out and let her have some time to herself.

They finally end at eleven pm, early for them to be having a comeback soon, and a sweat-soaked Jaemin plops himself on Isla's lap, all smiles.

"So," he says, taking a big breath, "What did you think?"

"It was wonderful," she says sincerely, you all did great. I'm sure the comeback will be the best one yet."

Jaemin's smile gets bigger, his eyes disappearing.

"Hey, Isla," Leo says, looking quite beautiful with his hair plastered to his forehead, "We're all going out to eat together. Why don't you join—"

"No," Jaemin says, sitting up so quickly that he nearly smacks Isla in the jaw with his head, "We're going home."

Leo raises his hands in surrender, knowing when not to poke the bear.

"Alright. See you tomorrow?" he questions, not sure if Jaemin plans on coming back again.

"Yeah, see you then, Leo," Isla says, nodding, giving him a polite smile.

She misses the dark look on Jaemin's face but Leo doesn't, flinching slightly before making his way to the others, glancing over his shoulder.

Her 'boyfriend' is just as chatty on the way home as ever, but Isla notices the slight slur of exhaustion on his words and how his blinks take longer each time he shuts his eyes. She has to help him into their apartment, beginning to run a tub of water to sit him in.

"No. No tub," he says, yawning, "shower."

"Are you good to stand up?" Isla asks as she's supporting most of his weight at this point.

He shakes his head.

"No. You help me."

"I don't think that's a good idea."

"Please," he whines, face pulled into a sleepy pout.

Isla sighs. He has to get clean before he goes to bed.

"Okay," she says, guiding him to the glass shower and warming up the water while he sits on the edge of the tub, head lulling slightly.

"Alright. Get undressed," she says once the water is warm enough, shaking her hand to dry it off.

Jaemin just raises his arms, eyes still closed.

It is rather adorable, Isla has to admit. She pulls the shirt over his head, giggling at the way his hair stands up straight on his head. She unties his shoes as he rests his head on hers, slipping them off along with his socks. She pauses slightly at his belt buckle, swallowing slightly before she undoes it with trembling hands, the sound of it hitting the floor seeming to echo throughout the room.

"You can do the rest, Jaemin," she says, unable to force herself to continue.

He whines, not even speaking real words. She gives in, knowing that he's worked tirelessly today and tries to touch him as little as possible. When she opens the shower door to usher him inside, he yanks her in a sudden bout of strength, the girl becoming drenched instantly as she stumbles, hands reaching out and grabbing Jaemin's arms to try and prevent herself from falling. When she looks up through her soaked hair, he's smiling mischievously at her, eyes still looking exhausted.

"Jaemin!" she shrieks, trying to move away but once again slipping as her shoes slide off the wet plastic.

"Mm?" he asks, letting the water hit his head.

"Why'd you do that?!"

"I wanted to shower with you," he mumbles.

"Why didn't you just ask?"

"You would have said no."

That's true.

Jaemin starts to tug at her clothing but she swats his hands away.

"Just bathe, Jaemin," she says annoyed, carefully moving to open the door and escape.

He's silent for a moment.

"Why . . . why don't you love me anymore?" he asks, voice small and broken.

"What do you mean, Jaemin? Of course I love you!" Isla insists, hand hovering over the handle, anxiety rising.

"You don't," he says quietly, sliding down the wall until he's sitting on the floor, legs pulled up to his chin, "You said you wouldn't lie to me."

"Jaemin–"

His voice catches in the beginning of a sob, shower water masking the tears that slip down his cheeks.

"Jaemin–"

He pulls himself closer, hands shaking.

Isla turns off the water, crouching down next to him and hesitantly reaching out to touch his arm.

"I'm–" he hiccups, "I'm not stupid, Isla."

He takes several breaths in an attempt to stop himself from crying.

"I know . . . that you don-don't love me anymore," his voice cracks, "You don't look at me the same anymore. You don't speak to me the same anymore."

Isla's head is swimming as she watches him have a mental breakdown, unsure of how to help, unsure of what to say.

"Jaemin . . . of course I love you. More than anyone, remember," Isla says, fishing for the proper words.

He shakes his head, refusing to look at her.

"You won't even let me touch you," he says.

His voice is hollow, completely void of any emotion. He seems so depressed that Isla finds herself feeling guilty even though she has no reason to be. She swallows, wet hair stuck to her skin, Jaemin under her fingertips.

For one awful moment, she doesn't know what to do. She's paralyzed under the implications, completely frozen.

Isla has only known Jaemin for little more than a week and it certainly hasn't been a romantic affair. She's done all she can to spend as little time with him as possible, to touch him only when necessary, to guard herself from his unpredictable behavior.

It's certainly not the situation to be thinking about sex, not at all.

Isla wants to brush him off like she did the first day she met him but something in his demeanor tells her that it could very well be the straw that broke the camel's back. Jaemin looks so fragile, pathetic and drenched and naked, the very definition of vulnerable. So, why does she feel like she's the one exposed?

Is this really how she wants to lose her virginity? What about the rules she set up?

Those and a million other questions fly through her brain but she can't focus on any of them, not with the utterly defeated look on Jaemin's face.

"I'm sorry, Minie," she says, standing up and reaching for his cold hands, "I never wanted you to feel this way. I'm just a bit overwhelmed at the moment."

She pulls him up, the man essentially dead weight. Jaemin crashes into her without a reaction, eyes glazed over. He doesn't even look at her when he falls onto the perfectly made bed, wet hair dousing the comforter. He only looks up at her, eyes wide with surprise, when she straddles him, wet clothes sticking to his skin.

"Isla? What are you—"

She cuts him off by connecting her lips with his.

Isla turns her thoughts off, giving in to the situation. She can debate the ethics and consequences of her actions later, but now Jaemin needs to stop looking like he wants to die more with every breath he takes.

Isla pulls away to find Jaemin's brown eyes blown wide, breathing heavier than before.

"Isla—"

She grinds her clothed core against his dick, ignoring the flush of heat that rises to her cheeks as she feels him stir from below her. His breath escapes in a hiss as his hand reaches to squeeze her hip. She's never done this before and has no idea if she's doing it correctly, but if the smut she's read in fanfiction is even close to accurate, she at least has some idea.

"Don't do that, fuck."

She ignores him, slowly grinding against him.

"I'm sorry, Jaemin," she says, feeling herself get breathless as well, the unfamiliar feeling of someone pressed up against her turning her on, "I'm sorry I've been so bad to you. I'm sorry I'm such a shit girlfriend."

She grabs the edges of her shirt, slipping the soaked material over her head and tossing it somewhere, "I'll make it up to you, I swear."

Isla isn't sure where this courage has come from, but she's thankful for it. Something tells her that chickening out halfway through would be the final nail in Jaemin's coffin.

Jaemin's breath catches and he props himself up, attaching his lips to her neck and sucking harshly against the skin, wanting to leave his mark for everyone to see. Isla's head falls back and she moans, not expecting it to feel as good as it does. Jaemin's fingers sneak around to unclip her bra, sliding the material down her arms and throwing it while sucking a new spot on her collarbone.

"Jaemin."

He growls, Isla squeaking in surprise as the man suddenly flips them, pinning her against the covers with his weight. Her bare breasts are smashed against his chest, Jaemin sliding down her body and swirling his tongue across her right nipple, causing Isla to grab his hair tightly in between her fingers. He slides it down her stomach, leaving goosebumps in his wake.

He unbuttons her pants, pulling the stubborn material down her legs, thankful that she'd taken her shoes off when she entered the house. Before she can say anything, he's tugging her panties off as well.

She shrieks when he runs his tongue over her slit, the idol having the audacity to laugh and place a kiss on her thigh before delving in, eating her out with abandon.

"Fuck, Jaemin!" she screams, back arching off of the bed. She tries to pull away but he presses on her thighs hard enough to prevent her from escaping as he licks her like a man starved.

"I'm—" she moans when he sucks her clit harshly, "I'm supposed to be - making it up to you," she says, half desperate to get him to stop as she hurdles to an orgasm.

He ignores her, continuing to do as he pleases until she freezes, moments away from cumming. Then the bastard pulls away. Glancing up at her innocently, slick all over mouth and chin.

"Oh my God," she says, collapsing on the bed and covering her eyes with her arm, feeling worn out and more embarrassed than she ever has before.

Jaemin laughs again, all traces of despair momentarily erased.

"I'm not done with you yet, angel," he says, voice low, deeper than she's ever heard it.

He pulls himself up and over her, resting on his forearms as he stares at her, intense emotion in his eyes. Before she can decipher what it is, he grinds his cock over her cunt, the head getting caught momentarily on her hood. Isla digs her nails into his back.

"Stop teasing me," she begs, head empty of every other thought than feeling him inside of her.

He does it again, wetting his dick but not pushing inside.

"What do you want?" he asks, loving the way she looks under him, the way her skin is flushed and damp, the way her lips are parted and her breathing is fast.

"You."

"What about me?" he asks, dragging across her a third time.

"Everything!" she says, not processing her words, "I want everything!"

Jaemin falters momentarily, fully having expected her to say she wanted him to fuck her.

He kisses her, slowly, hands in her head, pulling away only to catch a breath before diving back in again.

He chose correctly.

Isla whines one more time and he pushes in, pausing when she winces slightly. He doesn't understand why, as they've slept together before and she should be used to the feeling of him inside of her. Regardless, he peppers kisses all over her neck, waiting for her to adjust. When she nods, he pushes all the way in and bottoming out. Curses fall from his lips like prayers, her pussy squeezing him so tightly that he's not sure how long he'll be able to last.

"Move," she begs, once again pulling at his back.

Jaemin rolls his hips sinfully, pulling halfway out before thrusting back in, Isla's words reduced to nonsensical noises as she wraps her legs around his waist in a desperate attempt to get him closer.

"Faster," she demands, Jaemin all too willing.

The sound of skin slapping fills the room as he increases the pace, feeling his high get closer with each drag of his dick against her walls. He grinds his thumb against Isla's clit, desperate for them to cum together. Sooner than he would have liked, he feels himself falling over the edge.

"I love you! I love you, I love you, iloveyouiloveyouiloveyou!" Jaemin exclaims, nearly collapsing as he cums harder than he has in months, Isla's walls contracting as she cums right along with him.

He's slow to pull out, not wanting to leave the heaven between her legs. When he does slip out, he grabs a baby wipe from his bedside and glides it between her lips, incredibly satisfied to see his cum spilling out of her.

Isla's eyes are closed as she fights not to cry, hating how much she loved every second of it. She pulls herself closer to him, finding solace in the thing that messed her up in the first place.

"I love you, Isla," he whispers.

"I love you too, Jaemin."

9

Isla wakes up to sunlight streaming through the blinds, her body tucked gently into Jaemin's, his lean arms keeping her firmly against his chest. She's as naked as the day she was born, breasts squished against his hard chest.

Her mind is blurry and, for a moment, she panics, not remembering how she came to be in this situation before it all comes rushing back to her. Her cheeks instantly heat and she attempts to move away from Jaemin to go put some clothes on, but he groans in his sleep, pulling her closer. Jaemin nestles his face in the crook of Isla's neck, his even breathing tickling her skin.

He looks utterly at peace, sleeping with neither the look of total despair nor his expression of lust from last night evident at all. It reminds her of the numerous clips she's seen online when Jaemin was passed out due to exhaustion, his features arranged completely in a way that can only be described as innocence. Isla's heart flutters briefly and she takes her time to study his features, eyes trailing across his brows and down the slope of his nose before landing on his lips, the same lips that did a number of sinful things only hours ago.

How can he, this sleeping angel, be the same man who makes her afraid to breathe incorrectly in fear he'll snap? How can this same man be the one in front of millions, smiling and laughing happily like there's not a thing wrong?

Isla begins to feel her nose burn, a tell-tale sign of tears coming. She wrangles out of his grasp, stealing the sheet as she exits the bed and mumbles something about having to pee to the newly awakened Jaemin.

Thankfully, the toilet is in a closet of its own, letting Isla gather her emotions and steady her breathing. She bites her bottom lip harshly and forces herself not to cry, not to dwell on the fact that she just slept with Jaemin purely out of guilt and fear, not because she truly wanted to.

It makes her feel dirty, used almost. This is not how spending a night with someone is supposed to make you feel. There's no satisfaction, no dazed happiness, no love surging through her heart. Isla places her fist over her mouth, gagging slightly before swallowing the sensation down, refusing to upchuck.

A gentle knock comes on the door.

"You okay, baby?" Jaemin asks softly, voice clogged with sleep.

"Mmhm," Isla says, not sure if she'll be able to use real words.

"Okay."

A pause.

"I'll go make breakfast, okay? Would you like me to leave some ibuprofen out for you?"

"Yes, please," Isla says, shoving down all her emotions and realizing that she does ache slightly, her muscles sore.

Jaemin's bare footsteps fade away and Isla waits a moment before flushing the toilet despite not using it at all. She clutches the sheets against her body so tightly, her knuckles turn white. Jaemin's nowhere in sight, just those bright orange pills and a glass of water laid out on the countertop. She swallows all four at once and escapes into the closet, hastily pulling a pair of plain panties over her legs and tossing on a sports bra, not wanting to wear anything that might make her stand out. Then it's sweats and a plain black t-shirt, Isla plopping one of Jaemin's baseball caps over her unruly hair and calling it a day, too emotionally drained to put any real effort in.

When Isla figures she's stalled for as long as she can get away with, she heads into the kitchen, arms wrapped around her lower torso.

Jaemin's halfway through breakfast, fluffy pancakes stacked high on a plate.

"I was in the mood for something sweet," He comments as Isla sits at the table, staring blankly at the food.

"Baby?" Jaemin asks, suddenly in front of her with a knife and fork.

Isla jumps, startled.

"What's wrong? You're acting weird this morning," Jaemin comments, a soft, concerned look on his face.

"Just a bad dream," she lies, picking up a knife with trembling fingers and cutting cleanly into the pancakes on her plate, not looking at him.

"What was it about? Dr. Moon says talking about dreams can make them not so scary," Jaemin offers, upset to see his love so shaken.

Isla takes a bite, finally glancing up at him. Dr. Moon is his psychologist, the woman whose idea it was to bring her back to Korea in the first place. Bitter resentment floods her, Isla's grip on her utensils tightening.

"I don't remember," she says so quietly, Jaemin can barely hear her.

Isla feels hollow, almost like she switched places with Jaemin, empty and in need of comfort.

Jaemin's frown deepens and he rises to his feet, coming to stand beside her before crouching down.

"Hey," he begins, "You know you can tell me anything, right?"

Isla nods, the motion stiff and minute.

"I know, Jaemin. I just don't remember it. All I know is that it was scary."

"How about we stay home today, then, hm? We can relax, light some candles, maybe watch some movies," he tries reaching out to her, heart falling when she stiffens under his touch.

Isla shakes her head.

"No, I'll be fine, I promise," Isla says.

She doesn't have the strength to deal with his eternal hovering, not today. More than anything, Isla just wants to be alone with her thoughts. Sitting in the corner of OT2B's practice room will have to do.

Jaemin's eyes dart across her face. He doesn't believe her.

"Besides, nothing cheers me up more than seeing you practice," Isla says, faking a very weak smile.

He either buys it or his ego allows him to turn a blind eye to her blatant deflection.

"Okay. Eat up and then we'll go," Jaemin says, returning to his own seat and finishing his breakfast.

Knowing it'll be a million hours before they'll take a break and Jaemin will allow her to leave his sight to grab something to snack on, Isla eats every bite even though she wants to throw up every time she swallows.

An hour later, they walk into the practice room, the boys still surprised to see Jaemin. Isla's fairly sure that practice began quite a while ago since the others are already covered in a thin layer of sweat. No one says anything, though, and Jaemin begins stretching, chatting happily with the members. All at once, all five of them look at her and Isla tightens her grasp on her shirt, not liking the smug look on Seojoon and Daehyun's faces. If she felt dirty earlier, it's nothing compared to how she feels now.

The hours crawl by at a snail's pace, Isla desperately wishing she could get away with fucking around on her phone without Jaemin noticing and throwing a fit. It would at least give her a distraction.

But no, all she can do is watch him, watch him, watch him.

She doesn't even move despite her butt being numb from the hard ground.

How many people would kill to be in her position? How many people would have accepted his lies and manipulation without hesitation, simply happy to be in the presence of their beloved idol? Why couldn't Jaemin have selected one of those people? What did she ever do to deserve this?

Isla pushes down those thoughts, knowing that having a breakdown in the middle of practice would not end well for anyone.

She's finally given a break when someone (a manager, maybe?) comes into the spacious room and interrupts, all five boys halting their performance as Jaemin breaks away and stands closer to the man, wiping his brow and nodding.

Jaemin turns and jogs to Isla, plopping down on the floor beside her.

"My doctor wants to see me for a bit, okay? Why don't you grab a bite to eat down at the cafeteria?"

Isla nods, rising up and wincing as she stretches, sore from being so still for so long. Based on the light coming from the windows, it's already afternoon, maybe three or four o'clock.

Isla doesn't look at the other boys as she leaves, not wanting anything to do with them. She debates making a run for it, but she's quite certain that someone would catch her.

With nothing better to do, Isla wanders down to the cafeteria, once again noticing how empty it is.

Smash Entertainment is full of employees and idols and she doubts that most of them are off of work by now. It's not lunchtime, but still.

"This is for the idols only," a voice says from behind her.

Isla jumps and turns, not expecting to be followed.

A sweaty Leo stands in front of her.

"That's why it's always empty. In case you're wondering."

"Oh," Isla says, taking a step back, not feeling as comfortable around him anymore, "Should I just run out and get something then?" Isla suggests, hoping Leo will go along with it.

"That's not a good idea," he says, Isla's spirits falling instantly.

"But I can take you out, at least," he says, smiling slightly.

"Really?" Isla asks, perking back up.

Leo laughs. Isla is rather cute, especially when she's smiling.

For a moment, guilt rises up in the male. This is the first time she's seemed genuinely happy since he's met her and he knows it's because of what Jaemin is doing to her. And after what Jaemin told him happened last night, Leo can't help but feel bad for her.

It's why he followed her once Jaemin was successfully out of sight. On top of being crushed by the weight of Jaemin's demand, Isla is also all alone in a foreign country surrounded by people she can't even communicate with. Being the only other person her age who speaks English and being from the States himself gives Leo a conflicting sense of responsibility.

"Yes, really. The coach called break since Jaemin's headed out for a bit. I already said I was going to my studio."

"Let's go then!" Isla shouts, grabbing Leo's hand and dragging them out of the cafeteria, the rapper tripping a few times.

"Aren't I supposed to be leading you?" the rapper asks.

"Oh, yeah," Isla says, stopping abruptly, Leo bumping into her back, "I just got too excited, I guess."

Her cheeks are flushed. She blushes more than anyone Leo has met before.

Leo lets go of her hand and instead places his palms on her shoulders, leading her through deserted back hallways. There's a door they push through and suddenly they're outside in a small enclosed garden, birds chirping sweetly.

"I didn't know this place was back here."

"Mm," Leo says, "The CEO had it built a few years back. It's supposed to be a place for idols and trainees to take a break and clear their minds."

"That's nice of him," Isla comments.

Leo snorts.

"There's a reason it's empty. No one ever gets enough time to take a break. He mostly uses it as a selling factor for new trainees. It makes them think this place is better than it really is."

Isla frowns. She's heard that Hwang Hyungmin - the CEO and founder of Smash Entertainment - was a bit of a hardass but overall a good boss who values his idols.

"Really? That's surprising," she says.

"Don't get me wrong. He knows what he's doing and he lets more established groups have a bit more flexibility than a lot of other companies. But at the end of the day, it's a business. There's a lot more dirt hidden behind all the glitz and glamor than you'd think."

Isla isn't quite sure what to say.

"This way," Leo says, successfully changing the subject.

Isla watches in curiosity as Leo pulls back a section of a large rose bush, revealing a hole in the wall. She steps out of it and into a back alley, Leo following after her. They jump a fence at one end of the alley and walk through more back roads until they arrive at a small store, an old wooden sign hanging up with a faded picture of a flower painted on it. The door chimes as they enter and are greeted by a friendly-looking old woman who smiles at Leo, the two obviously well acquainted.

Just like the cafeteria, the place is deserted. However, the small restaurant has a cozy feeling, very similar to the vibe she gets when she's shopping in her local second-hand bookstore.

The couple settles down into a pair of well-worn wooden chairs, the elderly lady setting two cups of steaming green tea in front of them.

"This is nice," Isla says, blowing away the steam and taking a small sip.

"It's one of my favorite places to go when things get too stressful. It's been here since my great grandmother was a child but has fallen into obscurity behind all of these corporate buildings," Leo takes a sip, "So, I bought it."

"This is your restaurant?" Isla asks, somewhat flabbergasted.

She's absolutely certain that he can afford it no problem with how hugely successful OT2B is, but it still seems so bizarre.

"Legally, I guess, but I let the owners keep and run the place. They keep any money they make as well. I just didn't want it to go out of business."

"That's really sweet of you, Leo," Isla says, smiling at him.

He smiles back.

"I haven't told the others about this place. As much as I love them, I needed a space that was just my own, ya know?"

"I imagine it's hard being around someone twenty-four-seven whether you love them or not. Just a week with Jaemin hovering over me seems so . . . stifling," Isla says, voice softening.

Leo feels awkward, taking a long sip of his iced tea.

"Ah well . . . why don't you tell me a bit about you? I mean, I heard a lot from Jaemin, but now that I know that he's . . . ill . . . I guess it's a good idea to hear it from you."

"There isn't much to tell," Isla says, "I'm an only child but I'm estranged from my family. I didn't go to college and I work at a diner. Or I used to. I quit to come here."

"There's got to be more than that," Leo prods, trying to get the sad tone in her voice to go away, "What do you like doing? What are some of your goals?"

"Hmmm, well, to be honest, I spend most of my free time on you. Or rather, OT2B. Watching videos, listening to music, stuff like that."

"Thank you," Leo says.

"No, thank you," Isla says, "For being there for me. Even if you didn't know you were doing it. You guys have really pulled me through some rough stuff. And thanks for bringing me here. I really needed a break."

Leo softens. He knows that he and his band members have a positive impact on the lives of millions of people, but it's another thing to be face to face with someone he knows has experienced misfortune and hear how he helped get them through it.

"Of course. It'll be our secret," he says, winking at her.

Isla laughs briefly. As the sound dies down, Leo's expression grows more somber.

"So," he begins, lifting his cup to steady his hands, "How have things been going with Jaemin? He seems a lot better, but how are you?"

Isla is silent for a moment. Before she can open her mouth, tears well up in her eyes and spill over as a sob gets stuck in her throat. She grasps her shirt in an effort to suppress the sudden burst of emotion.

The tears fall anyway, and soon, Isla is hunched over, pain radiating through her body. Even though she'd tried to tell herself that she was okay, last night really messed with her. The memory of it has been flashing through her brain all day, making her feel sicker and sicker and even more alone than she ever has been before.

A piece of herself is gone, given to someone she's afraid of, someone who doesn't even love her. Isla knows that she can never get it back, never spend her first time with the love of her life like she wanted. She wasn't even sure if she was ready for sex, but did it because she felt she had to because she was terrified for him.

"Oh my gosh," Leo says, not having expected the sudden change. He fumbles around for a bit, unsure how to help her. But Isla doesn't pay him any mind. She's too busy spiraling, trapped by indescribable emotions, sobbing until there's nothing left of her , nothing left to give.

10

The blank clock ticking steadily on the wall is the only sound in the spacious room, Jaemin relaxing on the white chaise in Dr. Moon's office.

The space is boringly bland, everything empty and white. The psychologist has only just moved her office into one of Smash Entertainment's empty rooms, but Jaemin has a feeling there won't be any more personal touches added.

They've been meeting for a month now and Jaemin has discovered that she's just as boring as the blank walls around them. He doesn't know why he has to meet with her and no matter how much he asks her, the doctor won't tell him.

The woman sits still behind her glass desk, ankles crossed and shoulders pulled back, typing on her dimly glowing laptop and somehow not making a single sound despite her long nails.

Finally, she breaks the silence.

"How have you been feeling, Jaemin?"

Her voice is cool and doesn't fluctuate but it manages to be more melodic than robotic.

It's the same question she always begins with. But unlike normal, Jaemin finally feels something other than despair. The idol smiles, unable to stop himself.

"Happy. I've been really happy, doctor."

More typing.

"And what has been making you feel this way, Jaemin - ssi?"

"Isla. Always Isla. I'm so much better when she's around. Nothing hurts anymore. Things that made me want to scream make me smile now. I swear the sun's been brighter lately."

He speaks with the happiness of a love-struck teenager, blinded by sweetness. His tone causes dissatisfaction to spread through the doctor. Her jaw freezes in annoyance. How is it that a nobody foreigner can waltz her way in and change Jaemin's mood so swiftly when she herself hasn't made any progress with him in an entire month? Her thoughts cause her typing to stop for a moment before she continues on.

"How has your relationship been fairing?" she asks him.

Jaemin readjusts himself on the couch, tucking his forearms under his head like he's relaxing on a hammock in the middle of an island vacation.

"It's progressing really well," a smile, a beautiful, brilliant smile, "Really, really well. I love her so much."

Jaemin rolls his head to the side, looking at the doctor directly for the first time since he's walked in. Dr. Moon's heart stutters slightly.

"I want to spend the rest of my life with her."

His smile is so sweet, it makes the doctor pause once more, watching a euphoric glaze coat his eyes. She clears her throat.

"And what about him? Your hidden side? Has he shown up recently?"

Jaemin shakes his head.

"No," he says dreamily, "No, I haven't seen him. He doesn't show up when she's around, not at all."

Dr. Moon continues taking notes on her laptop, biting her lip slightly.

"And Isla still does not wish to speak to me? You've asked her?"

"Yes, ma'am, I have," Jaemin says, not faltering, "She's afraid of doctors, you see. She has been ever since she was little, when she got bitten by a snake and had to go to the E.R."

"Psychologists aren't the same as medical doctors," Dr. Moon says, raising an eyebrow.

"I know, doctor."

"Yeji," the woman says, words spilling out of her mouth before she could stop herself, "You can call me Yeji. I've been working with you for a month now, Jaemin - ssi. No need to be so formal."

Jaemin pauses. For a moment, Yeji thinks she's overstepped

herself too quickly, that she's ruined the progress she's tried so hard to make. Jaemin is a lot more comfortable in her presence than he was only a few weeks ago. The doctor would like to believe that it's all because of her, but something in the back of her mind hisses that his comfort and lack of hostility has nothing to do with her and everything to do with that curly-haired demon.

"You can't tell someone who is afraid of doctors that a shrink is any different, *Yeji*," he says, eyes hard.

He's clearly urging her to drop it but Yeji pushes forward anyway.

"Please try to get her to agree to see me, Jaemin."

"I promise," he says, standing up swiftly, "See you later, Yeji."

Jaemin leaves quickly, turning back only once to wink at her before the door closes softly after him. There is still an entire fifteen minutes left in their session, but she doubts calling him back is any good.

Dr. Moon continues to type on her keyboard, documenting Jaemin's progress.

Patient continues to have positive growth. Psychotic episodes continue to decrease.

The mindless nature of the keys against her fingertips lulls Yeji Moon, making her zone out without realizing. She jumps to attention when a soft knock sounds on the door, the face of one of OT2B's managers peeking from behind the door.

"Hello, Dr. Moon. Do you have a moment?"

"Ah, yes, come in," Yeji says, closing her laptop, "I can take a break."

The man comes in, moving to sit on her chaise.

"Here, please," she asks, pointing to the stiff chair on the other side of her desk.

No one is allowed to sit on that chair other than Jaemin.

The man redirects himself silently, sitting down.

"How . . . have you been, doctor?"

"Let's not beat around the bush," Yeji says, placing her chin on her perfectly manicured hand, "You're here about Jaemin."

The manager looks awkward, shifting in his seat.

"Is he doing well?"

"He seems to be," she says, looking the manager dead in the eye, "His girlfriend seems to be helping quite a lot. Only . . ."

"Only?" the man asks, anxiety rising.

"Only, I worry that he may begin to become overly reliant on her. She's here on contract, right?"

He nods.

"Yes. We were able to get her to agree to come back, on her terms."

"And Jaemin is unaware, correct?"

"Correct."

"And how are the other members handling it? Jaemin's said that their relationship is as strong as ever."

Manager Calm frowns slightly.

"I didn't . . . Jaemin said that?"

"Yes, he says everything is going well. Better than well, actually. That's not the case?"

Manager Calm shakes his head.

"Things have definitely been tense. Although none of the boys have spoken up about it, they're all on edge. The relationship between Jaemin and the others is definitely strained, if not shattered altogether. They never know if he's going to show up to practice and when he does, he's entirely invested into it . . . not the performance, but impressing her."

Yeji purses her lips.

"That's quite the opposite of what he's been confessing to me in our sessions."

"Is that worrisome?" the man asks, sounding concerned.

"I'm not sure, not yet. It would help a lot if Isla would agree to come and speak with me. No doubt she has the most candid impression of him. Her insight would be incredibly beneficial."

Yeji leans forward on her desk, head propped perfectly on her netted fingers. She smiles just so, satisfied when Calm's cheeks warm ever so slightly. It would be hard to tell for a normal person, but Yeji has been studying OT2B and the people who surround them for years now.

"Would it help if I asked her?"

"Yes, please."

He nods and stands, exiting the room just as quickly as he came. Knowing that it'll only be a matter of time until she gets her way, Yeji opens her laptop and begins typing again.

Downstairs, a happy Jaemin walks with a skip in his step, excited to see his Isla again, excited to feel her eyes on him as he dances. He swings open the door to the practice room and steps in, slowing as he realizes that it's deserted. His smile falls and panic rises before he remembers that he told her to grab something to eat at the cafeteria.

Reassuring himself that she's okay, that she didn't leave, Jaemin half walks, half jogs to the eating area, slamming open the door.

She's not there.

"Isla?" he calls even though he knows she isn't there, "Isla?"

Jaemin walks slowly through the room, half expecting her to jump out and yell "Surprise!"

He feels himself begin to shake, steps speeding up as he walks around the room. The idol then bursts out of the room, sprinting down the hallways in search of her, screaming her name at the top of his lungs. His vision blurs and he can't focus, bumping into people and tripping over his own feet.

By the time a hand reaches out to grasp him, he's nearly in tears, looking at the person with wide, frightened eyes.

"Where's Isla?" he asks, not registering the face of his closest friend.

Fear shoots through Seojoon as he sees the true damage in his friend for the first time.

"Jaemin, are you okay?"

The answer is obvious. His hair is messed up, his expression wild as a frightened deer caught in the underbrush. Jaemin doesn't even look like he's present in the current reality.

"Where's Isla?" he parrots, eyes searching Seojoon's face.

"I think she's in the cafeteria, Jaemin. Why don't you come back to practice, okay? I'm sure she'll be right back."

Jaemin shakes his head.

"No. She's not. She's not there. I checked. I did, I checked."

"Okay, okay," Seojoon says, watching as Jaemin works himself up,

"She's probably in the bathroom then. That's usually where people go after they eat, the restroom."

"The restroom," Jaemin nods, "Yes, yes, Isla's in the restroom."

He moves to walk away from Seojoon.

"Where are you going, Minie?"

"To the restroom. To Isla."

"You can't go to the women's restroom, Jaemin," Seojoon says, grabbing his shirt.

Jaemin flings him off harshly, startling his bandmate.

"Jaemin–"

"Why is everyone trying to keep us apart? Huh? Why?! Why can't you just be happy for me, hyung? Why can't you just be glad that I love her? Why?!" Jaemin explodes, grabbing Seojoon by the collar and shaking him.

Footsteps come running and Jaemin is grabbed harshly, and pulled away from the now crying Seojoon, ugly tears streaming down his face.

Daehyun and Woojin hold on tightly to Jaemin, both of them horrified by the sight they're seeing. Jaemin thrashes against them.

"Let me go! Let me go! Let me see . . . Isla!"

Jaemin instantly relaxes, a happy smile on his face as the girl rounds the corner.

It sours when he sees who she's with.

11

Leo stands and walks over to where Isla is sitting, trying to comfort her. But his hip accidentally bumps into the table and knocks his glass over, soaking Isla.

She jumps back, shrieking at the unexpected coldness. For a moment, she forgets her tears.

"Shit, I'm sorry," he says, reaching for a napkin and trying to dab up the liquid, feeling terrible.

It's obvious that she's struggling and all he's done is make it worse.

His attempts don't do much good at all.

"It's alright," Isla assures, wiping her eyes and standing up, "I'll just have to go home and change."

She sniffles once more before trying to straighten her wet clothes and replace that happy mask she's been wearing, burying her true feelings once more.

"I have a spare shirt I keep in my studio for emergencies," Leo offers, desperately wanting to help.

"You mean in case you spill something," Isla teases, more herself than she was moments ago.

The idol's cheeks warm slightly.

"But yeah, that would be great! I doubt Jaemin would let me go by myself," she continues.

Leo has quite the reputation for being a klutz. She's not incredibly bothered by the spill, knowing that it was an accident. It happened all the time when she was a waitress.

Leo says goodbye to the restaurant owners and the two of them head out, making their way back through the alleys and into Smash Entertainment. The hallways of the upper floors are as deserted as always. Isla learned from Leo over lunch that the upper levels are reserved for groups that are distinguished or really popular while new groups and trainees stick to the lower floors and are forbidden from venturing upwards, so the pair has no problem making their way to Leo's private studio.

Leo unlocks the door and Isla looks away as he inputs his password for courtesy's sake. The lock beeps four times and he opens the door, letting Isla in first.

"Oh, wow," she says, turning around in a circle, taking it all in.

She's seen Leo's studio a million times in behind the scenes videos and photographs, but it's another thing entirely to be inside of it. It's smaller than the cameras make it seem, every spare inch of space occupied with an instrument, equipment, collectable toy, or other piece of decoration.

"Sorry it's so messy. I've been in here a lot lately and haven't really had time to clean up."

"You're fine," Isla assures him.

The studio isn't really messy. Cluttered, sure, but nothing's really thrown around haphazardly.

"Working on anything new?" Isla asks, unable to stop herself despite knowing he most likely won't tell her.

"Hm?" Leo asks, rummaging through a small pile of clothes, looking for a clean shirt.

"You said you've been in here a lot lately. Are you working on anything new?"

"Sort of. Practice has been cancelled or postponed a lot because of Jaemin so I've had more time on my hands than usual. Jaemin's probably told you that we have a comeback coming up, but I can't really come up with anything I really like," Leo replies, procuring a clean shirt and handing it to Isla, turning around so she can change.

Isla drags the soiled shirt over her head and used the dry parts to blot at her skin before putting on Leo's shirt. It's huge on her since it's already oversized on the man himself, landing just above her knees. Deciding that it's a little too ridiculous to wear so long, Isla hikes it up, tying a knot in the fabric over her right hip.

"You can turn around now," Isla says, the man doing so.

"Do you wanna hear it?"

"Really?" Isla asks, excited.

That bright look is on her face again, the girl practically vibrating in place.

"Yeah," he says, making his way over to his desktop and clicking a few times, pulling up a complicated-looking program.

There isn't another chair in the space so Isla hovers beside him. Leo clicks on a track and a melody floats through the giant loudspeakers. It's choppy, still quite obviously in its early stages but it has a lot of potential.

"I like it," Isla says, "I could see you doing something great with this."

"Yeah?" Leo asks, "I'm thinking about scrapping it."

"No!" Isla shouts, startling Leo, "Take a break from it if you want, but don't scrap it," her words softening when she realizes that she'd shouted.

Leo chuckles.

"Okay. I'll keep it then."

Before either of them can say anything else, Leo's watch beeps.

"Jaemin's session will be over in five minutes. We should head back before he throws a fit."

"Okay," Isla agrees, folding her soiled shirt and tucking it under her arm.

The two of them head out, Leo's studio locking behind them. After a couple of minutes, the duo hears a commotion, turning a corner to find Jaemin and Seojoon in some sort of scuffle. Before

Isla can even react, Jaemin notices her and breaks into a happy smile.

"Isla! I-what are you wearing?" he asks, tone suddenly dark.

"What?" Isla asks, his emotion switch throwing her off.

"Those aren't your clothes. Those aren't my clothes. So, I'll ask you again, whose. Clothes. Are. You. Wearing?"

"It doesn't matter, Jaemin. I spilled something on myself," she says, trying to placate him.

Jaemin's eyes slide from her to the man beside her, the other members deathly silent. The atmosphere is so tense that Woojin actually holds his breath.

"Why is she wearing your clothes, Leo?" Jaemin asks, switching to Korean.

"She spilled something on herself, Jaemin. Calm down."

"Calm down? Calm down? CALM DOWN?"

Jaemin takes a large step forward, shoving Leo harshly.

"She is mine. Mine. You don't get to touch her, Leo. What about this don't you understand?" he asks, shoving Leo against the wall.

"Jaemin, stop it," Isla says, grabbing onto his arm.

"Why are you defending him? What did he do to you? Do you love him more than me? Is that why you're with him? Why weren't you in the cafeteria?"

"Stop it!" Isla yells, grabbing his arm harsher and pulling him towards her, "Stop being this way, Jaemin! Cut it out!"

"Cut it out? After you just cheated on me? After you lied to me? How could—"

Isla raises her hand and brings it down sharply across the side of his face, the resounding smack causing everyone to gasp. Woojin, the one closest to them, reaches out to grab her but stops when Jaemin brings his own hand up to his face, wincing at the sting in his cheek.

"Do it again," he says, advancing towards Isla until their chests touch, "Hit me again."

He grasps her waist, cold rings bleeding through the fabric of her shirt. Isla is bewildered, staring at him in shock. He can't be serious, can he?

"Hit me again. Shove me again. Scream at me, kiss me, sleep with me. Anything, as long as it's me you're giving attention to. Anything, as long as it's you."

His fingers tighten around the hem of Leo's shirt and he yanks harshly, the fabric ripping off of her frame.

"Jaemin!" Isla shouts, trying in vain to push him away.

"And you. You don't get to stomp over my heart like this. You don't get to hurt me like this. Every breath I take is for you," Jaemin says lowly, hand squeezing tight on her jaw, yanking her face up to his, "And every one of yours is mine."

12

To say that Isla is humiliated would be a gross understatement. Leo's shirt lay in tatters in Jaemin's hands, the girl's stomach exposed. She's not particularly exposed, having went running in a similar outfit several times. No, her embarrassment stems from the fact that Jaemin has done this to her, disregarded her comfort and personal space in favor of winning whatever imaginary pissing contest is going on between him and Leo. Isla shoves past him, glaring at Daehyun and Woojin who stand in her way.

"Where are you going?" Jaemin asks as she pushes by his bandmates, her footsteps quick and heavy.

Isla ignores him, clenching her fists so tightly, her nails dig uncomfortably into the flesh of her palms. If she was angry before, she's livid now.

"Baby? Don't walk away from me, please," Jaemin says, following her, completely disregarding what he's just done to her.

Thankfully, there's a bathroom not too far away. Isla opens the door to the room and slides into a stall, sitting on the lid, knees pulled under her chin. The restroom door opens not even ten seconds later; It doesn't take a genius to figure out who it is.

"Isla?" the idol asks, slapping one of the stall doors.

It's empty.

"Are you mad at me?"

Another empty stall.

"Isla?"

Jaemin's rings tap against her stall door.

"I know you're in there. Come out."

Isla doesn't respond, burying her face in her knees and closing her eyes. She wishes that her childhood delusions were real - that the monster couldn't see you if you couldn't see it.

But this is the real world. Monsters don't have talons and horns. They have disarming smiles and beautiful voices.

She's suddenly overcome with an epiphany, realizing that she can't do it. She can't stand being near Matoi Jaemin for one more second. He's just too psychotic to handle, too prone to reckless mood swings that make her fear every second that passes. No matter how much she adores him, she can't take this type of treatment - she won't.

Isla opens her eyes to find Jaemin laying flat on his back on the dirty bathroom floor, staring up at her. His hands clasp the bottom of the stall door, his legs still on the other side. She's not surprised that he crawled in here with her. Isla just re-hides her face, not being able to stomach looking at him.

"Are you cold?" he asks her, "I can grab you something of mine."

"I'd rather freeze," she says, refusing to look at him.

"Isla–"

"How could you do that to me, Jaemin?" she explodes, stomping her feet down on either side of his head.

He doesn't flinch, eyes boring into her from below.

"How could you treat me like that? How could you do such a thing? How could you embarrass me like that?!"

Jaemin is silent, not even blinking at her tantrum.

"I can't stand you. I'm going home," she says, standing up and reaching to unlock the door.

Isla doesn't get very far at all as Jaemin's hands wrap tightly around her ankles.

"Let me go, Jaemin," she says, the desire to kick him in the head flaring up before she shoves it back down.

"I'm sorry. I'm so, so sorry," he says, frozen exterior cracked to reveal a much more desperate man, "I won't do it again."

Isla kicks him off her left foot and opens the door, fighting to cover any ground as she literally drags Jaemin's body across the floor.

"Let go!" she screams at him, trying to shake him off with all her might but Jaemin doesn't budge at all, only drawing himself closer to her foot.

Utterly furious, Isla yanks herself out of the bathroom, using all her energy to walk back down the hallway, tugging a pleading Jaemin with every step.

"I won't do it again, I won't, I won't!" he promises, digging his nails into her skin and kicking like a two-year-old, making it nearly impossible for her to cover any ground.

But she's sick of it, sick of him, sick of everything. Isla digs her nails into every door frame, refusing to give in to him again, refusing to let go and coddle him and wipe away his tears over something he caused.

Isla is a bit surprised to see the rest of OT2B still hanging out in the same spot as before, all huddled together and speaking in whispered tones. Their conversation quickly ends when they hear Jaemin's wailing, watching in a mix of horror and fascination as Isla drags their brother down the hallway. Jaemin reaches up and grabs the band of her sweats, pulling himself up until his face is buried in the small of her back. The unexpected change of weight pushes Isla to the ground, the girl landing so harshly, her breath is knocked out of her. Her jaw smashes against the hard ground, teeth catching the tip of her tongue. Blood fills her mouth and tears spring up in her eyes.

Jaemin crawls up her fallen body, wrapping his limbs around her and completely immobilizing her as if he were a snake.

"LET ME GO, MATOI JAEMIN!" she cries, swallowing the unpleasant spit and blood mixture.

"No! No, no, no, no, no, no!" Jaemin says, somehow squeezing her even tighter, her ribs compressed until she can barely breathe.

Isla throws her head back, looking at the other shocked boys.

"What are you doing?! Get him!" she shouts at them, frustrated and angry, hating them for just standing there uselessly.

Her words shock them out of their state, all four men rushing to pry Jaemin's struggling body off Isla.

"STOP!" Jaemin shouts, "STOP IT! LET ME GO!!"

Woojin and Seojoon hold Jaemin a solid foot off of the ground, Jaemin kicking his feet frantically in an attempt to free himself. Isla lays still on the floor, eyes closed while she tries to gather her thoughts. Her brain is a jumbled mess, thousands of thoughts screaming at her. She's shaky on her feet, Leo reaching out to help stabilize her.

She slaps his hand away. She's mad at him too, even if offering his shirt to her was just a polite gesture and not intended to cause Jaemin to lose his damn mind.

Jaemin is still crying and spewing promises, fighting against his members.

"Will you ever shut up?!" Isla screams at him, hair sticking to her slightly dampened skin.

He stops at once, wet tear tracks glistening on his face. He stops fighting against Seojoon and Woojin, letting his body hang pathetically in the air. He sniffles slightly, looking at her in that kicked puppy way that squeezes her heart. It's that face that keeps her from storming out (well that, and her lack of a shirt) and racing straight onto the next plane back home. The girl feels guilty, looking at him makes her feel like the world's worst person, even though it's him who's treating her horribly. She rubs her head, an intense migraine beginning to form.

"Look, Jaemin, I'm sorry, okay? Why don't you just finish practice and I'll go home for the day. I think we need a break."

I need a break. I can't look at you anymore. I never want to look at you again.

"I don't think that's a good—"

Isla cuts Leo's words off with an intense glare.

"I'm going home," she says, words final.

She takes Woojin's offered sweater, daring Jaemin to say something as she zips it up despite the warm weather. He doesn't say anything, just sniffing once more. She leaves him there with the others, eventually able to find the elevator to take her down to the parking lot where a black van is already waiting for her. She doesn't question it, sitting in the comfy seat in Woojin's sweater, eyes closed, happy to let her brain be free of thoughts.

Once at the apartment, she grabs a bottle of water and downs it in one go, taking more headache medicine. Isla sits on the couch, studying her hands. The hands that are still in pain from hitting Jaemin, from clawing her way down the hallway.

Should she stay or should she go?

Isla bites her lip, finding her phone and quickly pulling up a list of flights from Seoul to her airport.

She doesn't get any time to even consider booking a flight because the door beeps, a sheepish-looking Jaemin walking in. Isla knows for sure that it hasn't been any longer than twenty minutes since she's seen him. Her body sags in defeat and she pockets her phone, her escape plans temporarily thwarted.

"Aren't you supposed to be at practice, Jaemin?" she asks him, watching him as he enters the apartment and sits on the couch beside her.

She doesn't stop him when he lays his head on her lap, curling himself into a ball.

"I'm sorry. I just . . . I don't like it when you look at other guys," he says, voice small.

He's ashamed of himself, hiding his embarrassment in Woojin's sweater.

"You can't be that way, Jaemin. You can't. Our relationship," she forces that word out of her mouth, "will fail if you can't trust me. It'll fail if you keep acting like this. You can't lash out, Jaemin. You can't act that way to me and your members," she says, patting his hair as he sniffs again.

If anyone should be comforted in this situation it's her.

"I am sorry."

"Actions speak louder than words, Jaemin. You can't be sorry and go straight back to acting like that again."

He nods.

"Do you forgive me?"

"No," Isla says, unable to keep the slight edge out of her voice, "I don't. You humiliated me today. You made me feel awful. You've yet to give me a reason to forgive you, Jaemin."

He nods again, bitter tears beginning to sting his eyes.

"I think it's best if I take the spare bedroom tonight."

"Okay," he says, voice cracking slightly.

The rest of the day is miserable. No matter how hard Jaemin tries, he can't get Isla to pay him any attention. He tries asking her questions, tries apologizing, even tries to get her to yell at him by being obnoxious. None of it works. Even though he's glued himself to her side, it's like she's not even there, like she's some ghost simply existing next to him. It's absolutely driving him crazy.

She won't even bathe in their bathroom, deciding to wash up for the night in the spare one all the way across the house.

"But there isn't the soap you like in there. Maybe you should just shower in here, hm?" Jaemin tries, watching her gather a few night clothes from his point perched on her side of the bed.

It's a subtle, subconscious decision, a way to make him feel like they're closer than they actually are.

She doesn't slam the drawers any harder than usual, doesn't glare at him with intensity. Isla just moves around like she's all by herself, like he doesn't exist at all.

"Please stop," Jaemin pleads, voice showing his desperation.

This is supposed to be their place, their home. He's supposed to feel safe and loved here, not discarded.

Isla doesn't pay him any attention. She finishes grabbing her essentials and closes the bedroom door softly behind her, not even wishing Jaemin a good night.

Alone in the room that suddenly feels unfamiliar, Jaemin pulls his knees to his chest, holding himself as tightly as he possibly can.

Had he really gone too far? In the heat of the moment, all he could think about was her smelling like someone who wasn't him, looking like she belonged to someone who wasn't him. He hadn't cared about who was there, hadn't cared about her in the moment. He acted on impulse and now she won't even look at him.

Jaemin brings his fist to his mouth, holding in his cry. He bends in half and buries his face in the sheets, taking deep breaths in an effort to take in her scent. The smell is faint but it's just enough to push Jaemin over the edge. He pounds at his temples with both hands.

"You fucked up," the voice says, the one he hasn't heard in a while, *"You fucked up big time."*

"Shut up," he murmurs into the sheets, "Just shut up. Please. I can't deal with you now."

There's a soft chuckle in the back of his mind before it dissipates, leaving Jaemin to an empty head.

The sheets wrinkle under his fingers.

What if she hates him now? What if she never wants to be around him anymore? What if she leaves him?

Jaemin wants to stomp into the other room and gather Isla in his arms, just to feel her heartbeat, just to chase away the bitter loneliness that plagues him. But based on what happened today, that will only make her angry with him, maybe even cause her to hate him even more than the people who hide behind computer screens do. Feeling like he might vomit, Jaemin stands up and quietly leaves their bedroom, walking over to the other side of the house and stopping right in front of the guest bathroom.

The shower is already running, steam streaming out from under the door. She's playing some music loudly, but the sound of the water hitting the ground prevents Jaemin from knowing what song it is.

He tries to imagine exactly what she's doing. Is she running the rag down her arms? Maybe she's just standing in front of the stream, letting the water beat down on her face. It's killing him that he doesn't know, the idol placing his hands on the door and pressing into the wood, wishing he could phase through and be reunited with her, that things could go back to how they were yesterday, when he got to know every inch of her skin.

He slips away when the water cuts off, curbing his urge to hear damp feet against cold tile. He retreats into the bedroom like a criminal, straining his ears to pick up any sound of her moving about the house. Maybe he's too far away or maybe she's being especially quiet, but he can't hear Isla at all, can't hear anything to prove to himself that she's here with him.

He paces the floor, scratching at his arm slightly to prevent his hands from grasping the doorknob and running right to her side. Jaemin plays mindless games on his phone for what seems like hours only to check the time and realize that ten minutes haven't even passed. He takes a selfie and posts it on Twitter just to have something to do. He can't bring himself to read the comments.

Jaemin scrolls through YouTube videos, deciding to watch some videos with more English vocabulary to practice. He hasn't had a difficult time conversing with her yet, but he knows his pronunciation needs work and he wants to be able to have deeper conversations with her, to ask her those burning soul-searching questions he's amassed over the past five years. Thankfully, this takes his mind off of the situation better than his other distractions. He pushes himself to memorize the big words with their seemingly endless amount of letters, saying them over and over until they roll off of his tongue just the same way as the stout-looking lady who teaches them.

He lets his mind wander to dreams about the two of them relaxing on an empty beach, away from all the lights and bodyguards. Her hair blows gently in the salty wind, head atop Jaemin's lap as seagulls squawk in the distance, their sound mostly drowned out by the sound of the waves crashing onto the sand. Jaemin asks Isla about her *aspirations* for their future. She tells him about her plan for the next *decade*, about how she wants to get married in a garden one day like she's always dreamed of ever since she was little. Jaemin tells her that a garden is the perfect *venue* because she's a flower of her own accord, just as sweet as the blooms on the bushes. She smiles then, that rare, gorgeous smile saved only for the best of times, and proclaims that she can't wait for their forever to start.

It's something Jaemin so desperately craves, to see that smile, to hear those words, to know she means them. Oh how he wants that to happen!

Jaemin pulls the covers up to his chin.

How many children would they have? Would they look like him or like her? Would their hair be the same hair he loves to play with? Will their lips produce that same grin he adores? Jaemin can imagine coming home to find the love of his life playing with their child, for Isla to look up at him as he comes in with bright eyes, eager to tell him what their child had achieved.

Looking at the clock, Jaemin notices that it's a bit past midnight. He wonders if Isla is asleep yet. He wants to check but he stops himself, remembering her words from hours prior. She wants to be alone.

And yet, Jaemin is unable to fall asleep. He even tries sleeping on her side of the mattress but he receives no comfort. His body is hyper-aware that Isla isn't next to him, leaving this huge feeling that something is missing - that something's wrong. He gives up when the clock hits two. He's tortured himself enough, hasn't he?

He's been away from her long enough. He's given her enough space. Isla couldn't have really believed that he'd be able to sleep without her in his arms, could she? She couldn't have. She's just upset, but surely, she'll understand that he can't go another second without being near her, without holding her.

Jaemin's feet pad quietly against the carpet and wood as he walks across the house. Isla is fast asleep when he unlocks the door to the guest room, peeking his head inside to look at her. The room is still, only her breathing disrupting the tranquil atmosphere. Jaemin slips inside, careful to close the door as silently as he can.

Isla is curled up on the left side of the bed, leaving room for Jaemin. His heart flutters, the man knowing that she must have done this on purpose. He slides under the covers and scoots over to her body, wrapping her in his arms and pulling her close. She stirs only slightly before cuddling up to him and falling asleep.

Jaemin buries his face in her hair, breathing in deeply and kissing her forehead softly.

He'd missed her. He'd missed her so much even though she was only steps away from him. He's missed her presence, how simply being around her was enough to make him feel calm and happy again.

He tightens his grasp on her body.

Jaemin doesn't think he can ever let her go.

13

When Isla wakes up, she is disappointed but not at all surprised to find Jaemin fast asleep next to her. She had hoped that maybe he'd actually listen to her request and give her space, but to be honest, he lasted much longer than she thought he would.

Isla sighs, rubbing her eyes and unlocking her phone to check the time. It's just after eight in the morning and the flight she booked last night before she went to bed is scheduled to take off at eleven pm. That's plenty of time to drop Jaemin off at practice and go and collect her money from CEO Hwang. She tries to scoot out of the bed but Jaemin grabs onto her and pulls her back, snuggling his face into her neck like she's some big teddy bear.

"Jaemin," she begins, sticking her nails under his arm to try and pry him off, "We need to get up."

He whines, wrapping his legs around her as well.

The action reminds her of an old interview he gave, stating that if he were to be an animal, he'd definitely be a koala because he likes cuddling so much. It had made her squeal back then but now all it does is make her wish he'd chosen a skunk or something equally as unpleasant.

"You have to go to practice, get up," Isla says.

Since today is the last day she'll ever see him, Isla tries not to get too frustrated with the idol when he ignores her again in favor of pretending to be asleep. He clings to her even tighter and quivers slightly like he's trying to stop himself from crying. Isla blows on his face softly, disturbing the strands and his shaking eyelids until he peeks his bright, glossy eyes open.

"What's got you so upset this morning, Minie?" she asks, voice soft.

"You're not . . ." his voice is deep and gravelly, starkly contrasting with his delicate appearance, "still upset with me, right? You know I'm sorry, right?"

Isla smiles, knowing it's better not to answer.

"Let's get up, Jaeminie. It's a beautiful day," she says, kissing him gently on the cheek.

This pacifies him enough to let her slip out of bed and begin to get ready, Jaemin not far behind her. Anxiety causes her to check her email more often than normal, refreshing to see if CEO Hwang has messaged her back. Her inbox still lays silent.

"What are you looking at?" Jaemin asks, coming behind her with freshly washed hair and a towel tossed over his head.

"The weather," she says without missing a beat, "Looks like it's gonna be hot today."

If there's one thing Isla has learned from all of this, it's how to lie.

Jaemin makes a non-committal noise and plops down in front of Isla, giving her those puppy eyes. Without a word, she takes the towel and begins to dry his hair, making sure to get behind his ears. She does it more tenderly than she usually would, taking more time than necessary. It's her own secret goodbye.

Jaemin's all smiles when they exit the apartment, hand in hand and wearing matching black t-shirts. Their shoes are also the same, those yellow Converse she'd fallen in love with years ago ever since OT2B had taken a photoshoot wearing them. She tries not to think about how he knows that she loves them. There's practically a bounce in his step as he swings their hands back and forth when they enter Smash Entertainment, happily humming some tune she's never heard before.

Isla doesn't make eye contact with the other members even though they're obviously staring at her, their eyes drilling holes in her being. It's suffocating, loud music pounding and stares shooting her anxiety through the roof.

Do they already know she's leaving today? Had CEO Hwang told them? Are they judging her?

The hours seem to pass slower than ever before. Each second seems to take an eternity. Isla doesn't know how many times the boys have run through their choreo or how many times Jaemin's shot her a bright grin whenever his time in the center came.

After sixteen lifetimes, practice is once again interrupted by a man coming in to fetch Jaemin, probably to speak with his shrink about his tantrum from yesterday. Isla promptly stands and leaves the room, ignoring Leo's shout to wait. Her footsteps are quick as she avoids him entirely, not even bothering to shut the door behind her. All that matters is getting to the CEO's office.

She raps her knuckles against the door rapidly and swings it open without waiting for anyone to answer. It's certainly incredibly rude of her to do so but she's rushing, afraid Jaemin will come back from his therapy session before too long like he did yesterday. CEO Hwang is there already, as well as quite a few of the Suits from her first trip to Korea. Whatever they were saying halts as soon as she barges in, closing the door behind her.

Isla feels a bit awkward in the room with so many eyes on her, like she's a child interrupting grown-up talk and will be shooed out with a juice box and a pat on the head. She stands her ground, though, straightening her posture and lifting her chin.

"I'm here to pick up my pay," Isla says, voice strong, "I know that you got my email. I can't stay here any longer. I can't be around Jaemin any longer."

The resident translator quietly murmurs her words, but still, no one moves, all just staring at her. An icky feeling crawls up her skin.

"Isla," one of the Suits begins, the one who's bilingual, "We've seen a great deal of progress in Jaemin's condition since we've introduced you into his treatment. Are you sure you wouldn't like to stay longer?"

His voice is condescending, reminding her of the time her middle school gym teacher, an old, balding man in his fifties, told her she couldn't play on the baseball team and called her sweetheart. Back then, she'd ducked her head and ran off with red cheeks, embarrassed and doubting herself.

Not today.

"Yes, I am absolutely sure that I'm ready to leave."

The blonde, suited man stands and walks slowly with dress shoes clicking on the hard floor until he's only two feet away from her, much closer than she'd like. Isla doesn't step back. She knows an intimidation attempt when she sees one.

"But there's been so much advancement. Surely, you don't want to disrupt that?"

"I don't know what you're calling advancement. Keeping me under his thumb all hours of the day, fighting with the other members, yelling at employees."

"Every celebrity has their dramatic moments," he says, completely dismissing her, "You're too caught up in the bumps. Jaemin's been eating better, performing better - even his morale is higher. Is it too much to ask for you to continue spending time with him? You're living a life others would kill for - living with your idol, dating him, *sleeping with him—*"

Isla bites her lip, wishing she could stop the heat flooding through her.

How does he know that?

"And getting paid for it. You're living the life, Miss Isla. It can't be too hard to continue being his medicine."

Isla clenches her fists, staring the man in the face.

"I'm a person, not a drug."

"He's addicted to you like you're one."

"That's not my problem anymore," Isla says, fighting not to explode, "I want my pay. I'm leaving today, stop trying to change my mind."

The tension in the room is malleable, both Isla and the Suit staring each other down like two circling lions.

"Fine," the man says eventually, wiping imaginary dust off of his coat jacket, "Take your pay and leave."

He produces a fresh, crisp check from his breast pocket and hands it over. Isla unfolds it to see more zeros than she'd ever thought possible. The girl slides it in her jean pocket, glaring at everyone in the room before exiting, leaning her back against the hallway wall and taking a deep breath.

"You're leaving?"

Isla shoots a foot into the air, her nerves making her more startled than she'd usually be. Leo stands across from her, posture relaxed, arms crossed casually.

Isla nods once, a quick, jerky movement before pushing off the wall and walking away. She wants to stop, to thank him for being nice to her when no one else has been, but she can't allow herself to get sentimental now.

All she has to do is smile for a few more hours, watch Jaemin bounce around for a few more hours, and pretend everything is okay for just a few more hours. After everything she's been through, it'll be easy.

Leo sighs heavily, watching her go. He'd really hoped that Isla being around would help Jaemin and it has, he supposes, just not the way he'd planned on. Leo and the rest of the members had been too naive to think a green-eyed beauty could waltz in and fix everything, even if Jaemin's therapist swore up and down it would.

Speaking of Yeji, Leo continues his journey to her office, desperate to speak with her. Yesterday's events have shaken him to the core, never having expected the quiet, loving Jaemin to act so violently. It also gives the twenty-four-year-old an excuse to see her.

Even before Jaemin began acting so . . . rashly . . . Han Leo has been a big fan of Dr. Yeji Moon's work. He first learned about her when he was a senior in high school and still lived in Washington. He'd been assigned a project to research an outstanding individual in the field of study he was interested in taking (which had been psychology before he'd been scouted at a global audition and realized that being a rapper wasn't such a far-off dream) and had stumbled across Dr. Moon. Despite only being his senior by three years, she'd already completed all the requirements for her degree and had become one of Korea's youngest psychologists. Not only was she incredibly smart, she was absolutely drop-dead gorgeous - all milky skin and long legs and flawless features. He'd developed a crush on her all those years ago and knowing that she's working with one of his members reignites that same interest he had in the past.

When he arrives in front of her office, Leo stills himself, taking a deep breath before reaching up and tapping his knuckles on the glass.

"Come in," a voice from inside wafts through the door.

Leo pauses for a beat and then swings the door open, eyes immediately drawn to the petite woman sitting with perfect posture behind the desk, typing away at her laptop. She looks up at him, an easy smile gracing her face. It causes Leo's heartbeat to speed up. He clears his throat awkwardly.

"Is it alright if I speak to you for a moment?" he asks.

"Sure," Yeji says warmly, "take a seat."

Leo sits right across from her, close enough to see her delicate eyelashes.

"How can I help you, Leo?"

"I . . . um . . . wanted to talk to you about Jaemin."

The doctor perks up instantly.

"What is it that's bothering you?"

"His behavior yesterday was so unlike him. It was so scary to see him behave so violently. I never would have thought that he'd try to hit me or literally rip the clothes off of Isla's back. No wonder she's leaving."

"Excuse me?"

"No one told you? I just brushed past her on the way here. She left CEO Hwang's office. She's going home."

"When?" Yeji asks, her tone urgent.

"I'm not sure. Probably soon."

Yeji looks like she's going to say something but stops herself.

"Well . . . why don't you tell me more about your relationship with Jaemin? I'd like a little insight into how things were before."

Leo is a little surprised by the sudden change of topic but he relents, beginning to speak about the lengthy history between him and Jaemin.

But soon, their conversation veers off course and Yeji is asking him about himself, his likes and dislikes, the little things that make him happy. And as Leo opens up, Yeji does too. Every word she says is enchanting to the other man. He doesn't even care that he's skipping practice to speak with her.

If he had a crush on her before, he's now on the brink of falling in love altogether. He feels as if he knows her, as if they've truly connected.

"But you know," Yeji says, just past nine, "It's really unfortunate that Isla is leaving. Jaemin has made phenomenal steps forward. I'd hate to think how her absence would reverse that."

Leo frowns slightly.

"It really would be best if she stayed," Yeji says, leaning forward and across the desk, her palms flat against the table, "Jaemin could quite possibly go off the deep end, never to return. I know CEO Hwang and the others had to make a little contract to get her to come back, but we really shouldn't let her go."

"But–"

"I know. I know it would seem mean to stop her," she's pouting, almost, "But think about it, Leo. Who do you value more? Jaemin -

the man who's like your brother, one of the people you love the most, or Isla - a complete stranger who you barely know?"

The doctor leans even closer. Leo is left speechless.

"I think we need to have an emergency meeting before she goes anywhere. It may seem cruel but I think it's best if she stays no matter what. And you know, Leo, I think I know exactly how you can help," she says, smiling sweeter than honey, lips just barely touching the shell of his pierced ear.

14

It isn't easy at all. If time moved slowly before, it's creeping along at a snail's pace now, Isla feeling like she's only breaths away from upchucking all her nerves. She tries her hardest for her facade not to break and Jaemin doesn't seem to notice, the idol being a master at seeing only what he wants to see. She almost cries when a sweaty, exhausted but elated Jaemin collapses into her lap, giggling but ready to fall asleep any moment, just after eight in the evening. Isla shoulders him into the big black van, letting him rest his head on her as he drifts into a light sleep on the way home.

'Home'.

That's a strange word. It means more than she thought it could.

Jaemin showers without complaint, too tired to whine about Isla joining him or suggesting late-night activities. Isla tries not to make it obvious that she's rushing things more than usual, eyes trained on the clock.

And finally, *finally*, Jaemin's asleep just before nine pm. Isla stuffs some pillows into his arms to escape, quickly grabbing her purse with her wallet, check, and passport and tiptoeing out of the apartment, out of Jaemin's life.

The taxi ride is uneventful, Isla tapping her nails against the car door to try and calm herself down. They're still pale pink from the last time Jaemin did them, a little imperfect heart painted on all ten fingers.

"It'll be fine. It'll be okay. Everything's fine," she repeats in her head, willing it into existence.

Isla arrives at the airport without any problem, her large hat covering most of her face. She sits at her terminal, waiting for her plane to be ready to board. She fiddles about, eyes on the clock, waiting, waiting, waiting.

Everything's fine.

Until it isn't.

Out of nowhere, Han Leo emerges, covered face blank, eyes cold and hard. Flanking him, a few hundred feet back, are a handful of security guards. This part of the airport, in particular, is mostly deserted, a few occupied looking businessmen too far away to be much help.

"Isla," Leo begins.

"No," she says, scooting seats away, "No!"

Leo takes another step closer.

"It's my job as leader–"

"NO!" she shrieks, raising her hands as if to protect herself.

"You can't leave, Isla. He needs you."

"I'm leaving. You can't stop me. I'm done, Leo, I'm done."

The rapper sighs once, a long, low breath that Isla sees more than hears due to her rapid heartbeat. She looks around desperately, noticing how this section of the airport is deserted, something she didn't realize until now.

"Flight J1013 boarding. Flight J1013 boarding."

Isla stands and makes a move to get on the plane, to leave once and for all.

"Get her."

Before she knows it, two strange men have their steel grips on her arms, one man covering her face with his hand while others form a protective circle around the altercation, keeping anyone from seeing the way Isla claws at the men, the way she kicks her legs out, the way her screams are muffled.

Pure terror surges through her nervous system, her sight becoming hazy as she enters the beginnings of a panic attack more intense than any other she's ever had. Her emerald eyes are blown wide open, throat running dry and coarse as the group shuffles her away from the terminal and towards an unused exit, the cold night air chilling her skin.

She's sweating, still trying her best to get away even though it's futile, the sheer number of captors outweighing any chance she has of escaping. She's tossed in the back seat of one of those horrid black vans, the doors locking and trapping her inside.

She screams, pounding on the glass and crying, heart beating so fast that she feels like she's gonna pass out any second.

She's being kidnapped. She's actually being kidnapped!

"You're not going to do anything but hurt your hands," Leo says from beside her, sitting there calmly like it's any other day.

"Leo, please! What are you doing? You've got to get them to let me go. I can't stay here, I can't be here!" she breaks down, hot tears streaming down her face, "I trusted you. I-I thought we were friends!"

Leo ignores the pain in his heart. Yesterday, he wouldn't have thought he could do such a thing, but after Yeji's very persuasive conversation and the meeting he'd been pulled into, he doesn't really have much of a choice - not when Jaemin's health and wellbeing is dangling out in front of him. He doesn't say anything to Isla, pulling her purse away from her and rummaging through it, pulling out her passport.

"What are you doing?" Isla asks, petrified.

Calmly, so calmly, he pulls a lighter from his pocket and flips it open.

"No!"

Isla tries to lunge at him but the car takes a quick turn, throwing her back against the car door so hard that her teeth rattle.

The flame licks the passport, gently at first, almost like a caress. Leo stares at her blankly as it grows and consumes her ticket out of this hell, as the smoldering ashes fall on the floor of the van. He lowers the window and throws the flaming item outside, Isla scrambling to press her face against the back windshield to try and see it.

Pure fury causes her to lunge at Leo once more, nails poised like claws to rip his throat out. It isn't much of a fight, Isla is barely able to scratch his cheek before he has her pinned against the backseat, their combined bodyweight causing the cushion to sink.

She's sobbing now, full out. Sobbing for the loss of her passport, the loss of her easy escape, the loss of herself.

"Let's get you back before he wakes up," Leo says somberly.

Pure hatred rolls through Isla as she glares at the perfectly expressionless Leo. Hatred more intense, hotter than anything she's ever felt before. She has the desire for the van to go spinning off the road and straight into a tree if only to wipe that overly blank, nearly inhuman look off of his stupid face.

He sits there, less than two feet away from her and yet she's unable to do anything about it. He has her purse, her whole life clutched in his hands. She wants to snatch it away from him and throw herself out of the car but she knows there's no hope in that being successful, Leo having already proved how easily he can win over her. And the doors have been child-locked, meaning Isla truly is stuck right where she is.

She glowers when the van pulls into the apartment complex just past midnight, arms crossed. Isla refuses to move, staying firm in her spot and glaring at Leo with all the anger she can muster. The rapper casually reaches into her bag and pulls out her cell phone, Isla's lock screen image illuminating the dark space. It only takes him a single try to unlock the device, revealing her home screen.

"It's his birthday. That's sweet."

"Go fuck yourself."

Leo ignores her, opting to scroll through her apps and messages for a bit before turning the device off.

"You won't be getting this back. I think it's safe to say that Jaemin isn't to hear a word about anything that happened tonight."

"I don't think he'd appreciate me being forcefully thrown into a van by a bunch of strange men," she snaps.

"I don't think he'd appreciate you attempting to leave him in the middle of the night like a crappy one-night stand either."

He has a valid point and they both know it but she's too riled up to relent so easily.

"You can't keep me here forever. You can't force me to stay here like this."

"We can and we will for however long it takes for Jaemin to be back to his normal self," Leo says, leaning over her to open the now unlocked door, "Go on up, I'm sure he's waiting for you."

Isla wants to continue sitting there in protest but one of the bodyguards gets out of the front seat to stand in the open doorway, the threat clear. She slides out of the van with as much dignity as she can muster, briefly making eye contact with the complex's guard before looking away, feeling vulnerable.

She considers making a break for it, but even if she did escape, where would she go? Leo stole her wallet so she has no way to pay for anything, no way to prove her identity or call for help. Her throat is dry when she realizes that she has no real way of escaping even as the streets lay empty and open in front of her.

Her feet are heavy as she drags herself after the guard, an overwhelming sense of doom lurking over her head, a complete breakdown just under the surface.

The guard stops at the end of the hallway, silently gesturing for her to finish the walk to the apartment, finish the walk 'home'. For a moment, Isla's eyes catch on the long railing just off to her left. Surely if she leaped from this height, she'd perish. Six stories would certainly leave her in a pile of blood and bones smeared on the concrete, it would certainly let her escape walking into the apartment once more.

But something tells her Jaemin would jump right after her, land right beside her in a puddle of his own. It makes bile rise up in her throat.

There truly isn't any way out, at least not yet.

And so, she takes a deep breath of the warm night air and punches in the code, the day she first arrived in Korea, and steps into the apartment.

Everything is still as the door beeps locked behind her. There's not a noise coming from anywhere, so for a moment, Isla allows herself to pretend. She perches on the couch and folds her hands in the way all the classy women on TV do. She closes her eyes and opens her ears, picking up on the slight hum of the air conditioner above. She pretends that everything will be okay, that everything that's happened to her is normal. The fantasy is so sweet she can taste it, can taste the cherry of Jaemin's Chapstick as he kisses her sweetly the way a real boyfriend would.

A single tear slips down her face as she opens her eyes into the darkness, allowing herself just that much before reeling all of her inner turmoil inside. Not even a moment before the salty tear lands onto her pants, the bedroom door opens, panicked footsteps rushing forward.

"Isla!"

She doesn't say anything but she doesn't have to, the idol easily able to identify her figure in the pitch-black darkness.

"Oh my God! I thought you left! You scared me!" Jaemin says, voice burdened with sleep, low and slower than usual.

His half-asleep brain has more difficulty pronouncing the foreign words, more of his accent slipping through than he'd normally allow. Jaemin sits beside her on the couch, ensuring that there's not a stitch of space between the two of them.

"Of course not, Jaeminie. Of course I wouldn't leave you. I love you too much," Isla says, her words an empty whisper, unable to pull any enthusiasm into her tone.

"What's wrong?" he asks, genuine concern echoed in his words.

So, she shatters. Slowly at first, just a sliver, but then all at once, her internal shield crumbling to dust. Feeling utterly alone and powerless, she crawls onto Jaemin's lap, holding onto his nightshirt with shaky fingers as her shoulders shake with sobs larger than any her body has ever experienced before. Startled, Jaemin isn't sure how to react at first but soon draws her closer to him, warm hand rubbing slow circles into her back and head propped onto hers, his body rocking her ever so slightly as she cries her heart out.

Jaemin doesn't say anything, doesn't ask any questions. He just holds her securely, a quiet softness to his actions.

How pathetic she is, taking comfort in the arms of the very reason she's trapped here, marooned in this awful place, this disgusting house. But if anything, she draws herself deeper into him, not wanting to part with the first moment of sincere solace she'd had since she arrived.

Jaemin still holds her when the sobs slow into soft cries and then uneven breathing, Isla desperately attempting to make herself silent.

"Can we just," a hiccup, "go to bed?"

"Of course, baby," Jaemin says, standing with ease and carrying her bridal-style back to bed where the sheets are tossed away haphazardly.

He walks on his knees over the mattress and lays Isla down. He doesn't move to grab her night clothes nor does he question why she's no longer in them, blinded by his concern for her wellbeing. All he does is pull the blankets over both of them and curl around her, pressing a lingering kiss on her temple.

"I love you," he whispers in the darkness, hands brushing over Isla's warm, swollen cheeks.

And for once, not to appease him or to cover up a lie, not to prove anything to anyone, Isla leans forward and kisses him. For once, wanting to know what it's really like. For once, wondering how it must feel, how he must taste.

Her heart breaks further when she realizes he's not sweet like cherries.

15

Leo sighs as he sits in front of Yeji, her words repeating in his head. Isla is leaving. He'd hoped that she would be the solution for all of their problems, hoped that the girl could do what he and the other members couldn't. It's been miserable these past few months, first discovering Jaemin's condition and then watching him wilt away with every passing day.

Nothing he'd done had helped. Nothing he'd done had brought even a smile back to his face, let alone restored his previous joy and demeanor. The boys had tried everything! They'd smothered him with attention, gave him space. They forced him to eat only to discover him passed out over the toilet, dangerously dehydrated.

Jaemin didn't even have the desire to dance anymore, the thing that brought him the most joy. He didn't want to mess around with the other boys like he loved to do. It was like he lost all of his energy, all of his being when Isla walked out of his life. Now that she's leaving, Leo isn't sure that there will be anything left of his little brother.

He thinks he might hurl.

To distract himself, he looks at his expensive watch, noticing that the meeting has been going on for half an hour already.

When he feels like he may implode from anxiety, the door cracks open and Leo is ushered inside to see all the execs huddled around a large table, panicked whispering flying so fast across the air that Leo can't catch any of what they're saying. The only silent one in the whole room besides Leo is Dr. Moon, the lady looking rather content and unbothered despite the drastic nature of their situation. She sends a quick wink towards Leo before slamming her hands on the table and standing up smoothly like a swan rising from water.

Everyone quiets down, not having expected the sound or the one who produced it.

"Gentlemen," she says, smoothing down her coat, "and ladies. All of this squawking is pointless. What we need is a solution, not an argument."

The voices rise again and the psychologist slams her hands down once more, urging them to quiet down. She gets a few unsatisfied looks - these people aren't used to being shushed - but no complaints.

"I believe that I have come up with just the solution,"

This is what Leo's grown to admire about the doctor. She was young but she managed to control a room filled with people nearly twice her age with ease. Yeji Moon has the charisma of a beloved politician, able to connect with people and understand them, make them understand her. It's what's made her such an amazing psychologist despite the relatively small amount of time she's been operating.

Everything about her checks out, every patient she'd had has made leaps and bounds towards (or even achieved) recovery. She has magazines written about her, praising her intellect and successes.

"As of right now, Jaemin is still quite unstable. However, each time he has visited my office, I gather that he's inching closer and closer towards rehabilitation. His physical health has already improved drastically. His eating and sleeping habits are returning to normal. I estimate, within a few weeks, he'll go back to his normal weight. None of this happened with the methods tried before Miss Isla's appearance, correct?"

Everyone nods. Again, nothing they'd tried motivated him in the slightest, not even the drugs he'd been prescribed.

"And the last time she left, what happened?"

The room is silent.

"Anyone?"

More silence.

"What happened," Yeji says, beginning to walk around the room, making as much eye contact as possible, "was a shutdown. Psychologically and mentally. Jaemin shut down. And now that he's come into contact with the thing - person, rather, that he's been so desiring, Matoi Jaemin will completely and utterly be destroyed.

He's an addict, one impossible of quitting cold turkey. Our best chance at saving him is to keep her around for as long as it takes before he comes to the realization that he doesn't need her at all. As I continue to work with him, he will realize that all of his memories surrounding Miss Isla are nothing more than delusions. Only then will it be safe for her to leave, only then do we no longer risk losing Jaemin to the voice inside his head."

"But she's leaving," someone voices, no longer able to keep silent, "And I don't blame her. The way Jaemin is . . . it's not healthy. It's scary."

"We convince her to stay," Yeji Moon says, ignoring her, "by any means necessary."

"She won't be convinced," a blonde man, the head of the international department, says, "You know that. She looked me dead in the face."

"You convinced her too softly. She cannot be allowed to leave."

"Are you suggesting we force her to stay? That's going too far," the man at the back says.

"The ethics are certainly questionable," Yeji says, coming to a stop and standing still right in the middle of the room, "But can you risk it? Are you willing to risk losing your idol," she turns to Leo, "your brother?"

Dr. Moon sits down as chaos once again erupts as people argue. Leo has to go to practice but he can't force himself to move, needing to know what the result will be. The decision makes him sick.

Dr. Moon makes her way out of the room, gesturing for Leo to follow her. He does, a large array of emotions bombarding him.

"It has to be you, Leo," the doctor says, ankles crossed as she sits on her big chair in her office.

"Yeji—"

"Dr. Moon," she corrects him.

Leo blushes, embarrassed. He'd called her Yeji during their discussion in her office and she hadn't minded.

"Dr. Moon . . . I don't think I can do this. I can't force her to stay here against her will, it just isn't right."

"Tell me something, Leo," the doctor says after a slight pause, "Do you have any feelings for her? For Isla?"

"What? Of course not," he says, shaking his head.

"Are you sure? Absolutely?"

Leo nods.

"You aren't taken with her? She's quite a beauty, you know. Surely you've noticed that."

Another nod, this one much more hesitant.

"You must pity her," Dr. Moon says, leaning forward, "Such a pretty young thing, trapped and afraid. You must feel like she's a bit of a kicked puppy, left out in the rain."

He isn't sure what to say to that.

"It's understandable, Leo. Truly, it is. It means you're a good person, a real big-hearted man. Admirable even."

Leo feels his face warm. He never thought the day would come where she'd compliment him, when praises would slide out of her perfectly-shaped mouth. Yeji's eyes are on Leo so intensely that he feels like he's being stared through, like every fiber of his being is getting analyzed. He takes this time to let himself look at her, really look at her. Her hair is as dark as pitch and bone straight, pulled into a very professional ponytail at the crown of her head. Still, her hair reaches to the middle of her back, slick and shiny. Her eyes are bright, on the smaller side but turned out ever so slightly at the sides. Even her nose is pretty, small and rounded, softening her appearance even further. She's truly gorgeous.

"But will you let your compassion for her - this complete and absolute stranger - stop you from saving Jaemin?"

Leo frowns, an uneasy feeling settling in his stomach.

"From what I can tell, things aren't as bad as she's making them seem. A little bizarre, sure, but certainly not dangerous. She has no reason to be afraid."

Is Yeji right? The scene Jaemin caused the other day in the hallway was certainly painful to watch but it didn't seem like Isla was in any real danger. Annoyed, definitely. But still, he didn't exactly hurt her. Right?

"Have you seen any bruises? Has she ever looked underfed or like she lacked sleep?"

"No. She looks fine."

"Then is there any reason for her to leave? Yes, Jaemin's behavior can be difficult to handle but we all have to do our part to help him along. It would be unfair for her to abandon her duty, wouldn't it?"

Now that Dr. Moon says it like that, it does seem like Isla is making too big of a fuss. And at the expense of Jaemin's health and wellbeing? Leo isn't sure he can just sit back and watch her leave his brother to rot.

"And she must have some affection for him," Yeji continues, "Quite a lot of it, for her to be so willing and devoted to him for all those years that she's been a fan. It's still the adjustment period, I'm positive she'll come around."

Leo bites his lip and begins to play with her fingers.

"Won't you help? For Jaemin?"

Leo takes a breath and nods.

"What do you need me to do?"

After running through the plan she created, Dr. Yeji Moon stands and ushers Leo out of the door, being sure to smile as nicely as she can.

"Remember, Leo, it's your job as a leader to protect your members. At any cost."

"At any cost," he parrots, looking at her once more before stepping away and heading to put her plan in action.

When the door shuts, she flops down in her office chair, eyes drifting to the chaise.

"Just a little more, Yeri," she says, rubbing her head as a headache builds, "Just a bit longer."

She takes a single white pill with a full glass of water. The voices are always louder when her head throbs.

16

When Isla wakes up, she's cuddled into Jaemin's side almost protectively. For a moment, just one, she's confused, wondering why she's not in her own bed, in her own home, in her own country. Why is she still in the arms of her psychotic 'boyfriend'? But then it all rushes back to her, the paycheck, the taxi ride, the near escape she had.

Leo.

The urge to vomit is real but she represses it, knowing that Jaemin will certainly wake up if she bolts out of bed and rushes into the bathroom. The taste in her mouth is disgusting but she swallows anyway.

What will she do now? She has no way to contact anyone to let them know that she's in trouble, no money to sneak her way out and stay somewhere else. Even if she could just run out of the front door, Isla has a sneaking suspicion that she's being guarded. There's no way she could make it to a police station or, even better, the embassy. Telling Jaemin is definitely out. He'd certainly have a freak-fit. What would she even say?

Isla supposes that she could tell him that Leo broke into their house and tried to take her away from him but that wouldn't be believable. The rapper doesn't have access to this apartment and even if he did, there's no way Leo could have actually taken her right from Jaemin's sleeping grasp, nor is there even a reason he should.

Isla bites her lip. The only thing she can think to do right now is keep her mouth shut and wait until someone slacks in their patrol and she can slip far, far away.

God knows how long that will take.

There's no way she's falling back asleep now, not with her mind running faster than lightning.

She shouldn't have come back. She shouldn't have been so worried about Jaemin, about the man behind the smile that lit up her dark days, the man behind the voice that lifted her spirits. Isla shouldn't have let her sympathy for him land her in this situation.

Bitter tears threaten to fall out of her eyes but she refuses to let them fall. She's cried enough recently.

Jaemin eventually stirs awake, slowly at first before his eyes widen almost comically, returning to their normal size as soon as he sees Isla snuggled into his side.

"Hi, baby," he says affectionately, moving to try and tame her hair a bit, "Are you feeling any better?"

Isla nods, wanting him to drop it.

"What happened? Why were you so upset?"

"Just a bad dream."

"Another one? You've been having a lot of those lately," Jaemin says, frowning.

"I know," Isla says.

"Any idea why?"

Because I'm surrounded by monsters.

Isla shakes her head.

"No. I'm just tired of having them."

"It must be because we've been eating so late. I used to have nightmares all the time as a trainee before my body got used to the weird schedule. We'll start eating earlier in the day, okay? You need a good night's rest every day or else you'll start to get sick."

"You'd know, wouldn't you?" Isla asks, words coming out before she even thinks.

Jaemin just nods and hums slightly.

"Mm, I would. It's best to get consistent sleep. You'll feel better," he says.

Isla is relieved he didn't explode or have some other irrational reaction to her slightly unkind question.

"Time to shower. Why don't you go back to sleep while I get ready and make breakfast, okay? Then we can head to practice.

Maybe seeing me dance will energize you," he says sweetly, a little giggle at the end of his words.

Isla nods, eager for any time away from him. She pretends to sleep while he goes through his morning routine, watching as he stops himself from 'waking' her to dry his hair like he always does. For the first time since she's been here, he actually does it himself. She must have drifted off, however, because the next thing she knows, Jaemin is shaking her awake gently.

"Breakfast, baby."

Isla rubs the sleep out of her eyes and tumbles out of bed, still in her clothes from her failed escape. Jaemin doesn't say anything but his eyes linger on her outfit, the question, the anxiety clear in her eyes.

Damn it.

She should have changed instead of drifting into denial-induced daydreams about cherry lips and healthy relationships.

"The uh . . . nightmare was pretty bad. I decided to take a walk around the complex."

"Jagi! That could have been dangerous! You shouldn't go out on walks in the middle of the night."

"Seoul is a pretty safe city. It isn't Chicago or anything. Besides, I didn't even leave the complex."

"Still! You can't just disappear into the darkness," Jaemin says, voice raised.

He's not yelling but his dissatisfaction is clear. Isla shrinks down a bit, feeling like a scolded child.

"I'm sorry. I just didn't want to wake you."

Jaemin's anger softens a bit and he places his chopsticks down.

"You can always wake me, Isla," he says, searching her face, "You know that, right?"

Isla bites her lip and then nods.

"I know, Minie. I'll wake you next time."

He smiles that breath-stealing smile she loves.

"Good. Let's finish up, okay?"

The couple resumes eating quietly, silverware occasionally clinking against their bowls. He made something new today and Isla has no idea what it is. It's pretty good though, nice and filling.

When they're almost done, Jaemin's phone rings and he excuses himself to fetch it from where he left it in the bedroom. Isla stops eating immediately and slumps in her seat, head back and staring blankly at the ceiling. She fixes her posture when his footsteps draw near.

Jaemin's face is pulled into a deep frown as he holds the phone to his face, coming to a stop by the table but not actually sitting back down.

"Okay. Thank you, Leo. Yes, we'll be extra careful. Thank you again."

Isla's tummy flips when she hears that name, wondering what Leo has up his sleeve.

"What's going on, Jaemin? Why do you look so upset?"

Jaemin sits down, picking up both of Isla's hands and squeezing them firmly.

"Leo just called to tell me that another idol's girlfriend just got attacked by a group of sasaengs. She's in the hospital. Apparently, they messed her up really badly. She has some broken bones and pretty ugly bruises."

"Oh my God! That's awful!" Isla says.

Sasaengs have always been the worst thing about being an Idol. There's nothing scarier than delusional 'fans' who believe they have some sort of control over you or your decisions, just because they are 'in love' with you. There have been way too many sasaeng attacks recently, vengeful, heartbroken psychopaths having the urge to lash out and hurt someone else to express their feelings.

"It is. CEO Hwang texted me and told me practice is cancelled until further notice. The attack was way too close to here for comfort. They're keeping it covered up so the paparazzi don't hear but they still want us to be extra wary."

Practice is cancelled? Oh God. That means . . .

"He also told me it's best if we don't leave the apartment until it gets sorted. No one wants to see you get hurt. Especially not me. I can't believe someone would be so sick and twisted to come up with a fantasy between them and someone they've never met and take it this far." Jaemin says, shaking his head with disgust.

"Me either," Isla says, hiding her bitterness as best she can.

The timing of this 'attack' is much too convenient for it to be real. This is obviously some ploy meant to manipulate Jaemin into keeping Isla locked away with him.

"Do you know how long we'll need to stay home?" Isla asks, praying that it'll only be a day or two.

"No idea. I'm willing to put it off as long as it takes to make sure you're safe," he says, leaning over the table to kiss her.

"Right. Safe . . ."

The rest of the day isn't terrible. Isla and Jaemin spend most of it doing laundry and other chores that eat up time. It's boring, but Jaemin doesn't do anything to freak Isla out or make any advances towards her beside the occasional forehead kiss. He even found some cherry Chapstick at the back of the medicine cabinet, only to toss it in the trash can.

"I don't like the taste of cherries, blegh. Why'd I even buy this?" he asks, ruffling his hair and wiping the offending wax off his mouth.

"I don't like cherries either," Isla says, watching the plastic tube as Jaemin chucks it into the trash can.

Isla is disappointed when Jaemin informs her the next day that they still need to be on high alert. This day is much slower as there's nothing really left to do. Jaemin showers her with attention, wanting constant cuddles, his fingers brushing softly across the band of her shorts. It's a clear question, one Isla pretends to miss entirely.

She just doesn't have any energy. Isla feels tired, oh so tired, just completely worn down by life's events. She can't bring herself to do anything but mope around, anything more than basic human functions requiring more energy than she has, even though she barely does anything but sleep. It worries Jaemin deeply. No matter what he says or tries, Isla just isn't herself. He's worried about her, worried that she's not okay.

Being trapped in the apartment only makes it worse. Isla is

struggling to accept that she's really stuck here in Korea and being stuck in an even smaller place with the person she tried so hard to escape from makes it nearly unbearable. Her inner turmoil is swirling around, growing and growing.

But there's one good thing about being in the apartment. It's mind-numbing. Sooner than it would usually take, Isla is less depressed and more bored out of her mind.

By the seventh day, even Jaemin is bored, resorting to singing around the house while Isla draws ugly pictures in a notepad she found on the bookshelf. Drawing isn't her strong point.

Day nine is when Isla really cracks, not wanting to see the same walls for even another hour.

"Let's go out, Minie, please," she begs him as he stretches in the living room, giving her a spectacular view of his ass.

It's a good booty, she can't lie.

"It's still not safe, baby," he says, walking on his hands and spreading his legs slowly until he sits into a perfect middle split.

"Come on, Jaemin! We'll be fine, I promise!"

"I don't know," he says, folding his torso forward and stretching even further.

God, this boy is flexible.

"Jaemin, please," she says, sitting right in front of him and making eye contact, pulling her best puppy dog look, "I'm so sick of being home! I want to go out."

"Isla," he says, rising and pulling his legs back until he's in a normal sitting position.

"I want to go explore with you, Jaemin, I wanna see Seoul. I've been here for almost a whole month and I haven't seen anything besides our house and the company."

"You saw the airport."

"Jaemin!" she whines.

Internally, she's cringing over how pathetic she's being but she's desperate. Being stuck with Jaemin is one thing but being stuck with Jaemin inside of an apartment is another entirely. Besides, maybe she'll be able to scout out an escape route or, even better, get away for good.

Jaemin frowns slightly before nodding.

"Okay. Okay, we can go out!"

Isla practically squeals in excitement, ready for the smell of fresh air and the feeling of sunlight on her skin.

"But I have one condition."

Isla practically vibrates in excitement in front of the front door, seconds away from just snatching it open and darting out, desperate for sunlight to warm her skin. Jaemin laughs lightly, a fond feeling untangling in his chest.

"When are we going, Minie? Come on, come on!" she says, looking at him with wide, beautiful eyes.

It's already been twenty minutes since he caved and agreed to sneak out with her to go on a 'date', but they're still in the apartment.

"Just a minute, just a minute," he says, bending down to tie his shoe before straightening and pulling a simple black mask over the bottom of his face.

He shakes his hands through his hair a few times and flips his head backwards before rolling his neck to the side and snagging another mask out of his pocket, lovingly placing it over her features and kissing her sweetly on the forehead.

"Do you promise you'll be safe?"

She nods.

"And you'll stay right beside me?" he asks, voice trembling ever so slightly, "Without letting go of my hand?"

"I promise," she says, feeling slight guilt as she makes eye contact with him, watching the apprehension and fear swirl around in his dark eyes.

"Okay," Jaemin says, taking her hand in his own, "I trust you."

The door beeps pleasantly as Isla and Jaemin sneak through hallways, avoiding their usual routes and sticking to the paths less traveled. They eventually exit the complex into a large garden, flowers and benches spaced throughout the area.

"I didn't know this was here," Isla says, watching butterflies float through the air on cool winds.

"Mm," Jaemin begins, "I don't come here often. This is the private property of the apartment complex so I have the right to, but it's always seemed like a place to go with someone you really care about."

The garden certainly does have that sweet, romantic vibe to it. It would be easy to see a couple setting up a picnic here, watching the clouds go by and smelling the roses.

"Maybe we should just have a date here," Jaemin suggests, "We're still on protected property, so it'll be safer."

Isla shakes her head. As beautiful as this place is, it's not enough.

"I want to see your favorite places, Jaemin," she says, squeezing his hand with hers, craving an escape, "We can come back here another time."

He looks like he's about to say something but Isla pokes her bottom lip out, pouting.

"Okay. Another day, then," he says, squeezing her hand back in return.

The couple continues to quickly make their way through the complex and nod at the security guard at the back, smaller gate. This man seems a bit jollier, not so ominous.

"Where are we going?"

"To some of my favorite places," he says, "Places I've always wanted to take you."

That pleasantly-delivered phrase sends a chill up Isla's spine.

"Like where?" Isla asks, having the desire to know where he's skipping her off to.

She doesn't have a phone and no one knows where they're going. Her breaths speed up dramatically and Jaemin looks at her in alarm.

"What is it? Is the mask too hard to breathe in?" Jaemin asks, stopping completely to look at her in concern.

"I just . . . want to know where we're going. I don't really like surprises . . ."

Jaemin frowns.

"There's this small cafe I used to go to when I was a trainee. I figured we could have lunch there. Why? Do you not want to?" he asks, voice small.

"I-I'm sorry, Jaemin," Isla says, shaking her head, calming down.

Leo's unexpected kidnapping of her has her suspicious of everyone, Jaemin included. But it would be counterproductive for him to take her somewhere dangerous or to want to hurt her himself.

"Being stuck at home for so long has got my head in a funk. What's this place like?" she asks him, pulling on an ever so slightly wobbly smile.

"You sure you're okay?"

"Yes, Minie. I'm feeling just fine."

Jaemin looks her over once more before nodding.

"Okay. Well, it's a really small place. Not many people know about it."

"Even though you've been there? Even Starlights from my country know all of your favorite spots."

"I haven't really taken any pictures there or anything. Most of the other members haven't been there either. Seojoon and I would stop by before we had to head off to cram school when we were still in high school."

"Ah," Isla says, "Well, I'm excited to be getting special treatment then," she says playfully, attempting to fully shake the mood from before.

It doesn't take an incredibly long time to arrive at the little hole in the wall cafe located behind a large bookstore. It would definitely have been faster if they'd hopped on a bus but that was too much of a risk for Jaemin to even suggest. What they're doing now is already dangerous enough. Isla doesn't mind. She hasn't been able to do a lot of walking since she's been in Korea, so the casual stroll is good for her soul. Even though it's still relatively early in the day, a bit before the lunch hour rush, plenty of people are on the streets, sitting at bus stops and walking with shopping bags. There are businessmen and women dressed sharply on coffee runs and talking quickly on shiny, brand-new telephones. A couple of teenagers are laughing loudly and posing for photos with their friends, causing a short burn in her chest.

All of these people are here, living their normal lives without worry. They have highs and lows, ups and downs, but all Isla feels is stuck. Stuck not only with Jaemin, not only in Korea, but stuck in her own life. Before that fateful Saturday morning, Isla was stuck in a dead-end job that made just enough for her to get by. She had very few relationships and none with any actual value. She rarely had anything to look forward to, rarely had anything that brought her intense emotion. There were things she enjoyed, sure, but nothing that squeezed her heart and occupied her brain late into the night. Nothing but OT2B.

Isla is snapped out of her reverie by a happy greeting, a middle-aged couple standing behind a counter in the little cafe. If she thought Leo's restaurant was small, this place is absolutely tiny. The counter takes up over half of it, a well-worn-in mat covering the exposed floor. Two short, brown little tables are placed on top of it, implying that patrons are supposed to be seated on the ground.

Isla slips off her shoes as Jaemin does the same, the man smiling at the older couple and talking easily, even tossing his head back to laugh as he guides the love of his life to the furthest table. It's quite obvious that he's well acquainted with them, making Isla feel like the odd one out. The fast-paced Korean flying over her head certainly doesn't help anything either, Isla is barely able to pick up a single word.

"Ah, angel, this is Mr. Kim and Mrs. Cho. They've run this place since I was a child," Jaemin says, politely attempting to bring her into the conversation.

Isla smiles as kindly as she can and bows her head slightly, spitting out the only Korean greeting she knows. Her ears heat up when the couple begins chatting loudly again, obviously complimenting her despite the little she's said. Unlike the embarrassed Isla, Jaemin is quite proud, practically glowing as some of his favorite friends compliment Isla, telling him that he's chosen well.

Jaemin brushes it off but smiles so wide his cheeks hurt. The couple has always been kind to him, not changing their attitudes once he and the other boys of OT2B hit it big. They never told anyone that he frequented the place, meaning that fan memorabilia does not decorate the walls like so many of the other places they've been. There isn't a sign pointing to his favorite table or a big star by his favorite meal on the menu. It's so refreshing.

Jaemin orders the two of them the cafe's prized cake, a slice to share, and orange raspberry lemonade, both of which are quickly delivered. The plating of it is gorgeous, a perfectly sliced six-layer piece of marbled cake with lemon drizzles crisscrossed on the ceramic. Isla hadn't expected something so grand from such a simple place, but as she's learned, appearances can be deceiving.

"I really shouldn't be eating cake but I wanted to split one with you," Jaemin says, picking up his shiny cake fork, "It's always reminded me of you."

"How?" Isla asks, avoiding the delicious-looking dessert in favor of sipping the chilled drink in front of her, teeth clinking against the glass straw.

"I had this the day I saw you," he says, sinking the sharp prongs into the delicate food. It breaks away with ease to sit tantalizingly on his fork.

Jaemin leans forward over the table, bringing the cake forward until it brushes on her lips ever so slightly.

"And ever since, the taste has come to mind every time I see you. Sweet, *soft*."

Isla stares at him as he guides the food into her mouth, the cake practically melting against her tongue. It's hands down the most delicious cake she's ever tasted, eyelids fluttering closed as she takes it in.

"Nothing else even comes close to it," Jaemin mutters, watching the way she breathes, watching the flushed color in her cheeks.

His eyes trail down to her exposed collarbones before slowly coming back to her face, watching the way her eyes open slightly, like she's just come down from a high. It's an expression she's made only one other time.

They don't talk much while they finish the surprisingly filling cake, Isla wishing she could have the recipe for it but somehow knowing she wouldn't be able to replicate it. Hand in hand, once again, they venture out, Jaemin taking her to a few of his other favorite places in

Seoul. They stop to take pictures whenever something fascinates Isla, which is more often than Jaemin had expected. They'd even stopped by some of his favorite stores, Isla having a blast looking through clothes (even though they would certainly be too short or too small for her, given the fact that she doesn't exactly fit into the short and bone-thin beauty standard here) and trying on accessories, Jaemin buying her a pair of earrings identical to ones he owns himself.

While she is busy looking around, Jaemin quickly buys them couple rings. It's cheesy, sure, but it's something he's always wanted to try. He pockets the box before Isla sees him, happily taking her hand and leaving the final store for today's adventure. They've already been out for several hours now, but there's just one more place he has to bring her.

"Where to now, Minie?" Isla asks, wanting this outing to last as long as possible before they're locked back up in their apartment under a fake threat.

"Someplace special," he says.

They walk away from the masses, away from the stores and glass fronts. This place is large with a dark granite front, standing like a soldier at the end of a street. An eerie feeling brushes across Isla's skin as Jaemin pushes the glass door open, a cold breeze washing over their faces.

"There are some people I want you to meet."

17

This date has been fairly successful in Isla's eyes. Besides the overly sexualized cake experience, their outing is normal and it allowed her to get a better idea of her surroundings. She mentally creates a map of roads and shops, remembering what connected to what and where places that could help her out in the future are.

Jaemin's been all smiles as well, nothing but a ball of happiness as he and the love of his life had a secret adventure. To be perfectly honest, Matoi Jaemin feels quite a bit like Romeo, taking his lover out under the noses of those who try and keep them apart. He's ecstatic that they haven't been caught and that no one has approached him or been caught staring. It's truly been the most perfect date.

But like all of Shakespeare's greatest works, there has to be an element of tragedy.

Jaemin is still excited when he leads Isla into the cold, dark building, overhead lights making the dark granite floors shine as they walk over them.

"What is this place?" Isla asks, clinging onto Jaemin a bit tighter.

Sure, there's nothing wrong with it, not on the surface. But everything is squeaky clean and somehow impersonal, despite the flowers and mementos housed in little glass boxes, imbedded into the walls and stacked as high as the ceiling.

Jaemin doesn't answer, but he doesn't really need to. It becomes obvious as they walk past small framed photos and well wishes encased in glass.

He stops in a seemingly forgotten corner, standing with feet in first position.

"Mom, Dad, this is Isla," he says, placing a hand on the cold glass.

Inside is a single urn, black with gold markings, and a bouquet of dead flowers falling apart. The gold-rimmed photograph is in color, almost too bright. There's a couple photographed, holding each other close and smiling in a way reserved for the happiest of couples.

"Oh, Jaeminie," Isla says, placing a hand on his back.

She's not sure what to say. What do you say to someone who brings you to meet their dead parents?

He looks away from the case and back to her, no pain in his eyes.

"I wanted to bring you to meet them ever since I fell in love with you," he says, tucking some hair behind her ears, "They would have loved you."

"I'm so sorry," Isla says.

Based on the single urn, it seems that both of his parents died at the same time. It's excruciating to lose a single loved one, Isla can't imagine what it must have felt like to lose two at once.

"Don't be!" he says, meaning it, "They've been dead for a long time now, ever since I was eight years old. It doesn't hurt so much anymore."

"What—" Isla begins before stopping herself.

She doesn't want to be insensitive.

"What happened to them?" Jaemin asks, picking up on her question.

"You don't have to tell me."

He shakes his head.

"No. I want to. I want to share my story with you. Genuinely, without leaving anything out. I want you to understand me," he says, placing her hand over his heart and looking into her eyes.

They're wide, bright and painfully honest.

"I want you to know who I am. Who I really am."

Isla licks her lips, a feeling something akin to anxiety forming in her stomach.

"Okay," she says quietly.

Jaemin sinks onto the floor, one leg extended and the other propped up.

"Sit down. This might take a while."

Isla dutifully sits beside him, staring straight ahead. She can't bring herself to look at his face.

"I had a pretty good childhood. Not remarkable in any way, but I was loved, I wanted for nothing. My parents rarely fought, we rarely ran into trouble."

He pauses, tilting his head up slightly.

"But it was just us. No uncles, no cousins. No grandparents," he chuckles slightly, a bitter, sad sound, "Or so I thought. My grandmother, my mom's mom, was very much still alive. Is very much still alive. The old bitch will probably outlive me, she's so stubborn."

Isla stays silent, suddenly finding her fingernails incredibly fascinating.

"That stubbornness is what made her and my mother clash heads. You see, my grandmother came from old money. The heir to a conglomerate. Filthy with money. Her whole life was planned out to a T. Where she would go to school, who she would marry. And she wanted that for my mother. She hated that she couldn't control her," Jaemin says, dragging a nail across the floor.

"My father was a normal man. Had a normal house, drove a normal car. He looked at my mother and saw a person, not an opportunity. So, she ran away, got married, had me. Happily ever after, right?" he asks, turning his head to look at Isla who can no longer avoid his stare.

His smile is still there but his lips tremble ever so slightly like he's been holding it for too long. Maybe he has.

"Until my grandfather got sick. Mother went to see him before he passed and grandmother threw a fit. Or I imagine she did, that's very on-brand for her. But anyway, she threw my mom out and my dad went to get her. A drunk driver drove them off of a bridge."

"Jaemin–"

"It doesn't matter. I suppose they died quickly. Doesn't matter. So, I went to live with my grandmother who I'd never met. She hated me," he laughs, "Oh, she hated me! How inept I was to be related to her, how snot-nosed and useless. I didn't have anything to offer her except a reminder of her only child, the only failure in her life. And even worse, I wasn't even fully Korean! My dad was Japanese. She hated my whole existence."

"That's awful, Minie," Isla says.

He shrugs.

"I would have preferred it if she had continued to hate me," Jaemin says, memories he's tried to repress forcing their way up to the forefront of his brain, "There was nothing worse than being loved by her. I still remember that day. The day the tutors told her I had potential, that I could grow up and continue her proud lineage, that my previous upbringing could be forgotten if I scored high enough, if I could play instruments like they were an extension of my very being. I could be perfect, just like her, if she guided me there."

He pauses.

"So, I was."

"What did I tell you, Jaemin?!"

"Not to speak to the help."

"And what did you do?"

"I spoke to the help."

The ruler hurt when it landed on his palms, but the sting was soon forgotten. The pain of reaching for the skies until it felt like his arms would fall off was much worse.

"She had expectations."

"Your tutor tells me you've made less than one hundred percent on your last two tests. That is unacceptable."

"But—"

"Do not speak back to me, boy," she said, voice sending shivers down his spine.

His grandmother never yelled. It was the deeply rooted power in her voice that made him tremble.

"I'm locking you in your room. You will not come out or have dinner until you've completed two hundred problems without a single mistake. If you mess up, you start over."

"About how I stood . . ."

"Back straight! Hold your head high, you're above them!"

". . .how I spoke . . ."

"Yes."

"Yes ma'am," she said, voice tight, "You speak to me that way again and I'll smack you in the mouth, do you understand?"

". . . what my interests were . . ."

"You're to be on the baseball team. Join math club and make sure you win student body president. Don't disappoint me."

"But there was one thing she encouraged me on. She loved my voice. Sure, anyone can learn to play an instrument, but to sing!" Jaemin throws his arms wide, "To sing is an ability very few can wield well. I sang at every party to the awe and envy of all of her stiff-necked enemies called friends. You should have seen the way she gloated, how far her chest stuck out as people threw compliments at her like my voice was just another thing she owned."

He looks at Isla, face contorted into something that looks like bliss but with a hateful undertone.

"Ah, I loved it. There were very few times when I was with my grandmother that I loved being her grandson. People would look at me with the awe-struck look people only get when someone exceeds their expectations. It made me feel powerful, like I was on top of the world. I loved it so much that I wanted more, I wanted people from everywhere to hear me sing, to see me dance. I wanted to perform."

Watching Jaemin tell this story, watching the emotions cross his face causes an empathetic pain in Isla. Her heart goes out to him, imagining the sweet child Jaemin once was drug through dirt, bend so hard he broke. What a cruel fate.

"Oh, she *hated* that!" Jaemin says, nose scrunching up, "She hated that I loved it so much my eyes started to drift from calculus problems to TVs where I watched idols command a crowd like I wanted to, like I craved to. For the first time since I met her, I had a dream of my own, something I wanted to fight for."

"She tried to stop it. She fired all of my music teachers and stopped holding parties. She forbade me from speaking to the few friends I had managed to make, afraid they would encourage me. And the things she would say . . ."

"You'll never make it out there, Jaemin. Look at you! Look how pathetic you are! You don't have what it takes!"

"You're too fat to be an idol, Jaemin. You'll make a fool of yourself!"

"They'll hate you. Who could blame them? I hate you too, ungrateful child. Ignorant child,"

"You have a purpose greater than to be a puppet on a stage. You have an empire in front of you. DO YOU HEAR ME? AN EMPIRE!"

Isla looks away, trying to blink away the tears in her eyes. They fall anyway, quick and hot.

"I suppose she had the right to be worried. Every day I stepped further and further away from her, stopped letting her influence me so much. But it really turned when I snuck out one day to go with one of my friends - Seojoon - to Smash Ent's audition. I'd been helping him prepare for weeks during lunches. I knew the song, I knew the routine. And when he went in, I couldn't help but feel a bit bitter about it. So, I did it right there in the lobby. I performed it like I was in front of the world!"

"And you got in?" Isla asks him, sniffing slightly.

Jaemin nods, grinning brilliantly and wiping away the remaining tears on her face.

"Don't cry, angel! It was the best day of my life! Well, one of the best days. Nothing can top you, Isla."

Isla's eyes are wide and glossy.

"I was ecstatic. But my grandmother was furious. Furious that I disobeyed her, furious that I got in. She demanded that I quit but I wouldn't. So, she kicked me out."

"How old were you?" Isla asks, shocked.

"Fifteen. I had just turned fifteen."

Isla feels sick. How could someone be so despicable to turn a child, their child, out into the world all by themselves? It hits too close to home.

"It was hard. I tried to hide it but the company knew something was up. It didn't matter too much, though. I didn't have anywhere to go except the dorms with the other members. I dug myself deeper and deeper into debt as I had to borrow money for everything - school costs, food, clothes. The lessons we had to attend. But it was worth it. The debut was worth it, my career has been worth it."

"Why then," Isla asks, angry confusion propelling her words, "Why would you risk your career for me? Why would you risk something so important, something you had to suffer so much to achieve?"

"Because, as much as I love the lights, the crowds, the fans, when I'm alone, when it's just me and my thoughts, I feel empty. Hollow. Like I still don't know who I am, like I'm unworthy to be where I am. I feel like a fraud, like I'm always caught in a lie. But you, Isla. You make me feel good. The darkness doesn't bother me when I'm with you. You make me feel *whole*."

For the rest of the day, Isla's excited nature is subdued. Her thoughts aren't overrun with escape routes. It's as if a little piece of the mystery has been solved, the enigma that is Matoi Jaemin made a little bit clearer.

She can't help but stare at him, trying to figure him out as they sneak back home. Something told her that he hadn't made up any of that story, not a single word of it. How had his grandmother affected him? How has the abuse she inflicted upon him shaped who he is today? What did it have to do with her?

One thing's for certain, it gives her a whole new perspective. It seems that Jaemin is a product of circumstance, the tragic result of a frightening childhood. Even if she wanted to hate him, Isla realizes that she doesn't - she can't. Every circumstance of him making her uncomfortable has been catalyzed by factors out of his control. He's not well.

"It's not his fault. He's the victim, it's not his fault," Isla thinks, truly believing it for the first time.

"Maybe I can - no! You're not his doctor, Isla."

It doesn't matter what her thoughts are. She knows she's already made her mind up. Just like she could never leave the baby birds that fell from their nests there to die, Isla can't bring herself to abandon Jaemin, not after he poured his heart out to her sincerely, not after the way he continuously seeks her out for love, desperately, like a child who's never been held the way all children should be. Just like the birds, Isla doesn't know why she's been put in this situation, why she's the person Jaemin has latched onto so tightly.

But she is. She is the person he's chosen and it's up to her to decide how to deal with it.

"Baby?" Jaemin asks.

"Mm?" Isla asks, looking at him.

"You've been really spaced out ever since we left the crematorium. Are you okay?" he asks her.

"Yes. I'm perfectly fine, Jaemin," she says.

Maybe the best thing for her - for the both of them - is for her to try, actually try to help Jaemin. All of the execs at Smash Entertainment are snakes, sinister with motives all of their own. They're using him as a pawn, a puppet, but if she joins him, maybe they can control the king piece.

Wouldn't that be best for them both? For Isla to no longer live in fear, for Jaemin to feel the love he so despairingly craves? Maybe he'd actually get better.

Yes, she's already made her decision. Isla is going to stop analyzing every word Jaemin says, searching for a lie, searching for manipulation. She will take him as he is and try and love him, try and save them both from drowning.

They make it home without issue, tiptoeing through the secret garden and back into their apartment like teens who've snuck out of the house. Jaemin even giggles when they make it inside, leaning against the door and pulling his mask off completely, all smiles.

"We made it!"

"We did!" Isla says, tapping her fist against his like they're elementary school friends.

"It was fun sneaking out with you! Better than anything I had ever dreamed of. I want to do it again, go on more dates."

"We should go to the garden next time," Isla says, "the weather has been so nice recently."

He nods, placing his shopping bags down.

"It has, hasn't it? The flowers are in full bloom, too."

She nods.

"I'm going to go take a shower really quickly, alright? I'm all sweaty now," Isla says, pulling her shirt away from her sticky skin.

She doesn't ask him to join her. She's not there yet. Baby steps, she's only just begun.

"Okay! I can start something to eat. I know you must be hungry," Jaemin says, already thinking of something quick he can make.

"Why don't we order something? You always cook for us, Minie, you deserve a break," Isla says.

Jaemin frowns.

"I don't mind! I like cooking for you."

"You sure, Jaeminie?" Isla asks, stopping in her path.

"Do you not like my cooking?"

Insecurity bubbles up inside of Jaemin. Has she just been humoring him the entire time? Has his cooking really been disgusting? He'd slaved over recipes with Seojoon for hours, even going a step further and taking cooking lessons from one of Korea's best chefs.

"Your cooking is delicious, Jaemin," Isla says, noticing the little cloud that forms over his head, "Excellent, even. But sometimes it's nice to take a break and let someone else do the work, you know?"

"Okay," Jaemin says, doubts instantly pacified, "What do you want?"

"You can choose!" Isla shouts from the bathroom, turning on the shower.

By the time the two of them are all freshened up, the food has arrived, Jaemin approving the delivery and a guard bringing it to their front door. He was apparently in the mood for something simple because the smell of delicious, freshly fried chicken quickly fills up the room. Isla sits across from him on the couch, wanting to be more comfortable than she can be while sitting at the dining room table. Jaemin doesn't question her choice, sitting on the opposite side with the bucket of chicken between them.

This couch probably cost more than Isla made in a month at her old job, but she tosses that thought out of her head, trying to get herself in the moment.

"So," she says, chewing on the side of her mouth, "What do you like to do?"

"What?" Jaemin asks, looking at her strangely.

Isla suddenly feels rather awkward, not having expected him to react in such a way.

"What do you like doing, Minie?" Isla asks.

Even though she's been here for weeks, even though she spends more time with him every day than she has with anyone since she was a child, she doesn't really know anything about him as a person - just his obsessive tendencies and his frightening responses to her leaving/ignoring him. So, maybe the best way to throw her plan into action is trying to connect to him as a person.

He frowns slightly, chewing on a drumstick slowly while considering his answer.

"I don't know. I like watching movies. I don't usually get a lot of free time so I usually watch shorter videos online. Why do you ask?"

"I just . . . I don't know, I realized I've never asked you any of that. We kind of skipped right over that getting to know you phase, you know?"

"I already know everything about you, Isla."

"Do you? Do you really?" she asks.

Isla still doesn't know just how much Jaemin has made up about her or how much he's gotten from stalking her and her acquaintances online.

He nods, smiling.

"Your favorite movie is anything in the cheesy rom-com category. You hate horror, it terrifies you. Your favorite color is the shade the sky turns just before sunrise. You aren't afraid of heights and you enjoy amusement parks. You—"

"Okay," Isla says, interrupting him and trying not to let how creeped out she is show, "But don't you think it would be nice to ask anyway? To do those awkward get-to-know-you sessions?"

"We can if you want to," Jaemin says, sucking on a chicken bone before grabbing another piece.

"I do want to," Isla says, "We don't talk much, ya know?"

"I guess we don't, do we?" Jaemin asks, he himself only realizing this now.

He's been so focused on having her, on her being beside him that he hasn't thought of much else.

"I'm a bad boyfriend," he says, stopping eating entirely.

His lip wobbles ever so slightly.

That's an understatement.

She shakes that thought out of her head. It's true, beyond so, but lamenting over it won't help anything. Isla has to move forward.

"You're not. Let's just . . . we can be different now," Isla says, struggling to find the proper words, struggling to try and make an effort that isn't to pacify him or plan a quick escape.

It's wordy and clunky and she feels so totally unsure of how to do this - how to try and spend time with him genuinely.

How do you try to like your tormentor?

Jaemin doesn't comment on her bizarre phrasing or her sudden change of attitude. All he hears is an admission, a desire for him to spend more time with her doing normal, coupley things like in those movies she loves - like he's wanted to do for almost half a decade.

Jaemin grins. Handing her another piece of chicken and sitting back into the soft pillows.

"So, what's your most embarrassing childhood memory?"

18

It was four more days before Jaemin informed Isla that they were in the clear and the group of sasaengs had been caught and punished. During this time, the two of them learned a lot more about each other than either thought possible. The idol seemed much more human than Isla first assumed. If she had met him normally, Jaemin is someone who Isla would have wanted to date. He's funny in the most bizarre ways and much more caring than Isla had known, especially towards his bandmates. The stories he tells about them are all laced with love and emotion that cannot be faked. He speaks about them as if they truly are his family and it causes Isla's heart to warm as she begins to see him as just another person with thoughts and feelings, hopes and dreams.

Jaemin becomes entirely convinced that his nickname for her is perfect - that Isla really is an angel. It's the subtle things, how she speaks about warm summer days of her childhood and stuffed animals she always wanted but never got that makes him fall deeper and deeper in love, to want to give her anything she could ever want just because he desires to make her happy.

Even though getting to know Jaemin has been wonderful, she's thrilled to no longer have to stay in the apartment. Isla hadn't been able to convince Jaemin to sneak out again so it would be wonderful to see a different place, even if it was the Smash Entertainment building she's grown to hate more with each passing day.

The only thing that dampened her glee was the thought of seeing Leo again. Isla isn't sure how she'll handle being around him - how she'll act. A part of her wants to sock him in the jaw the second his face comes into view while the other is completely terrified, remembering the ease with which he held her down.

Realistically, she knows that he won't do anything to her while she's in the company of Jaemin, but he might try something when he inevitably goes off to speak with his psychologist.

Would he take her outside and rough her up a bit? Maybe he'd just threaten her or grill her about the last few days she'd spent with Jaemin? And what about the other boys? What do they know? Are they a part of her kidnapping as well?

All of these questions cause her to be noticeably sluggish, Jaemin, eagle-eyed, noticing her lack of enthusiasm.

"What's wrong, baby?" he asks her, switching on his bedside lamp.

It's already late into the night and Jaemin is to report to practice in only a handful of hours. He needs to be sleeping, but he could care less about that. Isla's been antsy ever since he told her that they'd be going back to practice.

Does she not want to see him practice? Does she secretly hate his dancing? Or is it his body she doesn't like? He hasn't been going to the gym as much lately because he wanted to spend as much time with Isla as possible. Had he gotten fatter since then? But she hasn't said anything about his looks or his weight.

"I just . . ." Isla says, rolling over to look at him in the dim light, "Can I tell you a secret?"

It's a risky move, definitely. Telling Jaemin anything about Leo could prove catastrophic. But then again, it could work out in her favor. Maybe Jaemin will make sure that the rapper never gets close to Isla, never gets another chance to hurt her.

"Of course," Jaemin says softly, sliding over to her and watching the anxiety on her face, "You can tell me anything."

"I just . . ." she begins, cuddling closer to him, "It's Leo."

Jaemin stiffens significantly.

"Ever since I went to lunch with him, I haven't felt comfortable in his presence. It feels like he's hiding something - like he can't be trusted. He just gives me this weird vibe."

Jaemin frowns, running his finger across her brows to smooth out the small wrinkle that has formed there.

"Do you want me to talk to him? I already told him to leave you alone that day but I can do it again."

Isla shakes her head.

"No. I don't want any more violence. No more fighting, either. Just don't let him be around me, please? And don't tell him anything about us, okay? I just don't trust him."

That doesn't sit right with Jaemin. What had Leo done to make Isla feel so uncomfortable?

"Don't worry. You don't have to be around him. I'll make sure of it," he says.

Isla nods, pacified. Her anxiety settles a bit and she drifts off to sleep, crashing after her fit of anxiety. Jaemin stays awake, however.

The question won't leave his mind.

What had Leo done?

Checking to see that Isla is really asleep, Jaemin snags his phone from its charger on his nightstand, unlocking it and tapping through until he finds his secret applications and folders, which is where he keeps information stolen from Isla's phone alongside some photographs and contacts he wouldn't want anyone to know he had. Since Isla has been with him in Korea, Jaemin hasn't checked them, not feeling the need to since he's been with her nearly every second of every day.

His face morphs into alarm when his folder - the one that should have all of Isla's texts and messages - is completely empty. Not a single file, not a single message shows up. Did she somehow get his phone, find all of the files, and delete them?

No, the folder hasn't been accessed since weeks ago when Isla left, when Jaemin curled up in this bed all alone and sobbed while rereading some of his favorite things she sent to other people, wondering why he would receive nothing. The memory is dark and unpleasant, reminding the man of why he never wants her to leave him again, reminding him of how cold and empty he feels when she's gone.

But then why are the messages gone? The only way they would disappear would be if she wiped her phone completely. Why would she do that? As a matter of fact, where is her phone? Now that he thinks about it, Jaemin hasn't seen Isla's phone for quite a while now, not since their fight. He hadn't realized it, too happy to be spending time with her to notice the missing device.

Jaemin's mind is swimming as he clicks through, discovering that every one of the files he's jacked from Isla's phone is missing.

What is going on?

An unsettling feeling flutters in Jaemin's stomach.

Isla's missing phone, her dislike of Leo, Jaemin's missing files .. . what's going on?

The next morning, Jaemin is sluggish after not having slept properly due to his pondering over the Leo situation. He sees no other choice than to confront Leo about it, even though Isla asked him not to.

Jaemin watches Leo once he arrives at practice, eyebrows pulling together when he sees the way Isla glares at him from her spot in the corner. Leo doesn't react to her whatsoever, not even when the other boys notice her obvious distaste. No one speaks up, however, continuing to run through their routines, the newest unreleased song blasting through the speakers and instructors correcting small mistakes the boys make.

Around lunchtime is when the routine is interrupted as one of the managers bursts into the room in a flurry of loose papers and panicked movements. Everyone stops what they're doing, watching the man try and collect his breath so he can spit out whatever urgent news he has.

The man finally straightens himself out and speaks.

"The Berry Award Show has been moved to three weeks from today."

"What?" Seojoon asks, shocked by the manager's words.

"We just received notice a few minutes ago. There was a small fire in the usual venue so they had to relocate to a different stadium. It messed everything up,"

The rest of the boys all voice their complaints and concerns, Isla being left behind in total confusion. Whatever is going on must be important, as she's never seen the boys stress out as much as they are right now.

"Three weeks? That's a whole month early! Our next album hasn't even been released yet! We haven't even shot any of the music videos!" Leo explains, panicking.

"I know, I know! We're going to have to really cram your schedule for this to work. The other managers are calling to see if we can start shooting the music video tomorrow. The stylists are already pulling looks for the new theme downstairs, so you boys need to run along so they can fit you. The producers have all been called in so we can wrap this up as quickly as possible. Everyone, you're probably not going to get much sleep these next few weeks."

And with that, he gathers his fallen documents and leaves just as quickly as he came.

Jaemin jogs over to the dumbfounded Isla, extending an arm to pull her up.

"What is it? What's going on?" she asks, watching as the other boys clear out of the room rapidly.

"There's been a problem with the award ceremony we're supposed to be going to. Everyone's trying to figure out what to do," he tells her, grasping her hand tightly in his and hurriedly leading them both out of the practice room, taking her through a turn she's never taken before.

"Where are we going?"

"The basement. We need to get fitted for the music video."

"We?" Isla asks, stumbling as she tries to keep up with him, "I'm going to be in it too?"

"Of course!" Jaemin says, pressing the button on an unfamiliar elevator.

It dings and they both step on, descending several floors before they arrive at the lowest level. The temperature is noticeably colder here than it is upstairs, a cold draft wafting from around the seemingly endless stand-alone metal clothing racks, filled to the brim with plastic-covered garments.

"Welcome to Smash Ent.'s closet."

It's almost as if Isla's entered an alternative universe. Everything in the basement is filed away, the concrete floor littered with electrical tape ripped into arrows and letters, ugly fluorescent lights twitching up above.

To be completely honest, this looks more like a warehouse than Isla would have expected. She'd always envisioned vast closets and soft carpets like at the apartment. That wouldn't quite be practical, she supposes.

"Is everything you've ever worn down here?" Isla asks as Jaemin leads her down one of the aisles packed so closely that her shoulders brush plastic on both sides.

"Of course not," Jaemin says, slightly amused, "just items worn for performances, award shows, videos and stuff like that. It's not just us either, all of the other artists' clothes are here as well."

"Why is it so cold?"

"The stylists keep it temperature controlled. Some of these clothes are very sensitive to harsh temperatures and weather, moisture and such. That's why this whole place is monitored so severely. There's over fifty billion won worth of clothes here."

Jaemin says it so casually, the number seems insignificant until Isla can process that it's—

"That's like forty-something million dollars! Oh my God!" Isla says.

It's preposterous to think that there's anyone, even a whole group of anyones, who have that much money invested in clothes, arbitrary things. But the K-pop industry does not work in small numbers, not even on the consumer. Hell, the things she alone has bought probably paid for one or two of these designer shirts she passes by.

"We get a lot of donations from brands and designers. Us wearing one of their garments is better promotion than anything they can buy."

"That makes sense. Everything you touch sells out within minutes."

Jaemin nods, making a sharp right when the last rack in the row ends. Isla's finally able to hear voices, all hurried but quiet like university students cramming for an exam in the library.

Not that Isla would know, considering she never went.

They must be in the center of the huge basement, a large section empty of racks. Instead, there's a raised runway lit by overhead spotlights that shine brighter than the rest of the room. Woojin stands on one end of it, a very stressed-looking middle-aged lady tugging on the waistband of his slacks and sticking pins everywhere she deems necessary. Woojin winces when he gets poked but he doesn't say anything, standing as still as he can.

Daehyun is in a similar position, a different lady fussing with a very extravagant and blinged-out dress shirt. Isla notices the strange look he gives her and she squeezes Jaemin's hand tightly, an uncomfortable feeling washing over her.

Does he know that she tried to escape?

Yet another stylist seizes Jaemin and ushers him over to a rack at the edge of the clearing, holding up garments before tossing them away in frustration. And then, seemingly out of nowhere, the dreaded blonde man appears standing in front of her, arms folded and eyes scanning her in a completely emotionless fashion. Goosebumps race up her arms. In her mind, Isla tries to blame it on the icy temperature, but she knows it has everything to do with the man in front of her.

"Shouldn't you be off ruining lives or something?" she asks, bitterness lacing her tone.

He smiles. The bastard has the audacity to smile!

"I'd be careful of your words, Miss Isla," he says.

Isla feels more than sees a pair of eyes burning into the back of her head. A short turn confirms that Leo is glaring at her intensely, even raising a finger and pressing it against his lips as someone adjusts the lapels on his jacket.

If looks could kill, she'd be six feet under by now.

Isla doesn't respond to the Suit's words, angry that she doesn't have anything to retort with. They've got her in their palm and they know it.

Cocky son of a bitch!

"Now, let's not keep the wonderful stylists waiting, Miss Isla. They're very busy ladies," he says, uncrossing his arms to shoo her in the direction of a rather flighty-looking woman.

The suit remains by Isla's side as the woman grabs various shirts before abandoning them and disappearing into the racks. It's only a few moments until she returns with various dresses, one in particular catching her eye. It's long and white, small flowers embroidered in silver thread across the bottom hem. The lady urges her into one of the changing rooms on the far side of the clearing, Isla vanishing behind the heavy velvet curtain.

Momentarily, she looks around to make sure there aren't any

cameras. She doesn't see any, so she quickly disrobes and tugs on the dress. It's rather heavy to be a summer dress but the fabric is still soft to the touch. The full skirt flares out a few inches below her waistline, making her torso look longer than it really is. The top cuts elegantly across her shoulders, highlighting the dips in her collarbones. Unfortunately, it's too tight in the chest area, squishing her breasts tightly and causing them to spill out over the top more than she's comfortable with. Even her waist feels restricted.

It makes her feel self-conscious, not wanting to leave the safety of her small sitting room. It's obvious that this dress was meant for someone of a completely different build. It makes her feel rather boyish, like her shoulders are too wide. She supposes they are, at least when compared to the female idols she's seen.

"Are you quite finished?" a voice asks from behind the curtain.

It's the Suit.

"Well, yes, but—"

He doesn't wait any longer, snatching it open and causing Isla to shriek in surprise. She's technically decent, but she hadn't expected him to expose her.

Jaemin looks up from where his own clothes are being adjusted, glaring at the Suit in anger. How dare he invade her privacy like that? Anger flirts under his skin and Jaemin prepares to snap at him but he gets distracted when Isla steps fully out of the dressing room.

She looks glorious. The white fabric against her skin is radiant even in the horrific lighting. And her shoulders are out, those shoulders he loves, those collar bones he wants to dip his tongue into again. He feels a twitch in his pants and tries to shift his thoughts away from how beautiful his love is.

It appears that he isn't the only one to notice. The other boys have their eyes on her as well, admiring how stunning she looks. Jaemin isn't pleased, noticing how Woojin's eyes linger on the tops of her breasts more than he'd like.

"Watch yourself, maknae," Jaemin growls out, causing the younger man to jump and get stabbed by a pin.

"Sorry, hyung," he says, eyes downcast.

Isla crosses her arms in an attempt to cover up but only worsens it by accidentally pushing them up even further.

How long has it been since he's slept with her? Too long, much too long. They haven't done anything worth anything, barely even kissed since the last time and she appears like that? In front of everyone? Hell no.

A stylist comes out and blocks his view, muttering under her breath and measuring around her body, writing down her findings.

"She says you're too fat for it," the Suit says.

Isla's cheeks go pink and she looks to the floor. It's obvious that it was meant for someone else, but to insult her weight?

"Maybe it's because I actually have a figure," she says, glaring at the hateful man.

Deep down, Isla knows that she doesn't have a weight issue, not even close, but she certainly doesn't fit into Korea's harsh beauty standards. She's not short enough, not thin as a stick, not pale as a sheet of paper.

"If that's what helps you sleep better at night," he says, "But just know the rest of us have no idea why Jaemin likes a pig like you. And look at your skin, you're much too dark. You don't fit in."

His words are hurtful and bitter, falling from his smirking lips like poison. Isla begins to think that the poor lady hadn't insulted her at all and the Suit is using her as a scapegoat.

Even though his words sting and are untrue, Isla doesn't let them get to her, straightening her shoulders and standing tall, not about to let some racist prick with a stick up his ass make her feel worse than she already does.

"Do you sleep, Charles? Ah, excuse my ignorance, of course robots don't sleep,"

"My name isn't Charles. It's—"

"I don't care what your name is, Charles," Isla says, feeling pissed off, beyond pissed off, "I'm here in this too-small dress because of you and your buddies. I won't stand to be kidnapped and made fun of."

"Careful, he might hear you," Not Charles says, head gesturing ever so slightly towards Jaemin.

For the first time since they split apart, Isla looks at him. He's as gorgeous as always in his overly embroidered suitcoat, the material just a tad too big for his shoulders. But the thing that catches her off guard is not the way his clothes fit but the intense look on his face. It's somewhere between hunger and anger. His eyes look even darker than normal as he stares at Isla who panics internally.

Had he heard her? Did he know about her escape attempt?

Isla feels herself begin to sweat ever so slightly. The moment is broken when the stylist grabs another item and pushes her back into the dressing room. This goes on for hours, the look Jaemin gave her slipping her mind as boredom takes over.

Sure, she likes trying on clothes, but this is just ridiculous. She's switched in and out of at least twenty different choices by now. It's tiring and she's beginning to get hungry.

It does end, eventually, and Isla returns to her own clothes, noticing Jaemin waiting for her. Whatever emotion he's been experiencing seems to be over, Isla notices with relief. He's back to happy, smiley Jaemin.

"Are we done?"

"With the clothes, yes. We have to run to the salon now."

A sense of dread fills her stomach.

"Are they going to do something to my hair?!" Isla asks.

There are fifteen million ways that could go wrong. Maintaining her natural hair in Korea has already been hard enough since there aren't any stores that carry the products she needs, so she doesn't need some well-intentioned stylist ruining it.

Noticing his girlfriend's panic, Jaemin smiles.

"Of course not. Your stylist won't be here until the morning, I found out."

"Then what're we going to the salon for?"

"They're dyeing my hair."

"No!" Isla exclaims.

Jaemin's black hair is by far her favorite and he has it for so little time.

"What?"

"I like your hair like this. It's my favorite."

"It won't be much different. It's going to be silver."

"Silver is quite different from black, Matoi Jaemin," Isla says, her dissatisfaction clear.

"You won't like me with my grey hair?" Jaemin asks, pouting.

"Of course I will. I love silver. It's just not as good as black. At least it's not pink."

Jaemin gasps.

"Everyone loves me with pink hair."

"Pink is my very least favorite!" Isla says, laughing at Jaemin's playfully scandalized expression.

He seems happier today than usual. For once, Isla doesn't sense his usual hesitation. It's a glimpse at the real Jaemin, the one she hopes is real.

Every other member is here as well. Seojoon's head is already bright red, the color of milkshake cherries.

Cherries . . .

Isla shakes her head.

"I have to be here?" she asks Jaemin.

"Of course you do. I always want you by my side, Isla," he says as he sits in an empty salon chair.

Isla sits down beside him, wishing very dearly that she had her phone. She simply sits there, twisting the chair back and forth with one foot and playing with her own fingers.

"What happened to your phone, baby?" Jaemin asks.

She tenses at once. The stylist has him facing her so Isla is forced to make eye contact, not able to escape his invasive gaze. Her heartbeat skyrockets, pounding so loudly she swears he can hear it. What does she do now? What does she say?

Isla's eyes drift over to Leo, trying desperately to come up with an excuse.

"Why are you looking at Leo, baby?" Jaemin asks.

He's calm, much too calm.

"I was just wondering what color they're dyeing his hair," Isla says quickly.

Jaemin hums.

"But I thought you said he makes you uncomfortable. Why would you care about something so frivolous as the color of his hair?"

Isla licks her lips subconsciously, trying to combat the dry feeling in her throat. Jaemin's eyes linger on her mouth before trailing up to meet her eyes. She looks frightened, like a scared little animal caught in headlights.

"What are you and Leo hiding, Isla?" he asks, voice completely free of emotion.

"I . . . nothing."

"I thought we agreed on no more lies," he says.

Isla's eyes dart around the room, hoping to find a portal that would take her out of this situation. She wants to be anywhere else.

"Look at me when I'm talking to you, please."

She doesn't want to, but something tells her it'll only make him angrier if she defies his request. He's been mostly soft, whiney even, for the majority of the time she's been with him. Isla's mind briefly flickers over to the memory of her dragging him down the hallways while he pleaded with her. Where is that man? He certainly isn't the one sitting before her.

Isla raises her eyes to look at him, noticing the cold anger he hides just below the surface. His fingers grasp the armrest tightly, nails digging into the leather.

"I'll ask you one more time. What's going on between you and Leo?"

"Nothing," Isla says, sticking firm to her story even when it's obvious that Jaemin doesn't believe her.

He doesn't say anything, looking her over once more before breaking their staring contest as the stylist informs him that she has to rinse out his hair.

For the rest of the time they're there, Jaemin does not say a word to her. He doesn't even acknowledge her, causing her anxiety to run out of control. She has the desire to go hide in a bathroom somewhere just to escape the suffocating atmosphere, but something tells her Jaemin wouldn't stand for it.

So, she sits there for an eternity until the stylist switches off the blow dryer, Jaemin's grey hair shining as she runs oils through it and brushes it quickly.

He stands without thanking the stylist and extends a hand towards Isla, who silently says her prayers as they stride out of the room. Jaemin nods to the few members still remaining in the room.

It's dark outside now, probably around ten pm. Isla doesn't say anything as they board the standard black van, street lights casting light into the space and illuminating Jaemin's face. His features are set into a divine mask of carefully crafted indifference but Isla knows better. He's still angry, still unpredictable. Something tells her that the chance of making it to the apartment and going to sleep peacefully is exactly zero.

In the entirety of Jaemin's brooding, Isla failed to come up with a single story she could tell Jaemin that he'd believe.

Is this it? Is she really riding off to her doom?

Jaemin's silence is killing her. He doesn't turn on the lights when they arrive home, the only noise is Isla's uncertain breathing. His back is to her, Isla barely able to see the faint outline of his shoulders, his muscled arms.

He won't hurt her, will he?

Isla swallows.

"Why do you always insist on lying to me, Isla? Why do you always insist on running off with Leo every time you get the chance?"

"I don—"

"Shut up."

Isla closes her mouth so quickly, she almost bites her tongue, not having expected him to say that to her.

"Don't interrupt me when I'm talking."

Isla is still as a statue.

"Maybe he was right. Maybe I am useless. That's why you walk over me like this."

Isla wants to argue with him but holds her tongue.

He sighs like the whole world rests on his shoulders.

"I don't care anymore. I want you and I'm going to have you. You are mine, just as much as I am yours, do you understand me?"

"Yes," her voice is quiet, but Isla knows he's heard her.

"I don't think you do, baby. Angel, darling, love of my life," he says, turning around and stepping so close to her that their chests brush, "Do you think I say these words to just anyone?"

"No," Isla whispers, unable to look away from his piercing eyes.

"Do you think I fall all over myself for just anyone? Do you think I treat everyone like this?"

"No."

"So, we can agree that you've wronged me then, can't we, baby? We can agree that you've stomped all over my heart, can't we?" his voice is much too light for his hard-hitting words.

Isla stays silent, not wanting to say anything.

"Speak, Isla. Tell me I'm lying. Tell me I'm wrong. Tell me that you running off, having secrets with Leo, that all of that is just in my head."

Isla stays silent once more.

"That's what I thought," Jaemin says, voice hard, husky in the same way it is every morning, "go to the bedroom, angel."

Isla's breath hitches, a ball of lust swirling around in her stomach.

Jaemin is silent for a moment.

"Are you saying no?" he asks, lips brushing against the shell of her ear.

Isla finds herself shaking her head.

"What are . . . what are you going to do?" Isla asks.

He's too close, his presence is dizzying.

"I'm going to show you who you belong to."

His words shoot straight down her spine.

Wordlessly, Isla heads into the bedroom, Jaemin eyes on her through the darkness.

Anticipation. Pure anticipation surges through Isla like river rapids. She sits on the edge of the bed, legs pressed tightly together as her brain assaults her with the image from mere moments ago - Jaemin's beautiful face contorted in nothing less than fury, quiet, intense, cold fury that sends a hot shock straight through her nervous system, electrifying her to the point that every hair on her body stands at attention.

She tries in vain to hear what Jaemin's doing out there in the living room but can't make out anything over the sound of her own breathing.

This is so different from the first time. She's sitting here, waiting for him, wishing the seconds would pass faster so he'd appear, so he'd come and take her like he promised.

"I'm going to show you who you belong to."

Just thinking about his words has a blush racing across her cheeks and up her ears, the girl playing with her fingers to try and keep herself distracted from the inevitable. If she thinks about it too hard, she'll chicken out and go hide in the bathroom like a child. But if she's honest with herself, hiding is the last thing she wants to do right now. Isla wants to touch and be touched, to hear the breathy way he says her name when his fingers slide up and down her sides, to see his eyes heavy-lidded with lust.

The young woman shifts uncomfortably, suddenly aware that her underwear is sticking to her, dampened from her thoughts alone.

And then he's there.

Jaemin stands in the doorframe, lit suddenly by the lights flicking on. Isla's breath catches as she stares at him, noticing that his expression hasn't changed at all. He stalks towards her, causing her to move back on the bed, feet digging into the covers.

He isn't fazed at all, crawling towards her like a jungle cat, slow and deliberate. Isla's holding her breath by the time he reaches her, arms placed on either side of her left leg, causing the mattress to sink from the pressure he's applying. He leans his beautiful face closer before connecting their lips, kissing her deeply as he pushes both of them deeper against the pillows.

Isla's breathless when he pulls away, gasping but hardly able to pull in any air before he's kissing her again, his body weight pinning them both to the mattress as he moves his arms to tangle his fingers in her hair and pull her even closer.

She feels dizzy when he places a kiss on the corner of her mouth, trailing a damp line of licks and nibbles all the way down to the base of her neck where he parts only long enough to slide her shirt over her head and toss it to the floor.

"Minie," she mewls, thoughts a tangled mess,

The noise that he makes sounds much closer to an animal's growl than anything human. Isla moves her pelvis, causing Jaemin's fingers to dig into her skin as she brushes against his growing erection.

"Stop it," he says, unhooking the clasp of her bra, the material sliding down some before Jaemin tugs on it harshly, causing the material to rip and fall, now in useless pieces.

"What is it with you and ripping clothes, Matoi Jaemin?" Isla asks, voice husky.

Jaemin looks up at her from under those long lashes of his, sticking his tongue out to run over the skin of her chest, pausing at her collarbones to bite down and suck harshly.

"Jaemin!"

"What's with you and Leo, making me angry all the damn time, huh?" Jaemin questions, letting go of her skin with a slick pop.

The mark he's made is bright against her skin. No doubt it's going to be there tomorrow, no doubt everyone will get to see it when she shows up for the shoot. He's pleased with himself, moving to create another one higher on her neck as his right hand cups her breast, thumb flicking over her nipple, the bud hardening as he stimulates her.

"It's not what you th . . . ah!" Isla exclaims as Jaemin rolls his hips hard against her, the thick material of their pants leaving Isla desperate for more skin on skin contact.

She's never hated jeans as much as she does in this minute.

"I don't care," he says, dragging his lips just barely over her skin until he reaches her ear, biting on the lobe gently, "I don't care what you were doing. I don't care why you were looking at him all day. It doesn't matter what your reasoning is, baby."

He licks the skin just under her jawbone.

"You shouldn't have done it," the anger in his tone is palpable.

"Jaemin–"

He moves away from her entirely, sliding off the bed to watch her. Isla's all riled up, blushed and wet, hair messy and eyes unfocused. Jaemin hasn't even gotten into her pants yet.

"Finish stripping," he says, voice revealing just how much seeing her like this affects him.

"What?" Isla asks, response delayed as she blinks at him.

"Finish."

Suddenly, Isla feels overwhelmingly embarrassed.

"Ah, Minie–"

"Are you saying no?"

Isla shakes her head rapidly. Her eyes flicker away from the man in front of her as her fingers hook onto the waistband of her pants, raising her hips up to slide them down her legs and abandon them on the ground. Jaemin doesn't move, eyes darkening slightly as he notices the wet patch in the seat of her panties.

"Look at me when you take them off," he says, voice not leaving any room for arguments.

Isla bites her bottom lip harshly before doing as he says, now sitting on the bed as naked as the day she was born.

The room is silent as they stare at each other, Isla feeling more vulnerable with every second that passes. This is only the second time she's ever done this and she can't help but feel self-doubt, insecurity bubbling up inside of her.

"You're so beautiful."

"What?" Isla asks, surprised.

"You're so beautiful," Jaemin repeats.

The sharp edge in his voice has dulled, replaced by a softer, sweeter tone. Jaemin leans forward, placing both of his hands on the very tops of Isla's thighs, caressing the skin there.

"You're so beautiful," he says once more, fingers gliding up and down Isla's soft skin.

He captures her face and tilts it up, studying it so intensely that Isla feels as if he's peering right into her soul. Her green eyes are wide and bright, turned down at the corners ever so slightly. The beauty mark under her right eye stands out against her caramel skin, her rounded face and full lips red and alluring.

"So beautiful," he murmurs, "So mine."

Jaemin nuzzles Isla's cheek softly.

"Undress me,"

Isla's fingers skim the skin of Jaemin's stomach, pulling the fabric up and over his head, messing up his newly dyed hair. She presses a palm against his stomach, feeling the muscles under her touch. All those hours of dancing have certainly paid off.

Isla slides closer, unbuckling his bottoms and pulling them over his rounded ass along with his boxers, revealing that deep V that secretly drives her crazy. Jaemin pushes them both back, Isla's naked skin sliding on the silk sheets.

His fingers trail over her hips before teasing her just above where she craves his touch.

"Minie!" Isla protests.

Jaemin ignores her, repeating his action once more before pressing his thumb on her clit, sliding it around like a joystick. His love sighs, relieved to finally be touched. The sensation doesn't last long, however, as Jaemin slides a single finger into her before adding another, curling both of them upwards, repeatedly.

"Don't stop," she moans, eyes fluttering closed.

"Look at me," he demands, Isla's eyes fluttering open just in time to see him wrap his soaked fingers around the base of his cock, trailing her wetness all the way to the tip before popping them in his mouth and sucking, eyes hazy.

"Oh my God, Jaemin."

He doesn't say anything, laying on top of her before flipping the both of them over, Isla sitting on her boyfriend's lower abdomen.

"Ride me."

"What?" Isla asks, feeling Jaemin's muscles ripple under her.

"I'll help you," he says, hands gripping her hips tightly.

At this point, Isla wants him too badly to be embarrassed anymore. She reaches behind herself and grabs him by the base, squeezing his cock once before rising up, dragging the tip around her before sinking down slightly.

Isla winces slightly before continuing, sitting lower and lower as they both groan, Jaemin cursing under his breath as she bottoms out. She stays still for a moment, getting used to the feeling of being stretched out around him. When she's ready, she bucks her hips forward in experimentation.

"Fuck, baby."

Jaemin guides her, rolling her hips back and forth before she slides up and down him, her breasts bouncing with every movement. Jaemin could see this sight every day for the rest of his life and never get tired of it. Never grow used to the adorable look on his love's face. Her skin is flushed, mouth slightly swollen from the way he kissed her, lips parted and cute little noises escaping her every time she moves.

He can't take it anymore.

Jaemin flips them once more, catching Isla off guard. Her quiet noises grow louder as Jaemin rolls his hips quickly, the sound of skin slapping echoing in the room.

"Jaemin," she mewls as he begins to play with her clit, teasing and pressing and touching her so much, her head is foggy.

"Who makes you feel like this?" he questions, sweat rolling down his back.

"You," Isla says, tossing her head back.

"Leo?"

"No!" Isla says, nails digging into Jaemin's skin.

"Then who?"

"You!"

"Who?!"

"You! You, Jaemin, you! Only you!" she gasps after a particularly hard thrust.

"Who do you belong to?"

"You!"

"Who do you love?"

"You! Only you, Jaemin, only you!"

Those words send him over the edge, bringing Isla with him as he attacks her clit.

"Oh, baby. Oh, Isla!" he shouts out, Isla's walls clamping down on him as she sums so hard, her toes curl and her back arches off of the bed.

"Oh my God," Isla says, breathless and utterly exhausted as Jaemin slips out of her.

"Buckle up, angel, we're not finished."

By the time the morning rolls around, Isla is so sore that she can barely move. Jaemin's wrapped around her like a vice, still naked but back to being the soft boy he usually is. It took three rounds before he stopped being angry with her and one more before everything was completely out of his system.

Isla turns as best she can, watching Jaemin's peaceful expression as he sleeps. He looks so innocent, so heavenly that her heart flutters and doesn't stop, speeding up when Jaemin's eyes peel open as an alarm goes off on his phone. Thankfully, it's a pleasant sound, so neither of them move to shut it off. It's a little past five so the sun has just barely risen, morning light streaming in through their curtains.

"Good morning," he says, smiling sleepily at her.

"Good morning, Jaemin," Isla replies, moving his hair out of his face.

"You really aren't doing anything with Leo?" he asks, his voice small like a scared child.

"Of course not. Why would I look at anyone else when I have

you?" Isla asks, watching the shy smile that blossoms on his face.

What a beautiful, broken boy. He deserves to be loved. He truly does.

Jaemin giggles, peppering kisses all over Isla's face.

"Jaemin!" she whines, "We have to get up!"

He ignores her, kissing her on the mouth before pulling back with a grossed-out look on his face.

"Ew. Morning breath."

"Look who's talking!" Isla exclaims, smacking him with one of the pillows playfully before leaving the bed to walk to the bathroom.

She's quite a bit sore, her gait uneven to Jaemin's pure and utter delight. He follows after her, watching as her eyes grow large when she sees all of the bruises on her skin.

"Jaemin!"

"I'm not sorry," he says, kissing her temple before turning on the shower water.

Isla knows it's pointless to try and cover them up considering that she'll be changing clothes several times today. Annoyed (but not really), Isla hurries to get ready, putting practically no effort in since she knows she'll be getting all dolled up.

The stylists told her to bring her own makeup (unsurprisingly, since it's incredibly difficult to find anything in her color) and some of her favorite hair products as well.

The company van is ready and waiting when the couple rushes outside, afraid of being late. It's about a forty-five-minute drive to the shoot location, giving both Isla and Jaemin ample time to squeeze in a much-needed nap before they arrive.

"Ready, angel?" Jaemin asks her.

19

The shooting location is a large movie studio housing several fake rooms that must have been assembled in the night. There is a comfy-looking living room, the first-class section of an airplane, a grand stage, and a few other scenes hidden behind those. There's a little trailer off to one side which houses the impromptu hair and makeup stations. As soon as Jaemin and Isla arrive on site, they are whisked away by stylists, flat irons and brushes ready.

Isla is absolutely embarrassed by the marks littering her skin but she tries not to show it. To the staff's credit, no one comments on it, but their eyes do linger for a bit longer than they should, eyeing up Jaemin who is smug even across the room with his eyes closed as shadow is spread across his lid.

Isla's stylist, someone with features more similar to her own, is utterly silent, applying color corrector and concealer without a word. Isla flinches a few times, the bruises sore and tender.

"What's the aesthetic this time?" Isla asks, head tilted back so the woman can hide a mark right under her jaw.

"We're shooting the mv for Sanctuary, so it's supposed to be a mix of lots of glitzy, glamourous shots mixed with simpler scenes from everyday life," Jaemin mutters, eyes still closed.

Isla hums.

"What do I have to do, exactly? Why am I in this again?"

"Because you're my sanctuary, obviously," Jaemin says, unable to hide his smile, "The other boys chose places or things that are meaningful to them, Seojoon chose his dog. But nothing is more important to me than you, Isla."

But why? After all of this time, Isla still has no clue why she's the one he chose. Every time she asks him, he expertly dances around the question or answers with a response so vague it makes her head spin. Without knowing why she's there, Isla will still be at an important disadvantage.

Isla isn't sure what to say to that, but thankfully, her stylist moves on from hiding Jaemin's possessive claim on her body to applying normal makeup, starting with her eyeshadow.

Everyone else arrives and is styled and dressed within the next hour. It amazes Isla how quickly such a big group of people can move and work in harmony. So far, there hasn't been a single mess up or error, despite the entire shoot being tossed together in a matter of hours.

Isla doesn't speak to any of the members, but she does catch Woojin staring at her a few times, his expression unreadable. It's perfectly blank, any emotion masked by a face of complete and total indifference. It's unnerving, to say the least. She feels like an animal at the zoo under Woojin's cold analyzation

It's almost scarier than being stared down by Leo. At least with the leader, Isla knows where she stands, what the feelings between them are. Woojin is a completely different situation.

The first few scenes are shot without Isla. Today's filming will focus on the 'comforting' part of the video, so all of the boys are interacting with their chosen objects. Daehyun sits slumped over at an old piano, the keys dusty and the notes ever so slightly sour. Still, it's his expression that sells it, relief and pure happiness etched on every part of his face, fingers dancing over the keys with renowned familiarity.

Leo's scene takes place in some sort of underground club, the scene dark as the rapper stands on a small stage, the floor beneath him packed with extras. No doubt it's a reference to his days as an underground rapper, when no one had any real expectations of him, when he didn't have to carry the weight of his and his brothers' careers, when the world didn't have an eye on him at all times.

For a moment, a very tiny, miniscule moment, Isla pities the man. Seojoon is playing with his dog and taking photographs while

Woojin relaxes in a fake bedroom, smiling brightly as he plays video games and edits on his computer while eating snacks. In another set of scenes, Daehyun dances in a small room by himself, all wooden floors and smeared mirrors. Seojoon is cooking in the kitchen, smiling and dancing awkwardly as he sears meat and grills vegetables.

All of their scenes touch Isla's heart. She's watched these boys for five years, watched their struggles to find themselves while pursuing a dream so grand, it's hard to fathom. She grew up with them, she listened to their songs when she was sad, when she was happy, when she felt alone. Their videos made her laugh when things were grey, their words encouraged her when she felt lost.

How had she ended up here? How did Isla end up with the people she loved more than anything, how did she end up resenting them, fearing them, desperately trying to save them and not lose herself in the process? How had she passed that thin line between fan and idol? Or rather, why did Jaemin yank her over that invisible line, spewing lies with teary eyes and bright smiles?

Isla shakes her head gently, careful not to loosen her hair from the top of her head. She's not wearing that dress today, sporting some comfy leggings and an oversized sweater so soft she could fall asleep in it. It's finally her time to shoot and nervous energy spreads through her, the girl chewing on her lip slightly. She's afraid to mess up, to add yet another embarrassing moment to her steadily growing roster of regrettable memories.

Thankfully, she doesn't have any lines nor does she have to dance at all. Her role is rather simple, actually. All she has to do is sit on a couch and read a book and wait for Jaemin to ring the doorbell three times. Then she just opens the door and hugs him. Easy, right?

Still, she's afraid of messing up and having to shoot several takes for it.

The director gets her situated on the surprisingly soft couch, socked feet pressed against an armrest and a heavy leather tome open in her lap. The camera rolls and she tries to get into the role, reading the book (it's actually the Bible, which Isla doesn't know how to feel about given the situation) and flipping pages every so often. She changes her pose when told to (of course, Charles is here to give her instructions) and also pretends to sleep and watch a movie.

The time comes for Jaemin to ring the doorbell.

Isla opens the door and tries to mold her expression into shocked happiness but is unable to pull it off realistically. Her heart drops to her stomach when they have to keep repeating the scene, not wanting the staff to become annoyed with her.

On the fourth take, Isla swings open the door and is surprised when Jaemin drops his prop bags and races forward to hug her, arms tightening around her waist and face buried in her neck.

"I missed you," he says, voice throaty and choked up with genuine emotion.

Isla's expression softens and she hugs him back, closing her eyes and squeezing him close to her. She's startled when the director yells "Cut!", breaking the moment that felt oddly intimate. Jaemin doesn't let go of her right away, pulling away from her slowly and studying her expression before kissing her on the tip of her nose and grinning.

"I've always wanted to do that," he admits, "I've thought about it so often, especially on the days when I missed you the most, when I felt the most alone."

"Jaemin—"

He grins one more time, perfectly white teeth on display, and runs off as the director calls him over.

Day one wraps up late in the afternoon but pushes on longer when the members have to stay to allow the stylists to make a last-minute change to their wardrobe. By the time they're released to go home, it's dark out. Isla once again falls asleep in the car, giving Jaemin a chance to watch her even breathing and peaceful expression.

He can hardly believe, even now, that she's here with him, that he can touch and hold and kiss and love her like he's desperately craved to for over fifteen hundred days. She's so beautiful, so precious to him.

Isla's presence is soothing, silencing the voice in his head and making life seem brighter than before. His mind drifts to the first time she made him feel that way. His expression clouds a bit, remembering the weight of the phone in his hands, the artificial light from the screen. The floor was cold, his face was red, his palms ached and silence blasted his ears. But then she came along . . . his Isla.

Jaemin sighs, rubbing gently on the makeup on her neck to reveal one of the marks he'd made. He didn't know that was one of the things he'd enjoy doing, but he never felt such a connection with any of the other people he'd slept with, never felt the need to leave something on their skin.

Of course he didn't. None of them mattered to him, none of

them were Isla.

Jaemin doesn't bother to wake her up when they get home, knowing she must be exhausted from the long day. She's easy to lift, Jaemin supporting her weight under her knees and arms, the girl's head rolling into his chest while she slept, breathing not even changing.

He sets her down on the bed gently and pulls off her shoes as she rolls over into a ball, causing Jaemin to laugh under his breath.

How adorable.

The socks come next, then her shorts, Jaemin allows his fingers to skim across the soft skin on her legs.

God, he loves her legs. He left a few hickies there as well, one of which he kisses quickly. He slides a pair of pajama bottoms up her legs, knowing keeping her in only her underwear would certainly cause distractions in the morning which they (unfortunately) won't have time to handle.

Jaemin's more careful when taking off her shirt. He moves slowly as not to wake her, leaving her bra on until he's pulled on one of his t-shirts. If he takes it off beforehand, he'll surely wake her up. Last but not least, Jaemin retrieves some makeup wipes from their bathroom to take care of the paint on her face, knowing it's not good to sleep in makeup from personal experience.

When he's all done, he quickly handles himself and crawls into bed next to her, breathing in her scent.

He loves her so much. So, so much. She's his lighthouse in the darkness, the beacon leading him out of the fog.

When she first came back, Jaemin was anxious, afraid that she'd disappear again. But Isla is still here with him, still by his side. That only means one thing, that she's staying with him because she wants to. Because she loves him.

Jaemin giggles giddily, face buried in the pillows so as not to wake Isla.

Could he be happier?

Day two of the shoot doesn't involve Isla, so she can sit back and watch. In a way, it's exciting, getting to see the complete process of the creation of one of OT2B's iconic videos. She watches as lights are adjusted and music blares from the speakers. The boys dance the choreography Isla has memorized by this point, each of them in glittering outfits and decked out in accessories more expensive than some people's annual salary. They work hard, every one of them, and don't complain even when the director makes them run their scenes multiple times.

There are seemingly a million outfit changes, Isla keeping Jaemin company each time he lands in the stylist's chair again. They laugh and talk in a way that's almost normal. Isla teases him gently over one of his honestly hideous outfits, causing him to laugh along wholeheartedly to the disdain of the woman trying to touch up his makeup.

She even tells Jaemin about one of her high school memories when she suddenly remembers the story after Jaemin cracks a joke about one of his old school teachers. Jaemin eats it up, eager to learn as much about the love of his life as possible. Sure, he knows all of the facts about her like where she was born and who her family members are, but he can't tap into her mind, making every moment she shares with him a treat to his over-eager ears.

Jaemin internalizes the tale, trying to remember what he was doing at the moment when it happened, trying to link their lives as much as possible.

The second day's shooting runs even later than the first but everyone is ecstatic when the director calls wrap, a loud cheer coming from the boys and the staff. It was hard for them to pull off but, by some miracle, they'd been able to do it, giving the editors enough time to work with the footage and whip it up into something magical.

Jaemin swings an arm around Isla's shoulders, leaning against her playfully.

"Ah, I'm so tired," he whines, head propped up on hers.

"I'm tired just from watching you. You did amazing, Jaeminie."

Jaemin smiles at her, her praise always pleasing him.

"Really?"

"Yup! You looked amazing. I'm sure that the music video will be phenomenal."

"Fe ... what?"

"Phe-nom-e-nal. It means super amazing."

Jaemin smiles, happy to learn a new word.

"Phenomenal. I hope so. I really want the fans to like it."

"Oh, they will," Isla assures him, "You're going to break records with this one for sure."

Jaemin's heart flutters. Isla is always so supportive of him, always encouraging and reassuring him whenever he has worries or doubts.

Could he ask for a more perfect person to be in love with?

There's another busy day ahead of them tomorrow but, thankfully, they don't have to go in until later in the morning, allowing everyone to get more than four hours of sleep.

Isla turns in quickly and Jaemin follows, but not before sending a quick text. Lips set in a hard, cold line.

What did you do to Isla?

20

Isla remains fast asleep, breathing evenly and head empty of any and all dreams. Jaemin is relieved that she's no longer having nightmares. He himself knows how horrific your own mind can be, how hideous the images in your head can get. Isla hasn't been having them as much, thank God.

Jaemin slips out of bed, looking at the time on his phone. It's just past four in the morning, everything still and dead in the world around them. He places a kiss on her temple, lingering just to relish the feeling of her skin under his. Jaemin sits there for a moment, perching on the very edge of the bed, just watching her sleep. He could watch her sleep for hours - hell, he already has. There's something so comforting about it.

He'd been terrified of storms back then and would race on small feet to his parents' protection, his mother placing him against her breast while his father rubbed circles on his back. It didn't help him sleep but it relaxed him, made him realize he was safe from the storms raging outside.

Isla makes him feel that same way, except she chases away the storms in his own head, acting as the peaceful eye. It's a feeling of security he hasn't felt for over a decade. She's so precious to him. So, so precious. He wishes words existed that could properly express the totality of his emotion, the grandness of his adoration for her. He'd kiss the ground she walked on, praise every strand of hair on her head if he could.

Jaemin sighs, running fingers lightly over her arm before standing up and running his hands through his hair.

So, what does Leo have to do with this? With her?

Jaemin no longer believes that there's anything romantic going on. He doesn't even believe that they're conspiring on some plot together, not after the way Isla looked at his younger bandmate the other day. She was incredibly uncomfortable, angry even, although she tried to hide it. Jaemin's able to tell her emotions so easily, even if she only changes her expression ever so slightly.

He's obsessed, utterly enamored. Every expression she makes is seared into his eyelids, ingrained into his brain.

Something is definitely up and he's going to figure it out.

Jaemin casts one more look at his sleeping lover before

exiting the bedroom, slipping on some shoes on his way out. Quickly as he can without creating any noise, Jaemin makes his way downstairs to the shared apartment. He knows Leo will be there, undoubtedly too exhausted from all of the filming to head to the studio or his own place.

He unlocks the door with the code and enters, not turning on any lights. Everything is still and calm, the steady hum of the dishwasher being the only noise he can hear. A faint light is emitting from Woojin's crowded room, Jaemin peeking in only long enough to see the youngest member passed out and drooling over his keyboard.

He leaves, continuing down the hallway before doubling back, rolling his eyes as he grabs a blanket and tosses it over Woojin, knowing the man is too heavy for him to lift into bed. Jaemin switches the computer monitor off, being sure to save Woojin's editing before he does so. He closes the door behind him and walks until he stands in front of Leo's bedroom.

The door is shut but not locked, allowing Jaemin to waltz right in. Leo is snoring slightly and spread haphazardly on his bed, Jaemin able to make out the outline of his figure. He sits on the chair of Leo's desk, legs crossed and arms gripping the rests tightly.

Every second Leo spends asleep ticks Jaemin off more and more. How can he be fast asleep without a care while Jaemin is wide awake, head buzzing with questions sparked by the man a few feet away from him?

"Leo," Jaemin says, voice even and speaking at a normal level.

The rapper doesn't react at all, still blissfully unconscious.

"Leo," he repeats, voice slightly more strained.

Again, nothing.

"Leo!"

The man wakes up with a start, limbs flying everywhere and clonking his skull on the headboard. He curses, rubbing his head and wincing.

"Leo."

"Jesus Christ! Jaemin, is that you? Why are you sitting in the dark like a psychopath?"

Leo fiddles about and turns on the light, the switch located on the wall beside him. The room is illuminated but Jaemin doesn't flinch, remaining his posture and analyzing Leo with cold, hard eyes.

"Shouldn't you be asleep? And in your apartment?" the other man asks, voice scratchy.

Jaemin watches as Leo rubs his eyes and yawns, slumped over.

"You ignored my text."

"What text? You woke me up over a text?" Leo asks, disbelief in his tone, "C'mon, man! Surely it could have waited until you saw me tomorrow."

"You mean later today. And no, it couldn't have waited, I need to know now."

"Know what?"

"What did you do to Isla?"

Leo freezes and Jaemin grips the rests tighter.

He knew it. He fucking knew it!

"I don't know what you mean," Leo says after a moment of

silence, a touch too long, "Is something wrong with her?"

"Oh, no," Jaemin says, struggling to keep the ice out of his words, "She's perfectly fine. But for some reason, she seems to feel a certain way about you."

"About me? I'm not sleeping with her!" Leo explains, terrified that Jaemin thinks he's having an affair.

"I know. I have that well covered, don't worry. I know every inch of her body. Trust me, I'd know if anyone even tried to touch her," Jaemin says, satisfaction shooting through him as Leo squirms, obviously incredibly uncomfortable.

"You've done something to her to make her scared of you, Leo."

"No, I–"

"Shut up for once, please. Stop lying to me, I hate liars," Jaemin says, finally standing up to tower over Leo who's still sitting on his bed.

"You did, Leo. You did something to her. What was it?"

Leo is silent, half asleep and half terrified that Jaemin knows what's going on.

"Did you yell at her? Threaten her?" with every word, Jaemin feels himself becoming angrier, words spitting out with venom.

"No!"

"Why is her phone missing, Leo? Why is it wiped?"

Leo pales. How does he know they wiped her data?

"I don't . . . I . . ."

Shit. He has to come up with something and quick. It seems that they underestimated Jaemin in their haste to stop Isla from leaving. What to do, what to do?

"CEO Hwang . . . he was worried that she'd leak company information."

Leo regrets his words as soon as he sees the expression on Jaemin's face.

"She absolutely wouldn't do that. Isla wouldn't even *think* about doing that to us. How dare you accost her like that?!"

He's raging now, infuriated. Leo doesn't think he's ever seen Jaemin so angry.

"So, that's what you did?! You came up to her and stole her phone, yelled at her?!"

"No! No, Jaemin, no!" Leo says, feeling small, "It wasn't like that at all! CEO Hwang had me ask her very politely—"

"POLITELY, MY ASS!" he's screaming now, not caring about waking the others, "SHE WOULDN'T BE TERRIFIED OF YOU IF YOU'D ASKED POLITELY!"

"Jaemin, calm down!" Leo pleads, frightened by his sudden anger.

"CALM DOWN?! YOU WANT ME TO CALM DOWN AFTER YOU WENT AFTER ISLA, YOU LYING BASTARD?!"

Jaemin looks like he's three seconds from punching Leo right in the face. The younger man scrambles to his feet, putting as much room as possible between the two of them.

"Jaemin, please—"

"I'll tell you what, Leo," Jaemin says, suddenly calm and collected, persona completely flipped, "If you touch her again," he steps closer to the rapper who, in turn, takes another step back, hitting the wall,

"If you speak to her again," he's close now, too close, "If you so much as look at her again, Han Leo."

Leo closes his eyes, not wanting to look at Jaemin for one second more. When he eventually opens them again, breathing heavily, Jaemin's only a centimeter from him, eyes angry and staring into his soul.

"I will *fucking kill you*,"

And then he takes a giant step back and exits the room, slamming it shut behind him. Leo slides down the wall, heart pounding loudly in his ears. He's shaking slightly, not able to process what just happened.

Jaemin has never been so livid, so terrifying. But the scariest part is that Leo believes him. Oh, he believes him. Every word hit like a dagger, nothing but truth behind them. And if Jaemin ever finds out what he really did to Isla . . .

He thinks he's going to throw up.

Jaemin stalks out of the apartment, feeling slightly less angry but desperately needing to hold Isla in his arms. She's still asleep when he arrives, quickly slipping under the covers and pulling her flush against him.

"Minie?" she asks, words slurred with sleep, "waz wrog?"

Jaemin simply shakes his head, already feeling so much better. It's as if she's pulled all the negative emotions out of him, calmed his chaos.

"Nothing, baby. Just go back to sleep," he says.

Isla mumbles something incoherent before promptly falling back asleep, still pressed against him.

How could Leo even think to do anything to Isla, his Isla? To make her feel unsafe, afraid? Jaemin nearly growls just at the thought of it, placing a kiss on Isla's forehead.

He'll always protect her.

Always.

As promised, the next few days are pure chaos. Everyone is busy, including her. Isla had expected that she'd continue to follow Jaemin around like she usually does, but instead, she'd been put to work. While the boys practice with the background dancers Smash Entertainment hired for the big performance at the Berry Awards, Isla has been recruited by the stylists. For hours on end, she shuffles through clothing, pulling what they ask of her and running around like a headless chicken. Thank heavens that one of the stylists has studied in Canada, giving Isla her instructions with no problem.

She can't remember a time when she was so stressed out. It's ridiculous how many clothes and accessories the boys need to have ready. For the Berrys alone, they're changing clothes three times.

Isla begins to think that these poor women don't get paid enough for this. She swears a few years of her own life have been shaved off just from being here for such a short time.

At some point during the day, (Is it lunch? Dinner?) a sweat-soaked Jaemin comes to find her, surprising her by tossing his arms across her shoulder.

"Baby!"

Isla nearly drops the watch she's holding.

"Jaemin!" she exclaims, punching him in the shoulder playfully after noticing his happy expression, "You scared me."

The man makes some small noise, pulling her closely into a hug.

"I've missed you, Isla."

"You saw me this morning."

Jaemin whines, holding her even closer.

"Baby—"

Isla is vaguely aware of the stylists looking at them but she dismisses that fact.

"I missed you too, Minie."

It's not exactly a lie. She certainly would have preferred to be upstairs watching him and the background dancers than slaving away in this cold ass basement.

"Really?"

"Yep! How's it going?"

Jaemin grins.

"I'm excited about it. The other dancers are really talented. The choreographers have some really exciting stuff going on."

"I can't wait to see it then."

"Want to come with us? We're going out to eat, the boys and us."

"Yes!" Isla almost shouts, eager to escape the stylists.

Jaemin laughs, moving his arm to settle around her waist.

"Let's go then."

Isla hands the watch to one of the ladies, eagerly skipping to the elevator with a giggling Jaemin in tow, hands clasped.

It takes two black vans to transport them all to some restaurant Isla's never seen, a little place with giant grills in the middle of tables.

A BBQ place!

Isla's never been to one, causing excitement to soar through her. They settle in, Isla just now noticing a certain rapper's absence.

"Where's Leo?" Isla asks.

Jaemin's expression hardens.

"He had to do something else," he says quickly, shutting her down.

Isla shrugs, not really caring. She's not going to complain about her tormentor not being there to eat with them.

A lady comes out carrying trays of meat and vegetables, everyone perking up.

Back at Smash Entertainment, Leo paces the floor of his studio anxiously, constantly checking his phone.

Dr. Moon is supposed to text him so he can meet her and tell her everything about Jaemin. What's taking her so long? Exasperated, Leo decides to forget waiting around and storm up to her office to tell her right this moment. He gnaws on his upper lip, still remembering the pure fury Jaemin slapped him with, the waves of near hatred pulsing off of him.

Jaemin. His little brother, Jaemin. The one who always sought him out when he needed guidance.

What has happened to him? Precious, harmless Jaemin? And over what? Some girl? Some stranger?

He's got to talk to Dr. Moon.

Leo arrives at her office, preparing to barge right in. He stops short, however, when he hears hushed voices whispering behind the door. The man presses an ear against the surface, trying to discover if this is a conversation that can be interrupted.

"... Thursday night ... silk shirt ... ten twelve seventy ..."

Leo scrunches his face up. That's definitely not Yeji's melodic voice, certainly belonging to some male. He can't quite make out the owner of the voice.

"... don't ... my wife is ... whore ..."

He's only picking up on the smallest bits of the conversation, unable to get a feel for what the conversation is about. He steps back from the door and retreats down the hall when he hears the scraping of chairs against the floor, hiding in the shadows. It's the blonde foreign executive, the one who seems to hate Isla the most. He walks away from Yeji's office at a strolling pace, not once looking back. His blonde hair is messier than it was earlier today and his shirt is only half tucked into his pants.

What's going on? Why did he visit Yeji?

To Leo's knowledge, the only people who are supposed to have contact with the psychologist are the members, Isla, and CEO Hwang. The blonde man shouldn't even be speaking to her.

Leo knocks twice on the door, listening to the quiet "Just a moment," that comes from within.

His heart thunders in his chest in anticipation of seeing her again. Undoubtedly, she'll have the perfect answer of how to respond to Jaemin's not so little outburst. It'll come so easy to her that Leo will want to smack himself in the head, wondering why he couldn't think it up.

"Come in."

Leo strolls into the white office, eyes immediately drawn to Yeji's poised form. Her legs are crossed at the ankles, back straight and short, perfectly manicured nails clicking on her keyboard. She does not look up at Leo when he enters, simply making a small gesture to the seat in front of her.

For a moment, Leo wishes she would tell him to stretch out on the chaise so she would study him, pry into his mind and invade his privacy.

He takes a seat quickly.

"What was Hunter doing here?" he asks, his own words surprising him.

Yeji looks stunned for a moment before sighing heavily and rolling her eyes.

"He just decided to stop by and bother me. I can't stand him, you know. He's so full of himself,"

Leo smiles, any apprehension melting away at her words.

"I don't like him either," the rapper says, puffing up his chest a little bit, "I don't know how his poor wife deals with him. There's this rumor going around that he only married her because her father's rich."

"That wouldn't surprise me," Yeji says, "He definitely seems like that type of asshole."

Her annoyance fades as she looks at Leo, smiling brightly at him before placing a hand on his arm.

"Good thing my sweet boyfriend is nothing like him,"

Leo blushes furiously.

"Boyfriend?" he asks, nearly stuttering.

It's as if the lady snatched the moon and handed it to him.

"Of course," Yeji says, "I don't sleep with just anyone. Unless you don't feel the same way . . ." she trails off, smirking internally at the panicked look on his face.

Han Leo is so much easier to manipulate than she thought he'd be. She almost feels sorry for using him for her own agenda.

"I do!" he shouts before blushing even harder and lowering his tone, "I do. I was just a bit surprised is all."

Yeji moves her hand up, holding his jaw softly.

"You're so cute, Leo. Now, what can I help you with?"

And just like that, the mood is ruined.

"Jaemin threatened me. He barged in during the middle of the night and screamed at me for messing with Isla."

"He knows? Jaemin knows that we've forced Isla to stay here?" she asks, concern lacing her tone.

This is not part of the plan.

"I don't think so. If he did, he would have . . ." Leo's hand ghosts its way up to his neck, "He was violent. Angrier than I've ever seen him. And all over Isla. I don't think she told him anything either," Leo says, shaking his head, "I think he just . . . noticed. Just picked up her ill-will towards me without her ever uttering a word."

Yeji bites her lip, concentrating.

"Okay, Leo," she says, suddenly warm towards him.

She grabs one of his hands and squeezes it reassuringly, Leo's cheeks heating with color.

"Thank you for telling me. I'd say to avoid speaking to either of them for a while, just until I talk to him, alright?"

Leo nods, focused on her hand on his. It's so soft . . . so warm.

"Okay, thank you, Yeji."

This time, she does not correct him.

Leo lingers even though there isn't anything else to say, keeping her hand inside of his. It's awkward, inappropriate even, but the doctor doesn't reprimand him, instead, speaking up gently.

"Shouldn't you go off to practice? I heard there's quite a stir going on right now."

"Oh!" Leo says, turning scarlet and jumping up, dropping her hand clumsily, "Right, thank you!" he says, darting out of the office even though he's on a lunch break that won't end for another twenty minutes.

Yeji Moon watches him go, nails tapping against her flawless skin. She'd be an idiot not to notice how flustered he is around her. Maybe she can use that . . .

Leo sighs as he flops face-down on the couch in his studio. He'd made a total fool of himself, he can feel it. He can't seem to help himself! Yeji is just so beautiful, so smart. She's accomplished so much in her field even though she's only two years older than him.

The doctor no doubt thinks he's a dolt. Would she even be bothered to speak with him if she wasn't working for the company, if they had met of their own devices? Or does she view him as a child, someone not even worth wasting time on?

Ah, it's infuriating! Having a crush on his brother's doctor! But Leo doesn't think he can give it up. Just remembering how pleased she looked when he successfully kept Isla from running away turns him into a giggly mess, hiding his squeals of delight behind a tough exterior and a closed fist.

She doesn't know, does she? She can't possibly suspect that he likes her.

Can she?

Would that be such a bad thing?

Ugh.

Leo shakes his head, trying to stop thinking about her. He can daydream later. For now, he has to be happy that Yeji seems to have a plan for dealing with Jaemin, one that will hopefully stop him from hating Leo's guts.

There's a knock on his door, Woojin sticking his head in.

"Hyung? I brought you something from the convenience store."

Leo sits up, hoping his cheeks have cooled down.

"I thought you guys were going to a restaurant?" he says, taking the plastic bag and peering inside.

"Mm, we did," Woojin says, nodding his head, "But I had them stop by to pick you something up. I know you wouldn't have eaten anything and practice starts back soon."

"Thank you, Woojinnie," Leo says, opening a cup of noodles and standing to switch on the electric kettle he keeps just for these situations.

Woojin doesn't say anything, pulling out a soda and rolling the now-empty plastic bag into a ball, chucking it into the recycle bin. He watches Leo with calculating eyes, trying to figure out what part exactly he has in all of this Isla nonsense. From his observations, he has definitely noticed a weird air around the three of them, some complicated emotions being tossed back and forth.

He doesn't know Isla well enough to be able to tell anything important from her, but he knows his hyungs like the back of his hand.

"So, what's going on between you and Jaemin hyung?" Woojin asks, startling Leo so badly, he nearly spills the hot lunch all over his lap.

"What?"

"Something's been wrong between the two of you ever since Isla showed up here."

"I . . ." Leo slurps up a noodle, "You know Jaemin's not well, so he's been feeling some emotions that aren't really valid. He's very protective of her and tends to snap now and ask questions later."

Woojin frowns.

"Don't worry, though, Jinnie. He's getting better every day. Dr. Moon will have him all fixed up in no time. Until then, things might be a little bit awkward."

Woojin's frown just gets deeper.

Leo pats him on the back.

"Don't think about it too much, okay? Come on, let's get to practice."

21

Isla sits on the edge of their bed, chewing her lip in anticipation. The music video is set to drop in only a few minutes and she doesn't know quite how to feel. The teasers had been dropped two and four days ago, but neither of them contained any clips of her, not even from the hurried reshoot that had taken place six days ago when one of the editors decided that Isla wasn't in enough of the scenes.

She had adorned that Scarlet O'Hara dress that had (thankfully) been altered to fit her and ran around in some big, beautiful flower field. Isla isn't sure exactly how that fits in with the rest of the video's aesthetic, but it was quite fun to film so she can't really complain

"How much longer now?" Jaemin asks from his place beside her, always beside her.

"Two minutes," Isla says, staring at the screen of her brand-new phone.

Jaemin had gifted it to her, the device already decked out with a matching phone case and adorable lock screen featuring Jaemin's shyly smiling face. She knew instantly that he'd taken it for that exact purpose, recognizing the lamps in the background.

It's the cutest wallpaper she's ever had, hands down.

Needless to say, Jaemin's contact was saved with a heart in her phone. Isla hasn't gotten around to changing it, but she doesn't really think she will. He gets so puffed up and giggly whenever he sees it and she has no desire to take that simple happiness away from him. But for some reason, all of her other contacts have been destroyed completely, even though she synced all of her Gmail accounts. Bitterly, she expects that Leo has done something to them, tampered with her information.

"Are you nervous?" Jaemin asks her, placing his chin on her shoulder.

"Aren't you?"

"Nope," Jaemin says, popping the 'p', "Just excited to see how it all came together."

Isla wishes she could share the same sentiment but all she can think of is her performance. This will be the first time since Jaemin announced their 'relationship' months ago that Isla will be in the spotlight. She hasn't even so much as peeped at any of her social media accounts, not wanting to see thousands upon thousands of hate comments on top of all the other bullshit she's had to endure.

She shrieks when she gets the Twitter notification from Smash Entertainment, managing to click the link to the video with shaky fingers. Isla holds her breath through the entirety of the company's logo, releasing it when a black screen suddenly surges forth with color.

Five men walk out onto a stage, lights focused on them, the world silent except for their even, steady breathing. Leo lifts the mic to his lips and music bursts forth as fans in a huge stadium scream in excitement. The new song plays over clips from their last tour and the clips they shot last week. They all focus around the glamorous part of their careers, the fans, the planes, the money. But halfway through, clips of the boys' desires and wants for the simpler things in their lives appear, Isla nearly losing a lung when a quick clip of her smiling in a meadow flashes on screen for the world to see.

"Baby! There you are!" Jaemin shouts, Isla quickly smacking him on the thigh to wordlessly tell him to be quiet.

More scenes of life in the spotlight flash by, this time with the boys dancing to the song's choreo before finally cutting to the scenes of the boys getting to do things they love outside the realm of idoldom. There's Daehyun with his piano and Woojin with his editing. Daehyun dancing and Leo biking by the river. (She doesn't remember them shooting that.) Seojoon playing with his dog and Woojin working out. And finally, towards the very end of the video, Jaemin walks into the fake house and embraces Isla.

It's so different seeing it from an outsider's perspective. From here, Isla can't deny the softness in Jaemin's gaze, the way he hugs her so tightly. It's romantic, tooth-rotting sweet, a scene straight from a kdrama.

"Oh, Jaemin . . ."

Isla can't stop herself from watching the video three more times, breath catching on each of her scenes. The gravity of her being in this video hadn't hit until now, tears welling up in her eyes. There are a million other things Jaemin could have chosen, things he should have chosen. It could be his love for lazy days in bed, the thrill he gets from gliding around on ice, the way he loves his bandmates more than life. He could have picked the park he sneaks away to, the starry sky at night, the feeling of air blowing through his hair on long car rides.

All of these things are pieces of him, important things that make Matoi Jaemin himself. And yet . . .

"You chose me . . ." Isla says, voice warbling with emotion.

Jaemin blinks in confusion.

"Of course I did. I already told you, you're my sanctuary, Isla."

Isla tosses her phone on the comforter behind them, tangling her arms between his. She sniffles, lips barely pressed against his neck. Jaemin holds her as she bursts into tears, rocking her gently.

"What's wrong, baby?"

"I love you," she says, gasping over her sobs.

She's ruining his shirt but she doesn't care. The revelation is too all-consuming for her to care about anything else at the moment.

She loves him. Isla loves Jaemin. She does. She loves him. It isn't smart, it doesn't make sense, it happened too fast, but it's the truth.

It's painful. The feeling sits in her stomach like a rock, clogs her throat and makes her want to gag. She loves him. Isla loves Jaemin, this pitiful, broken, scary man. She loves him.

She loved him from the moment he first made her laugh on an awful day all those years ago when she'd first stumbled across OT2B. She binged videos when she felt lost, hopeless. But that love fled when she met him for the first time, was tapped down into a teeny tiny part of her being. But it's managed to grow in this terrible situation. Every time he looked at her, touched her, tried to please her for no other reason than making her happy, it grew. It grew whenever his doubts ran rampant, whenever he seemed small and alone. Her love grew more and more with every new thing she learned about him, with every despicable person she met who influenced him.

Matoi Jaemin is a pathetic shell of a man and she loves him for it.

Isla cries harder, hanging onto Jaemin for dear life.

She loves a sick man. A damaged man. A man who's fucked in the head. Isla just wants him to get better, wants him to be the bright, shining person she knows he can be.

But where will that leave her? When Jaemin is all better, when he realizes he doesn't truly love Isla and that everything he thought he knew was a lie, what will happen to her?

She knows. She knows that she'll be left in the dirt, thanked for her part but no longer needed.

Falling in love with Jaemin is quite possibly the stupidest thing Isla's ever done in her life but she can't take it back, can't press rewind and escape into a time when none of this was real.

"Are you okay, Isla?" Jaemin asks her, concerned by her sudden breakdown.

Isla sniffles and sits up, wiping her eyes and giving him a watery smile.

"Yeah," she says, "It was just a really good music video."

Jaemin bursts out laughing, wiping her tears away.

"It was a good video but not *that* good," Jaemin says, "You don't need to get so worked up about it."

Isla nods, already feeling the beginnings of a headache coming on.

"I'll get you some ibuprofen. We don't need you to make yourself sick."

"Okay," Isla says, watching him as he walks away, wondering what it'll feel like when he stops coming back.

22

Isla sits in the salon chair in front of her stylist (yes, she learned that Smash Entertainment had hired this lady just for her) as she plays around with her hair, trying to get it just so. She uses some floral-smelling hair spray every three minutes, Isla nearly choking on the fumes. It smelled nice the first few times she used it, but now that there's like three cans of the stuff in her hair, Isla is over it.

Today is the day.

In just a few hours, she and the boys will hop in a limo and slide up to the Berry Awards' blue carpet. She'll have to stand in front of cameras for the first time and try not to get blinded while hanging onto Jaemin like a loving girlfriend should.

Isla had tried to convince Jaemin that it would be best if she simply had a ticket to the show and sat separately from the boys, but he'd thrown a hissy fit, blatantly refusing to go to the show if she didn't stick to his side the whole time they had to be there. The only time she'll get a break from him will be when OT2B goes up to perform their song.

To be perfectly honest, Isla is glad that she'll have Jaemin only inches away. This is her first real public debut since the world (herself included) found out that she's his "girlfriend" and she doesn't know what to do with herself. How will it feel to have thousands of eyes on her at all times? Will the whispering make her skin crawl?

Isla sighs. She just wants it to be over.

"Something wrong, baby?" Jaemin asks.

His stylist is just now beginning on his hair, straightening it and flipping it so it frames his beautiful face perfectly.

"No. I'm just a bit nervous."

No point in lying.

"I was nervous the first couple of times I went to award shows too. After a while, you'll think nothing of them."

His words are supposed to be comforting but have the exact opposite effect on her. Isla can't help but feel like this may be the only award show she attends with the band. The next one she'll have to watch from her phone screen, snuggled up in pajamas and studying the way he smiles, remembering how much prettier it is in real life.

"When are we leaving again?" Isla asks, trying to change the subject.

"Well, the carpet opens at six and we need to be there at about that time. It's only a half-hour drive from here so we have about an hour and a half until we need to go."

Isla nods slightly, now limited to the stylist's firm grip on her jaw as she studies her face, trying to decide what makeup will go best.

Jaemin's prediction was spot on because they roll out at five-thirty sharp. Isla sits as stiff as a stone next to Jaemin, pretending to play on her new phone (much to Leo's disdain). When Jaemin turns away to say something to Daehyun, Isla flicks him the bird.

Really, she's a ball of nerves. What if she trips when they exit the car? What if someone shouts something mean at her? What if the other idols ignore her completely? And what about the fansites? Will she have her own fansites? The thought of being followed around with a camera makes her sick.

Isla closes her eyes, forcing herself to take deep breaths and ignore the trembling in her fingers. She doesn't need to open them to know that it's Jaemin who takes her hand, placing a soft kiss on her knuckles.

"You'll be just fine. Don't let go of my hand, okay? I'm here for you." he whispers into her ear.

Isla gulps before nodding once, still not opening her eyes.

Jaemin rubs his thumb over her wrist softly, giving her something else to focus on.

Much too soon, the limo comes to a slow stop, Isla already able to hear the photographers. She opens her eyes as the door swings open, OT2B filing out one by one.

Jaemin goes last, exiting the car but leaving his hand in hers, assisting her out onto the carpet. The heel of her stiletto sinks into the textile as she steps out, cameras clicking rapidly and voices shouting in words she can't understand. Her ears heat in embarrassment but Jaemin still smiles at her, easing her fear somewhat.

Every eye is on the couple as they stroll down the carpet hand in hand, Isla repeating a mantra in her head.

Left foot, right foot, left foot, right foot.

Jaemin and Isla arrive at the photo wall where the other boys are already standing, each looking dashing in their perfectly tailored designer suits. Everyone is dressed slightly differently, the pattern and color of their jackets, shirts, and ties varying. The only two who match are Isla and Jaemin, the girl rocking bedazzled Louboutins that make her taller than her lover and a blood-red evening gown, her hair framing her face perfectly. Jaemin's suit is all black, his tie being the same color as Isla's dress and his dress shirt littered with diamonds to match her shoes.

They look stunning, truly a celebrity couple.

Isla had asked Jaemin if it bothered him that she would be taller than him but he didn't seem to mind too much, too fascinated by the fact that they would be matching.

They also wear the couple rings Jaemin bought, each strung on a platinum chain around their necks. Isla couldn't stomach wearing one on her finger.

Isla tries to stand off to the side as not to interrupt the ot5 photos, but Jaemin yanks her closer and tucks her between him and

Seojoon. She tries her best to smile but she's almost certain that it doesn't look very genuine. Thankfully, they all move on quickly, finding themselves in front of tonight's hosts.

Isla zones out a bit, knowing she won't be able to understand anything. So, needless to say, she's shocked when one of the hosts, a man in his late twenties maybe, speaks to her.

"You're Isla, right? Matoi Jaemin's girlfriend?" he asks in a very friendly tone.

Isla nods her head, embarrassed that she got caught not paying attention.

"Ah, yes! I'm Isla," she says, wondering where this is gonna go.

"You made an appearance in the latest music video. How was shooting that?"

"Oh, it was a blast," she says, exaggerating slightly, "All of the staff were really professional. I think it came out really well."

He smiles at her and Isla feels Jaemin getting stiff next to her.

"And what is it like being OT2B's Matoi Jaemin's girlfriend? You're living out the dream of fans all over the world."

Isla frowns.

"I'm not dating OT2B's Matoi Jaemin," Jaemin freezes completely as does Leo, "I'm just dating Jaemin. At the end of the day, he's just a man, even if he does spend way too much money on clothes," Isla says, looking at Jaemin playfully.

He erupts into giggles and the audience swoons, no doubt a translator lurking around somewhere to express Isla's words. Leo almost sags in relief while the other boys just nod and smile.

Jaemin's on cloud nine, pressing a quick kiss right under her ear, the same place he likes to suck hickies. The thought causes her to shift on her feet, Jaemin giving her a look that says he knows exactly what he's done.

There are a few more stops, but soon enough, they make it inside the venue, led to their spots right in the front. It looks like no one told the organizers that Isla would be joining them because there isn't enough space for all of them to sit down. A very stressed-looking stagehand rushes up, uttering apologies and offering to grab another chair but Jaemin sits down and pulls Isla right down with him, readjusting her on his lap.

Isla doesn't think she's ever been so red. People are staring, some even open-mouthed at them, but Jaemin doesn't acknowledge it at all, propping his chin on her shoulder.

"Hyung!" Woojin says, surprised.

"What? I'm perfectly comfortable like this."

The others are still shocked, moving only once Daehyun has taken his seat, looking as unbothered as always.

There is still lots of time before the show starts, some other idols coming up to OT2B to chat and catch up. Jaemin doesn't move Isla, not even when he's talking to one of his friends who he hasn't seen in months.

Eventually, Isla grows comfortable on Jaemin's thighs, relaxing against him. The public is let in forty-five minutes before the show begins, Isla instantly recognizing the Starlights in the seats. There are lightsticks galore, dressy outfits accessorized with fansite items and bias picket fans. There's quite obviously a stir over her and Jaemin, cellphone cameras recording and photos being taken every second.

Isla tries her hardest to ignore it and by the time the show is starting, she's tuned them out completely.

Even though Isla has been a K-pop fan ever since she was fourteen, she's never bothered to watch an entire award show. She'd always just wait for the parts with OT2B in them to be re-uploaded by other fans.

It proves to be interesting at times. There are some cool performances by other artists but none to the grand level that OT2B's will be. The hours fly by quickly and, before Isla knows it, the boys are standing up to go behind stage to prep for their performance.

Jaemin pulls away from Isla slowly, winking at her as he runs off. "Wish me luck!"

"Good luck!" she says, waving at him.

It's a bit strange to be sitting all alone but Isla quickly forgets about it when the stage lights up to show the five of them adorned in new stage outfits, all bright and sparkly. They each have different colored mics, Jaemin's being the same color as her dress.

The performance is going beautifully until Jaemin accidentally trips while dancing. He doesn't fall to the ground but he misses the beat and completely screws up the synchronization.

Isla's heart starts to beat rapidly when she notices the distressed look on his face which he quickly hides behind a smile, rejoining the others as quickly as he can. For a moment, everything seems like it's going to be fine as Jaemin rotates into the center, mic pressed against his pretty lips.

And then his voice cracks.

Terribly.

The noise is so bad, Isla can't help but wince, instantly regretting it when she sees the look on Jaemin's face. He bites his lips harshly as a deterrent to the tears that want to gather in his eyes, his face feeling hot with shame.

Twice more. Jaemin's voice cracks twice more in the song and by the end of it, he's completely humiliated. He won't even look in Isla's direction no matter how hard she tries to catch his eyes.

Oh, Jaemin.

He's the very first one off of the stage, feet pounding down the little stairs on the side and disappearing behind stage.

Isla stands up abruptly, chucking off her thousand-dollar shoes and picking up her dress, rushing off to go find him.

The security guard gives Isla a hard time as she desperately tries to get backstage to see Jaemin. The stocky, burly man doesn't speak a lick of English and absolutely refuses to budge no matter how hard Isla pleads with him. All of her attempts to explain are completely futile. It stresses Isla out so much, she almost wants to cry. She's two seconds away from cursing this man out when Woojin's head pops out from behind the curtain.

Isla almost sags in relief when he quickly speaks to the guard and he *finally* steps aside, allowing Isla to past through. The girl shoots the nastiest look she can imagine at him before jogging after Woojin's hurried footsteps while trying not to trip over her dress.

Her mind is frazzled with worry. How bad is it? Is Jaemin beating himself up over it? Is he a mess of tears, desperately trying to hide from the world, afraid of criticism?

When Woojin pushes the door open, Isla discovers that it's so much worse than she thought. Instead of being a crumpled pile curled up on one of the leather couches, Jaemin sits on the floor, legs straight and off to either side, head facing his chest. It's the same position held by an old rag doll, splayed and lifeless.

"Minie?" Isla asks, squatting down beside him.

"He won't talk to anyone. He won't say anything," Leo says, genuine concern over the man showing through his shiny eyes.

Upon closer inspection, Isla notices that they're all teary-eyed, no doubt more upset over Jaemin's breakdown than his mistakes.

"Jaemin," Isla tries once again, sitting down on her butt right beside him and lifting his head with a perfectly manicured, trembling hand.

Dried tear tracks are over the man's cheeks, lines all coming together on his chin. His eyes are red and swollen, his entire face puffy. He'd cried and hard.

"It's alright, Jaemin," Isla says, panicking when his eyes remain the same lifeless way as before.

He doesn't respond at all.

Something he once said to her runs to the forefront of her brain and Isla decides to go with it. Shakily, hoping she doesn't make things even worse than they already are, Isla brings her other hand up, pressing her nails into his cheeks hard enough that they'll definitely leave marks.

One of the other members - Daehyun, maybe, yells something but Isla ignores them all, dragging Jaemin's face to hers and kissing him, pushing her nails even deeper into his skin. It's only a moment before he responds, closing his doll eyes and kissing her back.

Jaemin shudders, his self-inflicted shutdown ended by the girl kissing him. All at once, the tears start all over again, Jaemin burying his face in the crook of Isla's neck. He smears Isla's carefully applied lipstick all over her skin as he sobs, balling himself into her side.

"It's okay, Jaemin," she says, patting him affectionately, "It was a great performance. I'm sure no one even noticed."

That's definitely not true. No doubt his mistakes are already trending everywhere.

Jaemin doesn't seem to buy it either, sobbing even louder than before. The other boys and the staff wisely looking away and pretending that nothing is going on.

"I'm absolutely useless, Isla! Useless!" he says, choking up on his own words, "I messed it up so badly! Everyone's going to hate me!"

"Matoi Jaemin!" Isla says, voice hard as anger swirls beneath her tone.

Jaemin startles, not expecting Isla to sound so pissed. He gasps a bit, trying hard to stop crying.

"Look at me," she demands, forcibly lifting his frame so he's once again sitting up beside her.

Isla lifts Jaemin's drooping face so he has no choice but to look at her.

"Stop it. Stop saying that. No one is going to hate you, Jaemin," she says firmly, watching as bitter tears fall down his cheeks, "So what if you messed up a tiny bit? You're human. If you were perfect all the time, something would be wrong with you. It was a great performance! An amazing start to a new era. Are there going to be some people who talk shit about it? Of course there are! But they'd talk shit about it even if nothing went wrong. Haters will always find something to bitch about, even if there's not a single flaw. But you know what? Do you know what, Matoi Jaemin?" Isla takes a deep breath, "There are so many people who love and support you. So many. Millions of people *adore* you and for good reason. You deserve it. You deserve to be loved more than any person I know."

His cries have slowed down now, the idol only occasionally sniffling as he tries to catch his breath.

"I love you. Sincerely, deeply. I love you, Jaemin. A voice crack isn't going to change that, okay?" Isla says, voice softening tremendously.

"Okay," Jaemin says softly, "I love you too."

"I know," Isla says, wiping away his latest set of tears, "No more crying now. Let's get you cleaned up, alright?"

Isla stands, reaching a hand out to Jaemin. He takes it, standing somewhat shakily on his feet. Isla ushers him over to one of the stylists who quickly whips out some brushes and plops him down on a chair to fix his makeup, one of them rushing to touch her up as well. Under their magic hands, any trace of Jaemin's breakdown is erased and replaced with a fresh, beautiful face.

Isla turns to leave and return to her seat outside, stopped only when Leo grasps her wrist quickly.

"Thank you," he whispers to her.

Isla leaves without a word.

When OT2B returns to their seats, it's as if nothing happened at all. Jaemin is all smiles and happiness, perfectly okay on the outside. Isla notices the way he sits a bit closer than usual, the way his grip is tighter on her hands.

When they win the Artist of the Year award, Isla cheers louder than anyone else, Jaemin shooting her a brilliant smile from the stage as Leo grabs the mic.

"STARLIGHTS!"

The crowd screams, people waving their signs crazily, ecstatic that their favorite has won such a big award, even if they've been winning it for years.

The ride home is filled with excited chatter from the boys as they recount the memories that just happened. Isla is so tired that she wants nothing more than to pass out in the big fluffy bed back in the apartment. She doesn't let herself doze off, however, still monitoring Jaemin's behavior.

Even though he had perked up dramatically after her pep talk and winning the big award, Isla can tell that he's not quite himself.

The van drops them off and the couple makes their way home, Isla's fingers threaded between Jaemin's lightly.

He doesn't say anything as they take off their shoes, quickly heading into the bedroom. Isla hears the shower start as she plops down on the bed, tugging pins out of her hair and tossing them on the floor while rubbing her scalp to relieve the headache she's developing.

Jaemin's shower takes so long that Isla is about eighty percent asleep before he exits in a cloud of steam, towel wrapped around his hips and another on top of his head.

"Do you want me to dry your hair?" Isla asks, voice sounding groggy.

"No, it's fine. Go ahead and wash up, okay?" Jaemin says in a normal tone, retreating into the closet.

Isla quickly takes her own shower but by the time she reenters the bedroom, all of the lights are out and Jaemin is in bed facing away from her. Isla sighs, tossing on some pajamas and crawling into bed.

Jaemin is pretending to be asleep but Isla indulges him, sliding into bed on her side and scooting closer to him. She wraps her arms around his torso, pulling herself close to him. Isla can see his eyes move behind his lids in the darkness but ignores it, placing her ear over his chest and listening to his heartbeat.

"You know," she whispers, "There are so many things I love about you."

Jaemin's heartbeat speeds up slightly.

"There's the way your front tooth is slightly crooked. There's the way you fall over when you laugh. How frustrated you get when you lose a game. How excited you get whenever any of your members compliment you. There's the way you drag your fingers through your hair,"

Isla pauses, tracing patterns over Jaemin's chest.

"There's the way you try so hard at everything you do. There's the compassion you have for others. The generosity you have. There's the way you sing to yourself when you think no one's watching and how you always wear rings."

"But there are also things I hate about you, Jaemin," Isla says.

Jaemin stiffens, stops breathing.

"I hate the way you treat yourself. I hate the way you can't see how great you are. I hate how you always put yourself last. But most of all . . . most of all, I hate the way you think the world is against you, that you don't deserve to be loved."

Isla kisses his collarbone.

"Don't worry, though. I'll prove that you're wrong about yourself, even if I have to remind you every day."

Jaemin makes a small noise, the beginning of more tears.

"Good night, Jaemin," Isla says, rolling over, Jaemin scooting closer to her and crying softly in her hair until he wears himself out.

23

Despite what Jaemin believed, Sanctuary has been a tremendously successful comeback. There had already been millions upon millions of pre-ordered albums and the title track flew right to the top of the chart in countries all over the world. OT2B has been on music show after music show, Sanctuary beating the competition flat out.

This means that the boys are as busy as ever, having some sort of performance nearly every day. There's also a fan-meeting to be held next week in celebration.

How long has it been since Isla wished to be one of the lucky fans who could meet them, smile at them while they signed her album? It seems like another lifetime entirely.

As for Jaemin, he seems as normal as ever. He still lavishes Isla in attention, though it means more to her now. Every word, every smile, every caress holds meaning for her, meaning that surely will lead to her heart being broken.

Isla shakes her head. She doesn't want to think about it. Now is one of the rare moments where the boys have a bit of downtime, all five of them sprawled across the large practice room. Most of the members are playing on their phones. Daehyun is passed out in a lump in the corner, squeezing in as much sleep as possible, Isla supposes.

But Isla catches Woojin staring at her again, causing goosebumps to race across her skin. She's always known that Woojin has an intense power within his gaze, having been affected by it plenty of times back when she was just a fan. But she can't figure out what's up with him. His expression is so perfectly blank that Isla has no idea how he feels about her.

It's unnerving.

Jaemin sits right beside her, tapping on his phone screen while his eyebrows are knitted together in concentration.

Isla breaks eye contact with Woojin, looking over Jaemin's shoulder.

"Are you still stuck on that level?" Isla asks him.

Jaemin's been trying to beat this level on the game for three days now and he gets more frustrated each time he loses it. It's rather amusing to see him so worked up over something that doesn't matter at all. It's like Isla gets a glimpse at the inner child he has each time he runs out of moves and throws the tiniest of tantrums.

Ever since Isla brought up that she and Jaemin don't talk much, the man has made a much greater effort to speak to her and have both meaningful and absolutely stupid conversations. Some nights they lay awake in bed just talking about the world and revealing their closely held secrets while they fight about which fast-food chain is better on other days. They've truly become friends.

Isla's mood falters slightly when she realizes that Jaemin knows her better than anyone else.

"I think it's impossible. There's no way to win!" Jaemin explains, already pouting.

"Lemme try," Isla suggests, Jaemin handing his phone over to her immediately.

Isla fails it herself three times but manages to win with several moves left over, causing Jaemin to throw a whole whiny fit.

"Oh, come one, you big baby!" Isla says, laughing at Jaemin's expression, "It's not that important."

"But still," he says, lip poked out.

Isla kisses him quickly, removing every trace of a frown on his face.

"You'll be okay," Isla says.

Before Jaemin can comment further, Isla's second least favorite person on the planet walks in, blonde hair impeccably styled as always. Isla sours instantly.

"Miss Isla," Not Charles says, approaching her and Jaemin, "Your presence is requested."

"By who?" Isla asks, not wanting to have to deal with CEO Hwang again.

"Dr. Moon," he says simply.

That catches her attention. In all of the months that she's been here, she hasn't once seen the doctor who's taking care of Jaemin. Isla's been wanting to meet her ever since she came back but it just hasn't worked for some reason. The doctor was always busy or Isla had to do other things that stopped her from checking in.

Isla stands up, Jaemin following close after her.

"The doctor requested that Miss Isla come see her alone."

Jaemin looks unsure, eyes flickering between Isla and Not Charles.

"I'll be right back," Isla says, squeezing Jaemin's hand and smiling to put him at ease.

"I ... okay," Jaemin says, watching the two of them leave the room.

Isla doesn't say a word to the Suit while they walk through the seemingly endless hallways of Smash Entertainment, finally stopping in front of a normal door. Not Charles raps his knuckles against the door and a soft voice calls out. He swings the door open and gestures for Isla to enter alone.

The girl looks at him once before stepping foot into the office, the door shutting behind her.

Dr. Moon is a carefully put together lady, professional in her dress and styling. She doesn't even look up when Isla enters, tapping away at her keyboard.

"Miss Isla," she says eventually, startling her a bit.

"Ah ... yes?" Isla asks.

"Take a seat, please," she says, gesturing to the chair in front of her desk.

Her words are very clean and crisp, not even the smallest of accents peeping through. She sounds like she was born and raised in upstate New York. Maybe she was.

"I have to apologize for it taking so long for me to be able to see you," the doctor says, closing her laptop softly and pinning Isla with an intense stare. Her eyes are almost off-putting, dark and cloudy.

"It's alright," Isla assures her, feeling small despite being the bigger person in the room.

Dr. Moon is very petite.

"Now," she begins, "Tell me, how is your relationship with Jaemin?"

Isla blinks. It appears that the doctor is not one for pleasantries.

"It's . . . fine, I guess. Nothing too abnormal," Isla says, feeling uncomfortable.

"You can be honest with me, Miss Isla. Jaemin isn't here, you don't have to pretend."

Isla frowns.

"It was bad in the beginning, I admit. Really bad. Scary even. But," Isla licks her lips, looking out the window at Seoul's skyline, "But I realized that Jaemin was - is just desperate for affection. He craves it like he's been starved of it. And since then . . . Jaemin isn't a bad guy, not at all. He's sad, utterly pathetic at times, but he's sweet. He's funny and he's kind and a million other things. And actually," Isla says, looking back at the expressionless doctor, "I wanted to thank you for helping him. He deserves to be saved."

The doctor is silent, utterly mute.

"Um—" Isla begins, regretting her desire to come see this woman.

"It would seem to me that you've developed *feelings* for Mr. Matoi," she spits the word out with barely contained venom, "Is that correct?"

Isla blushes.

"I . . . yes, I'd say so," she says, voice quiet.

It hits differently to say it aloud.

The doctor takes a breath.

"Miss Isla. It appears to me that you've mistaken your place in this situation."

"What?" Isla asks, stunned by the woman's words.

"Mr. Matoi is quite charming, I understand. He's your idol, a man you've no doubt wanted for quite some time. The sex has probably surpassed whatever you came up with in your head."

"Excuse you?!" Isla asks, scandalized, "What are you implying?"

"What I am saying, Miss Isla, is that you've picked up on whatever signals Jaemin has dropped and interpreted them as him having genuine affection for you. Jaemin is not well, Isla. Whatever emotions you think he has for you aren't real. Are you in love with him? I thought you'd be smarter than that, doll."

Isla sits there, called out and utterly humiliated.

"You are nothing more than a tool to aid in Jaemin's healing process. As soon as he enters a normal state of mind, he'll drop you faster than you can say 'I love you'" the doctor says, voice pleasant.

"You do want him to get better, don't you?" Dr. Moon asks.

All Isla can do is nod, eyes cast downward.

"Then keep playing your role. You've done well at keeping him happy. Just don't let yourself think the glass slippers won't disappear when the clock hits twelve."

Hot, embarrassed tears well up in Isla's eyes, preventing her from looking up at the doctor.

"Well, I think that we're done here," the doctor says, standing up to open the door.

Isla rushes out as quickly as she can without running, tears blinding her. She bumps into someone and apologizes quickly but doesn't stop, feet taking her to the bathroom. Isla once more sits on the toilet and cries, trying to keep the noise down as much as possible.

Of course she knows that the doctor's words are true. How could Jaemin hold any true love for her? Isla knows that whatever fixation he has for her isn't rooted in her as a person but as something to keep the voice in his head silent. She hasn't done anything to earn his real affection.

Why'd she agree to do this?

Isla cries even harder when she realizes that if given the opportunity to turn back time, she wouldn't change a thing.

Woojin stands puzzled in the hallway, wondering why Isla sped off with tears in her eyes. His gaze trails her path and lands on that simple white door.

By the time Isla's sniffles have died down enough to the point where she can breathe without hiccupping, quite a bit of time has passed. Shaky fingers check her phone to find that it's been nearly half an hour since she's stormed into this bathroom. There are quite a few texts from Jaemin but she doesn't open them, stashing her phone in her pocket and exiting the stall, pausing at the sink to splash her face. Her skin is blotchy and swollen, giving away the fact that she's been bawling her eyes out.

Isla sighs, feeling a headache coming on. She's worn herself out and it's still rather early in the day. She bends down once again to splash her face, and when she comes up, Jaemin is standing behind her.

Isla shrieks, stumbling back and nearly falling. Jaemin grasps her by the wrist and yanks her upwards. Isla places her free hand over her speeding heart.

"Jaemin!" Isla scolds, "You'll give me a heart attack!"

Jaemin doesn't say anything, looking her all over.

"Why were you crying?"

"What?" Isla says, the shock of his arrival momentarily making her forget her state.

"Your face is red," he says with concern, "Why are you upset, baby?"

And Isla cries all over again, Jaemin's sweet tone reminding her of Dr. Moon's words.

If Jaemin is shocked, he doesn't show it, bringing his girlfriend to his chest and patting her affectionately.

"What happened? You went missing," Jaemin asks her.

Isla's face is buried in Jaemin's chest. She doesn't want to look him in the eyes, doesn't want to face him. So, instead, she stays silent.

"Did Yeji say something to you?"

"Yeji?" Isla asks, still not looking at him.

"My doctor. Did she say something mean to you?"

Isla sniffs.

"No, not really. I just . . . I don't know."

"She upset you, though. You can't deny that," he says, pulling her away from his chest to look at her.

Jaemin softens when he sees her bloodshot eyes, distress etched into every feature on her face. She should never be this upset about anything. Anger sparks inside of Jaemin as he thinks about what the doctor could have said to *his* Isla to make her cry.

"It's not a big deal, Minie. I just got a little bit . . . sensitive."

"I'll talk to her," Jaemin says, mind made up as he rubs his thumbs over Isla's heated skin, "Don't you worry about it."

"Don' t–"

"I'll talk to her," Jaemin says once more, not leaving any room for arguments.

Isla is too tired to argue with him further.

"Okay."

"Do you want to go home early?"

Isla shakes her head.

"No. I just need to take some medicine and I'll be alright, I think."

"Are you sure?"

"Yeah. You still have a lot left to do today."

"You can go by yourself," Jaemin offers.

"What, really?" Isla asks, surprised.

In the months she's been with Jaemin, he'd never been one to let her have any time to herself on purpose. He's always as close to her as he can be, paranoid that she'll disappear.

"Of course. I don't want you to be here if you're not feeling well. I can call the driver and he'll be here in just a few minutes."

Isla nods. Nothing sounds better to her than painkillers and a nap right now.

Jaemin kisses the top of her head and messages one of the drivers, walking Isla down to the parking garage and sending her off. As soon as the car fades in the distance, Jaemin stalks back into the building, walking quickly and with a purpose. He's supposed to be in a meeting right now, but Jaemin doesn't give a damn.

Why do people seem determined to make Isla upset? Why is someone messing with her every time he turns his back for just one second? First Leo and now Yeji? What's wrong with them?

Jaemin opens Dr. Moon's office door without knocking, taking the woman by surprise. She slams her laptop down and quickly stands up, stumbling on her heels. She can't allow anyone to see her precious collection of files, not even the object of her desires.

"Jaemin! You aren't supposed to be here!" Yeji says, voice cracking slightly.

"Never mind that. What did you speak to Isla about?"

Yeji smoothes her clothes out.

"I can't disclose private conversations, Jaemin. You should know that," she says, walking around her desk and sitting on the edge of it, legs crossed and back straight, a pretty smile on her face.

Jaemin is not impressed.

"Cut the bullshit, Yeji. What did you say to her?" he growls, arms crossed in an effort not to snatch her like he did Leo.

"Why does it matter?" Her composition is now back entirely, smile growing slightly bigger with each moment that passes.

She's enjoying this - taunting him.

"It matters if you want to keep your fucking job. If you're going to be difficult, I can be difficult too."

Yeji's smile droops.

"Fine. Take a seat," she says, pointing him to the chaise lounge.

"I'd rather stand."

Yeji dismounts the desk and walks toward Jaemin, stopping right at the edge between professional and overly friendly.

"Jaemin," she places a hand on his shoulder, "Miss Isla and I simply talked. There was a bit of a misunderstanding between us but we quickly realized that we're on the same page," Yeji smiles at him, "We both want what's best for you."

"And what is that?" Jaemin asks, removing her hand.

"I can't tell you."

Jaemin cocks his jaw, annoyance spreading through him like wildfire. If Yeji dances around his questions one more time, he's going to blow his top.

"Look," he begins, "I don't care if you're on the same page or in different galaxies. You said something to hurt her, something to make her upset. You will not do it again. If I even think you've done something to irritate her, you'll be on your ass on the concrete before you can even blink, do you understand me?"

Yeji blinks at him, not having expected Jaemin to be so fiercely overprotective of Isla. Sure, in their sessions she's noticed that he is attached to her, but Yeji could have sworn that it had to do with his delusions, that his attachment would weaken with every moment he spent with her.

Yeji's face hardens significantly. It looks like Miss Isla will be more of a threat than she originally thought.

"I understand, Mr. Matoi," Yeji says, retreating from him to sit back at her desk, mustering up an air of indifference.

She waits until he drags his hand through his hair and walks out, shoulders back and strutting like he always does, perfect and so untouchable, even now. Once his footsteps fade far into the distance, Yeji stands up quickly, grabbing one of the decorative sculptures on the bookshelf behind her and chucking it to the ground with all of her effort, barely holding in the scream building in her chest.

The doctor unbuttons the first three buttons of her shirt, fanning herself. She can't get too heated, too angry.

"Looks like someone's in a mood," an amused voice calls from behind her.

Yeji jumps, nearly slipping on the shards underneath her.

"Oh, it's just you," she says, looking at the tall blonde man.

"You don't seem particularly happy to see me, toots."

"Oh, shut up, Hunter. What are you doing here?" Yeji says, straightening herself up.

The blonde man leans against her desk, grinning at her.

"I just stopped by to say that little miss princess went home today all ugly and red-faced," he sounds satisfied.

"Oh, I am well aware. Jaemin came in to speak to me about it just a few minutes ago."

Hunter raises an eyebrow.

"Is that what your little fit was about? Baby got scolded?" he walks over to her, placing his hands on her waist, "There are better ways to get aggression out, you know?"

"Can you go three minutes without making a sexual innuendo?" she says, slapping his hands away.

"Oh, come on. It's been two weeks, Yeji."

"And?" she snaps, in no mood to deal with him, "This isn't exclusive. Go out clubbing or something."

Hunter frowns.

"You've been sleeping with other guys?"

"What I do or don't do doesn't concern you," Yeji says, going to fetch the dustpan from under her desk and sweep up the pieces.

"So, that's how this is, huh?"

"Unless you've got something important to say to me, you don't need to be here. I have to review some files."

Wordlessly, Hunter leaves the room.

Yeji sighs, dumping the shards in the trash bin.

Why are men so hard to control?

And as if things couldn't get any worse, the doctor's phone rings. Quickly locking her door, Yeji sinks down onto the chaise, stretching her body out across the fabric, wishing Jaemin was there beside her.

"Hello?" she says, stuffing all of her angry and bitter emotions down deep inside of her.

"Hi, baby sis! How are you? You missing me?"

"Yeah, I'm good. Miss you lots," the doctor says, fighting to keep her lunch down at her sugary sweet, completely untrue words.

She relishes every day she doesn't have to see her stupid sister's perfect face.

"Miss you too! But my patient is doing well! Hopefully I won't be gone much longer."

Yeji locks her jaw, hiding the desire to scream.

"Oh?"

"Yeah. I'll keep you updated. Hey, I gotta go. I'll talk to you later. Bye."

Yeji hangs up, not wishing her sister well. Bitterly, she hopes that her plane would crash and burn, or that she'd be kidnapped in her sleep. The doctor tosses her phone on the floor, rubbing her head, trying to relieve the ache there. Soon everything will be better.

Soon.

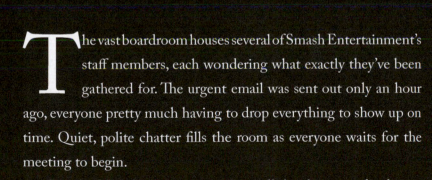

24

The vast boardroom houses several of Smash Entertainment's staff members, each wondering what exactly they've been gathered for. The urgent email was sent out only an hour ago, everyone pretty much having to drop everything to show up on time. Quiet, polite chatter fills the room as everyone waits for the meeting to begin.

Finally, CEO Hwang rises, causing all the chatter to die down.

"After the success of One Thousand Times Bright's latest album," he begins, "We have decided that now is the perfect time to go on an international tour."

Small murmurs break out.

"But we just finished a tour," Daehyun pipes up.

"I am aware. However, I feel like there is enough new material to warrant another one," the CEO retorts.

Daehyun sits back in his chair, arms crossed.

"Where exactly are we going?" Leo asks.

"We are in the process of booking venues, but hopefully you'll be making stops in North and South America, Australia, Europe, here in Korea, and in Japan."

"So, everywhere," Daehyun says.

"We're not going to Africa," Seojoon says, laughing at Daehyun's expression.

"When is the tour going to be announced?" Jaemin asks.

"Sometime this month. Tickets will go on sale a week or two after that. And if all goes well, the tour will start in three months."

"And how long will we be touring for?" Woojin asks.

"Four or five months."

All five of the boys speak up, all talking over each other. When it becomes apparent that no one is going to shut up, CEO Hwang raises his voice.

"Quiet! Quiet, now, boys! What's the issue?"

"It's not that we don't want to go on tour," Leo says, picking his words carefully, looking each of his bandmates in the eyes, "It's just that we just finished one. And tours are exhausting."

"We have to strike while the iron's hot," CEO Hwang says, voice firm, "While there's such a widespread buzz about the new album. We could wait, sure, but the outcome won't be as spectacular."

"Not to toot our own horn, but I'm pretty sure we could sell out a tour at any time," Daehyun says.

The others nod with him.

"Too bad," CEO Hwang says, growing annoyed, "You still have three months before the tour begins. That's plenty of time to rest up. Now, if you're done whining," he stands, pushing his chair in, "Meeting adjourned."

"Wait, CEO Hwang–" Jaemin speaks up before anyone can leave.

"Yes, Jaemin - ssi?"

"What about Isla?"

He shrugs.

"Bring her with you, I don't care."

Jaemin smiles. He can't wait to tell his girlfriend.

The boys remain in the meeting room once everyone else has left, some of the members fuming.

"Are you upset, Daehyun hyung?" Leo asks.

"How are they just gonna spring a tour on us again? Don't they know how exhausting and damaging they are?!" the rapper exclaims, "I mean Woojin fucked his leg up just a few months ago."

"Hyung . . ." the youngest says, feeling uncomfortable.

"What?" Daehyun asks, turning to look at him, "It's true! I just don't want any of us to burn out."

"Then we've got to make sure to rest up while we can," Seojoon says, "I'd like to go on another tour or two before I have to go off to the military."

Silence lays across the room like a thick blanket.

It's an unspoken rule not to speak about Seojoon and Daehyun's inevitable enlistment. It's not that the boys don't want to go or to serve their country, it's that they don't want to leave OT2B, to step away from the lights and the fans they adore. There's always the fear that when they return, no one will be waiting for them, that they will have been forgotten in the time they were away.

"Well, I guess it's been settled then," Daehyun says, standing up and walking out of the room swiftly.

Jaemin doesn't hesitate, standing and going after him.

"Hyung," he calls after him, "wait up!"

The man ignores him, continuing to walk away. Jaemin jogs to catch up, placing a hand on his hyung's shoulder, stopping him.

"Daehyun hyung," Jaemin says, "Are you okay?"

"I'm fine, Jaeminie," the man says, sounding defeated, "Just tired."

"You know you can talk to me, right, hyung?"

"Can I?" Daehyun asks, looking at him, their eyes meeting, "I don't even know who you are anymore, Jaemin."

The rapper's words are malicious, a manifestation of his anger. He usually wouldn't say something like that, even though the thought has been hovering around the back of his brain ever since Isla Montgomery showed up. It seemed that everything was fine. He felt comfortable in his usual routine, comfortable with those who surrounded him. But her appearance pulled the rug out from under his feet.

This time, Daehyun does brush Jaemin's touch off, continuing down the hall, not once looking back, knowing he'll just make it worse if he sticks around.

He naively never thought Jaemin's mental illness would have such an effect on him.

"Hyung . . ." Jaemin whispers, feeling something inside of him crack.

When Jaemin returns to the meeting room, he musters up a smile.

"Ah, Daehyun hyung says he isn't feeling too well . . . and I promised Isla I would check up on her, so . . ."

And then he's off, trying not to think about the way Daehyun looked at him, about the words he said to him.

"I don't even know who you are."

Jaemin's footsteps increase rapidly as those words bounce around in his head.

"I don't even know who you are."

"I don't even know who you are."

"I don't even know who you are."

Even as he walks into the parking garage and slides into one of the black vans, he can't shake Daehyun's words.

How long has it been since the older man looked at him with such disdain? Jaemin strains his brain to remember. Sure, the two of them didn't get along at first, but that could be said of anyone. Being shoved into a one-room apartment with four complete strangers and enduring the stress of being a trainee tends to bring out the worst in people. But in the entirety of the five years since they've debuted, Jaemin can't think of a single time when Daehyun was so on edge. Even when things got hard and the future looked grim, the man could easily be cheered up with some encouragement from the other members.

So, why is it so different now?

He nearly sighs in relief when he comes home to find Isla relaxing on the couch, stretched out like a cat in the sun.

"Isla!"

She winces at the loud noise and looks up only to be bombarded by limbs as Jaemin practically yanks her upward, hugging her tightly.

"Jaemin, what are—"

He squeezes her even tighter.

"Jaemin, what—"

"I just need to hold you for a moment," he says, lips against her skin.

Isla obliges, wondering what happened. Had speaking with Dr. Moon brought his spirits down? Maybe it didn't go as well as he'd hoped.

"Are you okay?" she asks once he's loosened his grip enough for her to speak and breathe properly.

"I just . . . do you know who I am, Isla?"

"Of course I do," she says in confusion, "What do you mean?"

"I just . . . no reason," he says, shutting down.

"Jaemin," Isla says, voice low in warning, "We said no more secrets, remember? So, what do you mean? What's bothering you, baby?"

Jaemin nearly breaks then and there but he remembers the headache she's been suffering with. It's probably not the best time to dump his feelings and insecurities on her.

"Later," he says, "I'll tell you once you feel all the way better."

Isla's heart flutters. This is the second time today he's being considerate of her. It's so starkly different from how he behaved when they first met, when he always put himself first, even if he thought he wasn't.

"You sure?" she asks, not liking the heavy look he's trying to hide.

"Yeah," he says, nodding.

"Don't think this means I'm gonna forget!" she says playfully, hoping to cheer him up some.

"I won't."

"You promise?" Isla asks, raising out a pinky.

"Promise," he says, grinning at her.

But before Isla manages to get it out of him, Jaemin has to go back to Smash Ent for practice. Despite the man insisting it's okay for her to stay home, her headache has completely vanished. Isla isn't particularly fond of the idea of returning, but she's worried about Jaemin.

The last thing she needs is for him to have another episode.

The rest of the day passes in relative normalcy, the rest of the boys noticing something off between Daehyun and Jaemin, which is concerning to say the least. Woojin notices more than anyone, his worry increasing. Jaemin's already having problems with Leo, now Daehyun?

A sick feeling begins to blossom in Woojin's stomach, his eyes once more landing on Isla's form in the corner.

Is it because of her? What is she doing to Jaemin?

If only he could speak to her! He's never wished he had studied

English harder than he does now. If he'd kept up with the lessons, he could at least find out more about her.

When Jaemin and Isla return to their apartment, she pushes him down on the sofa, not planning on letting him get out of telling her what happened earlier.

"Spill it, Matoi," Isla says, sitting down beside him, "What happened with Dr. Moon?"

"Oh, her? I just told her to be more respectful towards you."

"So, she didn't upset you?"

Jaemin shakes his head, grey locks brushing his lashes.

"She doesn't have the capacity to upset me."

Isla raises an eyebrow at that. What does he mean?

"Well, what happened after that?" she says, deciding to move on.

"We had a meeting. Nothing really went on. CEO Hwang just told us we're going on tour."

"Is that a problem?" Isla asks, studying his expression, looking for even the slightest change.

Sure, they'd just come from a tour but would that make him act the way he had earlier?

"Not for me. Daehyun hyung had a problem with it, though. He kind of stormed out towards the end and I went after him . . ."

Jaemin falls silent, looking down at his hands crossed in his lap, a sad look on his face.

"And I tried to comfort him . . ." his voice gets choked up, "And he said . . . he said to me . . ."

Isla leans forward, placing a hand on his shoulder. She doesn't push him, knowing that whatever Daehyun said must have been really hurtful.

"He said that he doesn't know who I am, Isla . . . like I'm a stranger or something."

Jaemin looks up at her with big, glossy eyes, tears just barely hanging on.

He sniffles and Isla feels her heart shatter.

"Oh, Minie," she says, holding him close and patting him reassuringly, "I'm sure he didn't mean it. You said he was upset, right? I'm certain he didn't mean to snap at you like that."

A single tear falls and she wipes it away.

"No more tears, baby. I hate to see you cry," she says, kissing him softly.

Jaemin sniffles once more but no more tears fall.

"But . . . you're going on tour, right? Are you excited?" Isla asks, trying to change the subject.

"Yeah," he says, a watery smile gracing his face, "And you get to go with me!"

"I do?" Isla asks, surprised.

"Of course! I can't go anywhere without you. I love you too much," he says.

"I love you too, Minie. More than you know," she says, her own words hurting her.

He places his head on her shoulder.

More than I should.

Isla pretends that everything is alright, stroking his hair, trying to ingrain the feeling of it deep into her memory.

25

While the company bangs out any tweaks in the tour schedule, the boys get a bit of a break. As soon as it's announced, however, the boys will have to go straight into preparations.

Jaemin is ecstatic to have some time to spend with Isla before the big tour. There are still so many things he wants to show her in Korea. There are a million and one things to do in Seoul, not to mention all of the fun stuff he wants to do in his hometown, Busan.

So, bright and early on their first day of break, Jaemin rouses Isla from her slumber, heart melting at her adorable half-asleep expression. He doesn't think he'll ever get tired of seeing it.

"Minie? What time is it?" Isla asks, sitting up, the covers slipping away from her shoulders.

"Just past six. Come on, sleepyhead, get up," Jaemin prods gently, poking Isla's cheek.

She grumbles and sinks back down into the sheets.

Jaemin, incredibly amused, stands up from his position perched by her bed and yanks all the covers off in one swoop.

"Jaemin!" Isla whines, voice high-pitched as she struggles with the sheets, trying in vain to keep them over herself, "Aren't we off today? Why aren't we sleeping in?"

"It is our day off," Jaemin says, pecking her lips, "And I want to take you out on another date. Come on, baby, I have lots of plans. You need to get up now."

And suddenly, Isla is fully awake, heart pounding in her chest. She opens her eyes fully, looking at the ecstatic Jaemin standing over her.

"A date?"

Jaemin nods eagerly.

"Yes! Let's go on a date, baby."

"Okay," Isla says, rolling out of bed, her curly hair a hot mess.

She's never been able to sleep in a bonnet no matter how hard she tried. No matter what, Isla would wake up in the morning to find the silk head covering buried under the sheets.

She knows damn well that skipping along and doing cute coupley things will only make her hurt more in the end, but right now, she can't bring herself to care.

Using Jaemin's vague instructions of "cute but comfortable",

Isla rummages through their closet. There's about a million things she hasn't worn yet, but she finds herself drifting to his side of the ginormous closet. Her fingers brush against the fabric before her eye catches on a familiar piece of clothing.

Isla removes the shirt from its hanger, quickly slipping it over her head and tucking the edge into her shorts and lacing her Converse up.

When she exits the closet, the already dressed Jaemin is lacing his own shoes.

"I didn't know we had matching pairs," Isla says, pointing at his feet.

Jaemin looks up, momentarily surprised to see Isla wearing his shirt. It causes a slight blush to warm his cheeks. There's something so domestic about sharing clothes.

"Of course we do," Jaemin says, "Most of the shoes you have are shoes I have too. Except, well, like your heels and stuff."

Isla nods.

"So, where are we going?"

"It's a surprise," Jaemin says, grinning at her.

"Are the drivers here yet?"

Jaemin shakes his head.

"No. We're taking my car this time."

"You have a car? But I thought you couldn't drive?"

Jaemin blushes, embarrassed. Because idols have to be chauffeured around so often, it isn't really necessary for them to be able to drive themselves and thus many don't bother with it.

"I got my license recently. I wanted to be able to take you places."

"You're actually adorable, do you know that?" Isla asks him, flattered.

The surprise turns out to be an entire day at Lotte World, a famous theme park in Korea. Isla had seen it plenty of times in OT2B videos or on YouTube, but it's quite another thing to actually be there. The two of them spend all day going on ride after ride and eating ridiculous food, wearing matching fluffy hats and holding hands.

Isla is sure that they've been spotted since neither of them really tried to hide their identities, but the guard looming across their shoulders keeps her from being too worried.

By the time night falls, Isla is so exhausted, she feels dead on her feet. But she's happy, unbelievably so. It's been an absolutely perfect day.

The rest of the week passes in a similar fashion. Jaemin wakes Isla up early in the morning and then takes her to one of his favorite places in Seoul. They go biking next to the Han river, shop in Myeongdong, and eat at secret restaurants.

And during this time, Jaemin comes to realize something. All of the years he's been in love with Isla, all of the times she's made his heart flutter, none of them are even close to the way he feels about her now.

It's the subtle things she does, like the way her eyes squint ever so slightly when she's thinking or how she always stops to hear birds sing in trees. It's the way her hand feels inside of his, soft and warm but tight in his grasp.

It's the way that she always pours an obscene amount of honey and sugar into her tea, how she wrinkles her nose before she sneezes, the way she cuddles up next to him while she's sleeping.

There's the way she always supports him, the way she always knows exactly what to say to make him feel better. It's how she laughs and plays with him, the feeling of her fingertips against his chest, the way she dries his hair.

There are a million new things Matoi Jaemin loves about Isla, a million things he never knew about or even wondered about until recently.

And the fear.

Oh, the fear that Jaemin will look up one day to find her gone has faded into nothingness. He slowly finds himself worrying less and less about keeping her, knowing that she'll be there even if he looks away, even if he leaves. Isla will still be there for him even when he cries on the floor or leaves bites littered across her skin.

She'll still be there.

"Isla," Jaemin asks, the waves on the beach cresting and crashing softly against the sand.

"Mm?" she asks from beside him, hypnotized by the wide ocean in front of her.

"Why do you love me?"

"There are a million reasons why," she says, eyes still lingering on the waves, "It would take me forever to tell them all to you."

"Even though . . . even though I'm the way I am?"

His voice is vulnerable, nearly impossible to hear over the sea.

"I don't love you despite the way you are, Jaemin," Isla says, finally looking at him, "I love you because of it. And I'll still love you if you change."

"Really?"

"Yes, really," she says, fingers squeezing his in the sand and smiling in a way that throws all doubt from his head.

"Busan is really beautiful," she speaks after a moment of silence, "I could sit here on the beach all day just watching life go by."

"Maybe we'll do that," Jaemin begins, "One day, maybe you and I will sit out here when we're old, listening to the waves and remembering this day."

"I'd like that," Isla says, "I'd like that a lot."

26

Even though breaks are few and far between and thus should be treasured, Woojin spent the entirety of his week off thinking about work. No matter how hard he tried to toss himself into leisure activities or get immersed in movies, hell, even try to take a nap, his mind would inevitably wander back to the goings-on at Smash Entertainment.

Something is wrong, he knows it. There's something majorly off and it's starting to destroy the band. First, there were tensions between Leo and Jaemin - a pair who'd always been close - and now, Daehyun and Jaemin are having issues as well. It doesn't take a genius to notice how cold Daehyun has been to the younger.

But why?

Woojin is completely in the dark and it's driving him insane. Leo is dismissive of his concerns and Jaemin hardly ever speaks to anyone without Isla being right there next to him. And as for Daehyun . . . well, he's tossed himself head-first back into work. And Seojoon is either in denial or somehow oblivious to the destruction that's hurtling towards them all.

But he's not sure what he can do or who he can trust. Those he had previously leaned on, members, managers, staff members, do they even care about him? What are their actual intentions? Over the years, Woojin has grown to trust those around him wholeheartedly, but he no longer has such blind faith.

He's truly on his own, at least until he knows who is actually on his side.

With that mentality, Woojin kisses his mother goodbye a day early, deciding to do some snooping of his own.

He tries to calm his racing heart on the drive back by listening to calming music on the radio, but to no avail. He just can't shake the feeling that something terrible is going to happen.

He nods to the overnight security guard, pulling his car into the employee parking lot, stepping out into the night. It's just past ten, meaning most of the regular staff members should have left by now. No doubt the stylists are still awake and working hard in the basement, but he doesn't plan on popping down there.

As carefully and quietly as he can, Woojin makes his way to the upper levels of the building, trying not to look suspicious. He nods curtly at one woman he passes, keeping his gaze ahead and walking swiftly. Before long, he makes it to manager Calm's office, thinking up an excuse as to why he would be here instead of on vacation.

Thankfully, he doesn't have to say anything. The office is empty when he peeps his head in. Woojin sighs in relief. Unfortunately, since the door was left open, the manager will probably be back shortly. Without hesitation, Woojin dives in, opening drawers and flipping through files. He's not sure what he's looking for or even if it could be found in a document, but he still looks anyway, hoping something will stick out at him.

It doesn't.

Fifteen minutes of searching proves to be totally fruitless. The only thing he found even remotely interesting is a document about Dr. Moon, but it appears to be an online article the manager printed out. A brief skim told Woojin that the article is nothing special, just recounting some of her many success stories.

The sound of footsteps causes Woojin to switch off the light and quickly dive behind the coat rack, thankful that his manager always keeps a full stock of sweaters and coats despite the season.

His manager comes inside, muttering something under his breath. Even in the dark, Woojin notices how tired the man is. In one hand, he carries a stainless-steel cup which no doubt contains coffee, and in the other, he has a thick stack of files. He places them on his desk, not noticing the slightly disheveled state of the items on top.

He stops to take a big swig of his drink and then he leaves again, rubbing his head.

Woojin makes a mental note to buy him something nice in thanks for all of his hard work.

Once he thinks it's clear, Woojin peeks his head out of the office, quickly making his way down the hall. Maybe he'll have better luck if he goes snooping in CEO Hwang Nim's office. As he passes by, Woojin peers inside. For a moment, he thinks it's empty, before he notices two figures moving in the darkness. Woojin presses his face against the glass in an effort to more clearly make the scene out, but he can't see anything.

Deciding he'll come back later, Woojin pushes off, heading to his last destination.

The hallway to Dr. Moon's office is completely empty and quiet, Woojin's breathing being the only sound in the hallway.

Once again, he peeps, even knocking on the door lightly. Woojin doubts that the elusive doctor would be here this late and his prediction proves to be correct. No one is inside the office, so Woojin creeps in and closes the door softly behind him.

He's never been inside of this office. Woojin spends several moments just taking it all in, light from the city giving him enough visibility to see the furniture and sparse decorations. He wonders what it was like for his hyung to lay on that chaise. He wonders if Jaemin spilled all of his secrets, if he confessed things to a complete stranger that he doesn't even know.

It makes him feel sick to his stomach.

Looking away from the offending chair, Woojin turns to face the desk. Dr. Moon hasn't left anything out except for her closed laptop. He decides to start with the many drawers instead. He begins pulling them open, disappointed to find superficial things like Chapstick and hair ties in the first one. The next drawers contain similar items - pens and papers, scissors and a stapler, just normal desk things.

Woojin's almost ready to call it quits when he tugs on the last door, noting with surprise that it's locked.

Finally, something interesting!

Woojin looks around for the key, rummaging through the other drawers again in case he missed it. He even looks over the shelves behind the desk, finding nothing inside or under any of the knickknacks

Woojin sighs. The doctor probably has the key with her.

But why?

It's perfectly reasonable to assume that the locked drawer contains confidential company information or some of Jaemin's files, meaning the doctor has nothing abnormal going on. But something in Woojin's gut tells him that that's not the case, that whatever is in that drawer is important.

Deciding he'll check on it another day, Woojin sits in the doctor's very comfortable desk chair, pushing himself closer to the laptop and opening it, the artificial blue light casting shadows across his face.

It's password protected.

Woojin sighs, becoming frustrated. He clicks the 'Forgot Password?' link and the clue pops up.

"Debut," Woojin reads out loud.

It couldn't be . . .

Carefully, Woojin types 041414 (the date OT2B debuted) into the bar, surprised when it actually unlocks the laptop. Deciding not to look a gift horse in the mouth, the man quickly double clicks on one of the icons. It opens up a document, which Woojin scrolls through quickly.

There doesn't seem to be anything wrong with it. In fact, there isn't anything wrong with any of her icons, all of them being simple patient reports. However, as he begins snooping through all of her files, he notices something odd. At surface level, there doesn't seem to be anything abnormal about this file, except for the ending.

When Woojin clicks on it, a screen pops up asking for a password. Woojin leans forward, inspecting the screen closer.

Why would one single recipe file have a password lock? He's always been suspicious about the doctor Smash Entertainment hired. Something about her sets him off and this locked file only deepens his concern.

Determined to satisfy his burning desire for an answer, Woojin tries the same password as before but this time it's denied. He plugs as many others as he can think of, eventually cracking it open using a trick one of his gamer buddies taught him a while back.

Woojin isn't sure what he had been expecting, but it certainly wasn't this. His eyes widen as he takes in what's on the screen, and his fingers begin to shake.

"Didn't your mother teach you not to snoop?" a voice calls out, scaring Woojin so much he squeals.

Woojin doesn't even get the chance to turn around as Dr. Moon grabs the large decorative vase from the shelf and slams it across the younger man's skull as hard as she possibly can. It shatters and Woojin crumples over in her desk chair with blood leaking from his scalp, sticking his hair to his skull.

Yeji Moon sighs, tossing the cracked bottom of the vase to the side and dusting her hands off.

What a mess. She never expected the quiet one to be so nosy. Grunting, the petite woman places her arms under the unconscious idol's armpits, dragging him out of the chair and down the hallway, careful not to drip blood on the floor.

"Why are you so fucking heavy?" Yeji asks the unconscious man as she struggles to drag him across the floor.

After what seems like forever, Yeji makes it to the back, barely used stairwell. She knows for a fact that the upper levels of the company don't have any cameras, at least not anymore. Her routine hookups with the CEO insured that.

With one hand, Yeji opens the door to the stairwell, shoving Woojin down onto the floor and kicking him down the stairs.

His body rolls down, hitting sharp edges and smacking into the wall occasionally. The momentum brings him down until he's face down on the landing below, crimson streaking over the stairs.

Yeji watches him, making sure that he's still breathing. When she notices the shallow breaths his body still takes, she turns around and shuts the door behind her.

She's sacrificed too much for her plan to fail now.

27

The call comes early in the morning. At first, Jaemin doesn't register the sound of his phone ringing, sleep clogging his senses. But after the buzzing doesn't stop, Isla rouses from her slumber, groaning slightly.

Absentmindedly, the girl pokes her boyfriend, trying to wake the sleeping male.

"Minie. Your phone. Minieee," Isla whines, wanting the buzzing to stop.

Jaemin peeks a single eye open, hand slapping around blindly for his phone. He finds it eventually, swiping to answer the call without looking at the caller I.D.

"Hello?" Jaemin asks groggily, half listening.

"Jaemin! Oh, thank God! I need you to get up right now."

At the urgency in his Manager's tone, Jaemin shoots upright, feeling more alert.

"What? What's going on? What's wrong?"

"It's Woojin," the man says, voice hurried, "There's been some sort of accident."

"Accident?" Jaemin shouts, "What happened?"

The volume of Jaemin's distressed question rouses Isla even though she has no idea what's going on. The girl turns on her lamp, rubbing her tired eyes.

"What's happening, Jaemin?" she asks.

The man ignores her.

"I don't have time to tell you. They're transferring him to the hospital as we speak. I've already sent a van, so be prepared."

The manager hangs up, leaving Jaemin with a million questions. He tosses the covers off, scrambling into the closet to pull on something decent.

"Get up, angel," Jaemin calls, "There's been an emergency. A car's coming to get us."

This wakes Isla fully, the girl sliding out of bed and tumbling into the closet after her boyfriend, just snagging something and tugging it on.

The car arrives fifteen minutes later, Isla and Jaemin sliding onto the spacious backseat. The idol is tense, leg bouncing and fingers clenching and releasing over and over. It breaks Isla's heart to see him so stressed. She grasps one of his hands and squeezes reassuringly.

"I'm sure everything will be alright," Isla says, trying to soothe him despite her own worry.

Jaemin smiles at her shakily, tugging her as close as their seatbelts will allow. He places his head on her shoulder, squeezing her tightly to comfort himself. Isla rubs his arm, relieved to feel his racing heartbeat start to slow some.

"I don't know what I would do without you, jagiya," he says, nuzzling her.

Isla doesn't comment, not wanting to admit that she's feeling the same way.

When they arrive at the hospital, the couple is escorted to one of the upper levels of the hospital and into a private waiting room. The other boys are already there, a somber mood hanging over the space.

A manager is whispering into a telephone in the corner when they arrive, looking up and hanging up promptly. The man rushes up to them.

"We're waiting to hear from the doctor," he whispers to Jaemin.

"What happened to him? What was the accident?" Jaemin asks.

The manager takes a breath, a pained look on his face.

"A janitor discovered him face flat on a stair landing about an hour ago. There was," he pauses, "A large gash in his head. It looks like he tripped and tumbled down the stairs."

"What was he even doing at Smash Entertainment?" Jaemin asks, "We're supposed to be on vacation."

"I don't know. We'll just have to wait until he wakes up and can tell us what happened. It's just a waiting game now," the manager says.

Jaemin quickly relays the information to Isla, both of them sitting down to wait. The clock on the wall clicks endlessly, everyone in the room trying to fight their restless desire to get up and pester the staff about Woojin's condition.

Finally, a nurse peeks in.

Everyone jumps up at once, eager for whatever news she has.

"There's good news and not so good news," the lady begins.

"The good news first." Seojoon insists.

"Mr. Park is stable," the lady says, "All of his vitals are normal."

"And the not so good news?" Leo asks hesitantly.

"We've had to put him into a medically-induced coma due to some swelling in his brain."

The room is silent as everyone struggles to process this new information.

"Will he be alright? He'll come out of it, right?"

"He should be alright, yes. As for how long he'll be under, I'm not sure. It depends on the person. It could be a few days or even a few weeks."

Jaemin feels himself beginning to tear up.

"He can have visitors now. Two at a time, please," the lady says, bowing before leaving the room.

Leo and one of the managers go first, leaving the others to torment over Woojin's condition. Jaemin's restlessness only increases with every minute that goes by. Even though the nurse told him that Woojin is stable, Jaemin won't feel comforted until he sees his bandmate for himself.

When Leo returns, face perfectly free of expression, Jaemin darts up, getting ready to see Woojin. Before he can take a step in the direction of his room, Daehyun and Seojoon are up, the former bumping Jaemin rather harshly as he brushes past him.

Jaemin almost trips, feeling himself growing pissed. He gets that Daehyun is upset with him, but now is not the time to be playing games.

Isla's fingers brush against the skin of Jaemin's arm, pulling him back down.

"You'll get to see him soon," Isla says quietly, "Don't worry. He'll be okay."

Jaemin intertwines his fingers between hers, desperately needing the comfort she provides. Isla helps as best she can, continuously rubbing patterns over Jaemin's skin to try and distract him.

Finally, after what feels like forever, Jaemin is allowed to go and see Woojin. His grip on Isla's hand is so tight, she winces, but does not pull away. She can't even begin to imagine what Jaemin must be feeling right now, never having experienced a tragedy like this in her life.

Woojin is propped up in bed, some bandages wrapped tightly around his head. Various tubes are placed in his skin, the gentle whooshing of machines being the only sound in the room.

Jaemin chokes on a sob, plopping down on the chair beside the bed.

"Oh, Woojinnie," he says, hesitantly reaching out to touch him, bailing out at the last moment, hand only centimeters from

Woojin's fingers.

This isn't right. Woojin shouldn't be here in this place, looking like he's fast asleep. He should be resting at home, enjoying the last bit of his vacation. He should be with his parents, annoying his older brother, laughing at the movie he's been wanting to see for months.

Anything, anywhere but here.

"Woojin," Jaemin whispers, feeling himself begin to shake.

Isla wraps her arms around his frame, noticing the beginnings of a panic attack creeping in on him.

"Let's go get some air, alright, Jaemin?" the girl suggests, brushing his hair out of his face, "Let's let Woojin rest up."

The man nods jerkily, standing up slowly, leaning his whole body on Isla's frame. She walks him out, the couple passing the waiting room where she makes eye contact with Leo before continuing onward, finding an empty balcony that overlooks the city.

The air is somewhat chilly but Isla doesn't pay it any attention, focusing on the zoned-out man beside her.

"Breathe, Jaemin. Breathe, baby," Isla says, patting his back.

He doesn't respond, eyes glazed over. It's obvious that he's in his own world right now, struggling to come to terms with what he just saw.

Isla bites her lip.

Perhaps it's best if he has some alone time without her hovering over him? She wants to help, but she knows that sometimes people just need to be alone.

Isla pats him one more time before rising, getting ready to head back inside and maybe grab something to drink when Jaemin's hand darts out, latching onto her like a vice.

"Don't," he says, voice so quiet she can barely hear, "Don't leave me. Please don't leave me."

He sounds utterly destroyed, Isla sinking back into her previous spot.

"I won't," she says, Jaemin's head leaning against her shoulder, "I promise."

Two whole days. It takes two days for Park Woojin to wake up. Two days of worrying, anxiety, and fear. Two days of fearing the worst.

The news is like a breath of fresh air into a dead corpse, everyone feeling revitalized. The members break the hospital's visitor rules, all five of them crowding around the somewhat disoriented maknae, all relieved to see his eyes open.

"We were so worried!" Seojoon says, grasping Woojin's hand, "So, so worried!"

"Don't ever do something like that again!" Daehyun scolds, angry demeanor fading almost instantly, "Don't scare us like that."

"Guys, guys!" One of the managers begins, "Keep it down."

The boys settle down somewhat, each of them still watching Woojin like a hawk. The man in question reaches for the cup of water on his bedside, Daehyun handing it to him quickly. He drinks it all down in one go.

"I," he begins, voice raspy, "What happened? Why am I here?"

Leo sucks in a breath.

"You don't remember what happened?" he asks.

Woojin shakes his head, wincing slightly.

"No," he says, "Can I have more water?"

Daehyun quickly refills Woojin's cup, handing it to him. The man once again downs it quickly.

"What's the last thing you remember then?" the manager asks.

Woojin frowns, thinking.

"Um . . . helping my mom in the kitchen back home. Or maybe going to bed that night. What day is it?"

"The twenty-fourth," Jaemin says, "You've been out for a few days."

Woojin groans.

"I don't . . . I don't know."

"It's okay," Leo says, "Don't worry about it. You focus on resting up, alright?"

The boys leave him alone as the nurse comes in to administer medicine, everyone retreating back to the waiting room.

"He doesn't remember anything?" Daehyun asks in disbelief, "Not anything?"

"Maybe it'll come back to him," Seojoon offers, "He did just wake up."

"I hope so. It doesn't seem like Woojin to fall down a flight of stairs. He's never been particularly clumsy," Leo says.

"And why was he even there? He should have been back in Busan, not anywhere near Smash Entertainment," Jaemin pipes in.

"Something about this isn't adding up," Seojoon says.

"Let's leave it for now, focus on Jinnie getting better. I'm sure someone will check the cameras and we can see what really happened," Leo offers, a sick feeling in his gut.

Silence blankets the room, everyone letting their mind wander.

What really happened?

Woojin stays at the hospital for a few more days before he is released with the stern warning to take it easy. His discharge is a huge relief for everyone around him, some just glad that he's okay while others are relieved that the tour won't need to be reworked. They move along with the schedule, a pouting Woojin sulking in the corner because he's not allowed to practice for another few days until the members are perfectly convinced that he's alright.

He had somehow managed not to break anything despite his tumble down the stairs, lady luck shining down on him. Besides the yellowing bruises littering his skin, Woojin looks perfectly normal, still as gorgeous as ever.

There's only one thing that's bothering him, one huge elephant squeezed into the corner of the practice room. The idol doesn't remember anything about that day. He doesn't remember why he was at Smash Entertainment or how he managed to fall down a stairwell he didn't even know existed. And to the management's bafflement. None of the video cameras on the upper levels were operational. All the CCTV had managed to pick up was Woojin parking his car in the garage and heading up into the building.

It screams foul play.

But who? And why? Or had Woojin really done this to himself? Had he really managed to take a tumble down the stairs of his own accord? But that doesn't make sense, it doesn't add up.

There's a tension over the room that stems from that elephant in the corner, a tension everyone tries their hardest to hide with smiles and laughter that is two degrees too forced to seem natural.

Isla is worried about Woojin, but she is more worried about Jaemin. Out of everyone, he seems to be struggling the most. Isla knows that the Sanctuary performance was traumatic for him, and that Woojin's accident only made him more stressed and anxious. He's regained some of the doubt and heightened clinginess that he's lost in the last few months, looking towards Isla each and every time he has a small blunder or feels upset with himself.

While she doesn't mind being his support, it does worry her. She fears that Jaemin is heading towards a regression, that all of the progress he's had since she came back will disappear.

And that's why Isla stands outside of Dr. Moon's office, trying to build up the courage to knock on the door. She can't help but remember the woman's words to her, the way the doctor made her feel so insignificant and small. She hesitates for so long that her phone rings, startling her. Isla jumps before quickly answering the phone, not wanting to alert the doctor of her presence.

"Hello?" she asks, walking away from the door.

"Baby? Where are you? You usually don't take this long to go to the restroom," Jaemin says.

Isla can hear grumbling in the background. No doubt he had everyone stop practice so he could call her.

"I'm headed back now, Minie. I just stopped to grab a snack."

"Okay," Jaemin says softly, "Hurry back. I miss you."

"I miss you too. I'll be right there."

Isla hangs up with a click, glancing at the door one more time before turning around and quickly heading to one of the vending machines, buying the chips she knows Jaemin loves and going back to the practice room to see the boys (minus the still sulking Woojin) and the backup dancers going over their group performance.

However, as soon as Jaemin sees Isla, he breaks formation and bounces right up to her like an overly eager puppy, wrapping his sweaty arms around her and kissing her quickly.

"Baby—"

Isla got over the embarrassment of Jaemin's PDA a long time ago. Now she wouldn't even flinch if he kissed her on National Television.

Isla sends him off gently, gesturing for him to go back to practice and taking a seat next to Woojin.

If the man is surprised by her action, he doesn't show it, studying the other dancers intently with fire in his eyes. It's painfully obvious that he's dying to get out there and practice his own songs for the tour, to learn the choreography with the backup dancers. It reminds Isla of a child stuck in time out, watching his friends all have fun at recess.

Isla opens the bag of chips, popping one in her mouth and chewing it, watching Jaemin's laser focus in the mirror. He knows every part of his body well and has mastered how to move it, something Isla is all too familiar with from the countless times he's proved it in the bedroom.

By now, the girl has most of Jaemin's choreography memorized, knowing exactly when he's going to toss his head or roll his hips. She continues to snack on the chips she bought, glad that her little white lie ended up with her actually having something to eat before lunch break in two more hours.

Isla cocks the bag towards Woojin, wordlessly offering him some of her treat.

"No, thank you." he says quietly, not much of an accent clinging to his words.

Isla shrugs mentally before continuing with her snacking, noticing Woojin looking at her from her peripheral. The girl hasn't forgotten about the way he always stared at her so intensely and sitting next to him was an attempt to try and figure out why.

Isla isn't dumb, she knows that his staring wasn't even remotely sexual or romantic, but it held something more mysterious than that, something deeper. She knows he suspects her of something, but of what? And why? He didn't stare at her like this when she first arrived, it's a fairly new development.

He's struggling to remember, struggling to make sense of Isla and Dr. Moon and what the relationship between them is. Strange stuff has been going on ever since the two of them showed up. Something more than Jaemin's illness is going on but he can't figure out what.

She once again offers the bag of chips and Woojin actually takes one, chewing it without taking his eyes off the dancers in front of him. Slowly, the two of them finish the bag, neither one saying a word.

"Are you okay?" she asks him, eyes still watching Jaemin.

"Yes. Thank you for asking," he replies.

It's a bit more obvious that he's somewhat unsure of the words. It's times like this that Isla wishes she understood Korean. One would think that after living in Korea for an extended amount of time and being surrounded by Koreans that she would have picked *something* up, but she doesn't know any more than she did when she lived back in her own country. She just hasn't had the time or energy required to learn a new language and Jaemin seems fine with her only being able to converse with him and a select handful of others.

Maybe now's as good a time as any to start learning.

"No problem," Isla says, feeling the conversation die down.

She can tell that they won't be doing much talking, especially when someone calls for a break and Jaemin comes running over to her, causing a smile to break out on her face.

And for the next several weeks, the routine continues. Isla follows Jaemin to practice then makes some excuse to leave in an attempt to go and speak with Dr. Moon, but she can never catch her. Either Jaemin interrupts her before she can gather the courage to knock or an 'Out of Office' sign hangs on the woman's door.

It's like she fell off the face of the earth or something, which is baffling to Isla. You'd think Jaemin's specially hired oh-so-secret psychologist would be in her office as much as possible to make herself available to Jaemin in case he needed her.

And speaking of Jaemin, her boyfriend still sees the Doctor on the regular. Isla has half a mind to ask if she can piggyback along with him just so she can catch this lady, but she knows that wouldn't be right. His therapy sessions are private and should remain that way without her butting her head in. The last thing he needs is for her to interfere.

And before she knows it, it's only two weeks before OT2B jet off for their first stop on this months long tour. Isla really hasn't stopped to think about how she feels about trailing around the world after Jaemin. Now that she thinks about it, her whole world has revolved around him ever since all of this started. It seems so long ago that she was just some aimless girl floating through life with no ambition, but it causes Isla's heart to drop when she realizes that she's still the same girl.

Her only goal is for Jaemin to get better, and once that happens, then what? She doesn't have any personal goals, doesn't have a dream job or house. Isla shakes the thought out of her head, deciding not to worry about that now.

Isla knows in her gut that it'll only be harder for her to talk to Dr. Moon when they're on tour and traveling. If Isla wants to talk to her about her concerns with Jaemin, she needs to do it now. Thankfully, the boys are all heading out to have a celebratory dinner tonight, one that Isla politely declined an invitation to, explaining that the boys need time to themselves without her lurking.

Despite some pouting, Jaemin agrees to go without her, the other members looking relieved when she doesn't slide into the black van with them. Isla doesn't take it personally. She knows that it must be tiring for her to hang around them all the time. Jaemin hasn't been out with just his bandmates in the entire time she's been around.

And so, Isla waves them off before retreating into the apartment, taking her hair down and rubbing her scalp. It was pulled into a tight ponytail all day long, causing shocks of pain to shoot through her whenever she smiles too hard. Isla plugs her near-dead phone into the charger by the bed and heads out. She's quickly stopped by one of the omnipresent bodyguards always hovering in the background.

"Where do you think you're going?" he asks, voice all gruff, hand on her wrist.

Isla shakes him off.

"I need to go back to Smash Entertainment. I left my phone," she says, wiping her hands on her pants, glaring at him.

He doesn't comment, simply opening the door to yet another van. Isla climbs inside the van claiming shotgun while the driver pulls away. The ride doesn't take long, but Isla feels like it goes by slower. Her heart beats faster than normal despite her trying to calm herself. It's just Jaemin's doctor. The lady is harmless, albeit a bit mean. Her boyfriend sees her regularly, she has no reason to be nervous, right?

Right?

Isla leaves the van, making the now-familiar journey up to Dr. Moon's office. This time, she forces herself to knock without hesitating, heart beating so loudly it's all she can hear.

No one answers the door, so Isla tries once more, knocking.

Once again, no one answers. Isla tries the door and is surprised to find it unlocked. The doctor must have stepped out for only a moment, meaning Isla should be able to speak to her soon. Isla takes a seat at the chair in front of the woman's desk, twitching slightly as she tries to calm down.

But minutes continue to pass without the doctor showing up. So much time passes, in fact, that she fears the guard will get suspicious if she doesn't leave soon. Sighing in disappointment, Isla stands up, deciding to leave a note on the woman's desk.

Isla sits down in Dr. Moon's spinning chair, opening one of the drawers to look for a pen. She accidentally brushes against the open laptop, waking the already unlocked computer. The sudden light catches Isla's attention and she looks, only to be frozen by what she sees.

"Oh my God!"

Pictures. Thousands upon thousands of photographs are stored in this open file. Photos of Jaemin laughing, smiling, looking pissed off. There's photographs of him out and about, of him eating, of him heading into the restroom. Every photograph is one he isn't posing for, every one of them is one that was taken without his permission.

Isla continues to scroll, feeling sicker and sicker every second.

There are photos of him from years ago, photos of him dancing alone in the practice room, photos of him out to drink with friends. And each and every photograph has red markings on them, scribbled notes she can't read. There are red circles around bruises on his skin, around his lips curved into a smile, around the imprint visible in the tight pants he wears.

Shakily, Isla opens up a subfolder, this one outlining everything he's ever worn in public, a checklist of sorts. There are notes on his favorite products, the brand of underwear he wears, bookmarked fanfiction involving him blindfolded and gagged.

Another subfolder, this one containing journals. Hundreds of entries, some in Korean but mostly in English.

Isla stops to read one, shivers racing up her spine as her eyes scan the document.

Nov 5

There was something off about him today, everyone who went to the fanmeet said so. He wasn't as happy as usual. Idiots on Twitter are all speculating about it, but I know the truth. I know him better than anyone, I know what he did last night.

I should be angry – I am angry. I'm saving myself for him and he brings home some idol trainee slut? How could he? How could he cheat on me like this? He loves me, I know it.

Don't worry, I still love you.

Don't do it again.

Another entry, this one from just a few months ago.

Feb 26

I'm sorry. I'm so, so, so sorry, baby. I had to. I had to do it! And besides, you can't be mad at me! You broke your promise first. You did it first! I had to!

It didn't mean anything, I swear. It didn't even feel good.

I thought of you the whole time. I'll always think of you. It'll always be you.

More entries, all of them vague, all of them making Isla feel like she's been transported into a horror movie.

April 11

When you sat in front of me today and your eyes closed . . . ah, Jaemin. Jaemin, Jaemin, Jaemin, Jaemin, Jaemin!!! Your lashes are so beautiful! I can't wait to pluck them all out one by one. Your lips are so soft! I can't wait to make them bleed.

I can't wait until you're mine. All mine! Mine, Mine, Mine, Mine, Mine!!!

Then you can finally stop pretending to love Isla. That bitch. That evil, two-faced cunt. I can finally free you from her jagged clutches.

She'll never love you like I do. She'll never understand you like I do. She doesn't know you like I do.

Don't worry. I'll take care of her soon. And then it'll just be me and you. You and me. Ah, I can't wait until you're home!

"What do you think you're doing?" a voice asks.

Isla's heart rate spikes when she hears it, swiveling around to see the woman she's been searching for standing in the doorway.

Yeji Moon sighs, running a hand through her uncharacteristically messy hair. Isla is frozen in place, mind still processing what she's just seen. The doctor, ever calm and collected, locks the door behind her, stepping deeper into the room.

"I've been having a lot of snoops, lately," she says, voice stable, "People today really have no manners."

Yeji isn't bothered one bit, closely coming to stand right in front of Isla.

"I'll take care of you better than I did the last one," she whispers.

And then she lunges at Isla, hands poised to wrap around her neck. Adrenaline kicks through Isla's bloodstream and she dodges, darting out of the chair and off to the side, sprinting for the door.

Yeji is quick on her feet, spinning around to yank Isla by her hair and snatching the locks harshly, Isla falling backwards and hitting the ground hard enough to knock the breath out of her. Yeji is on her in a minute, straddling the other woman's hips as she covers her mouth with one hand, squeezing down harshly with the other.

Isla's screams are muffled as she tries to claw the woman off of her, surprised by the strength this small woman possesses. As black spots start to dot her vision, Isla digs her nails into the woman's face, nails scraping one of Yeji's eyes. The doctor lets go of Isla's neck as she muffles her own screams, blood trickling from where Isla cut her. Isla lets out a loud scream, bucking her hips to toss the doctor off of her.

Once again, she is thwarted by the now angrier doctor, the woman's hands balled into fists.

"Why wouldn't you just die quietly? Why must everything be so difficult?" she hisses out, insanity etched into her features.

Yeji snatches the laptop off of her desk and chucks it at Isla's fleeing form, causing her to go down, her vision starting to swim from the force of the impact on her head. Tears spring up in Isla's eyes but she hardly has time to let them fall, Yeji once again attacking her. Isla twists around and punches her as hard as she can square in the face, hearing a satisfying cracking noise as Yeji's nose begins to bleed.

"You bitch!" the doctor growls, picking up her leg to kick Isla right in the ribs.

Isla falls to the ground, Yeji kicking her harshly once more. It's getting hard to breathe, Isla's face covered in tear tracks as she struggles to pull in oxygen. She feels weak, head throbbing so loudly, she can't even hear her own thoughts. Feebly, Isla once more tries to sit up, only to be backhanded right across the face, her cheeks stinging and the room spinning.

"I'm sick and tired of people always getting in my way. Always trying to stop me from doing what I want. Well, that ends today," Yeji says, blood dripping onto her cardigan.

She reaches for one of the statues from the bookcase behind her desk, a large metal angel.

Isla closes her eyes tightly, not wanting to look her end in the face. But the blow never comes.

Isla opens her eyes to see Jaemin standing in front of her, the idol having overpowered the smaller lady. The door has been kicked open and splintered, obviously taken down by Jaemin. Pure fury dances in his eyes as he shoves her against the bookshelf harshly, hand tightening around her throat. Yeji claws at Jaemin's hand but he doesn't even loosen his grip, holding her higher until her toes don't scrape the floor anymore.

"Stop," Isla protests weakly, barely able to speak, "Minie, you'll kill her. Stop."

At the sound of her voice, Jaemin drops the woman to the ground, rushing over to Isla.

"Oh my God," he says, scooping her up as gently as he can, "Oh my God! I thought she killed you!"

Jaemin is full-on sobbing now, his body shaking violently.

He knew something was wrong when Isla didn't answer his texts during the celebratory dinner. He grew even more paranoid when she didn't answer any of his calls either. Without even bothering to make up an excuse to the other guys, Jaemin hailed a taxi home, bursting inside only to think the very worst when he couldn't find her.

The guard informed him that she left towards Smash Entertainment some time ago and hadn't returned. The memory of Woojin's accident was fresh in his mind, so he got there as soon as possible, only to hear the love of his life scream.

He'd been blinded by anger when he arrived in the office only to find Isla passed out on the floor, the vindictive doctor poised to deliver the final blow.

Something dark had taken over him and all he could think about was killing her, killing Yeji for hurting Isla, his Isla, the person he loves more than life itself.

Yeji lay gasping on the floor, trying hard to pull in air. She coughs loudly, regaining the crying Jaemin's attention. He moves to attack her again but Isla grasps onto his shirt.

"Stay with me. Please," she asks, unable to stop the world from turning dark any longer.

Isla goes limp in Jaemin's arms, causing him to panic.

"No! Isla! Baby! No! You can't do this! You'll be okay!" Jaemin shouts, shaking Isla gently.

Hysteria overcomes him as he tries to revive her, so focused on his mission to save the love of his life that he doesn't notice Yeji stagger away, escaping the room.

"You'll be okay, baby! You'll be fine!" he says – promises – to her as he grabs his phone with sweaty fingers, dialing 112, the police's number.

"Stay with me," Jaemin begs, voice choked up, "Please stay with me. Don't leave me alone. I can't do it without you."

The idol's tears slide down his cheeks and drip onto Isla's bruises. He holds her like she's made of fine China, desperately afraid that she'll break if he moves her incorrectly. Her curls are matted and bloodied, the girl looking more like a stomped rose than the beautiful island she usually resembles.

"You can't," he cries, "You can't die. Help will be here soon. It's all gonna be okay. You'll be okay," Jaemin repeats, trying to stop himself from spiraling out of control.

It seems like it takes forever for the paramedics to arrive. A team loads Isla's body on a stretcher while Jaemin holds her hand, afraid he'll never see her again if he lets go.

28

Matoi Jaemin never knew how much he hated hospitals. The sterile smell, the impersonal staff, the hardback chairs and boring, pointless artwork hung on the bleak walls. He hates the tile flooring, the sound of hurried footsteps, the thin gowns the patients wear.

But more than anything, Jaemin hates seeing those he loves hooked up to machines, sleeping in that unnatural near-dead way. He hates sitting by bedsides and holding hands that don't squeeze back, hates the bruises that litter skin.

To say that everyone else was surprised would be an understatement. No one knew what to expect when a hysterical

Jaemin called, sounding three seconds away from having a breakdown, blubbering something about Dr. Moon and Isla and a fight and statues. So, once again, the private waiting room on the top floor is packed, all five members sitting uncomfortably, waiting for news on her condition. All their managers are there too, as well as some of the stylists Isla worked with and CEO Hwang himself.

Everyone waiting, pretending that everything is fine.

Jaemin has isolated himself into a corner, balled up with his chin placed on his knees, arms wrapped so tightly around himself in an attempt to keep himself together, to not fall apart while the love of his life is locked away in a room that feels a lightyear away.

The other boys all feel guilty, all blame themselves for not being able to comfort him in any way. Jaemin doesn't respond to anything, not to questions, food, or touch. It's like he's dead inside.

But none of the members feel as guilty as Leo. Leo can't even bring himself to look at his bandmate, blinded by his disgust for himself.

His nails dig into his skin, nearly drawing blood as Leo berates himself over and over again.

How could he be so blind? So stupid? How did he allow himself to be played by someone who meant Jaemin harm? How could Leo have fallen for Yeji's tricks? Her laugh, smile, every touch he mistook for being genuine.

How had he gotten in so deep that he didn't question when she asked for more? How could he have let her in, kissed her, hugged her, made love to her? How had he been happy, ecstatic even?

He felt understood, challenged by someone who viewed the

world the same way he did and it had led him to act mindlessly, to become part of the problem.

Leo had slept with and loved an attempted murderer. Someone who drove him to hurt Jaemin, to hurt Isla, someone who was only trying to do the best she could. Someone who had wacked Woojin across the head to try to get him to forget what he'd seen about her.

Apparently, hearing that your attacker has harmed someone else works wonders for recovering memory.

Leo can't bring himself to speak, to admit to all he has done. He deserves punishment just as much as Yeji does, deserves to be hated and scorned.

And yet, selfishly, he keeps his mouth shut in an attempt to keep the weak ties he still has. He doesn't want to lose any more than he already has, to wake up one day and know that he ruined everything beyond repair.

On the other side of the room, another man thinks just the opposite. CEO Hwang hadn't suspected the doctor for being anything more than he knew she was - a freak in bed, oh so willing to do just what he asked for an extra sum added to her paycheck. She used to visit him in his office after work hours, the part of the day he always looked forward to the most.

He's disappointed - not in her true character, but that he's lost a partner. Most of his other conquests became boring after he slept with them once or twice, but not Yeji, never Yeji. She always had something new up her sleeve, something nasty she wanted to try. She kept the CEO excited, made the mundane everyday more interesting.

He leans back in his chair, the beginning of a headache creeping up on him.

Now everything is a big mess. The tour is supposed to start in two weeks but Jaemin is obviously in no condition to do anything other than mope and wait for his girlfriend to wake up. The other boys are just as frazzled, every one of them more stoic than ever before. CEO Hwang hadn't expected the foreign girl to make such an impact on his artists and it's becoming a pain in the ass.

Not only that, the police have been pestering everyone for statements and such, attempting to solve the case and determine what actually occurred with this psychotic doctor.

There's never been a bigger shit show in the entirety of his career and CEO Hwang can feel himself aging because of it.

After God knows how long, a nurse pops her head inside the room, immediately catching Jaemin's attention.

"Family of Miss Isla Montgomery?"

Jaemin is on his feet immediately, rushing over to the lady as fast as he can.

"Isla? How is she? Is she alright?" he asks the lady, grasping onto her hands.

The nurse is taken aback but doesn't remove her hands from Jaemin's grasp despite her obvious discomfort.

"She is awake and talking now."

"Can I see her?" Jaemin asks, "Please?"

He thinks he might actually die if he goes one more minute

without seeing Isla.

The nurse nods, leading Jaemin out of the waiting room and towards Isla's room.

Everyone else seems to deflate a bit when Jaemin leaves, the man taking the majority of the depressing aura with him.

Seojoon leans forward, placing his chin on his knitted hands.

"Why has everything been going wrong lately?" he asks, more to the universe than anyone in the room.

"It really seems that way, huh?" Daehyun says, "Really does."

"Maybe it's not so bad," Woojin says, trying to lift spirits, "I mean, it's good that we found out about her sooner than later, right? And I'm okay, and Isla will probably be okay, right?"

No one says anything and Woojin quickly quiets down, sinking down into his seat. They all know that nothing is truly alright or okay in this moment, and they're not sure if it ever really will be.

Jaemin walks swiftly with the nurse, having to stop himself from sprinting like a madman down the hallway. They finally make it to Isla's room, the nurse reaching up to tap her knuckles against the door before swinging it open and allowing Jaemin inside.

The room is dark, blinds shut and curtains drawn, only the light from a singular lamp illuminating the space.

"Baby?" Jaemin asks, whispering into the darkness.

"Minie," Isla says.

She sounds sleepy, voice quiet as a mouse.

Jaemin sits next to her bedside.

"Hey, baby," he says softly.

Isla readjusts herself so she's looking at him, wincing slightly as she moves.

"Be careful," he warns, brushing some of the hair out of her face, "I don't want you to get hurt any further."

Isla nods softly, movements slow. It's obvious that she's still under the influence of pain medication.

"Thank you for coming to my rescue," she says, smiling at him, "I wouldn't be here without you."

Those are the words that break him, fat tears welling up and spilling down his cheeks. Jaemin hides his face in his palms as he sobs, shoulders shaking. Isla places a weak hand on his arm, trying to comfort him.

"Hey, don't cry! I'm okay, Jaemin. I'm just fine," she says, rubbing him gently, "There's no need to be upset."

"I almost lost you," he says, looking up through his fingers, "I almost lost you for good. I was so scared. I've never been so scared in my entire life."

He craves to hold her in his arms, to feel her heart beating against his chest, to have her breath brush against his skin. The time without her has been pure agony, even worse than when she left him all of those months ago.

Isla doesn't really know what to say. Truthfully, she has never been so frightened either. The root of her fear didn't stem from concern about her own safety, but rather dread over what Yeji had planned for Jaemin. From what Isla could gather, it would be nothing less than disastrous if whatever she had planned actually manifested.

She wanted to save him, to protect him from her and she'd failed. Instead, it was Jaemin who ran to her rescue.

"Why'd you do it?" she asks him once his breathing evens out and he can go more than ten seconds without gasping for air, "Why'd you jump in instead of just calling the police?"

"Are you joking?" Jaemin asks, suddenly sitting upright, anger in his tone, "You can't be that fucking stupid, can you?"

Isla blinks, not having expected his switch in character.

"There's no way I was just going to stand by and watch her try and kill you. No fucking way."

"You could have gotten hurt," Isla protests weakly.

"I could have gotten hurt? Me?! Baby, you're the one in the hospital right now. I don't give a damn about me getting hurt, not when it comes to you."

Jaemin's anger simmers down when he sees the look on Isla's face.

"Even if she'd had a gun, I would have stepped in. I would have jumped in front of you without a moment's thought."

Jaemin traces the edge of Isla's full lips, feeling how soft they are despite the circumstances.

"Always. I'll always put you before me. I love you too much to even pretend otherwise."

Isla is silent, gaze caught on the emotion in Jaemin's face. After a moment, she pushes herself to the far edge of the hospital bed, patting the empty space beside her.

"I can't–" Jaemin begins.

"Please," Isla asks, "I just need you to hold me."

Without another word, Jaemin climbs in beside her, Isla laying her head on his chest, snuggling as close to him as she can and ignoring the ache in her chest every time she takes a breath.

None of that matters right now. All that matters is Jaemin's heart thumping in time with hers.

29

All things considered, Isla manages to get off rather well. Yeji gave her a mild concussion and some scrapes and bruises, but besides some soreness, Isla is alright. Her chest is still tender from where her ribs have been bruised but the girl can't complain, knowing that things would have been much worse if Jaemin hadn't shown up when he did.

And speaking of her boyfriend, Jaemin refuses to leave her side for even a moment. His paranoia has skyrocketed to the point that he won't even go to the restroom without Isla following him. Instead of Isla coddling Jaemin like she's done in the past, Jaemin caters to every one of Isla's whims, just wanting to make sure she's alright.

"You sure you're okay, baby?" Jaemin asks, twirling a piece of her hair.

They're cuddled up on the couch, watching some mindless drama that Isla mentioned she had wanted to see. But Jaemin isn't watching it at all, studying Isla's face with the TV illuminating his.

"Mmhm," Isla says, resting against him, "Thank you for taking care of me these last few days."

She leans forward, pressing a kiss against his cheek.

"Of course, baby," Jaemin says, "I'll always take care of you."

The peaceful moment is interrupted by a knock on the door.

Jaemin sighs, wanting to ignore it but standing up anyway. He knows the only people who could be at his doorstep are his members or managers. Isla peers curiously from over the back of the couch, being careful not to move too suddenly or twist her body too much.

Jaemin cracks the door open slightly before swinging it all the way open, his hand resting on his hip in annoyance.

"What are you doing here?"

Leo stands awkwardly in front of him, not quite sure what to do with himself. Before, he had never felt unsure about interacting with Jaemin but now it's as if he's a stranger meeting someone new for the first time and desperately trying to make a good impression.

"I . . . well, actually . . ."

Seojoon steps out from behind Leo, hands carrying some dish wrapped in foil. One by one, the rest of OT2B reveal themselves, all smiling shyly.

"I . . . we thought it would be a good idea to stop by and bring dinner. Since you've been busy taking care of Isla . . ." Woojin says softly, trailing off.

Jaemin hesitates, not knowing if he should let them in or not.

"What are you doing, Minie? Aren't you going to let them in?" Isla asks.

It's rare to see all the members hanging out together outside of practice or their schedules anymore.

Slowly, Jaemin steps aside, gesturing for the others to come in. They shuffle inside the apartment, looking around at the space with curiosity. It's then that Isla realizes that the members haven't really gotten the chance to see Jaemin's apartment. The girl pushes herself up to greet the guests.

"Baby!" Jaemin protests, rushing over to grasp her arms when she winces as she rises.

"I'm okay," she says, but still leans against Jaemin's side as they walk over to the group.

Seojoon offers up the dish with a smile. Isla returns the grin, reaching her hands up to take the container. Jaemin beats her to it, taking it and placing it on the kitchen counter. Everyone then semi awkwardly shuffles into the dining room area and Jaemin doles out portions. There aren't enough chairs to host all six people, so a few of the members sit in the living room.

Light chatter breaks out as people eat, everyone using Seojoon's food as a springboard for conversation. Isla stays silent, knowing that this meeting is more about the boys reconnecting with Jaemin than about concern for her wellbeing. She's noticed how withdrawn he's been from them and the last time they had spent some quality time together had been interrupted by Jaemin dashing off to Isla's rescue.

She frowns lightly, noticing Jaemin adding to the conversation very minimally. Isla reaches for Jaemin's hand under the table, squeezing it three times.

The silent message is clear.

He smiles at her warmly, caressing the back of her hand with his thumb before piping up when a very animated Daehyun makes a comment. Within minutes, they're all laughing loudly, Jaemin's eyes disappearing behind his bright smile.

When was the last time he'd laughed so wholeheartedly?

Isla finishes her meal, cleaning the plate entirely. Jaemin's focus is on Woojin who appears to be telling some sort of story, the girl's boyfriend totally enthralled. She stands, quickly retreating back into their bedroom. She's tired, still exhausted from the fight and more than willing to let Jaemin hang out with his friends alone.

Ever so carefully, she changes into her softest pajamas, crawling into bed and turning on her lamp and reaching for the book Jaemin bought her a while back. She hasn't gotten much time to get through it so she takes the opportunity, settling into the pillows as laughter rings out in the living room.

Three chapters later, there's a knock on the door.

"Come in," Isla says, confused.

Jaemin never knocks.

The door creaks open and Leo steps inside, shutting the door behind him.

"What do you want?" Isla asks on edge.

She's too worn out to fight with him.

"I . . . I want to apologize."

For a moment, silence stretches in the dimly lit room.

"What?" Isla asks, voice quiet as a whisper.

"I want to apologize for everything I've done to you. There's no excuse for the pain and heartache I've caused you," Leo says, gaining courage, "I was wrong, oh so wrong, and I'll never be able to apologize enough to make up for it."

Isla places her book down in her lap, not sure what to say.

"But please," he says, voice trembling, "Please don't tell Jaemin about what happened. I've . . . I don't want to lose him. I can't lose him. He's my brother, one of the most important people in my life. If he finds out what I did . . . please, Isla. Please don't tell him what I did."

For the first time in forever, tears well up in Han Leo's eyes as he thinks about what could happen, about Jaemin saying he wants nothing to do with him ever again.

"I know you don't owe me anything. You have every right to hate me - to despise my very being, but please don't tell him."

"Just," Isla says, finding her voice, "Why? Why were you so cruel to me? I already felt so alone being stuck here. You were the one person I thought I could befriend while I was here but . . . why did you turn on me?"

Leo hangs his head in shame.

"I just . . . Yeji . . ."

He doesn't need to say anymore. The pain in his voice gets the message across.

"I don't know if I can forgive you," Isla says, Leo flinching at her brutal honesty, "But . . ."

The rapper holds his breath.

"But I won't tell him. At least not now."

Leo sighs, sagging in relief.

"Thank you, Isla, really I–"

"Don't get it twisted. I'm doing this for Jaemin. He's already suffered enough. He doesn't need to lose you. Any of you."

She pauses, looking at the man she once admired, noticing how flawed and imperfect he is.

"Whether you believe it or not, he treasures all of you more than anything."

"Not more than you," Leo says quietly.

Isla is silent, her grip on the book tightening.

"Get out."

He leaves wordlessly, shutting the door quietly behind him. Isla shuts off her lamp, replacing her book on the nightstand and shuffling under the covers. The girl presses the button on her phone, illuminating the screen and displaying her lock screen. She runs a finger over Jaemin's smiling face, lingering.

How much longer will it be before this is all she has? Glass memories and forgotten smiles?

She turns her phone off, placing it face down on the nightstand and trying to force herself into a fitful sleep.

It doesn't work. Isla doesn't know how long she lays there, trying to convince herself to fall asleep. She doesn't move when the bedroom door opens, Jaemin's familiar footsteps padding across the carpet. She hears him go into the closet and return moments later, presumably in pajamas.

He slides into bed, pulling Isla close and kissing her temple. She falls asleep to the sound of his even breathing.

30

The sound of water dribbling against the cold cement is beginning to drive Hunter insane. He's been waiting in this leaky basement for half an hour already after Yeji's frantic text.

The man huffs in annoyance, watching the ever-growing puddle in the corner. Whatever Yeji wants had better be good, especially since she called him out here to the middle of nowhere. Briefly, the man worries about the very shiny and expensive car he's left outside. With this kind of sketchy area, it would be no surprise if some scumbag tried to steal it.

He chews on his lips, checking his watch.

Oh, the things a man will do for a forbidden fuck.

Hunter startles when the door slams open, hurried footsteps pounding down the creaky wooden steps.

"I never thought you'd be this excite— holy shit, what happened to you?!" Hunter asks in alarm.

Yeri trips on the last step, wincing when she comes into contact with the hard ground. She's already been beaten up enough for today, she doesn't need to add anymore bruises to her collection.

"Everything's gone to hell," the woman says, looking up through her messy hair at her partner in crime, "I've been found out."

"Who would beat you up because they discovered you've been sleeping with me? That seems rather extreme," the man says, offering a hand to help her up.

Yeri swats it away, standing up with the last of her strength.

"No, you dumbass! I've been found out! My cover is blown! Cops will probably be surrounding this place any minute."

"What?!" Hunter asks in alarm, "What did you do? What's going on, Yeji?"

At the sound of her sister's name, Yeri floods with rage, letting out a loud shriek and pounding her fists against the concrete wall, not caring about the scraps she inflicts on herself.

"Don't say that bitch's name ever again! It's all her fault! Stupid Yeji! Always having to be better than me, smarter than me! Even this happened because of her! I hope she fucking dies!" Yeri rages, "I hate her! I hate Yeji! She should never have been born!"

Hunter backs away from the woman, alarm bells ringing in

his head. Something is clearly not right and he's not going to stick around long enough to find out what it is. The first step creaks when he places his foot on it, catching Yeri's attention.

"Where do you think you're going?" Yeri asks, madness swirling around in her eyes, "You're in this with me. You're almost as disgusting as Yeji is."

Hunter is obviously confused. The dumbfounded expression on his face causes her to scoff.

"You know," she begins, "I've never liked men. Every man I ever knew was weak or cruel. My own father couldn't stand up to my mother's smothering ways. He never stepped in no matter how much I cried to him. And as I got older, as I finally got to interact with the real world, all men did was ridicule me - make me feel inferior to my fucking sister. Everyone always wanted something!"

She's shouting now, completely losing herself. A bolt of fear slides down Hunter's spine.

"No one ever wanted to get close to me. They always wanted to use me to get to my sister. I hate her so much. Perfect Yeji, reaching out to give a hand to her poor, helpless, fragile twin sister. Even as an adult I couldn't get away from her! I couldn't go out on my own and figure myself out. The only people who made me feel like more than a tragedy were OT2B. So, when I got the chance to meet them, to see them, I had to take it. I've never been so thankful for my idiotic sister's naïve trust. All her passwords were the same. All I had to do was go snooping while she was out secretly visiting a high-profile client in Peru. It was too easy."

Hunter has no idea what the woman is saying, no idea about what's going on.

"But now it's ruined," Yeri says, sounding much too calm, "All that's left is to handle unfinished business."

Her tone causes Hunter to make a run for it, dashing up the stairs and out the abandoned house to his car, unlocking it and coming to a sudden halt when he notices all four tires have been slit.

"Oh, fuck." he says.

In a panic, he grasps at his cell phone, trying to call out for someone, anyone. However, he realizes that the device has no service.

"Give it up, Hunter." a voice says.

Trembling, the man turns around to find the feeble woman with hands much too sturdy holding a small handgun pointed right between his eyes. He has no idea how she obtained the illegal weapon, but Hunter is quickly becoming aware that whoever this is, is out of her damn mind.

"I never liked your kind," she says, "The self-entitled type who believe they're God's gift to women. The type to lead girls on and break hearts just because they can. The type to lie to their wives about their whereabouts while sliding in some young chick from the office."

Every word is spat out with unbelievable venom, bitterness amplifying with each syllable.

"I always thought you were obnoxious. Overly confident. You have the smallest dick out of all three guys I had to fuck to get what

I wanted. All puffed up on an ego you don't deserve."

Should he run for it? But if he does, she's going to shoot, right? Maybe he can talk her down.

"Yeji–"

"Shut up. That's not my name. Yeri's the one who's played you all this time. Don't give that accomplishment to my sister. Yeri's the one who strung you along like a puppet. Not her. Me. I did it."

He opens his mouth again but stops when he hears the click of the safety being turned down.

"CEO Hwang never made promises. He knows exactly what type of man he is - never lied to me or anyone else about it. And Leo . . ." she laughs, "What a pitiful idiot. Too sweet for his own good. Just like a kicked puppy. But you. You deserve to go down with me."

"Please," he mutters, eyes beginning to tear up.

Yeri nods, smiling with the most peaceful expression Hunter's ever seen.

"I'll see you in hell."

The man crumples to the ground before he can even scream.

Sighing, Yeri tosses the gun in the back seat of her car, walking around to open the passenger door before picking the body up by the arms, dragging it all the way to the open door and flopping his body inside. It's left a nasty trail of crimson on the ground but Yeri doesn't care. This place is one of the most popular sites for gang activity around. She knows it's not the first time someone's been murdered here and it certainly won't be the last.

She wipes her hands on her shirt, coughing loudly and bending over, head swimming. Everything in her hurts, aches, groans, cries out in pain but she pushes herself to complete her task. She shuts the door and hobbles over to Hunter's now abandoned vehicle, hunting around in his dash before coming up with what she's looking for. Flicking on the lighter, Yeri drags the flame across his precious cloth seats, watching with glee as the fire snakes up and starts to devour the interior.

Yeri makes her way back to her car, shutting the passenger door and sliding into the driver's seat. Reaching over the corpse, Yeri clicks the seatbelt into place, propping his head onto the headrest and closing his eyes with dainty fingers.

"Safety first," she says, switching on the radio and turning up her CD, the melodic notes of Sanctuary wafting through the speakers.

She puts the car in drive and starts towards her final destination. Yeri sings along with Jaemin's verse, fingers tapping on the steering wheel, the familiar exhilaration she gets only from him coursing through her veins.

Even though her plan failed, Yeri tries not to be bitter. He'll never forget her, she realizes with an eerie grin. Never, not even when he dies. Matoi Jaemin will always remember her, will always have her voice, her face etched in his mind. The crazed look on his face when he choked her is ingrained in her eyelids

That makes her press the pedal down even harder.

Really, she's done it, hasn't she? Lived the life the other fans could only imagine.

"Oh, Jaemin," she sighs, remembering the feel of his voice dancing through her ears, remembering every expression, remembering the way his body lay across the couch in her office.

It was worth it. Definitely worth it. Yeri would do it all over again, except this time she'd make sure to take him quicker, to keep him with her where he belonged . . . to get rid of Isla.

Yeri glances at her passenger seat.

Why hadn't she done that sooner? Hunter is so much more enjoyable when he keeps his mouth shut. As a matter of fact, there are lots of people who should join him. Yeji, her mother, all the people from her high school. Surely the world would be a better place without them.

She makes a turn, then another, foot steadily pressing the gas harder, the speedometer ticking up higher and higher. People begin to honk and throw on breaks as Yeri speeds through lights, never stopping, never slowing down. She doesn't even blink when sirens begin to wail, lights flashing in her mirrors.

It doesn't matter. They don't matter. Nothing matters but the end.

Yeri cranks the stereo up as loud as it can go, opening her mouth and belting out each and every word that she's had memorized ever since the album came out.

She can see it. There, there, in the distance, growing closer, closer, closer, closer.

Mapo Bridge.

Yeri jerks the steering wheel sharply, urging the car to go faster and faster until it bursts through the barriers, weightlessness overcoming Yeri's body as she grins and smiles, singing the last note of the song as the car plunges head-first into the deep, water filling her lungs.

31

Jaemin sits anxiously, fingers tapping against his thighs. The plastic chairs in the police station are cold and hard, not giving him any sense of comfort. Unable to keep still, he drums his right foot against the tile floor, glancing at the clock on the wall opposite him.

Why is time moving so slowly? He could swear that the clock hasn't changed at all in the last five minutes.

Sitting next to him, the very vision of calm, Isla scrolls on her phone languidly, earbuds playing relaxing music as she reads an article about the miracle of super smoothies. She knows that there's no point in getting all worked up, that it'll just wear her out and cause her to crash in the middle of the day.

Manager Calm sits a few chairs down, scribbling on some paperwork and muttering to himself. In the entirety of her time in Korea, Isla has never seen this man take a break. He almost works harder than the idols themselves. And behind him, off to the side, stands two stoic bodyguards, their hands clasped behind their back, eyes constantly scanning the room for the slightest hint of danger or suspicious activity.

Everyone looks up when a man in uniform steps into the room. "We're ready for you."

Jaemin and Isla sit next to each other on the other side of the commissioner's desk. The middle-aged man types on his computer, taking notes of what the couple recounts about the accident.

"And did you see where she went after the assault?" he asks Jaemin.

The idol shakes his head.

"No. I was too worried about Isla. I needed to make sure she was safe."

His voice trembles and he squeezes his girlfriend's hand, needing to feel her presence.

The commissioner opens his mouth to continue but the phone on his desk rings. He pauses.

"Yes, we're wrapping up. Send her in."

"Her? Who?" Jaemin asks.

The sound of high heels clicking against the hard floor catches the couple's attention. A petite woman with a perfectly slicked back ponytail and immaculate clothes walks in the room. She doesn't even make it more than three steps before Jaemin is out of his seat and lunges at her, hands poised to finish what he started.

The woman shrieks, stumbling backwards and falling flat on her butt as Jaemin's own bodyguards restrain the struggling man.

"Jaemin ssi! Please calm down, Jaemin ssi!" The commissioner says, scrambling to his feet.

"What are you doing here, you whore?!" Jaemin shouts, the stunned woman still on the floor, "You should have escaped when you had the chance!"

Jaemin's nails claw into the skin of the guards, trying his hardest to fight his way over to the woman who dared to hurt his Isla.

"There's been a misunderstanding! This woman is not who you think she is! Please calm down, Jaemin ssi!" The commissioner shouts.

Jaemin goes still instantly.

"What?"

"Please retake your seat, Jaemin ssi," The commissioner says, "All will be explained in a moment."

Hesitatingly, Jaemin does as ordered, sitting beside Isla and watching the lady be helped up by the commissioner. Someone fetches another seat and the woman sits down, smoothing her now wrinkled clothing.

"What's going on?" Isla asks Jaemin, eyeing the woman now sitting a bit off to the side.

"I don't know yet," Jaemin says, "But it'll turn into a homicide if someone doesn't start talking."

"Please introduce yourself," the commissioner asks.

"I'm . . . Yeji Moon. Psychologist," the woman says in that familiar voice, "But I'm not the woman who hurt you. This is actually the first time I've met any of you," she says.

"What? That doesn't make sense."

"I've been abroad in London working with a client for the past six months. I only came back to Korea yesterday, after I found out what happened."

"Then who's been running around Smash Entertainment for the last several months?" Jaemin asks, growing angry.

No one's speaking fast enough.

The woman opens up her handbag, pulling out an old, slightly faded photograph. She places it on the edge of the desk, pushing it towards Jaemin with shaky fingers.

The idol snatches the photo, eyes growing wide.

Two identical girls smile back at him, matching pigtails and green summer dresses.

"My sister, Yeri," Yeji says, voice quiet, "I never . . . I would never have thought she could have done something like . . ."

Tears well up in the woman's eyes but she blinks them away before they can fall.

"Yeri is . . . she hasn't exactly had the easiest life. She–"

"Hold up!" Jaemin interjects, "You need to start from the beginning. How could she have pretended to be you? Why didn't you know it? Where is she now?"

The woman takes a breath.

"This is going to take a while."

"Yeri!" A small, overly excited voice shouts, small feet running through the house despite all the times Mom and Dad have warned against it, "Yeri!"

Arms swoop in and scoop the young girl up, Yeji giggling as her father tosses her up in the air.

"Now what did Mom and I tell you about running in the hallways?"

"Not to," Yeji says cheekily, peering around her father's head to glance at her sister's closed bedroom door, "Can Yeri come and play?"

Her father sighs, placing her down gently on the floor and squatting beside her.

"You're a big girl now, right, Yeji?"

The little girl nods eagerly.

"Right! I'm six years old, you know!"

"I know," the man says affectionately, patting her head, "Let me explain something to you then."

The girl's eyes are wide and bright, always curious about learning.

"You know Yeri is your twin sister, right?"

She nods.

"What does that mean?"

"We look the same!" the girl says excitedly.

"That's right! You have the same birthday and are the same age too. You even shared mommy's tummy together."

"Really?"

"Mmhm," the man says, "But when you were both in mommy's tummy, Yeri had a hard time growing as big and strong as you. So, when you were born, she had to stay in the hospital for a long time."

"She did? Did I have to too?"

He shakes his head.

"No. You've always been our strong little girl. But Yeri was very sick for a long time. And even though she's better now, she's still not all the way healthy."

Yeji frowns, peeking at Yeri's door.

"So, she can't play?"

The man shakes his head.

"No, she can't play."

"Never?"

"Maybe! Yeri gets better every day! Maybe one day you two can go play outside together. Are you still saving the other swing for her to use?"

Yeji nods.

"Good. Run along then and go play!"

Peering out the window, Yeri places a small hand on the window, watching her twin play outside in the yard, laughter floating up.

"Come away from the window, Yeri," her mother says.

"Why can't I play with Yeji?" she pouts.

"You know you have to stay inside, Yeri."

"But, Mom!"

"Now, Yeri. You know it's not safe for you out there,"

"Yeri! Yeri!" Yeji says, running into her sister's bedroom without even bothering to knock.

The girl in question looks up from her desk where she'd been struggling to understand the multiplication problems she's been assigned.

"Oh. You're back. Is it time already?" Yeri asks, watching her sister toss her backpack on the floor and climb on her bed.

"Mmhm. Whatcha working on?"

"Multiplication," Yeri mutters shyly.

"Multiplication? I learned that last year! Here, let me help you!" Yeji says, butting her sister over so they both perch on the small desk chair, "It's so easy. All you do is . . ."

"It isn't fair! You've been saying I could go to normal school if I kept my grades up and I have! Why won't you let me go?!" Yeri asks, exploding at her mother at the dinner table.

"Yeri! Don't use that tone with me. You know that it's danger–"

"It isn't dangerous! It's high school! Yeji gets to go and live a normal life! Why can't I?!"

"Yeri," her father warns.

The girl stands up and storms to her room, the door slamming shut.

Her mother sighs, rubbing her forehead.

"What are we going to do with her?"

"I could watch over her," Yeji offers, "Make sure she's doing well with classes and everything. That way she can go to school like she wants to."

"That's very sweet of you, Yeji. But you don't have to. We don't want her to be a burden."

"She won't be!" Yeji insists, "It wouldn't be a burden at all. Really, I think it would be quite fun to have Yeri at school with me. We would get to spend more time together . . ."

The teenager trails off, getting lost in her thoughts. Despite spending their whole lives together, Yeji and Yeri spend very little time with each other. They lead totally different lives which never seem to overlap.

"Just . . . please. Let her go with me . . ."

"You can't move out, Yeri!"

"I'm twenty-one! Am I supposed to stay with you for my whole life? Yeji's already moved out!"

"Yeri—"

"You wouldn't let me go to college, you won't let me leave the house, what am I supposed to do, Mother? I won't live under your thumb forever!"

"Then just move in with your sister. Would that make you happy?

Living in Seoul?"

"Yes! Anything to get away from *you*."

"Yeri has been living with me for almost half a decade. Even though we're twins, I've always had to look out for her and take care of her because she had developmental issues when she was younger. Even though those issues were resolved in childhood, my mother always had an overly protective attitude towards Yeri. Yeri being so sick really messed my mother up."

Yeji wets her lips, aware of the gazes of everyone on her.

"She got her first taste of freedom in high school. She was so excited to finally be let out of the house, to get a chance at being normal. But . . . there were some bullies that made her have a hard time. She withdrew even more, became angrier and more prone to fits. But when she moved to Seoul to come live with me . . . it was like she flourished. She had found you guys, found OT2B. Every time I came home from work, she would rush to greet me and tell me about something you had done. She's gone to every concert, has every album. Knows everything about you . . ."

She looks at Jaemin, locking eyes, the emotion and clarity in her irises taking him by surprise.

"Especially you. Yeri is head over heels infatuated with you, Jaemin."

"What?" Jaemin asks, shock running down his system.

"I never thought it was as deep as it was. I didn't know that

Yeri was a sasaeng. She hid everything so well. I didn't know how unstable she really was. But she must have broken into my office while I was gone and read my emails before I could see them. And once she found out about Jaemin . . ."

Yeji sighs heavily.

"I'm so sorry that this happened."

"Sorry won't cut it," Jaemin growls out, absolutely furious, "You let your psychopathic sister be around confidential information–"

"I didn't know–"

"You should have known!" Jaemin shouts, standing up quickly, his chair falling harshly to the ground, "You should have known! You're the psychologist! How can't you tell your own damn sister is insane?!"

Tears well up in the woman's eyes, her face becoming blotchy.

"Jaemin, calm down," Isla says, trying to soothe him even though she feels the same way.

"Calm down! I'm not going to fucking calm down! A sasaeng has been pretending to be my doctor for months, months! And she tried to kill my girlfriend! Sorry isn't going to cut it!"

The woman's sniffles continue as Isla draws Jaemin's shaking form closer to her, trying to comfort the both of them.

"All we can do is move forward," Manager Calm says,

"Miss Moon, do you have any idea where your sister could have gone?"

At that moment, a young police officer busts in.

"Sir!" he exclaims, "We've just pulled a car out of the river! It's unregistered, but two bodies were found inside. One of them matches the description of the woman we're looking for."

Yeji dissolves into sobs, her shoulders shaking violently.

Jaemin would be lying if he said he felt even slightly bad.

32

Jaemin," Isla says, peeking her head in the bathroom as the man brushes his teeth, staring at himself in the mirror.

"Mm," he mumbles, looking away and locking eyes with her through the reflective surface.

"So, about therapy..."

Jaemin slams his toothbrush down on the counter, glaring at Isla intensely. He spits the foam out of his mouth and drags his hand across his lips.

"Drop it," he says, "I'm not going."

"But Jaemin," Isla says, fully stepping into the room, "You need–"

"Don't tell me what I do and don't need, Isla," Jaemin says, face hardening, "I told you to drop it."

Isla flinches, not having expected Jaemin's harsh tone.

"No, baby, I'm sorry," Jaemin says, instantly softening, walking over to Isla and holding her close, "I just . . . I'm scared, okay? You were just attacked by that psychopath. For months, she said all of that stuff. Fed all of this into my mind and I . . ."

Isla sinks into his embrace.

"That's alright, Jaemin," she assures him, "But you can't hide from it. You can't just let all of this - all these thoughts and emotions just fester in your brain forever. You need to talk to someone, someone real this time. It has to—" she cuts herself off, emotion wrapping around her words, "It has to be brought to light eventually. You have to let it all out so you can be better."

Now that's it's been revealed that who everyone thought was Dr. Moon was in fact the fraud twin sister, Isla has realized that Jaemin has progressed even further than she expected. If he's already so much better, so much more himself due to his own strength, how healthy would he be with proper assistance?

Her time is coming nearer, she can feel it. And yet, she cannot bring herself to grasp onto him, not when he could be all the way healed and in the right state of mind. She knows he'll be so much happier, being able to stand on his own two feet without having to grasp onto her for stability. And so, Isla pushes for her own heartbreak, her own demise.

"Are you sure? Can't you just hug it better?" Jaemin mumbles into her hair.

"I wish I could, Minie, I really do. But I'm just a woman, not a superhero."

"You're my savior, Isla. Don't doubt it for a moment."

The girl clenches the fabric of his shirt.

"I'll return my manager's calls then," he says, sighing when she doesn't change her mind.

"You know he's just worried about you," Isla says, "With the tour coming up soon, you need to be in tip-top condition."

He kisses her head before leaving her in the bathroom to make the call as promised. Isla leans against the wall with her eyes shut, trying to calm herself down. She doesn't need to be upset. She doesn't have the right to be upset.

"Baby," Jaemin calls, "Your phone is ringing."

"Coming!"

Straightening up, Isla walks into the bedroom, grasping her buzzing phone from the bedside table. She doesn't recognize the number and is tempted to just forward the call, but stops herself. Very few people know her number. There's a good chance it could be someone from the company.

"Hello?" she answers.

"Miss Isla?" a gravelly voice asks, "This is CEO Hwang!"

"Oh," the girl says, "Can I help you?"

She'd been expecting it to be one of the managers or the stylists who called, not the man in charge.

"Yes, actually. I need you to come to my office. A car is already outside waiting. And don't bring Jaemin!"

"But—"

Before she can protest, the man hangs up on her, effectively ending their conversation.

Isla blinks at her phone's black screen. She's not sure what to make of the CEO's sudden demand. The girl hasn't forgotten the way he and the other execs have treated her (and the boys) making her increasingly more suspicious.

Should she just ignore it? Pretend that she never got the call? Something tells her that if she does that, one of the burly security guards will just muscle his way into the apartment and take her by force.

"Who was it?" Jaemin asks, walking into the room.

"One of the stylists," Isla lies, "She needs me to come in so she can take some measurements."

"Oh? I can come with you," Jaemin says, "Just give me a minute to finish getting ready!"

"Actually, why don't you stay here? I don't want to rush you," Isla says.

Today was one of the rare days where Jaemin actually slept in late, meaning Isla is up and dressed while Jaemin is still in his night clothes. It probably has something to do with all the sex they'd had the night before. He always passes out afterwards.

"You sure?" he asks, always willing to drop what he's doing to cater to her.

"Yep," Isla says, kissing him quickly.

Jaemin melts into her affection, pressing his fingers into her cheeks and smiling into the kiss.

"I love you so much," he says once she's pulled away.

"Love you more. I'll be back in a flash," Isla says, slinging her purse over her shoulder, "Don't forget to call your manager about therapy."

"I won't," Jaemin promises, watching Isla walk out the front door.

He sighs when she disappears, already wanting her back in his arms. The fight with Yeri terrified him more than ever before. It woke him up a bit, forcing him to realize that the world isn't as supportive of him as he thought. He never would have believed that someone wanted to hurt her so badly that they would act on it.

The attack has impacted Jaemin worse than Isla. Fear has lurked around in his head, making it harder for him to sleep at night even when Isla is safely sleeping right beside him. Those nasty thoughts have started to pop back up, the idol blaming himself for not being strong enough to protect her like he's supposed to. Even though he's tried to hide it from Isla, she hasn't been easy to fool, always pushing him to go seek help.

Sitting down on the couch and tearing his eyes away from the door, Jaemin picks up his phone, smiling at his lock screen, a photo he had taken of Isla back when they were visiting Busan. It's by far his favorite photo of her, the serenity of the image soothing his panicked mind.

The phone only rings twice before his manager picks up.

"Hello? Jaemin?"

"Hi, Manager Calm," Jaemin says, sounding bashful, "I'm sorry

I've been dodging your calls."

"It's alright," the man says, "Are you feeling better? The tour is just around the corner, you know . . ."

"Yeah, I know," Jaemin says, "And . . . no. I'm not feeling better. I can't sleep at night. I can't focus. I'm constantly feeling anxious and worrying that someone's gonna hurt Isla again. I . . . I worry that I won't be able to stop it this time. The voices are coming back and," the idol's voice cracks, "Isla . . . she thinks that I should go to therapy like you suggested," he says, regaining a bit of strength in his voice, "And I'm tired of feeling this way. I want to go back to normal."

For a moment, the man on the other side of the phone is silent.

"I'm glad you opened up to me, Jaemin. You know that I just want the best for you."

Jaemin believes him. Their manager has stuck by him and the other boys ever since they were nobodies with nothing keeping them going but dreams. If there is anyone he trusts at Smash Entertainment, it's him.

"Yeah. I know," Jaemin replies.

"I'll make you an appointment with a therapist I trust. He helped me get through everything when I was going through my divorce."

Jaemin winces. He's always felt like he had a hand in his manager's divorce. His wife was angry that his manager spent so much of his time with OT2B. More time than he did with his family. It stressed their relationship to the point where it broke beyond repair.

"Okay. Thank you, manager nim."

"Of course, Jaemin. I'll see you at practice tomorrow?"

"Yeah. I'll be there," Jaemin says.

It may be a small step, but Jaemin already feels a bit of weight lifted off of his shoulders, finding it a bit easier to shove the voice in his head back into the void where it belongs.

He's going to get better.

Isla stands in front of CEO Hwang's office, debating whether or not she should go inside. In all honesty, she doesn't have much of a choice, but stalling seems like a good idea. She doesn't want to be in the same room as him - the man who is supposed to be in full support of Jaemin and the others - the man who failed horribly. A part of her places the blame solely on his shoulders even though there is still a large mystery surrounding Yeri Moon and how exactly she came to corrupt the system. Isla has no idea what CEO Hwang knows about her - if anything, making him a perfect scapegoat to thrust all of her anger upon.

She knocks swiftly on the door before opening it herself and stepping in, shoulders back as she stares dead ahead at the man sitting behind the desk. An interpreter stands off to the side of him, face expressionless.

"You called?" Isla asks, crossing her arms.

She knows she's being incredibly rude, but she can't bring herself to care.

"We have lots to discuss. Sit," CEO Hwang says, gesturing towards the seat in front of his desk.

It reminds her of her meetings with Yeri.

"I'd rather stand."

He doesn't look satisfied but doesn't protest.

"As you know, the tour is fast approaching. We're not nearly as prepared for it as I would like, but we've already sold out every arena on the tour. There can be no postponement or cancellations. They have to be able to perform."

Isla nods. She's figured as much. Even though it's obvious that Jaemin needs more time to cope, she's actually been surprised by the amount of time he's already gotten. Isla had half expected one of the managers to come knocking their front door down when Jaemin began to ignore calls and skip out on practice for the tour.

Most likely it was that one kind manager who always seems to care a bit more than everyone else.

"And for Jaemin to be able to perform in any capacity, you'll need to be by his side. Which would be rather difficult, considering Leo burned your passport."

Isla isn't surprised he knows. CEO Hwang was probably one of the people who told the rapper to do it in the first place.

"I managed to pull some strings with some friends of mine," he says, suddenly tossing a small blue item onto his desk, "So, we won't have any issues getting you through the gates."

"Is that?" Isla asks, picking the item up, "How'd you–"

"As I said, I have friends in high places. It'll work just fine. Don't let Jaemin know it was missing, alright?" he says.

Isla opens up her new passport, flipping through the pages. It looks perfectly fine, exactly like the one that had been destroyed.

"That's all, Miss Isla," the man says dismissively.

The girl turns to go, pocketing her passport. She makes it halfway across the room before pausing, still facing away from the man.

"I hope you take better care of him," Isla says, staring at the door, "Never let anything like this happen again."

The girl turns her head, her intensity startling the CEO.

"Do you understand me?"

She leaves without waiting for a response.

Isla walks down the hallway angrily, coming to a stop when she sees a group of managers talking amongst themselves. Not wanting to be the center of attention at the moment, Isla turns, walking blindly through the building and cursing herself for still being able to get lost in the vast building after being there nearly every day for eight months.

She tries a door, pushing it open to find herself outside in the same place Leo had taken her back when she thought he was her friend. Isla huffs in annoyance, moving to head back inside before she hesitates.

She's alone now. No guards in sight, no eyes watching her every move. Her passport is in her back pocket. She could go now, run and escape through the hole in the fence and flag down a taxi to take her to the consulate. Isla could take shelter there and wait to go back home, to put this all behind her, escape these awful, self-serving people.

She could. Temptation brushes against her lightly like a caress. Before she can let it affect her too much, Jaemin's face pops into her head.

Isla couldn't do it, couldn't leave him. She won't.

Isla crouches down by one of the flower bushes, picking one of the blooms and tucking it beside her ear. She takes a deep breath, letting the sunshine kiss her skin before heading inside to try and find her way back to the garage.

The apartment is quiet when Isla enters, pausing to take her shoes off.

"Jaemin?" she calls out, only met with silence.

She opens their bedroom door only to be met with a scene so funny she laughs instantly, the sound catching her dancing boyfriend's attention.

"What are you doing?" Isla asks him as he rushes towards her, grasping her hands and twirling her around with him wildly to the silly music playing from his speakers, eyes crinkled up with glee.

"Just having fun, baby," he replies, spinning her away from him before pulling her close.

"It's good to see you enjoying yourself, Minie," Isla says, wrapping her arms around his neck, "The world is so much brighter when you smile."

The man blushes, nuzzling his nose against hers.

"The world is brighter with you in it, Isla."

Isla kisses him, pausing their movement entirely. Jaemin responds instantly, melting into her touch and pulling her closer. She pulls back, reaching into her hair and transferring the pink bloom into his hair.

"I love you so much," she says, looking him straight in the eyes, no hint of the lightness that had been present only moments ago,

"So, so much. And I–"

Isla cuts herself off, her words getting choked in her throat, begging to come out cleanly, to express how much he means to her, to tell him she never wants him to leave.

"Stay with me. Please," she says, her vulnerability causing Jaemin to tuck her under his chin, rubbing her back comfortingly.

"Always. I'll always be with you, Isla. No one will ever be able to make me feel like you do."

"Do you promise?" Isla asks, not able to look at him.

"What's wrong, baby?" Jaemin asks, concerned with her out of character behavior, "Are you okay? Did someone say something to you?"

"I just don't want to lose you, is all. I just have . . . this feeling," Isla says, trying to backpedal.

What was she thinking? Why'd she say that? Now she's got him all worried.

"What feeling?"

"It's nothing," Isla says, "I'm just a bit tired, I guess. I didn't sleep super great last night."

Jaemin is visibly skeptical.

"You look very pretty," Isla says, brushing the skin under the flower she put in his hair, "Let's get packed, okay? We have a lot of traveling to do."

33

The first concert takes place in Seoul. Days before the event, Starlights line up around the arena, camping out to try and secure the best possible spot next to the stage. Everywhere Isla looks, she sees someone wearing OT2B merch, some people going so far as to dress like the boys themselves.

Isla gets to wander around the arena, getting the first hand behind the scenes experience. She watches the lights and camera crew set up and move their equipment around to best capture the boys who loiter around on stage, dressed in their everyday clothes.

Jaemin toys with his mic, twirling it around in his fingers absentmindedly, waiting for adjustments to be made. Woojin and

Seojoon are horsing around playfully, not paying much attention to any of the crew while Leo and Daehyun speak with one of the managers.

"Baby!" Jaemin calls, waving ecstatically when he spots Isla from the stage.

The girl migrates over to him, maneuvering around the safety gates and placing her arms and chin on top of the tall stage, looking up at him.

"Hm?"

Jaemin bends down, gently booping her nose.

"Give me your hands. I wanna show you something."

"Are you sure? I don't think I'm supposed to be on the stage, Minie."

"It'll be fine. Hands," he demands.

Isla willingly lifts her hands, Jaemin catching them and pulling her up like she weighs nothing. Isla's sneaker landing on the edge of the stage as she steps upwards. Jaemin smiles at her, turning her away from him so she looks out towards the tens of thousands of seats in the arena.

"Isn't it beautiful?" Jaemin asks, sounding amazed, "So many seats, and they'll all be filled with people in just a few hours. People who come from different backgrounds, who live different lives. But they have all come to see us. For a little while, they'll forget their troubles and just be happy. It's the most amazing thing."

Isla knows that feeling all too well. She's used OT2B as her own security blanket, her own vest against all the hard and painful moments of life.

"I bet it is," Isla says, trying to imagine it based on the photos she's seen, "I wouldn't know what it's like to be surrounded by that type of presence."

"Right," Jaemin says, frowning, "You haven't been to a concert before."

"Correct."

"Well, don't worry, baby," Jaemin says, stepping up to stand beside her, "You'll get the best seat in the whole house."

Oh, how right he is. Isla watches from behind the wings as the boys race across the stage, singing their hearts out to the adoration of loving fans. The lights shine nearly blindingly but Isla can't look away, the halo surrounding Jaemin as he sings being too mesmerizing to blink for even one moment. He's in his element.

For a second Jaemin's eyes wander over to Isla hiding behind the curtain, gaze softening as he whispers three words before turning back to the crowd, closing his eyes as he hits a note so sweetly, Isla feels tears gathering as she watches him.

He's an angel. Truly ethereal.

As one of the many concert VCRs plays on the gigantic screens outside, Jaemin and the other members rush backstage, stylists poised with their outfit changes. There's shouting and rapid talking, none of which Isla can understand, but it doesn't matter. Her boyfriend comes into view with the biggest smile she's ever seen him wear, gathering her into a tight hug before she can even open her mouth.

Isla doesn't even mind that he's absolutely drenched in sweat, skin shining almost as bright as his smile.

"Did I do alright?"

"More than alright," Isla says, pulling back so she can see his face, "You were amazing, Jaemin."

"It's because I knew you were watching," he says, "I was singing for you."

Someone yells something to him and Jaemin replies loudly, kissing Isla swiftly before running off to go get changed for the encore stage. Before Isla can return to her watching spot, he races back to her, catching her in one more kiss.

"For good luck."

He doesn't need it. Jaemin does phenomenally, enjoying spending time with his members and fans, sheer joy etched into every one of his features. There isn't even a trace of the shy, paranoid and terrified man she met what seems like forever ago. He's back to being that bright star, beautiful and perfect.

And even though Isla knows he'll return to her side as soon as the night is over, he feels further away than ever, more unreachable than the stars twinkling up above.

As fireworks boom far above, the boys finally return backstage for good, congratulating each other on a job well done. Exhaustion is overcome by exhilaration as they all chatter eagerly about their performance, more alive than Isla can recall ever seeing them.

She tries to stay out of the way as staff and crew bustle around, packing up and preparing for tomorrow's show, leaving her pushed in some corner. She passes the time by scrolling through Twitter, wanting to look at the clips posted about the concert. Impulsively,

Isla snaps a photo of her next to a speaker, deciding to post it after being silent on social media for months. She isn't sure if it's allowed, but she'll be damned if she has to listen to the Smash Ent execs' rules.

Isla doesn't bother to add a caption or to tag anyone in it. She just has the sudden urge to give herself something to look back on when it's all over.

"Baby! There you are!"

Jaemin's sudden shout catches Isla off guard. She looks up as the man bounds over to her.

"Oh, Minie!" Isla says, smiling, "Are you and the boys going out to eat? That's what you usually do, right?"

Jaemin shakes his head.

"No. I want to do something else. I want you to come somewhere with me."

Isla's brows draw together in confusion.

"Aren't you tired?"

"Yup. But there's something I want to do before we have to leave Korea."

Jaemin takes her hand in his, leading her through people and waving goodbye, promising everyone that they'll have another great show tomorrow.

"Where are you taking me?"

"It's a secret," Jaemin says.

Wordlessly, the couple walks through the near labyrinth of backstage before emerging behind the building, entering one of the many black vans the company owns. Jaemin's grasp on Isla's hand never falters, warmth from his palm seeping into her own and making her feel not so alone.

The girl isn't sure how long the drive is, but soon enough, they arrive in front of some building she has never seen before. She looks up at Jaemin, trying to decipher what his plan is. He doesn't acknowledge her, leading her into the empty building.

There isn't a soul in sight, their shoes squeaking against the marble flooring. Jaemin takes her up a flight of stairs to the second floor, where the scene in front of her makes her speechless.

"Surprise," he whispers into her ear.

The entirety of the floor is free of furniture, marble covered by softly flickering candles and assorted yellow flower petals. In the center of it all is a large pillow fort, sheets draping across the structure to transform it into a castle.

"What is . . ." Isla begins, not quite able to form her thoughts into words.

"I've noticed that you seem a little upset recently. So, I thought it would be nice to get away and spend some time together - just the two of us, before we have to travel the world.

"Jaemin," Isla says, turning to him with emotion welling up inside of her, "Thank you."

"Of course," he says, pulling her close and resting his chin on her shoulder, "I just want you to be happy."

It turns out that some time away is exactly what Isla needs. The two of them spend hours just talking in the pillow fort, snuggled up. For once, the girl isn't worried about losing Jaemin or about his health and safety. Isla just enjoys spending time with him, living in this special moment with each other, savoring the sound of his voice and the feel of his skin.

34

Jaemin bites his lip, foot tapping against the carpet floor. His eyes wander, skimming over the motivational posters and smiling people hung up on the walls. This place is too cheesy, too bright. It's nothing like Yeri's sterile, cold office where he could view his reflection in the floor. The therapist's office almost feels warm. The seats are worn in and a pleasant smell wafts through the air, a white noise machine purring softly across the room.

"Are you nervous?" Manager Calm asks.

"I . . . I don't know. More anxious, I guess," Jaemin says.

He's trying to be honest. He doesn't have to be a doctor to know the first step is being truthful with yourself and others.

"You'll be fine. Dr. Kim is a very kind man. You have no need to worry."

Jaemin smiles at him, thankful for the reassurance even though he doesn't quite believe it. For the millionth time today, Jaemin wishes Isla were here with him. He'd tried his hardest to get her to at least come with him to his session, but Isla had refused, telling him that it's something he needs to do by himself.

The idol craves the moment from just two days ago when the two of them were alone in the pillow fort, just talking and talking for hours upon hours. He's never felt so close to someone before, so able to be himself without any barriers or boundaries. It was comforting and that comfort is something he desperately needs at this moment.

The door on the wall next to Jaemin opens and a kind-looking middle-aged man appears, smiling warmly.

"Mr. Matoi?'"

Jaemin shoots to his feet.

"Ah, that's me," he says, trying hard not to stutter.

"Come right this way."

With one last look at his manager who gives him a thumbs-up, Jaemin follows the man through a large room before entering a smaller one with the door open.

"Take any seat you like," Dr. Kim says.

Jaemin perches on one of the very comfortable stuffed chairs, watching the therapist shut the door before he comes and sits down next to him.

"I'm Dr. Kim," the man introduces, "And I'll be working with you from now on."

"Hi," Jaemin says nervously.

"So, I've been told that you've been going through some trauma. Why don't you tell me what's happened?"

Jaemin licks his lips, his throat feeling dry.

"I . . . there's this voice . . . in my head. I don't hear it all the time, but whenever I feel awful or stressed out, it comes out to taunt me."

"Whose voice is it?" the man asks.

He's actively listening, not writing down every word like Yeri did.

"Mine," Jaemin says, voice just barely above a whisper, "It's my voice, but it doesn't listen to me. I can't control it."

"What does the voice say?"

Jaemin licks his lips, squeezing his hands together to try and anchor himself.

"That I'm not good enough . . . that everything is my fault . . . that I'll never amount to anything."

"Do you listen to the voice?"

"Yes . . . it's so loud. And I can see him."

"You can see him?"

"In mirrors. He stares back at me and mocks me with this . . . sneer," Jaemin says, beginning to grow angry, "Like he's better than me and knows everything that I don't."

"Do you see him often? Or hear him often?"

"Not as much anymore. Not since . . ."

"Since what?" the therapist urges.

"Not since Isla."

Instantly, Jaemin brightens up, the therapist taking note of his change in demeanor.

"Who is Isla?"

"My everything. She's the love of my life. My favorite person of all time. I don't hear the voice when I'm with her. I don't have those thoughts, either. She's like . . . a buffer for all the bad things in life. I don't know how'd I function without her."

Isla lays upside down on her and Jaemin's massive bed, playing a mobile game. It's a mindless way to pass the time, the girl progressing through levels with relative ease. She's all packed and their suitcases are already at the company, ready to be loaded onto OT2B's private jet early in the wee hours of the morning.

Now all that's left to do is wait for Jaemin to get back from his first therapy session. Isla pauses her game, laying her phone down on her upturned stomach as she thinks about how hesitant he'd been this morning.

Jaemin had been more jittery than she'd ever seen him, constantly buzzing with nervous energy. He changed his outfit three times before Isla informed him that he'd make himself late which only spurred more anxiety. He'd begged her to go with him to the session but Isla gently refused, knowing that he'll most likely do better without her being there.

The door beeps and Isla rolls over, hair falling in her face just in time to be bombarded by Jaemin.

"Baby!" he shouts, jumping onto the bed right beside her and wrapping his arms around her waist, rolling the two of them over so she's laying down on top of his stomach.

Isla blows her hair out her face in vain, trying to flip it out of the way by shaking her head. She would just rake it upwards, but Jaemin's got her arms pinned down.

"Someone's hyper," she says as her boyfriend moves her hair for her, allowing her to see his grinning face, "I take it therapy went alright."

"Yeah," Jaemin says, "I really like him. He listens very well and actually has helpful input."

"That's great, Minie."

"Hopefully he'll help me get better."

"I hope so too," Isla says sincerely.

Jaemin nuzzles her affectionately, the girl shrieking as he tickles the sensitive skin on her neck.

"Minie! Stop! That tickles!"

He ignores her, continuing to tickle her relentlessly before giving her a break, catching her lips in a kiss that takes her breath away.

"Thank you," he says.

"For what?" Isla asks.

"For pushing me to do this. I already feel this . . . burden lifted off of my shoulders after just one session. Just knowing that I've taken a step to stop feeling this way makes me feel so much better. And I would never have done it without you."

His tone and the wide-eyed look he gives her causes Isla to move her hand up to brush away his hair, looking at his long lashes.

"Of course, Jaemin. I'll always be there to support you and try and help you in whatever way possible. You mean the world to me."

Jaemin grasps Isla's hand, intertwining their fingers and squeezing.

"What did I ever do to deserve someone as amazing and wonderful as you?" Jaemin whispers, studying Isla's face.

"I ask myself the same thing every day."

The next morning, the pair sleepily makes their way into a black van that brings them to the airport, hurrying through the airport as cameras flash so brightly, Isla wishes she'd brought shades. Jaemin doesn't let go of her hand for even a moment, making her feel secure.

The inside of the private jet is gorgeous. Large plush seats line either side of the plane, a giant table decked out with fruits and snacks galore situated between four chairs.

"Oh wow," Isla says, the only one phased by the grandeur of their transportation.

The other boys flop down on seats, settling in and pulling out headphones and other devices to keep themselves occupied for the very long flight they have ahead of them.

Isla snags an apple before sitting down next to one of the windows, pulling it open a bit to peek out at the dark sky. Jaemin sits in the aisle seat beside her, pulling his face mask down to reveal his lips.

"Are you excited?"

Isla nods, hair bouncing around her shoulders.

"Yeah. This is such a nice plane."

Jaemin laughs, raking his hands through his hair. The stylists once again changed the boys' hair colors, Jaemin now rocking white-blonde locks.

"You're absolutely adorable, you know that?"

Isla rolls her eyes.

The plane takes off smoothly, Isla reading a book on her phone. As she finishes a chapter, she looks over at Jaemin, intending to rant to him about one of the character's stupid life choices but stops short, a slow smile spreading across her face instead.

He's passed out, mouth open slightly as he sleeps, head rolled over to her side. Isla records a short video, her hand brushing across his face gently. Unexpectedly, Jaemin presses his cheek into her palm, eyes fluttering open lightly before smiling gently and falling back asleep.

Isla's heart melts with his innocent action, removing the armrests between their seats and scooting closer so he can rest against her shoulder.

"I love you. Always."

35

Paris.

Isla takes in a big breath of air, watching as people bustle to and fro in the busy streets. No one pays her any attention, all busy with their own loves, own struggles.

It's refreshing.

The chill of a gust of wind causes the girl to pull her thin sweater closer to her body, trying to block out the cold. She steps forward into the mass of bodies, letting the stream of people pull her along as she glances from side to side, wanting to soak everything in. She doesn't bother to pull out her phone, knowing millions of pictures exist of this place already. Isla wants to soak it all in with her own eyes, to remember the feel of cobblestone under her sneakers and the sound of foreign languages licking deliciously in her ear.

A small shop off to the side catches her attention. With some slight difficulty and several hurried apologies for bumping into people and stepping on toes, Isla emerges from the pack in front of the store, peeping in through the large glass window at the items inside. She spies some overly frilly looking masks fit for a ball, puffed up jackets, sparkling necklaces and something that glitters in a way that takes her breath away.

A small metal bell tings when Isla walks inside, the smell of old books entering her nose. The place is obviously some sort of vintage shop, everything looking like it's been well-loved. Isla greets the shop owner - a petite man looking to be in his sixties or so - before wandering around the shelves and racks, fingers brushing across soft fabric. One jacket in particular catches her attention, so she pulls it off of the rack to holds it up to herself. It's an old leather biker jacket, brown and thick.

The price of it is surprisingly low considering that it's certainly made of real leather. Isla lays it over her forearm, wanting to continue exploring the shop. Most of the items are rather uninteresting or useless, but Isla stops in front of a jewelry case, eyes landing on a slightly tarnished locket. With careful hands, Isla lifts the necklace, turning it over in her hands, the smooth metal having quite a bit of weight to it.

On one side, the round locket is engraved with symbols and swirly patterns, the back of it being smooth and shiny, a year carved into it. 1928. Surprisingly, the locket opens easily, no image inside of it. But in the concave of the front panel, in writing so tiny Isla has to squint, reads words that take her breath away.

She leaves the store with both of the items, giddy. Pulling out her phone, she curses slightly, realizing that she was supposed to be back at the hotel half an hour ago. She has several missed calls and texts from both Jaemin and one of the managers, no doubt trying to ease the idol's mind. Isla presses one on speed dial, Jaemin picking up before she can even put her phone up to her ear.

"Isla!"

"I'm fine, Minie," Isla says, already knowing what he's going to say, "I just got a little sidetracked."

"Are you sure? You aren't lost, are you? Do you want me to come and get you?"

"Stay your pretty behind right where you are, Matoi Jaemin. I'll be there soon."

"You promise? You don't want me to send a guard?"

"Nope. I'll be right there."

"Promise?"

The girl rolls her eyes playfully.

"I promise, Jaeminie."

"Okay."

After a moment.

"I love you."

"I love you too, Jaemin. More than anything."

"Okay."

"You can hang up now, Minie."

"I know," he says, voice soft.

Isla chuckles to herself, heart fluttering. No matter how much progress Jaemin's made, he'll always be the same. He might not send the entire guard out to find her, but he'll stay on the phone until he can confirm that she's safe.

And sure enough, when Isla walks into the hotel, Jaemin is there in the lobby waiting for her, phone pressed against his ear. He smiles as soon as he sees her.

For the most part, Isla stays out of the way, really only seeing Jaemin and the rest of the boys late at night. On top of having to prepare for concerts every few days, their schedules are packed with TV and radio appearances, photoshoots and interviews. It hardly seems like there's any time to breathe, but the boys are thriving. There's this glow that seems to surround all of them as they work tirelessly to the point of near exhaustion. It's the way they smile, the way their shoulders are straighter and voices stranger.

Each and every one of the boys are having the time of their lives, doing what they love more than anything. It's what makes them leave their friends and family, their country behind. The euphoria that comes from emerging on stage in front of thousands of adoring fans, those who raise them up and love them more than anything.

And somehow, between it all, Jaemin still manages to go to therapy twice a week, either in person or over Skype, depending on the other man's schedule. Isla hasn't met the therapist who's helping Jaemin and that gives her a sense of anxiety even though she knows he's in good hands. Every time one of their sessions end, Jaemin seeks her out, the two of them spending time together wordlessly as Jaemin processes whatever happened during the hour he spoke with the doctor.

Sometimes Isla asks how it went, but mostly, she keeps her mouth shut, not wanting to hurt herself any more than necessary. But from the small bit Jaemin does tell her, it seems that they talk about everything. His parents, his grandmother, the other boys, her, hell, even the dreams he's having. But regardless, Jaemin's personality hasn't changed or been altered in any way. He's the same man she loves, the same try hard, lovable goofball he's always been.

"Do you wanna watch?"

Leo's voice snaps Isla out of her thoughts.

"What?"

"Do you want to watch tonight's performance? It's the last one in Europe, you know."

Isla nods.

"I know."

It's kind of hard to believe that the tour has been going on for weeks already. And in that time, Isla and Leo have come to form some sort of shaky alliance. Neither of them are going to open their mouths to tell Jaemin about what happened with her first passport, but that's about it. They certainly aren't friends, not even close. However, Isla can't bring herself to maintain hating him. It's draining and she'd rather leave all the nasty things that happened in the past and focus on the good that's going on in the present.

"But I think I'm going to sit this one out. I don't want to distract Jaemin," she continues.

"That's a fair point."

Every time Isla watches one of their shows, Jaemin is even more flirty and playful than usual. While that's not necessarily a bad thing, he also has a bit of a harder time focusing. Thankfully, he hasn't messed up because of her, but his performance is definitely different when she's in attendance.

Leo nods before walking away, speaking with one of the staff members running around backstage. Isla heads off, intending to find Jaemin and tell him that she'll be chilling out in the hotel tonight. It doesn't take long to find him, Jaemin practicing his dance absentmindedly and singing to himself, getting in the right state of mind to perform.

"Baby!" Jaemin says, eyes lighting up as soon as he sees her.

Isla will never get tired of the way Jaemin looks at her.

"Hi, Minie," she greets, kissing him quickly, "Getting ready?"

He nods, hair getting in his eyes. The mop on his head is getting rather long, but Isla doesn't mind. It rather suits him.

"You're staying, right?"

"Not today. I think I'll just relax at the hotel. Maybe watch a movie."

Jaemin pouts cutely.

"You sure?"

"Yup! And Woojinnie's been bugging you to do a livestream with him too. You should do that tonight."

"You won't miss me?"

"Of course I will. But I know you'll be there when I wake up."

He grins at her, pulling her into a hug.

"Damn right," he kisses her forehead, "Always."

And with that, Isla leaves, heading back to the hotel, ready to spend some time on her own, relaxing and pampering herself. She takes a long bath, using some of the delicious smelling oils that were provided, jets massaging her back.

When the water turns cold, Isla exits, wrapping herself in a plush robe and changing into some comfy PJs. She ignores the pretty lacy lingerie she packed, knowing it'll be beyond late when Jaemin returns. Instead, she turns on a movie, becoming invested in the film even though it doesn't have English subs.

From what she can gather, the story is about some princess stolen away in the middle of the night by a man who turns out to be a dragon. The sets and costumes are gorgeous, making the film look right out of a fairytale. She writes down the name of the movie, wanting to watch it again with proper subtitles.

Eventually, Jaemin sends Isla a text stating that the concert is over and that he's headed back to the hotel to stream with Woojin. By that time, Isla can barely keep her eyes open, drifting off to sleep with her phone playing their live.

"Baby! I'm back!"

Silence greets him.

Jaemin tiptoes in to see Isla passed out, unable to stop the grin on his face. She's so adorable. He's so lucky to have her.

The idol showers quickly then crawls into bed with her, falling fast asleep.

36

"I have something very important I want to ask you, Jaemin."

Unlike most of their sessions, Dr. Kim is actually in front of Jaemin, the man settled into a very plush-looking chair by a closed window. The Europe leg of the tour has ended, the boys getting a few days off before beginning their shows in North America.

"What is it?"

The discomfort has faded entirely, the idol feels very comfortable around his therapist.

"I've gathered a lot about you from our previous sessions, but something has always bothered me."

Dr. Kim leans forward, hands resting peacefully in his lap.

"Don't you notice it?" he asks, "The inconsistencies in your memories. Or what you perceive as memories?"

"What?" Jaemin asks, eyebrows drawing together in confusion.

"Listen to me very carefully, Jaemin. Focus on every word I'm saying. You tell me the same stories over and over again but they're different each time. When did you first realize you had feelings for Isla?"

Jaemin clenches his fists, an icky feeling washing over him.

"Two years ago. When I saw her at her first concert of ours."

"Last week you said it was three years ago when you coincidentally met in the park. And that her first concert had been with you in Seoul last month."

"I . . . no. That isn't . . . yes, that's right. It was three years ago at the park. I don't know what came over me," Jaemin stutters out.

Dr. Kim leans back.

"But two weeks ago, you said it was the very first time you saw her in person a year ago."

"I–"

"Listen to me, Jaemin. Think very carefully. Your memories with Isla . . . I don't think they're real."

"Of course they're real! What are you suggesting?" the man demands, rising to his feet, feeling very much like a caged animal.

"You're a very tortured soul, Matoi Jaemin. A lot of terrible things have happened to you. And when the human brain experiences trauma, it does its best to cope in any way possible. I don't have all the answers. The only person who can really know the truth is you."

Dr. Kim stands up before Jaemin can even begin to process his words.

"I'll be leaving now. I have a long flight back to Korea. You know where to find me if you need me."

Jaemin doesn't respond, the therapist exiting the room quietly.

They're not real. His memories aren't real.

"No," Jaemin says, standing up and clutching his shirt, trying to calm his suddenly racing heart, "Stop being ridiculous. He doesn't know what he's talking about. Dr. Kim is crazy. He's lost his mind."

"Has he?"

The voice slides up Jaemin's spine like cold fingers, making the man catch his breath.

"Is it truly Dr. Kim who's crazy?"

"No," Jaemin whispers, drawing into himself, "Not now. Not you."

Jaemin tries to shove the voice away, back into the confines it came from.

"She's not here. Your little crutch isn't here. It's just me and you, Jaemin."

"Shut up. Please," Jaemin begs, beginning to hyperventilate.

He crumples, falling down onto one of the chairs, hands finding their way into his hair.

"They aren't real. None of it is real. It isn't real. It isn't real," the voice repeats like a mantra.

"Quiet. Quiet," Jaemin chats, trying to put himself in his happy place.

"Look in the mirror. Look, Jaemin. Tell me what you see."

No matter how hard he tries to resist, Jaemin finds himself walking over to the large mirror mounted on the wall, hands covering his eyes, not wanting to look, afraid of what he'll find.

"Look," it whispers.

Shakily, Jaemin lowers his hands, peering into the cool surface. Instead of seeing the terrible sneer of the voice inside of him, Jaemin only sees his own terrified face.

"None of it is real, Jaemin. Not your memories, not me. It's all some pathetic attempt to make yourself feel better because you're too much of a bitch to handle real life."

"I–"

"Wake up! Stop living in your own head!"

Jaemin stumbles backwards, tripping and landing harshly on the floor, pain radiating through his limbs.

All at once, thoughts and memories swarm his head, his mind struggling to make sense of it all. There are moments that flash by that Jaemin tries to latch onto, only to discover that he can't hold onto them at all, that they're fuzzy before turning into ash. Jaemin's breathing increases rapidly as, suddenly, all he knows and felt comfort in crashes down, his barriers falling away to reveal his true, vulnerable state. His voice catches, a plea for help getting caught in his throat as an image comes to the forefront of his mind. Isla's face, completely and totally petrified, looking at him like a stranger, confusion and fear in her eyes. The pain that flashed across her face the first time they had sex. Her confused answers when they had lunch with his bandmates.

The idol doubles over, barely able to make it to a trashcan before puking his guts out, retching so violently, his head spins, fingers damp and trying to hold onto the plastic bin like a lifeline.

He can barely breathe, throat burning as he vomits again, sweat sticking his hair to his forehead.

Isla. The things he's done to her.

Jaemin wipes his mouth, holding onto his arms and sitting in a ball next to the trash can, trying to comfort himself.

Isla. How can he face her after realizing that everything he's ever thought, every memory about her that he's held so closely to his heart for the last six years is a complete fragment of his imagination? His heart aches, imagining her face, the feel of her skin, the words she utters every single day.

"I love you,"

His eyes sting.

"I love you."

That's all fake too. It has to be. He's essentially kept her as a prisoner for months upon months, forcing her - a perfect stranger - to deal with him, to council him, to love him, to protect him in a way she never should have had to deal with.

He bites his lip so hard that it bleeds, the tang of blood coating his tongue.

What has he done? What has he done?

The laughter they shared, all the secrets, the stars in her eyes whenever she looks at him.

Fake. All fake. All done to try and keep him from jumping off of a building.

Jaemin rests his head on the rim on the trashcan, letting the hot tears cascade down his cheeks, sobbing silently. He's never felt so much pain in his life, so much raw unadulterated agony. In the moment, Jaemin wishes it would stop, everything would just stop. His thoughts, his tears, his heart. Nothingness, emptiness, those are what he craves, the sweet release from all the suffering he has placed upon himself.

But he doesn't deserve it. Death would be too merciful. It would be much too easy of an out for him. Jaemin doesn't deserve it.

What he feels right now must be nothing compared to what Isla has felt for all of these months being beside him. How much worse has it been for her to endure all the stress and responsibility Jaemin has lumped onto her shoulders?

His phone ringing barely manages to catch the shattering man's attention. His phone screen seems to burn his eyes, the photo of Isla serving as a reminder of what he's done these last few months.

Jaemin allows the phone to keep ringing before it stops, a text message popping up.

Where are you, Minie? Shouldn't you be back already?

Isla.

For a moment, he smiles before it turns bitter.

I'm coming, baby. See you soon.

For a moment, he'll pretend that everything is okay. At least until he's strong enough to let her go.

"Wahhhhh," Isla groans, belly-flopping face down onto the wide expanse of the hotel bed and spreading her limbs out like a starfish, causing Jaemin to chuckle softly.

It's been another long flight as once again they had to travel across an ocean. Isla never knew jet lag could be so brutal.

Jaemin settles in beside her (as best he can, given that Isla's taking up eighty percent of the bed) and props his legs up, also drained from the flight. Isla's heart melts when he begins to play with her hair, head rolling over so she can look at him.

He has a faraway look in his eyes, the same that he's been maintaining for the last few days. Isla desperately wants to push him to tell her, but she knows from experience that he'll just brush off her concerns and act like everything is okay. Whatever it is that's bothering him, Isla hopes it passes soon. She misses his carefree attitude.

"It's good to be back home," Isla says, trying to break the silence, "It feels like forever since I've been in my own country."

"Have you missed it a lot?"

Jaemin sounds sad, borderline upset. His tone causes Isla to frown, sitting up abruptly, Jaemin's hand sliding weakly out of her hair.

"Of course. It's my home. But I haven't missed it so much to be sad about it. Besides, I've been with you all this time. You're my new home, Jaeminie."

Instead of smiling like he usually would, Jaemin frowns slightly, a hint of sadness flickering through his eyes.

"Okay, spill," Isla says, unable to stop herself from prying, "What's been wrong lately?"

"I . . . I feel like I've done something awful," he confesses, looking away from her bright eyes.

"Awful? Like what?" Isla asks, desperate to get the weight off of his shoulders.

"It's just a . . . weird feeling. I can't really explain it. I'm sure it'll pass."

Isla looks at Jaemin with wide eyes.

"You know you can tell me anything, right?"

Jaemin softens, guilt festering inside of him, threatening to eat him alive.

"I know," he says so softly, Isla would have missed it if she hadn't been focusing on him so intensely, "Let's just nap. I'm exhausted from the flight and it's making me loopy."

Isla nods, slipping off her shoes and unbuckling her bra, not wanting to sleep in the uncomfortable clothing. She also slides down her pants, leaving her in only enough to stay covered. The girl crawls between the cool sheets, snuggling in and looking at Jaemin who hasn't moved an inch.

"Aren't you gonna get more comfortable?"

"What?" Jaemin says, sounding slightly startled, "Yeah."

Quickly, he strips down, sliding next to her. But unlike his usual self, Jaemin stays towards his side of the bed, not reaching out to touch Isla.

She feels hurt but doesn't do anything, knowing that his mind is probably running a million miles a minute. But as her breaths start to slow and mind empties, warm arms slide around her waist.

Jaemin is silent as Isla drifts off into sleep, struggling to keep his breathing even, forcing himself to tamp down the impending doom that wafts above his head.

He's stalled as long as he can, desperately trying to hold onto her. But with every day that passes, this sinking, inky feeling grasps Jaemin stronger and stronger, guilt crashing over him in violent waves. He doesn't want to let her go. Doesn't want to brave the world without her light. She's been his biggest support, his closest friend. Her very presence has stopped the darkness from taking control of him and tossing him into the abyss.

And he loves her. Truly, with every fiber of his being. Jaemin adores Isla. The months that he's spent with her have been the happiest in as long as he can remember, a joy saved for the memories he's shoved far, far away.

The idol curls into a ball at her back, feeling moments away from cracking. He knows he promised himself that he wouldn't leave her until he's strong enough, but earlier, he came to the realization that he won't ever be.

There will never be a moment when he doesn't need her. Not because she makes him forget but because he wants to spend the rest of his life with her.

He inhales deeply as he remembers the day in Busan when the two of them sat on the beach and spoke of the future. Her words sounded so sweet. Heavenly. He can still feel the salt in his lungs and her voice in his ears. But they were only uttered to placate him, to protect him from falling any deeper.

They held no meaning no matter how desperately he wants them to.

Carefully, so as not to wake her, Jaemin slides his fingers across her soft stomach, wanting to remember how wonderful her skin feels. His eyes rake over every inch of her face, trying to embed every feature, every mark and curve of her face for the days when he'll no longer be able to do so. He forces himself to memorize the way her hair falls across her face just so, the sound of her heartbeat.

All of these are things he knows are futile to attempt to remember, but he has to try. It's the only comfort he can give himself.

When Isla wakes, the other side of the bed is empty. Groggily, she sits up, the sound of the shower running alleviating any questions about Jaemin's whereabouts. She stretches like a cat and slides out of the sheets, walking towards the bathroom.

"Minie?" Isla calls, knocking on the door

No response. She tries the handle. It's unlocked.

Jaemin's naked body is wrapped in steam, his hand pressed against the shower wall, head bowed as the stream pounds into his back. His hair is drenched, little drizzles of water cascading down his cheeks to drip off his nose. He doesn't move when the door whooshes open and steam escapes the shower, nor does he flinch when hands land on his back.

"Did you sleep alright, Minie?"

The man hums in response, dragging his head up, water dripping from his downturned lashes.

"Are you sure?"

He certainly doesn't look like he slept worth anything, if he fell asleep at all.

Jaemin pauses, turning around, looking at her with hesitant eyes. But the look disappears before Isla can speak up.

"Can I wash your hair?" he asks her softly.

"Hm? I ... sure, if you want to, I guess," Isla agrees.

Jaemin whirls Isla under the showerhead, soaking her locks and avoiding her gaze. As gently as he can, he rakes his fingers through her wet hair, detangling it to the best of his ability. He squirts the entire bottle of hotel conditioner in his palms and pulls it through her hair, working to saturate every strand. Every movement is calculated and careful, Jaemin's heart racing in his chest. His nails scrape against Isla's scalp in small circles.

"Minie–" Isla begins.

"Don't talk, baby. Please. Just ..." he interrupts, torturing himself.

Isla falls silent, closing her eyes and getting lost in the sensation. Her lashes flutter when a warm kiss lands on her jaw, Jaemin dragging his lips softly across the expanse of her neck. Isla's hands move to his chest, feeling the muscles move under his perfectly flawless skin.

But before anything can move any further, Jaemin pulls away, rinsing Isla's hair and turning the water off.

"I have to go. There's a meeting I need to get to."

"Okay," Isla says, being left alone in the bathroom.

The girl bites her lip, reaching up to touch her softened hair.

Something about the way he's acting makes her anxious. She can't exactly put it into words, but she knows that something isn't right. When she finally dries off, Jaemin is already gone, nothing but a note left in his wake.

Don't wait up.

37

Isla sighs heavily, watching fancams of the boys' performance last night. She had attempted to stay and watch but had rudely been informed that she'll only get in the way. The girl supposes the staff member was right. All she ever really did was mull around while workers rushed back and forth to make sure everything went perfectly. She'd probably be annoyed too, if she were them.

Isla tosses her phone to the side, not watching as the device bounces slightly on the dense mattress. She's sick of all of these hotel rooms with their spectacular views and foreign beds. She wants nothing more than to fall asleep in her own bed with Jaemin beside her, the smell of the familiar sheets and the sound of their apartment buzzing softly lulling her to sleep.

But it'll be a long time before that happens. There's still months left on this tour, months before she can stop living out of a suitcase. A very large and glamorous suitcase, but still.

She can't help the pout that pulls at her lips. She knows she's being childish but all she wants is to snuggle with her boyfriend and for him to tell her he can't wait for it to be over as well.

Isla checks her watch. Sure, she could do sightseeing - there's plenty of time left in the day - but she just doesn't *feel* like it. She doesn't feel like doing anything other than pouting. She sighs again, rolling over the unmade bed until she's cocooned herself in sheets like a five-year-old.

"What are you doing?"

The sudden voice startles her, causing her to roll off the bed unceremoniously, landing with a hard thump on the ground.

"Ow," she groans.

Hands pull at the sheets until a bemused Jaemin comes into sight, a large grin on his face.

"What are you doing, love bug?"

"Minie!"

Isla attempts to scramble to her feet but ends up tripping, Jaemin grabbing onto her with ease.

"You're back. I thought you had a meeting today."

"I did," he says, smoothing her hair, "But it got cancelled."

"You didn't want to hang out with the boys?"

The question causes guilt to flare up in Jaemin's chest but he stamps it down.

"I wanted to spend a day with you. I haven't gotten to spend a lot of time with you lately . . ." he trails off, knowing that it's entirely his fault.

Jaemin's been avoiding her to try and lessen his own pain but he'll allow himself just one day. Just one more day . . .

"Really? Well, there's this Russian movie I saw a little while ago . . ."

And with that, the couple falls back into their routine like nothing ever happened. It makes every moment a bittersweet one in Jaemin's eyes. For the most part, everything is normal, but Jaemin's hands never leave Isla. He's always touching her, playing with her hair, ghosting kisses across her jaw. His touches are innocent, fleeting but purposeful and they relax her.

Contently, Isla lays her head on Jaemin's shoulder, watching the film she's come to love. Jaemin doesn't pay the movie any attention, instead, focusing on her, watching the way her eyes light up when certain scenes play and the way she crinkles her face when others happen.

It's these moments he'll miss the most.

When the end credits begin to play, Jaemin kisses Isla's temple.

"Why don't I run us a bath?" he suggests, fingers soft against her shoulders.

"Are you sure? It's still kind of early."

Jaemin just hums against her skin.

"I have something planned," he says softly, breath causing her to get goosebumps.

"Okay," Isla breathes out, watching him as he stands up and walks into the ensuite.

She brings her arms up to rub the skin where he was, shivering slightly. Just the implication has her reeling. It's been nearly three weeks since they've had sex, and even then, it was only something quick, Isla working to bring the stressed man to orgasm without getting anything back in return. It would be a lie to say that she didn't mind, but she's been completely understanding of Jaemin's incredibly tight schedule and how exhausted he's been. Even if there have been moments where something could have happened, Isla favored him resting, his health being the most important thing to her.

Isla can hear the water turn on as Jaemin fills the tub, settling herself at the edge and playing with the hem of her shirt.

Before long, Jaemin returns.

"It's ready."

Isla stands up, taking his outstretched hand and letting him lead her into the massive bathroom. A fresh tub of gently steaming water is before her. Jaemin lets go of her hand to stand behind her, his fingers making their way to her bare stomach, sliding around on her skin before grasping her shirt and lifting it over her head, tossing it to the side. Swiftly, he draws her onto him, arms hanging loosely around her waist, head propped on her shoulder.

"I love you so much, you know that?" he asks, emotion in his tone, "I wish I had better words to explain it. I feel like the word 'love' doesn't explain it well enough."

"I love you too, Minie."

He never knew how much those words would hurt him.

With her back pressed against his chest, Jaemin's hand wanders lower, popping the button of Isla's pants before tugging them down gently, letting the material pool on the floor. Isla lifts her foot, flinging the pants right next to her abandoned shirt.

The idol makes quick work of her undergarments, holding her hand as she eases into the steaming water. Isla quickly grows accustomed to the temperature, the oiled water softening her skin.

Jaemin takes his time undressing, not breaking eye contact with Isla for even a moment. He watches as her eyes dilate ever so slightly and her breathing quickens, blood rushing to her cheeks. He smiles gently, taking his spot beside her in the massive tub.

Neither of them say anything, the couple simply relax together. It's so peaceful, Isla nearly dozes off, only awakened by Jaemin beginning to glide the washcloth across her skin.

"Thank you," she says, eyes opening to watch him.

He hums before continuing his job until she's all the way cleansed. He goes to also bathe himself but Isla protests, taking the rag and getting on her knees, rising up out of the water and placing one wet hand on Jaemin's bare chest, running the rag gently across his face, cupping his cheek and giggling quietly.

"I've always loved your skin. It's so soft and clear. And it gets so blushy. You're absolutely gorgeous, Jaemin."

"I pale in comparison to you, angel," he says, meaning every word.

Isla smiles brightly when she kisses him, her lips molding onto his. When she goes to pull away, Jaemin grasps the backs of her thighs, pulling her down to his lap to deepen the kiss, making Isla's head swim. When they finally part, Isla gasps, taking deep breaths of air and looking at Jaemin's dazed expression.

While he hadn't been hard beforehand, Isla's breasts pressed into his chest and her sitting on his lap has changed that.

Her hands begin to trail lower but Jaemin stops her, shaking his head.

"Stay here for a bit."

Isla watches in confusion as Jaemin stands up swiftly, water trailing down his stomach and across his thighs. He shrugs on one of the plush robes. She sighs as he leaves the bathroom, settling back into the deliciously warm bath. Fifteen minutes or so pass before Jaemin calls out to her.

"Baby! Can you come here?"

She empties the tub, donning the remaining robe and stepping back into the bedroom only to be completely floored by what she sees.

"Jaemin . . ."

Flowers, stems and all, are scattered all over the floor, their scent spreading across the room. Fairy lights twinkle everywhere, a large blanket spread over the floor with dozens of different desserts placed on fancy trays.

And in the middle of it all is Jaemin himself, smiling shyly.

"Do you like it?"

"I . . . oh my God, it's perfect," she says, thrilled by his surprise.

"I realized I've never done anything quite like this. Made a night of it. Treated you like you deserve to be treated," he walks over to her, raising her hand to press a kiss on her wrist, "I want to spoil you."

Isla is absolutely glowing. Her face makes Jaemin's heart pound so loudly he can hear it.

"Come this way."

Jaemin leads her through the maze of flowers, sitting beside her on silk pillows before the desserts.

"I got a variety of things for you to try. Here."

He raises a chocolate-covered cube of cake to her lips, Isla's teeth scraping on the cool fork. The cake practically melts in her mouth, her eyes closing, a slight moan escaping her throat.

"That's so good,"

Isla only manages to make it through a few more desserts before Jaemin pops one in his mouth.

"Hey!" Isla protests, "There was only one of those."

"Come taste it then," Jaemin says, his voice husky.

It sends a tingle right down her, and she moves to straddle him, closing the distance with a kiss. Her tongue glides across the seam of his lips, gaining instant passage. The chocolate on his tongue is sweet, his battling hers in a wet tango.

Jaemin doesn't protest when Isla begins to trail kisses down his neck, pushing his robe out of the way.

"We'll finish the dessert later. I want you now."

In one swift motion, Jaemin stands up, his forearms tucked

under her bottom. He carries her over to the bed, placing her on the mattress. Grinning, Isla tugs him down with her, trapping his torso between her things. Their kissing gets deeper with every moment that passes, Jaemin's hand trailing down to skim over her thighs before tenderly swirling around her center. She's already wet, lubricating his fingers.

"Are you excited?" he asks teasingly, bringing his fingers up and popping them in his mouth.

Her breath catches.

"Don't tease me."

He grabs her hips, rolling the two of them over and sitting up, tugging her robe until it reveals her breasts. He kisses her again, dragging his tongue down her neck and rolling her nipples in his fingers.

"Where's the fun in that? I'd rather push you to the edge first."

"Jaemin," she moans out, grabbing his arms.

She rolls her hips, causing the smug look on his face to be replaced. The sound he makes causes her to do it again, laughing slightly.

"I get what you mean. This is fun."

He kisses her again, hands moving away from her hardened nipples to cup her face.

"I've created a monster."

"Oh yeah?" Isla asks, moving his own robe out of the way to reveal his hardened shaft, getting rid of any barrier between them, "What are you gonna do about it?"

"Love you," he says, "Make love to you until you're the sweet little angel I know you are."

Isla is momentarily surprised. He's never called it that before.

Jaemin uses her pause to snake his finger back to her center, rubbing her sensitive nub, wanting her to be properly prepped. He slips a finger inside of her, curling it upwards and watching as Isla's head falls back in bliss. Jaemin kisses her exposed throat, adding another finger and then one more.

"No more. I want you, not your hand," Isla says.

Laying down, Jaemin entangles his fingers with hers, holding her hand. She exhales when he sinks into her, his plump head stretching her out just right. It takes an unbelievable amount of restraint for Jaemin to stop himself from bottoming out, wanting to give her enough time to adjust. Thankfully, it only takes a short time before Isla nods at him, signaling him to continue.

Inch by inch, Jaemin pushes inside of his love, her warmth and tight grip causing him to hold onto her hips tightly. It's a feeling he'll never tire of, a feeling he'll miss after tonight.

Slowly, tantalizingly slowly, Jaemin rolls his hips, hissing at the sensation. His grasp on her hand tightens.

"I love you. So, so much. Never forget that."

"I won't," she says, wrapping her legs tightly around his waist, trying to pull him deeper, closer.

"Promise me. Promise me you'll never forget."

There's a tear gathering in his eyes but she can't see it, her head turned in the opposite direction. By the time she makes eye contact with him, it's gone.

"I promise."

38

Jaemin paces the hallway in front of the hotel room, trying to work up the courage to open it. He's been outside pacing for twenty minutes already, mind running wild as he tries to calm himself enough to begin what he knows he must do. But no matter how much he reassures himself that his actions will be necessary for Isla, for her health and happiness, he just can't bring himself to grab the handle.

His heart pounds so loudly, it drowns out the sound of his uneven breathing, hands growing clammy.

Jaemin closes his eyes, Isla's face coming to mind. He has to do it for her. He's been selfish the entire time they've been together. He has to put himself last for once.

With that shaky resolve, Jaemin opens the door, face settling into a blank mask reserved for the times he has to deal with those he hates the most.

He doesn't say anything as he walks into the suite, dropping his bag on the ground and rolling his head to the side. His eyes scan the room for Isla, heart melting when he sees her fast asleep on the couch. Jaemin pushes the feeling deep down inside of himself, striding up to her with careful nonchalance. Roughly, he pokes her, shoving her hard enough that she wakes up instantly.

He fights the urge to apologize, to check the skin where he was none too gentle. Instead, he remains silent, watching her with a bored expression as she sits up and rubs the sleep out of her eyes.

"Minie? You're back from your session early. How'd it go?"

Jaemin skipped therapy this week, not wanting to see the face of the man who brought his perfect fantasy crashing down. He can't help but be bitter about it.

He shoves his hands in his pockets to prevent himself from reaching for her. With a slight sneer, he cocks his head to the side, looking all too relaxed.

"Look here."

Isla's brows draw together in confusion over his tone. He's never once spoken to her in such an uninterested way.

"Isla. I've got to apologize for dragging you into this mess. I know that you're just some fan who happened to be in the wrong place at the wrong time."

"I ...what? You're not making sense," Isla says, concern deepening with every word he says.

"I saw the therapist today. We had a major breakthrough. I realized that all of this," he waves his hands in the air between the two of them, "Is fake. Nothing more than something I conjured up to cope with my anxiety and depression."

Isla stands up rapidly, reaching out to Jaemin, flinching when he cooly steps away.

"Jaemin–"

"Thank you, really. For being there for me when I needed you even though you had every right to leave," Jaemin shoves away the growing lump in his throat, "I appreciate it. But it's over."

"Jaemin!" Isla shouts, grasping onto him tightly, ignoring the shake in her fingers, "What are you saying? It's over? We're over?"

Disbelief clogs her words as she struggles to process what's going on. Only yesterday he'd thrown her a lavish surprise, only yesterday the words 'I love you' fell from his lips like a prayer, only yesterday they made promises of forever.

"There's no nice way to say this. Management suggested I just leave it to them but I thought I owed you at least this much,"

"I . . . what about everything you said? Everything we did? Are you–"

"Fake. All of it was fake, Isla. What about this don't you understand? I'm sorry I'm being an asshole but I have a lot on my plate. I don't have time to sit down and explain that I lied every time I said I love you. I have to work, I can't tell you every little lie I said."

Isla is stunned. She stops moving all at once, struggling, desperately trying to make sense of what he said.

"But I . . . I love you," she says suddenly, glistening eyes searching his, "More than anyone. I, please, Jaemin. Don't do this to me."

Slowly, so slowly it feels like time has stopped, Jaemin grasps Isla's hand, removing it from his shirt.

"I don't need you. I don't love you. Don't you get it, Isla? I'm sorry this happened to you, I really am, but I can't change the past. All I can do is move on . . . without you."

Isla's heart breaks slowly with every word Jaemin says, fragile fragments falling off and stabbing her in the lungs so she suffocates on reality. Her lip wobbles, and with one blink, a single tear slides down her cheek.

It's a fight for Jaemin not to gather her in his arms, to say that it's all a sick, cruel joke, that everything is fine and always will be.

"Please don't do this to me. Please," a sob rises in her throat as more tears fall, the girl's face growing hot, "I love you so much."

He has to break her. Destroy her so completely she'll never want to think about him ever again. Hurt her so deeply she curses his name, every scrap of love burned away.

"You love me?" Jaemin mocks cruelly, a twisted laugh following, "You don't even know me, Isla. I was so fucked up, no trace of myself was even left. How can you love someone who doesn't exist?"

Isla hiccups, folding into herself as if that can protect her from the white-hot pain surging through her.

"Jaemin–"

"What does that say about you, huh? You knew I was so fucked I'd do anything for you. What type of love is that? Don't delude yourself. Did you think for one minute I could love someone like you? Someone so pathetic she drops her whole life just to try and save someone she's never even met?"

He shoves her shoulder harshly, watching while she falls to the ground. At this point, Isla is unable to stop the loud sobs that escape her throat. Every inch of her is shaking violently, hands trying in vain to find purchase on the slippery tile ground.

"But if you loved me at all," he says, crouching next to her, "You'll do as I ask. It's over, Isla. Go home."

With that final remark, the idol stands, trying to hide the glaze in his own eyes. He grabs his bag and walks out, letting the door slam shut behind him, the sound causing Isla to startle.

All alone, Isla curls into a ball on the floor, crying so loudly the sobs bounce off of the wall, taunting her. Her head pounds angrily, feeling as if her skull's gonna split in two. Snot dribbles out of her nose no matter how hard she sniffles, mixing with her tears and turning her into a mess. After what seems like forever, she manages to pull herself to her feet, stumbling into the bathroom, hands landing with a painful smack against the freezing countertop.

The sight in the mirror makes her cringe. Her hair is completely destroyed, sticking up in every which way. Even worse is her blotchy, swollen face. She's pink and puffy, shiny trails crossing her skin. She can hardly stand to look at herself but she won't look away. She absorbs every ugly detail, never wanting to forget it, never forget this moment, this pain and utter wretchedness.

"You knew," her voice croaks out, "You knew this would happen. Why are you surprised? Why are you upset?"

Her reflection has no answer for her. The sad figure in the mirror looks just as lost and hurt as Isla feels.

"Why are you crying? You knew it would come to this. You knew it would end this way. But you didn't care. Fucking masochist."

Another tear slides down her reflection's face, and before she knows it, Isla is in a lump on the ground, holding her legs to her chest, losing herself to the agony of heartbreak.

On the other side of the hotel door, Jaemin is kneeled over, tears falling silently as he listens to his lover's sobs, wanting to claw his way back inside to comfort her. But knowing that what's been done cannot be undone, Jaemin places a hand on the wall, walking blindly with hurried steps that turn into a full sprint, the man running through the halls barely able to see through his sorrow. Eventually, he can go on no longer, collapsing onto the floor and weeping for his lost love and his sorrow, knowing that there will never be a day that has shone as brightly as those he spent with her.

His hands grab fistfuls of his hair, wanting to rip them out to feel something besides total devastation.

Why'd it have to be this way? Why couldn't Jaemin have met Isla like a normal man, pursued her and had a normal relationship? Why'd he have to be fucked up, utterly insane, completely useless?

Jaemin punches the wall, ignoring the stinging in his knuckles and the red dripping down his fingers.

He ruins everything.

In the wee hours of the morning, the five members of OT2B crowd into a transport van, preparing to head to the airport to fly to the next venue.

"Where's Isla?" Woojin asks, eyeing his exhausted-looking bandmate.

"She's not coming," Jaemin says, voice barely above a whisper, "She won't be coming ever again."

39

Isla sighs heavily, trying to psych herself up. She smiles at the slightly grimy gas station mirror, but it looks unnatural no matter how many times she attempts it. The girl even smears lipstick across her lips and floofs her hair up, trying to look more presentable.

It doesn't work. In a fit of anger, she rubs it away, smearing the red stain across her face before trying to erase it with the single ply tissue provided. The shadow of it can still be seen when she leaves the restroom, sweater pulled tightly around her frame.

Isla loiters through the aisles, picking up some powdered donuts and a Dr. Pepper, placing them on the counter for the very tired-looking clerk to check out. Her eyes wander the shelves behind him, looking at the locked cabinet of cigarettes.

"One of those too. The off-brand ones."

Sleepily the man does as asked, ringing up the pack of cigs as well, not even bothering to card her. As he bags everything up, Isla looks at the carousel display of magazines, twirling it around absently until a familiar face catches her attention. There on the cover is her smiling face right next to Jaemin's, the couple looking head over heels in love.

Bitterly, she turns it away, mumbling thanks as she takes the cheap plastic bag and exits the store, leaning against the run-down brick facade. It's nighttime, yellow lamp illuminating her face as flies buzz around the light. She resists the urge to check the phone that weighs heavily in her pocket, not wanting to look at her screensaver.

She knows she'll cry if she does.

Before long, a familiar sedan pulls up, the brakes squeaking loudly. The passenger side window rolls down and Isla's aunt waves excitedly.

"Hey there, girly!"

Isla walks over to the car, pulling the door open and hopping in.

"Hey, aunt Rue. Thanks for picking me up so late,"

"Sure thing, bub. I was just up watching Lifetime movies. But what are you doing here? Aren't you supposed to be in Korea with that superstar boyfriend of yours? Nancy from the knitting circle showed me a magazine and - hey, are you crying?"

Rue ceases her babbling when she sees the fat streaks falling from Isla's eyes. Even though the woman has never been particularly good at picking up social cues, she knows that now is not the time for questions. So, she stops talking altogether, letting all the windows down, the humid air washing over Isla's face.

The girl takes a swig of her soda, the carbonation tickling her throat. In a few minutes, the entire thing is gone and she chucks the bottle out the window. She closes her eyes and lays her heavy head on her crossed arms, wind fluttering her hair. Even though it's hot and humid, it's familiar and comforting, the lull of the car rocking Isla to sleep.

It's just past four A.M. when Rue shakes her niece awake, feeling guilty for disturbing her obviously much-needed nap.

"We're here, bub."

The bottoms of Isla's old converse hit the gravel and she walks up to the slightly rusty screen door, pulling it open.

"Where are your bags, bub?"

"Don't have any," Isla murmurs.

She couldn't bear to take any of the dozens of outfits she brought for the tour, not when all they did was remind her of what she just lost. When Jaemin told her to go home, she'd been a mess, not wanting to stay in that hotel room for even a moment more. But her fear of running into any of Smash Entertainment's staff was larger, causing the girl to huddle inside until the black SUVs left, carting the boys off to the airport for their flight.

And once they were gone, once it sunk in that Jaemin really had abandoned her like she always feared, Isla scrounged up enough to pay for a cab to take her as far away as she could afford, dropping her off at an unfamiliar gas station where she called her aunt to fetch her.

"You hungry? I have a couple of those freezer meals left from the last time you stayed over."

"No thanks, Rue. I think I'll just go to bed."

Her words are lifeless, her body exhausted from the mental strain. Rue nods.

"Good night then," she says, shutting the door to her bedroom, not knowing how to comfort the obviously lost girl.

Isla hadn't expected anything more of her aunt. Her father's sister was never good at feelings, causing all of her relationships to fall apart. Isla is the only one in her entire family who still has anything to do with the woman.

Isla stares at her aunt's closed door for a moment before walking over to the guest bedroom right beside it. Her feet feel as if they weigh one hundred pounds each, causing the girl to flop down onto the ancient, squeaky mattress. Laying on her stomach, Isla looks at the blank eggshell-colored walls, wishing there was something there to distract her from her rampant mind.

She takes the box of cigarettes out of her pocket, opening the carton. She turns a single stick around in her fingers for a minute, watching it twirl, remembering who used to do the same. She pushes off of the thin mattress and crawls over to her bedside table opening the wooden drawer and hunting around for a lighter. It doesn't take her long to find one, fluid sloshing around inside the red plastic. Isla rolls over to her back, sliding her thumb across the course metal, watching the flame spring to life.

She lights the cigarette, tossing the lighter to the side haphazardly.

The rancid smell appears instantly, bitter smoke floating upwards. She holds it above her face, watching it burn. The smoke is heavy in her lungs but she doesn't notice, too focused on the glowing end to care.

She always wondered how her mother could find comfort in something she knew was bad for her, something she knew could only end poorly. But still, her mother smoked a pack a day until she kicked the bucket when Isla was thirteen. Never once did the woman even attempt to quit, attempt to stop herself from reaching for the lighter.

Isla always hated her mother for that. Her self-indulgent ways, her lack of care about the future. Bitterly, she realizes that she might be a lot more similar to the woman she hated than she thought.

Curiously, she takes a drag, lurching upwards to cough hideously, dropping the cigarette on the old laminate floor and stomping it out.

Smoking holds none of the sweetness of Isla's own addiction. It makes her lungs burn while Jaemin made her heart soar. It causes her to cough in pain while Jaemin made her laugh until she couldn't breathe.

Isla stares at the crumpled cigarette on the floor, her eyes once again watering.

What is she doing? She doesn't know, she doesn't know anything. All she can focus on is the pain of being discarded, the total humiliation and heartbreak of being left alone to cry with no one there to comfort her.

She misses him. She misses Jaemin so much that it overshadows any anger she could muster up. All she wants is to wake up to him asleep beside her, to realize that the last twenty-four hours have been nothing but a horrible nightmare. She longs for his touch, his presence, his voice.

It's painful, so painful that she's not sure if she'll ever lose this ache in her chest, ever shake the feeling of complete and total despair.

And what of her life? If Isla had nothing going for her before Jaemin, what does she have now that he's gone? She tasted a life of excitement, a life where she was always on her toes. A life she shared with someone even when it got hard and she wasn't sure what would become of her next.

She doesn't give a damn about the money or the expensive clothes she wore. She misses the comfort of home, the feeling that she belonged and had a purpose. Now, the girl is left alone and with what? She doesn't have anywhere to go, anyone to lean on. Her so-called family hasn't even attempted to speak to her in months and her shitty waitressing job has certainly been filled.

Isla is faced with the realization that her life is now akin to that empty, ugly wall. Cracks and splinters and nothingness.

She has nothing left.

What does she do now?

40

The muted screaming of fans makes Jaemin's head pound as he sits backstage, too many people hovering around him, all speaking too loudly, touching him too much. One set of hands fans his sweat-soaked skin while another flutters his clothing, trying to get him to calm down.

But his mind isn't in the moment as it should be. The idol's brain is blank, just firing synapses enough to keep him functioning. He wordlessly takes a water bottle and chugs it, throwing his head back while someone pats his forehead with a damp towel.

"Jaeminie . . . ah . . . Jaemin . . ." hazily, Jaemin looks at the source of the voice, Leo's concerned face coming into view, "Are you alright?"

He can barely hear him over the screaming, the chanting, the voices calling his name.

"Bae Daehyun, Kim Seojoon, Matoi Jaemin–"

Somehow, he musters up the energy to nod, though the action was far from convincing. A voice barks at the bodies to move away from him, to give him space to breathe. Dots start to appear as his vision swims, the man pacing a trembling hand on the wall behind him to stabilize himself.

"You went too hard out there," a voice - Daehyun? - says with concern.

Jaemin can barely process the words, his breathing heavy.

"Hey! Hey! You alright?" Another voice, another someone.

Jaemin slumps against the wall, feeling moments away from collapsing.

"Just," he begins, voice hoarse, "Give me a minute. I'll be fine."

"Sixty seconds!" a stagehand calls, giving the members a heads-up.

The screaming, all he can hear is the screaming.

Hands tug his jacket off of him and replace it with another. He stumbles to his feet, the world tilting under him. He stumbles, grasping onto another body, another someone.

"Jaemin . . . ah!" it's Leo again, "Are you alright? Do you need to sit this one out?"

"Forty-five seconds!" the stagehand says before Jaemin can even open his mouth.

"I'm okay," Jaemin insists, standing upright with his determination alone, "I'll be fine."

"Get in position!"

Jaemin shrugs off the remaining hands and walks towards the platform, climbing on with the other members and ignoring their worried glances. He doesn't have time to reassure them, to lie to them. He takes a breath and the screaming increases tenfold as the members pop back up onto the stage, grinning at the faceless crowd.

"Starlights!"

Jaemin forces a smile on his face, gripping his mic tighter to hide the shakiness in his fingers. There's only a single moment before the music starts, his body moving to the beat, lips producing the words like he has a million times.

But even though Jaemin is there, he isn't present. Performing doesn't hold the same allure it did only weeks ago. All he can focus on is the ache in his body, the heaviness of his limbs as he forces them to move how they're supposed to. Normally, the aura of the crowd would replenish his energy even if he was exhausted, but it's having the opposite effect. Every voice, every word, every chant drains him more and more, time seeming to slow down every time he blinks.

He stumbles slightly but recovers, making brief eye contact with Seojoon, pretending he doesn't see the alarm in the man's expression.

Just a little more. Just a little more . . .

But then what? A little more suffering and then the concert will end, then they will rest but have to do it all over again and again and again. The repetitive, vicious cycle that pains him every time he thinks about it. More, there's always more. Someone always wants something more. Another performance, another song, another autograph.

He's tired. Tired, tired, tired. But what right does he have to rest? Even if he stops, his mind won't, the exhaustion won't. Jaemin could sleep for one hundred years and still feel as awful as he does now.

The song winds down, he moves into position, sweat streaming down his back and the world spinning so violently he has to stop himself from dry heaving. And finally, sweetly, the last note rings through the air and he breathes, only to hop back up to start all over.

As fireworks burst overhead, the members descend into darkness. Jaemin barely manages to make it off the platform before the dizziness overcomes him and he stumbles, blacking out before he hits the ground.

Giggling. Soft laughter wakes Jaemin up, the man opening his eyes slowly against the warm sunshine.

"You fell asleep, silly."

He knows that voice. Jaemin sits upright instantly, looking around for that voice, for *her*.

Laughter sounds through the air once more and Jaemin rises to his feet, following the sound desperately.

"Isla?! Isla!"

No matter how hard he runs, Jaemin can't move from that

perfect spot. The grass is soft under his bare feet, birds chirping and a beautiful picnic blanket placed beside some wildflowers.

"Where are you?!"

"Over here!" her voice calls from behind him.

He jerks around quickly, only to be met with emptiness. The laughter continues but grows slower, more sinister until the beautiful scene bleeds away from him, replaced with smoky darkness.

"Isla!" Jaemin calls again, trying to work himself through the fog, "Isla!!"

He's growing more hysterical with every passing moment that he can't find her. Stumbling forward, Jaemin trips over something and lands harshly on the ground, wincing. The horrifying laughter grows in volume until Jaemin is forced to cover his ears. He can't move, the tendrils of smoke turning into cold, slimy snakes that wrap around him so tightly that he can't move a muscle.

He struggles, but his efforts are in vain. The ground underneath him begins to give way and he's sinking, sinking, sinking down below. But finally, her face comes to view, hovering over him like a spirit, an angel descending from above. He tries to reach for her, to call her name, but inky darkness enters his mouth instead, muffling any noise he tries to make. He can't free his hand, can't reach for the light she's emitting.

Completely helpless and terrified, the ground closes over Jaemin's face, leaving him to suffocate under the dirt.

"Jaemin!"

A hand touches him and Jaemin jerks awake, cold sweat stuck to his skin. The blinding light burns his eyes. He blinks rapidly, the room he's in finally coming into focus.

"You were screaming!"

Jaemin's heart is pounding so hard, he places one hand on his chest and the other over his forehead trying to calm down. Once it feels like he's no longer going to implode, he rolls his head over, finally taking in his surroundings. White walls covered in health posters and emotionless artwork greet him, along with the concerned faces of his manager and Leo.

"What? What happened?" he asks, voice gravelly.

"You passed out after the last concert. The doctor said it's exhaustion."

Jaemin sighs heavily before sitting up, attempting to swing his feet off of the bed.

"What do you think you're doing?" his manager asks, pushing him back onto the hospital bed before he can stand.

"I'm awake now. We can go. We have more performances to do."

Jaemin tries once more to stand but is pushed down again, this time by Leo.

"You're not going anywhere. You need rest and to get your fluids back in."

"I'm fine," Jaemin says.

"People who are fine don't blackout from exhaustion," Leo says seriously.

"It won't happen again. I promise that I'm okay. Let's just go," Jaemin insists.

A third time he tries to rise but is pushed back down.

"Cut it out!" Jaemin snaps, his sudden anger startling the two others, "I said I'm alright. I wanna get out of here. I hate hospitals!"

Seeing the determined look on his face, the manager stands.

"I'll go find the doctor. We'll see what she says."

The door shuts firmly behind him, leaving the two bandmates alone.

"What's been wrong with you? Ever since Isla–"

"Don't say her name," Jaemin nearly growls, glaring at Leo with suck passion he's reminded of the threat he gave him in his bedroom all those months ago.

"Ever since . . . the two of you broke up, something hasn't been right."

Jaemin opens his mouth to protest.

"Don't even say it. You know something's wrong. You've been pushing yourself too hard. You're always working out, practicing, staring off into space. You don't smile anymore . . . I'm worried."

Emotion clouds Leo's features as he looks Jaemin over, noticing the weight he's lost and the bags under his eyes.

"Every day I hope that you'll get better, that one day you'll heal from whatever happened. But every day it gets worse, every day you recede into yourself more and more. I just . . . I want you to be okay. I want you to be yourself again, so please, please tell me what I can do.

I don't want you to waste away. I don't want to lose you. I love you, Jaemin, more than I love myself, so please!"

At his words, bitter tears spring to Jaemin's eyes, a sob forming in the back of his throat.

"I fucked up. I fucked up so badly."

41

Lyra. What did I tell you about sharing?"

Isla crouches beside the pouting four-year-old, a soft yet stern expression on her face.

"Lyra," Isla probes.

"You said it's important."

"Mmhm, and what else?"

"That sharing is caring," the child mumbles.

"And you care about Mindy, don't you? She's your friend, isn't she?"

The little girl nods.

"Then it's not good to hurt Mindy's feelings. Why don't you let her play with the car for a bit? The two of you can take turns."

She nods once more before running off to go share the toy, Isla standing and stretching her sore legs. She never knew how much toddlers could wear you out until she started working at the local daycare three months ago. She used to go home to her aunt Rue's house sore and exhausted from having to wrestle with squirming tots, head pounding from the shrill screaming and crying that would happen each day.

But slowly, she grew to really appreciate working there. Children have the potential to be so caring and compassionate that Isla often finds her heart warmed by just how sweet some of the kids can be to each other.

"Lyra can be sweet when she wants to," a voice says.

Isla turns around to see the daycare coordinator, a kindly old woman in her sixties.

"Oh, hi, Maggie! Yeah, she really can be. She just needs a little push, ya know," Isla says, smiling warmly.

"Oh certainly. Quite a few kids are like that. They just need a little love and attention and they're perfect angels," Maggie says, chuckling warmly, "But don't let her cuteness distract you, now. You've got that class in half an hour, don't ya?"

"Oh shoot! I do! Can you handle everything right now?" Isla says, already heading towards the door.

"Yes, ma'am. Sarah's heading this way now. I can head the fort while you're gone."

Isla waves goodbye, leaving the small daycare, smiling at the happy sunshines and animals painted in bright colors on the walls.

The building is old but well maintained and greatly loved. It's been around since Aunt Rue and her father were little. They even received care here.

Isla hops in her car, an old thing she got for eight hundred dollars last month. It's not pretty but it's mechanically sound, and most importantly, it's hers.

Hers.

Such a funny word to think about. Isla believed many things and people were hers in the past but they managed to slip away from her each time, breaking her heart and leaving her with nothing.

But now this little car is hers, truly hers and so will that cute little apartment down the street be in a few weeks. She just has to save up a bit more, enough for the security deposit and she'll be out of her aunt's hair, truly ready to start over again.

Isla cranks down the windows, unable to stop the brief thought that passes through her brain, unable to stop herself from thinking about him. Four months. Four months is no time and forever all at once.

The first month was the hardest, Isla barely even leaving her room at her aunt's. All she did was cry her heart out, to internalize the pain and suffer because she was convinced that she deserved it.

Isla deserved the pain. After all, Jaemin was right. What type of person falls in love with someone they know is sick? A terrible, deplorable excuse of a human being. For weeks, that's what she would think, bullying herself deep into the night until her head was swimming with vicious thoughts and bitter tears pricked at her eyes, tears she wouldn't allow herself to release, wanting to endure the pain because she deserved it.

But after her twelfth pack of cheap cigarettes (she'd even managed to smoke a whole one without dying), her aunt had had enough. In an out of character bout of parenting, Rue told her to get up and go make something of herself so she'd stop crying about not having anything.

"Go be somebody. Damn, I didn't know who I was when I was your age, nobody does! You've got to figure that out before you can really fall in love. I know you've been caught up on that boy but trust me, if a man makes you feel that horrible, he doesn't deserve you. Everyone makes mistakes but the ones worth keeping are the ones who atone."

That same day, Isla enrolled into the local community college if for no other reason than to try. Try and be someone, even if she doesn't know who.

The girl pulls up to the small campus, manually locking her car and patting its hood affectionately as she passes. A quick check on her phone (a used one she'd bought off of eBay, selling the one Jaemin gave her to help buy her car) tells her she still has ten minutes left before class starts, meaning she doesn't have to run to get to class. She'd been late once and her teacher locked her out of class, motivating her to never let that happen again.

The classroom is mostly empty but there is one familiar face there, Isla sliding in next to her friend.

"Hey, Becca!"

"Isla! Hey! How was work?" the girl greets.

Becca is eighteen, fresh out of high school and trying to pursue her dream job of being a professional musician. She's only in college to give her parents peace of mind.

"It was good. The kids were pretty well behaved today."

"That's good! I'm glad none of them were being brats," she says, giggling.

"What about you? What have you been up to today?"

"Ah, I went over to visit my cousin. My mom's been bugging me about it."

"Oh, yeah, you told me about that. Was she as awful as you thought she'd be?"

"At first I thought so! I went into her room and they were covered in posters of these Asian pretty boys and I was like 'Oh boy'. But she made me listen to some of their music and it's actually really good! Do you listen to foreign bands?"

Isla's stomach flips, not liking the direction the conversation is going.

"Uh, no, not really."

"Well, you should check them out! You might like them too, they're pretty good. The group is called OT2B. I'm just now getting into them, but they seem right up your alley."

The sick feeling increases as Isla smiles at her friend, not wanting to let her know something's wrong.

"Maybe I will," she says, barely even able to muster the words.

Even though she feels a ton better than she did right after

Jaemin left her like a pile of flaming hot garbage, she still avoids any mention of OT2B as much as she can. She's blocked their names and anything she can think of relating to them from her searches on all platforms to try and avoid accidentally giving herself heartbreak. She even deleted all of her social media again after she checked and found out that OT2B had blocked her on Twitter and deleted any tweets mentioning her.

That hurt more than she thought it would and still does if she thinks about it. With a few clicks, Jaemin can delete her out of his life and go on his merry way while it's an uphill battle for her to forget him. It makes her bitter.

But thankfully the teacher starts class before Becca can say anything else, pulling Isla into a mind-numbing economics lecture.

Once the class is over and Isla is sufficiently stressed about the upcoming test in a few weeks, it's dusk, yellow and pink streaking around the sky, birds soaring languidly. A breeze ruffles her hair as Isla heads home.

Her aunt is in the middle of a Lifetime movie when Isla arrives, prompting the young lady to kiss her on the forehead quickly before retreating into her room to study. She plugs in a pair of cheap earbuds and drowns out her thoughts with Bach and Beethoven as she scribbles notes and bookmarks confusing sections in her textbook.

Her stomach rumbles loudly, so she decides to take a break, looking at the clock to realize that it's already half-past eight. She shuffles into the tiny kitchen, opening the refrigerator door, pale light shining on her skin. She frowns when she realizes that it's practically empty.

"Aunt Rue!" she calls, "I'm going grocery shopping! I'll be right back!"

"Let me give you some money," the woman calls back.

"I got it! Don't worry about it!"

Before she can even move, her aunt is coming out of her room, a couple of bills in her hands.

"Aunt Rue . . ."

"No complaining now! It's groceries, I can buy that."

"You really don't have to. You don't even charge me rent or make me pay bills. The least I can do is buy groceries," Isla says, pushing her aunt's hand away gently.

"You've got to save up as much as you can. I know that your job doesn't pay too much and you've got to pay for school yourself. And you bought that car not too long ago. I got it."

Rue opens Isla's hand, placing two twenties and a ten on her palm.

"I wish I could do more for you than I do. I love you, you know that."

Isla smiles, touched. No one in her family is any sort of well-off, meaning too often people have to scrape by. Slight guilt flares up when she thinks about the nest egg Smash Entertainment dropped in her account a few months ago, but she refuses to use it, not wanting to have anything to do with the company.

"I know, Rue. And you do enough as it is. Thank you for taking care of me. I'll be right back, okay."

"Don't forget that Piggly Wiggly closes early now. You may have to go to Seven Eleven."

"Alright," she says, shrugging on a jacket.

It's not super cold yet, just a bit chilly when the wind blows too hard. But the stores are infamous for blasting the AC year-round.

Isla hops in her car, her aunt's money in her pocket. She drives by Piggly Wiggly, noticing the empty parking lot and deciding to just head on to Seven Eleven.

The cashier greets her, used to her face due to all the trips she made down to get cigs.

"How you doing?"

"Good, you?"

He nods and Isla resumes browsing, grabbing bread, eggs, milk and a few other necessities, including the off-brand soda her aunt really likes. She walks to the freezers and grabs a small thing of ice cream and shuts the door, only to be startled by what stands in front of her.

Her breath catches in her throat and she makes an effort not to drop her items. There, no more than four feet away from her, stands a ghost.

His skin is pale and sickly looking, big bags under his eyes and a general pallor spread all over his body. His clothes hang off him in a way that says they used to fit and his posture is slumped. His dark hair is a shock of dark ebony against his complexion, well-trimmed but disheveled. Blinking, Isla's eyes widen, disbelief clogging her throat.

"J-Jaemin?"

There's a phantom of a smile on his face.

"Baby," he says, taking a step towards her.

Isla moves back instantly, wanting to be as far away from him as possible. Her heart is beating so quickly, she feels faint. She blinks, trying to make him disappear. She can't process what's in front of her.

"Isla," he says quietly, a faint frown pulling his skin down, making him look even sicker.

"Don't," Isla says, turning away from him, wanting to escape this confrontation, not wanting to think about why he would be at some gas station in the middle of nowhere - trying not to let the obvious answer sway her.

"We need to talk," he insists, voice cracking slightly, pressing his fingers into her sweater.

Isla reacts violently, shoving him away so hard that he stumbles, pretending not to be concerned by how thin he feels. All of her items fall to the floor at his feet, bruised and broken just like her.

"The hell we do. What the fuck are you doing here, Matoi Jaemin? You made yourself perfectly clear. There's no reason you need to show up in my life ever again!"

Her words are a poison so bitter that Jaemin visibly flinches and then has the gall to look ashamed.

"I know. I know what I said. But–"

"I don't want to hear it. I don't care. Whatever it is, I don't care. I don't care about you and I certainly don't care about whatever the hell you're about to say!"

"Isla–"

"I don't take bullshit, Jaemin. Maybe I used to. But there's something about being left in a hotel room like some two-dollar whore that makes a girl grow a backbone."

"You are *not* a whore!"

Isla is momentarily stunned by the sudden fire in Jaemin's eyes, the fierceness in his tone. Only moments ago, he seemed as fragile as a rotten leaf in autumn and now he stands with the presence of a tiger.

"I–"

"Just let me talk to you. Please. It's been eating away at me for months. Every day I hate myself more and more for not just telling you the truth, for letting the best thing that's ever happened to me slip away, so please. Just an hour. That's all I ask. One hour and then you can walk away and never see me again. You can hate me every day for the rest of your life. Just please let me explain."

The sincerity in his words is not lost on her. Her breath catches at the look in his eyes, his hands which have suddenly moved to capture hers.

When did he get so cold?

Isla pulls her hands away, stuffing them in her pocket and ignoring the hurt both in Jaemin's expression and her own heart. She wants so badly just to throw herself at him, to love him again like in a fairytale. But this is real life and no matter how naïve Isla still may be, she knows that there's no excuse for what happened, no excuse for how he tore her down to a level so low she couldn't even see the surface.

"Fine. One hour," she relents.

He smiles again and Isla's heart flutters. She hates herself for it.

With a space between them too wide to be natural, they head towards the front, Isla stopping by to apologize for dropping the food.

"No problem, shit happens," the usual cashier says, "But hey, you okay? You don't look so good."

Isla smiles but it's shaky.

"Yeah. Hard day," she says.

Before she can turn to leave, the guy calls her over, handing her a pack of those off-brand cigarettes.

"You look like you need this. Consider it a gift,"

"Thanks, Chuck," she says, her smile a little more real.

Isla ignores Jaemin's questioning look.

"You smoke now?" he asks as they walk out into the night.

Isla doesn't reply, opening the carton and plopping down on a warped bench with a dip in the middle, the crumbly gravel covered in old gum marks and littered with cigarette butts.

"Start talking," she says, biting the tip, rolling it around her teeth gently, careful not to tear the paper and accidentally swallow tobacco leaves like she did once.

Jaemin sits beside her, stiff and uncomfortable. It satisfies Isla, knowing that he's just as on edge as she is. She's just better at hiding it.

"I don't know where to start," he says, looking down at his hands.

For once, they aren't covered in shiny rings.

"I'm so fucked up. But you know that," he begins, catching her eyes, wanting to connect with her, "You know that better than anyone."

Isla doesn't say anything but she suddenly wishes Chuck had gifted her a lighter as well, yearning for the familiar heat to calm her down.

"I've been fucked up for a long time. Ever since I can remember. I told you about my grandma, you know all the shit she did to me. It really messed with my head. And then, as a shitty coping mechanism I guess, I started talking to myself. Started giving my voice to all of the negativity in my life, let it beat me down."

He pauses, looking up at the sky, not seeing a single star.

"It was so hard when I debuted. Everyone has a fucking opinion, you know? They always have something to say about something that doesn't concern them. But instead of realizing how pathetic and meaningless people like that were, I internalized it. It haunted me. Every day, all I could think about was how ugly I was. How fat and untalented. How utterly undeserving I was for anything."

The old urge to reassure him that none of that is true flares up in Isla so violently, the cigarette slips from between her lips and falls uselessly onto her lap. But she bites her tongue before the words can escape, ignoring the stinging pain that radiates from her mouth.

"And of course, I already thought those things. I was just a teenager, after all. I was already insecure, and suddenly, I was thrust into the spotlight I so wanted to be under and it was too much. The hate was too much for me to handle. I broke down so often but I couldn't stop myself from reading tweets and comments, from hurting myself more and more and more. And . . . and I couldn't tell anyone. Mental health has such a stigma, you know? It's bad here but it's even worse in Korea. I thought if I told anyone - even the other members - they would tell me that it's something I just had to deal with. That I signed up for it when I wrote my name on the dotted line. And in a way, that's true. Being in the public eye means everyone thinks they own you and can dictate you, jerk you around like a puppet."

He kicks a loose chunk of asphalt, sending it tumbling a few feet away.

"And so, I pushed everything down until it made me so sick I wanted to die. It felt like there was no way out. My dream had become my undoing, so I tried. I locked myself in the bathroom one night under the guise of being sick and tried to kill myself."

"Jaemin!" Isla shouts out in surprise, refusing to be silent any longer.

"I know, I know," he says with a small, reassuring smile on his face, "It's never the answer. But I couldn't see any way out. And I was so tired. So, so tired of hating myself every day. I just wanted it to be over. So, I was looking through more comments, wanting to read something that would push me over the edge, make me O. D. on the pain pills I stole. But instead," he sounds astonished, "But instead, in that very moment, I saw your comment. You . . . I," he looks at her with tears in his eyes, happy, grateful tears, "In that moment, when I was at my lowest, I found you. And of course, my English was shit back then but I could understand what you said with the help of a translation app. I'll never forget those words: 'Matoi Jaemin is an angel sent straight from above. He'll be the greatest idol ever. I believe in you, Jaemin!"

Isla doesn't even recall that tweet.

"It meant the world to me. I sat there crying on the bathroom floor because I was so relieved. You truly saved me that day even if you don't remember. I can never thank you enough for that day. Or any of the days we spent together.

"So, that's how you found me? Through one comment?" Isla asks.

Jaemin shakes his head.

"It started there. I wrote your username down on a slip of paper and kept it in a drawer to pull out whenever I needed encouragement. But soon it stopped being enough. So, I looked your account up again and started following you on my secret profile, started binging your tweets and comments. Suddenly, everything you did was interesting to me and I wanted to know more. And I thought . . . I guess somehow I thought that since you knew everything about me, since you always tweeted about how you wanted to be friends with me that we *were* friends."

Jaemin swallows.

"And it kept spiraling and spiraling and I didn't even know. I put you on this pedestal created of things I made up. I would daydream for hours about things that we would do and say and how close we were. But I wanted more. You made me feel so good, Isla," he says, looking at her with a pained expression, "You made me feel euphoric. Such a high compared to all the lows I was experiencing. I wanted more and more and more and then I wanted you to be mine. And so you were. Just as quickly as I imagined us being best friends, I imagined us dating and it was so much better. I would dream about how soft your skin felt and how you would look sleeping beside me. I wanted to know what you were doing always, so I paid someone to get me access to every part of your life possible. I know you had posters of us on your walls because of photos posted on your old Facebook. Every search you made went straight to my phone, which only fueled my obsession more and more. But it broke when you went on a date with whoever that guy was."

His words are bitter. Shivers crawl over Isla's skin and she pulls her sweater tighter. Of course, she knew that Jaemin must have stalked her in some form, but it's another thing entirely to hear him talk about it.

"I felt so betrayed. I physically hurt, I felt sick. So, the LiVe happened. I wanted the world to know that you were mine. It wasn't something I ever thought about until it seemed like I might lose you. And everything I ever did to you . . . Isla, I am so sorry. Words cannot explain how sorry I am for all the terrible things I did to you over the course of our relationship. When Dr. Kim pushed me to a breakthrough, when I realized that all I ever thought about you was a lie, that I had Mythomania, I couldn't even look at you without wanting to vomit because I was so appalled at what I'd done. And so, I hurt you in the worst way possible. I wanted you to hate me like I hated me."

"Why didn't you just tell me the truth? Why would you hurt me so badly? I don't think you know how shitty I felt laying there on the floor, crying my heart out and feeling like the most pathetic person in the world. The moment was something I'd been fearing for months and you managed to stab me in every weak spot I had left."

Jaemin's eyes widen.

"Why were you fearing us breaking up?"

"Are you joking? I know you're fucked up, Jaemin, I always have, ever since you made that stupid livestream. But, somehow, I managed to love you anyway. I loved you so much. I loved you more than anything or anyone with every fiber of my being."

Jaemin's breath catches.

"I always wanted you to get better. I just hoped I'd still be around once you were."

"I want you to be. Even though I'm an asshole and don't deserve you, I still want you around because I love you. Even more than I used to after realizing how terrible I made your life and how amazing you made mine. I adore everything about you and I swear that I'll spend every moment of my life proving it to you. Just please. Stay with me."

Jaemin grasps Isla's hand softly, pressing something cold into her palm.

"Please stay with me."

"Jaemin," Isla says, a multitude of emotions swirling through her so violently, she doesn't know whether to laugh or cry, "You can't do this. You can't just waltz into my life just when I'm starting to finally make something of it and pull me back in. Being without you forced me to realize how little I really had. And even though I don't have much now, I have myself. I'm getting to know who I really am and I can't do that with you."

A single tear falls down Jaemin's cheek, Isla's own eyes glistening.

She presses the ring back into Jaemin's frigid hand, not even looking at it.

"Take care of yourself, okay? Not for me, not for Starlights, but for yourself."

Isla stands up, pocketing the cigarettes and beginning to walk back to her car.

"Just once more. Please say it just once more," Jaemin begs, wilting.

"I love you," Isla says, looking back at him, barely able to choke down her sob, "But we both have to learn to love ourselves more."

"Please don't leave me," Jaemin calls out, beginning to tremble, "Please."

"This is goodbye, Matoi Jaemin. Maybe not forever, but certainly for now."

Isla puts her car into drive, watching Jaemin's figure grow smaller and smaller in the rearview mirror as the ache in her heart expands tenfold.

42

Did you ever get the midterm grade worked out with your teacher?"

A peaceful noise machine hums in the corner, offset by the occasional swoosh of a humidifier. Isla is relaxing on the very comfortable plush couch next to the kind psychologist she's grown to know very well over the last several months.

"Yeah, I did," Isla says, nodding, "She fixed it after I explained what happened."

"I bet you're relieved, huh?" the psychologist says, smiling at her.

"I really am! I was so worried about it," Isla says, "But it all worked out well!"

"And that's the last class you needed to get your technical degree, right?"

Isla nods enthusiastically.

"Yes! I get my diploma in about two weeks."

Isla is practically glowing with excitement. It's been a tough two years attending courses at a technical college while working part-time to support herself.

"You know, sometimes I look back at where I started and it nearly brings me to tears. I don't have a lot by any means but I'm in a place that I can be proud of. I thought I'd end up like everyone else in my family - a deadbeat with no ambition and too much time to add more problems into my life. But instead I managed to pull through and find something I enjoy doing and provide myself with the tools necessary to do it."

"And you should be proud of yourself. Especially considering the trauma you've been through in the last few years. It takes a great deal of strength and determination to pull yourself through and heal. I've met with a lot of people in my career but none as resilient as you, Isla."

She smiles, standing up as her watch beeps on her wrist.

"This is it, huh," Isla says, "Our last session."

"Yeah, it is. You've come a long way. I'm confident that you have the tools necessary to face whatever life throws at you."

"I feel that way too," Isla says, "I have this sense of liberation almost. Meeting with you these last few weeks has really helped me out."

Her therapist smiles at her.

"I'll check in on you in about three weeks or so, to see how you're doing. And of course, feel free to book an appointment any time."

Isla leaves the office feeling light on her feet. She hums happily in her car, driving through the mostly empty streets to her now-familiar apartment building. She parks in her assigned spot and locks her car manually, smiling at the old thing.

Isla hasn't gotten around to trying to find a newer car and doesn't think she will any time soon. Even though the car she bought two years ago is older than her parents, it still runs smoothly and Isla has gotten accustomed to it, taking comfort in the familiar cushiness of its slightly torn seats and the stick the passenger seat belt has.

With a quick pat on the car's hood, Isla strolls into her apartment building, waving to the elderly gentleman at the front desk. He's the man who owns the building and is very polite, if not a little bit absentminded.

"Good afternoon, Mr. Henry."

The man looks up from his daily newspaper.

"Hello, dear," he says, immediately returning to a gripping story about the local grocery store's increase in the price of bananas.

Her keys jingle as she unlocks the door, stepping into the cinnamon-scented air. She stumbled upon Bath and Body Works when they were having a phenomenal sale and snatched up some of their wallflowers. Isla shrugs off her shoes and places them on the rack by the door, padding around the aged wood with her bare feet. She walks into the clean kitchen and opens the refrigerator, pulling out a soda and popping the tab, setting it down on the counter as she fishes her phone out of her purse.

As a general rule, Isla always turns off her phone before meeting with her therapist so she doesn't get interrupted. It takes several minutes for the old device to boot up, giving her ample time to settle down onto her couch and prop her feet up, wiggling her toes before covering them with a throw. She sips the Dr. Pepper as her phone's home screen pops up, displaying a photo of a cute kitten she found on the internet.

It turns out that in her time at therapy, she missed a call from her aunt. She redials the number, the other woman picking up after a few rings.

"Hey, Rue! Sorry I missed your call."

"It's alright. I know you're a busy girl," her aunt says.

"Anyway, what's up?"

"You know that guy Phil?"

"The mechanic you've been telling me about?" Isla says, taking a sip.

"That's the one. We went out for drinks today!"

Isla sits up excitedly, almost spilling soda all over herself.

"Rue! That's so exciting! How'd it go?"

For a good half hour, Isla's aunt gushes about the man, sounding more hyper than Isla has ever recalled her being. They hang up with Rue promising to keep Isla updated and wishing her a good rest of the day, playfully scolding her to come and visit.

But Isla's happy mood sours quickly when she notices the unread texts from Jonny, a guy she went out on a date with a few weeks ago. He was nice, sure, and handsome too. But there just didn't really seem to be much of a connection. Isla got more pleasure from the delicious food she ordered than the conversation she had with him.

Sighing, she decides to just continue ghosting him. He'll get the picture eventually. Isla turns her phone screen off, placing it face down and sitting on the couch, her shoulders slumped.

In the two years that have passed since she left Matoi Jaemin at the gas station by her aunt's house, a lot has changed. Every day Isla grows more satisfied with her life, feeling proud of herself for making it through technical school and finding a job she's passionate about. She loves working at the local preschool and can't wait until she can work there full-time. She has her own place, pays her bills on time, and has even started up a small succulent garden on her back porch that she takes care of.

Every decoration in her home is one she picked out with loving care, making the space really feel like her own. Even her wardrobe has gotten a boost now that she lives near some really great consignment and thrift stores. Her mental health has never been better. She feels confident in her own skin and truly loves herself.

So, why does something feel like it's missing?

Her mind goes back to that night. She remembers every moment of it in great detail, the chill of the night, the paleness of his skin, the taste of tobacco.

Isla can't bring herself to regret her decision even though she often wonders what would have happened if she'd chosen differently. Would the two have been happily married or would they have fallen apart, too focused on not losing the other to remember not to lose themselves?

Isla finds herself grabbing her phone, typing the numbers she has memorized in, thumb hovering over the call button.

She's done this once or twice but has never gone through with it, hiding her phone away until she felt in a clearer mindset.

She'd said goodbye, but even back then, she said it wouldn't be forever.

But maybe it will be.

Jaemin could have easily moved on. She knows that he's doing alright - that all of the boys are. A quick search tells her that they're just as busy as ever, especially now that Jaemin's returned early from his military service. He could have forgotten her, filed the whole thing away as some unfortunate experience he never wants to repeat. There really is no reason for her to call. He probably doesn't even have the same number.

But while Isla's fighting an internal battle, her hand slips, thumb gliding over the call button. She only realizes it when the dial tone starts blaring loudly, startling her. Frantically, she tries to hang up, but before she can, the person on the other side picks up.

She holds her breath, not even moving.

"Hello?"

Isla gasps loudly.

"I . . . Jaemin?"

On the other side of the world, awoken by his ringing phone,

Matoi Jaemin squints at his phone in the darkness, sitting up quickly when he hears that voice, the voice he thought he'd never hear again except through videos.

"Angel?"

"I'm so sorry!" Isla says, panicking, "I don't know what came over me. I'll hang up now."

"Don't—" Jaemin shouts, startling Isla once more, "I-I didn't mean to shout. Just don't hang up."

"Okay," Isla says.

For a moment, neither of them say anything.

"So," Jaemin says, "Miss me?"

His sleep-deprived brain spits out the question he's dying to have answered. He panics when he realizes what he's said, opening his mouth to take the question back.

"Yeah," Isla says, voice soft, "I really have."

43

Y ou look exhausted."

Plopping down on the computer chair, Jaemin dries his hair with a towel before resting it around his neck.

"I *am* exhausted," he complains, placing his elbow down and leaning forward, putting his face closer to the webcam.

"You should get some sleep then," Isla says, "You can always talk to me later."

"Nooooo," Jaemin whines, "I want to talk to you more than I want to sleep."

Isla giggles.

"You talk to me almost every day, Minie."

Ever since the accidental phone call a year ago, Isla and Jaemin have slowly been rekindling their relationship. At first, it was awkward, painful even, but after one day where he had a ten-hour flight and Isla had nothing but time to kill, they'd opened up, talked about the help they've gotten and the way they've changed since they last saw each other.

"I miss you being here. That way I could snuggle up to you while I fell asleep like we used to. God, I miss doing that."

"I miss it too. You always ended up wrapped around me. It was adorable."

Jaemin blushes, smiling shyly. Despite being twenty-seven, Jaemin still has his boyish charm.

"I love you, you know that?" he says suddenly.

"Mmmhm," Isla says, "I know."

It only took a month of them talking again before Jaemin confessed to still being in love with her, even after all the time that has passed. Going to therapy only strengthened his feelings, only made him miss and appreciate her more, only wanting to get to love her again.

"Do you really?" Jaemin says, suddenly serious.

The change in demeanor makes Isla sober up slightly.

"Of course I do."

He suddenly looks nervous, readjusting himself in his seat and raking his hands through his hair.

"Then, will you ... do you want to come here? To Korea? Do you want to see me?"

Isla pauses, surprised. While the two of them have talked about reuniting in person, it was never in much detail.

"Yes! God, yes!" Isla exclaims.

Jaemin's nervousness melts into a smile.

"Okay. I'll send you a ticket then," Jaemin says, unable to hide his excitement.

Two weeks later, Isla boards a private jet, preparing to once again fly all the way across the world. She's incredibly jittery, trying and failing to distract herself with all manner of things. Isla stares out of the window, she plays games on her phone, she watches fifteen minutes of an inflight movie and tries to sleep.

But all she manages to do is make the flight seem to go even slower. By the time she actually lands in Korea at the private airport, she's completely exhausted, looking forward to crashing at the hotel that's booked for her.

Fate seems to have other plans. As she wheels her suitcase over the marble floor, every step feeling heavy, something swiftly approaches her, a person running at top speed. Before Isla can even process it, he crashes into her, arms wrapping around her tightly.

Isla drops the handles for her suitcase, embracing him just as tightly, amazed at feeling his skin once more after all that has happened.

Jaemin pulls away slightly, studying her face with fervor, warm palm resting against her cheek. The roundness in her features has diminished some, but she's still as soft as he remembers, emerald eyes just as bright, hair still as curly, still every bit as beautiful.

"Isla," the man says, completely breathless.

Jaemin's hair is different now, not so long and poofy but just as brightly colored, his locks dyed a brilliant orange. He has three more ear piercings than he did before and tiny tattoos are sprinkled across his right arm. A small scar has appeared under his left eye from a strange accident about a year ago. Jaemin is even taller, the two of them no longer being close in height. The locket she bought so long ago hangs around his neck, all shined up and glistening. It catches her eyes immediately.

"You found it," she says with wonder.

She had snuck the locket in his bags before their breakup all those years ago. To be honest, she'd forgotten all about it. It was supposed to have been a gift. She'd even had a small photograph of the two of them paced inside it.

"Of course I did," he says breathlessly, voice filled with awe, stunned that she's really there with him.

Isla rises up, lips meeting his, putting as much emotion into the moment as possible. All the pain, all the anger, all the sadness melts away into this moment of pure bliss and happiness.

It's been so long and so much has happened. She's grown and changed and so has he but the love she had for him never went away, not even when she wanted it to.

"God, I've missed you so much," Jaemin says, tears gathering in his eyes.

"Don't cry!" Isla says, her own eyes prickling, "You'll make me cry too."

She hits him playfully as tears fall from her eyes as well. Jaemin giggles, kissing her once more before wiping away her tears only for more to fall until she's sobbing into his embrace, clinging onto his shirt and breathing in his familiar scent.

Isla never knew how much she really missed him until this moment. "I love you," Isla confesses. "I love you more," Jaemin exclaims.

Once the two of them have calmed down enough to go more than one minute without bursting into tears, Jaemin grabs Isla's suitcase handle, leading her through the airport, his hand holding hers tightly. Jaemin doesn't let go of her hand even when he's driving his car, the smile never leaving his face. He hums an old love song happily, thumb swiping across the back of her hand. The girl gazes fondly through the car window, watching the familiar Seoul streets pass by, remembering all the memories she made when she was last here.

"We're here!" he announces, pulling into the parking garage she once saw every day.

"Are we headed back to the apartment?" she asks him.

Jaemin shakes his head.

"I sold it. I couldn't bear to stay there any longer."

Isla nods solemnly. As many good memories their old apartment held, it was also full of terrible ones.

"We're going to visit the rest of the members. They were almost as excited as I was when you agreed to come visit."

Isla giggles.

"Oh yeah?"

"Mmhm. Woojin especially, He was mad that he never got the

chance to say goodbye."

In the last year, Isla had actually begun to form a relationship with the other members of OT2B as well. She never connected with them while she was here, resentment preventing them from making a genuine effort to get to know her as a person. But once the others realized how much she truly meant to Jaemin, they reached out, wanting to understand her better. She's gotten to know all of them, but she's exceptionally close to Woojin. The two of them are the same age and have a lot of the same interests.

Jaemin raps his knuckles against an apartment door only for it to be thrown open only seconds later, the couple being pulled inside and immediately enveloped in a group hug. Loud chattering as everyone talks over each other, all trying to speak to Isla, causes a smile to grow on her face. She's passed around and hugged tightly by everyone (even Daehyun) while Jaemin playfully pouts, whining that they're hugging her more than he got to.

Seojoon has a wonderful lunch prepared and Isla's stomach growls in excitement. She hadn't realized how hungry she is over all her nerves. While everyone loads up, Isla chit chats with all of the boys, using the Korean she's learned since she began talking to Jaemin again. Her boyfriend is actually a great teacher and he beams with pride every time Isla adds to the conversation or laughs at one of the boys' stories.

They sit there for hours, catching up and growing acquainted. As the evening draws to a close, Jaemin excuses the two of them, stealing her away for some private time. The couple makes their way out to the balcony, breathing in the fresh air, Isla looking out onto the city.

"I really missed this view."

"I did too," Jaemin says, tone making it clear that he's not talking about the skyline.

Isla looks over to him, starlight illuminating her features.

"I'm so glad that out of all the accounts in the world, it was yours I saw that day, that it was you I chose," he says, licking his lips nervously and grasping her hands gently, "And I mean this with my entire soul when I say I want the honor of being able to choose you for the rest of my life."

Isla gasps as Jaemin lowers himself onto one knee, never breaking eye contact with her.

"Isla Montgomery, will you marry me?"

Tears shine in her eyes like jewels.

"Yes."

epilogue

The waves crash serenely against the sand, gulls flying overhead. High-pitched laughter is heard as a small child builds sandcastles only to knock them down over and over again, amusing himself.

Isla chuckles, watching her son play, the sight warming her heart.

"He's so precious," Jaemin says, kissing his wife's temple, "So wide-eyed and innocent."

"He gets that from you," Isla says, smiling at him fondly.

Jaemin laughs, digging his toes into the sand and looking out at the ocean, hypnotized by the waters.

"I'm pretty sure he gets it from you, angel," Jaemin says, the wind blowing his hair, "He's as sweet as his mommy."

Isla giggles, blushing. Even after all these years, every compliment from her husband sends flutters to her stomach. Or actually –

Isla gasps, catching Jaemin's attention.

"What? Is something wrong?!"

She grabs his sandy hand, placing it on her small baby bump.

"The baby is moving," she says, grinning, "He or she is quite the active little blip."

Jaemin presses his hand against her stomach, not being able to feel anything. He pouts adorably.

"You'll be able to feel the kicking soon enough," Isla says.

Jaemin lays down on the warm towel, tugging his wife down with him, snuggling her close to him.

"I love our little family. I don't think it's possible to be any happier than I am now," Jaemin says, eyes fluttering closed.

Their two-year-old son laughs again before standing up, waddling over to his parents.

"Look!" he says, thrusting his small hand out, a tiny seashell in his hand, "Pwetty!"

"Very pretty!" Isla says, "Good find, Ducky."

The child laughs at his nickname, quacking cutely like the ducks at the pond do. It's so sweet that Jaemin scoops him up, tossing him in the air as he laughs excitedly, the seashell all but forgotten.

Isla watches the two loves of her life zip across the Busan sand, wondering how she got to be so lucky.

Before too long, their son has fallen asleep, head bobbing to the side as he struggles not to fall backwards. Jaemin lifts him up into his arms while Isla folds their blanket and collects his toys, pausing to caress her beautiful baby boy's face.

He has his father's lips but his mother's nose, soft baby cheeks and long eyelashes topped with a mop of silky hair. The child truly looks like an angel gifted from above. Isla wonders briefly if their second child will look similar.

The drive home is long and tranquil, soft music playing over the radio as Jaemin holds Isla's hand in his like he always does, absentmindedly rubbing the back of her hand. She can hardly believe that it's been three years since they've been married.

So much has changed. OT2B officially went on indefinite hiatus, the boys still working on music and occasionally releasing something while having enough time to spend with their own families and pursue other interests and hobbies. They still see each other almost every week though, always dropping by each other's homes to hang out like they have for over a decade.

They love to spoil Jaemin's baby, always bringing toys and treats for him.

Isla is so grateful that her child has the support system she never did as a child. She knows that her son will grow into a wonderful person who will make a positive impact on the world.

Jaemin tucks the sleeping boy into bed before turning to Isla with that familiar look in his eyes, dragging her off to their bedroom while Isla only laughs, knowing that she won't be getting much sleep tonight.

No matter how much Jaemin's grown and changed, some things always stay the same.

"I love you, you know that?" he asks, hands around her waist, lips on her neck.

"I know," she says, "More than anyone, more than anything,"

"And I'll never stop loving you."

Afterword

As I sit here writing this, I am overcome with a sense of disbelief. Even though I've taken the steps to make Mythomania into a published novel, it still feels unreal to me. Nearly like a dream that I never want to wake up from. But dream or not, there are several people I want to thank for staying by my side during this difficult process.

First, I'd like to thank my mother, my number one fan and biggest supporter. You've always been there for me and I know you always will be. I would have never been here without you. Thank you for putting up with my exhausting self and for loving me for who I am. There's never been a sweeter mother.

Second, I want to thank my friends, those both near and far.

Trinity, thank you for being my ride or die, for always thinking of me and encouraging and uplifting me. I miss you every day. I hope there will come a time when we won't have to be so far apart.

To everyone who has ever said something nice about me or my work, thank you. To everyone who's ever supported me financially, or wished that they could, thank you. Know that it's your support that got me to where I am today. I'll never forget your kindness.

Thank you to everyone who edited, proofread, designed, and

created art for this story. You guys really made it come alive.

And finally, thank you to those who are reading this right now. Thank you for giving my baby a chance. I hope you enjoyed the story.

I hope to write many more novels in the future and to meet many more amazing people. I know my journey is just beginning. Hope to see all you guys there.

Rose

CPSIA information can be obtained
at www.ICGtesting.com
Printed in the USA
LVHW080106250220
648107LV00019B/1083